A SAVIOR IS BORN

DALTON SHIFTED HIS WEIGHT and followed her gaze out of the window and across the land, which lay peacefully under the light of the late afternoon suns.

"You are the Farloon, or Chosen Protector, of the Centaurs."

"What's that?" Her hand strayed to the pendant around her neck. She had always wondered what the word "Farloon", which was engraved on it, meant.

"It is a sacred position, one that puts you as high in the Centaurs' tribal order as Igentis, the leader of all Centaurs. It is an oath made between the Dragon Riders and the Centaurs that binds their two Kinds together."

She shook her head. "But what if I don't want to be? I don't even remember swearing an oath. How does that count? That's not fair."

Only silence answered.

Taking a deep breath, Dalton continued, his voice quiet and meek. "You are the only child of Lord Drox and Lady Andromeda Lavoisier. And you are the chosen and prophesied protector of Duvarharia—a warrior called to rid Ventronovia of Thaddeus, his dragon Kyrell, and Veltrix once and for all. You are the *Shelesuujao* of the Duvarharians, the child of the Dragon Prophecy."

Dragon Bone Publishing titles by Effie Joe Stock

The Shadows of Light Series

Child of the Dragon Prophecy

Heir of Two Kingdoms

Anthologies
(as editor)

Aphotic Love: An Anthology on the Depths of Romance

Other Publications

What Darkness Fears Anthology (Twenty Hills Publishing)

Fool's Honor Anthology (Twenty Hills Publishing)

CHILD OF THE DRAGON PROPHECY

EFFIE JOE STOCK

First Installment of <u>The Legends of Rasa</u>

©Copyright 2022 Effie Joe Stock

Child of the Dragon Prophecy

Book 1 of The Shadows of Light

ISBN:

979-8-9860641-3-0 (paperback)

979-8-9860641-4-7 (eBook)

979-8-9860641-5-4 (hardback)

Published in Hackett, Arkansas USA by Dragon Bone Publishing 2022.

2022 Second Edition.

First edition originally printed in 2021.

Cover and illustrations are created by and copyright of Effie Joe Stock.

Edited by H.A. Pruitt.

To my 12-year-old self,

A girl who saw fantasy lands all around her and decided to write her own.

This is to show her that despite what some people said, it really is worth the world to chase your dreams.

"While you remember the light, and while the Light is still in this world, believe in the light, so that you might then become *The Shadows of Light.*"

–A Long Forgotten Teacher

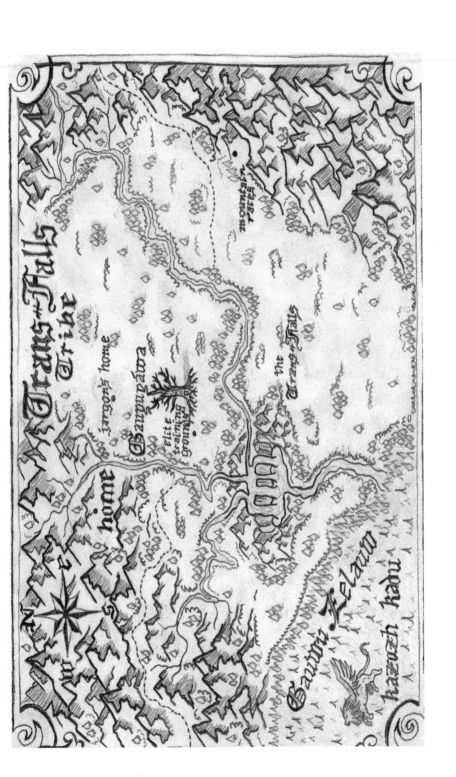

Pronunciation Guide & Glossary on pages I-VII in back of book.

BOOK 1

THE SHADOWS OF LIGHT

CHILD OF THE
DRAGON PROPHECY

EFFIE JOE STOCK

THE DRAGON PROPHECY

Dragon Palace, Duvarharia

Year: Rumi 5,210 Q.RJ.M (Quźech raź jin mraha– After our Lord)

Time Counted Since the Beginning of the Great Lord's reign

DAWN ROSE OVER the powerful empire of Duvarharia, the land of dragons, on a brisk autumn day. The larger sun of the day blazed across the sky as it took part in an amazing spectacle of solar bodies in their great dance across the heavens. It was on this day that all the heavenly bodies came together to demonstrate the awe and power of the Great Emperor who commanded them. Stars shone brightly and comets raced across the sky as the large moon and the smaller, rarely seen moon passed amongst both the greater and lesser suns of the day.

This particular astronomical occurrence was one that only happened once every five thousand years.

Two moons and two suns ruled the day and night sky over the planet of Rasa. Legend said that these heavenly bodies, along with the stars of the sky, were not just simple stars, moons, or suns, but that they were actually creatures—creatures who were infinite and immortal and who ruled the sky realm, Hanluurasa. Their movements across the heavens displayed their wars, their dances, and most importantly of all, the past, present, and future of Rasa.

As the great armies of the Centaurs stared into the sky on this fateful day, their eyes unaffected by the blinding light, they found more than just the future of Rasa; they found the end of it.

"We must tell the Igentis." A chestnut-colored Centaur turned fearfully from the flashing lights and the roaring of thunder in the sky.

With another Centaur close behind him, the chestnut broke into a gallop. He masterfully weaved his way through the forest, his long mane and tail snapping in the wind and his hooves thundering into the ground, kicking up the soft, moist, mossy soil. Just ahead of the chestnut, a pure white Centaur stood rigidly still, his hands behind his back, and his head tilted up to the sky, a dark look on his solemn face.

"Igentis, sir." The chestnut dropped to his knees, his head bowed reverently before the leader of all Centaurs. "The stars, they—"

"I know." The Igentis, Artigal, fixed his eyes on the Centaur before him, their eyes meeting. Artigal sighed heavily and stamped one of his white hooves. "I have read them already. Time has run out for the Duvarharians. The end of this life is near, and the Emperor is preparing his return."

The Centaurs around Artigal gasped, their weapons falling lifelessly by their sides, some of their eyes wide with awe, others with excitement, and even others, with fear and anger.

"Igentis, so it is true, then?" The chestnut Centaur's voice quivered with fear.

Artigal nodded slowly. "Yes. The day of the Prophecy is upon us. Indeed, it has already begun."

§

THE DRAGON PALACE, capital city of Duvarharia, was buzzing with energy and excitement as the streets filled with dragons and their riders. Each face—beast and man, young and old, male and female, rich and poor alike—turned to the sky. The Duvarharians shielded their eyes from the blinding glare with their hands or magic. People crowded each other, pushing and shoving, as they tried to see as much of the astronomical spectacle as they could. The large, sparkling buildings of the Dragon Palace loomed tall over the citizens, and many of the creatures were trying to not be in the inner city's tower shadow. The inner city itself appeared to be one large palace, looming high into the sky, almost into the clouds; some places were as high as some of the mountains which protectively encircled the grand city.

The Dragon Palace was no usual city made of mortal stone, granite, wood, or earth; instead, it was a city made out of Pure Magic. Buildings had been constructed by the many thousands of talented magic wielders of the land. For those who had built their own homes out of magic, their dwellings shone brightly with the color that marked their magic trace, their walls appearing to be of fine granite or even gems. This was the only city in the entire country of Ventronovia that had been designed like this. Nowhere in Duvarharia had another city been made entirely out of magic.

In one of the grand buildings and high above the rest of the city, Tabor tuned one of his measuring instruments. When he looked up, his exuberant apprentice was spinning a telescope back and forth on its stand as the young man attempted to study all the sky at one time.

"Steady now! That equipment is fragile." Tabor crossed his arms, shaking his head at his student.

As the leading scientific expert and recorder in all the land of Duvarharia, it was Tabor's duty to make sure that the knowledge of everything significant that went on in Ventronovia—whether it be the weather, a new hatching of dragons, new abilities of magic that were discovered, or the uncovering of old, forgotten information—was properly recorded and stored. It was also his job to make sure that the libraries were being run efficiently.

His knowledge vast, and his age climbing ever higher, Tabor had found himself a young man who showed the same spirit for knowledge and had taken him in as an apprentice. The boy's name was Quinlan, and he was, by far, the most willing to learn and ambitious young Dragon Rider that Tabor had seen yet.

Even now, it was hard to keep the bouncing, blonde-haired teen from flying his young dragon high into the skies, abandoning all concern for safety, simply to gain a better view of the suns and moons.

"By the Great Lord! I don't think I have ever seen anything more amazing in my life!" Quinlan laughed and brushed a lock of his messy, blonde hair out of his eyes before peering down the telescope. While human telescopes could only see so far as to observe the moons in a bit more detail, Duvarharian telescopes had been so enhanced with magic that one could see craters in incredible detail on the little astronomical satellites that circled Rasa's greater moon.

"The solar flares are absolutely stunning! I can see why the legend would depict it to be something like that of a ribbon dancer's ribbon, the hair of a dancing girl, or perhaps even the mane of a Sun-Flash dragon! Incredible!"

Shaking his head, Tabor couldn't control the fond smile that spread across his face. Quinlan's passion for knowledge reminded Tabor of himself when he was young.

Tabor quickly glanced toward the table at his right. A large, open, blank book was quickly being written in by a curious, glowing, blue apparatus. Instead of being a quill with ink, like what the humans used, this odd contraption was a simple charge of magic. Having been formed by Quinlan, this *juufu* was recording everything that Quinlan himself was seeing and feeling, instantly transforming the experiences into words and hastily converting it to the page. This was the most common and efficient way of preserving information, especially events.

Quinlan's *juufu* was leaping and skipping across the page at an alarming rate. The pages flipped so fast, it seemed as if they would be ripped from the book. It seemed Quinlan had forgotten to stem the information he was transferring to the book.

Tabor shook his head, hiding his amusement. Most of the wording would have to be edited out, leaving only the most significant events. It took a long time to be able to master channeling the flow of information so that your every mundane thought wouldn't be recorded.

He too had his own *juufu* recording what he saw. However, his was a warm bronze, matching the color of his dragon, and it wasn't scribbling nearly as violently as Quinlan's.

The wind tore through Tabor's dark hair. Though he himself was nearly 180 years old, he was only just beginning to show signs of white at the root of his hair, and his stone-gray eyes sparkled as youthfully as his apprentice's.

The light blue sky slowly began to darken, a little at first, and then more by the second.

The whole land went quiet.

The only thing that could be heard now was the occasional humming of the Moon-Shone dragons and the Sun-Flash dragons. Occasionally the keen trill of a Comet dragon could be heard mingling with the other dragons' songs. After a few long minutes, these special dragons took flight. As they soared into the sky, they themselves looked like little suns, moons, and stars, all shining in the sky.

The beautiful sight reminded Tabor of the legends that said these dragons had a special connection with the sky realm and, during certain times, these creatures were able to communicate with the heavenly bodies and possibly even absorb the power of Hanluurasa.

Quinlan ceased his constant peering through the telescope to watch the dragons as they abruptly disappeared into the suns, the moons, and the sky.

"Gods of all. They really are a part of the sky, then."

Tabor shook his head and fiddled with one of his instruments. What had happened to the dragons? What did this mean? How was this possible? None of his science could explain this.

Quinlan's mouth hung open, his eyes wide with wonder.

A great shadow covered the mountain range in darkness and rapid-ly approached the Dragon Palace.

Quinlan snapped out of his trance and pointed his telescope back to the suns. "Look, Tabor! It's about to happen!"

Tabor turned once more to the heavens. The instrument slipped out of his hands and clattered to the patio floor. "By the gods."

§

THE SKY RENT apart with the roaring of thunder and flashing of light against darkness. Wind howled around them, tugging violently at them and their records. Stars rained down from the sky—great balls of fire against the darkening expanse. Strange lights snapped across the sky in fantastic blues, greens, purples, and even red and yellow. The pages on the books beside the two Dragon Riders began flipping furiously, the wind threatening to tear them from their binding. Quinlan faintly heard Tabor say something about keeping the manuscripts safe before the mentor snatched them up and retreated into the observatory.

"Gods of all." Quinlan's eyes widened and he let the telescope drop from his hands.

Turning around, he surveyed the entire heavens above him, completely awed by the sight.

The moons and the suns were no longer just heavenly bodies. A dragon moon and a dragon sun, along with a man and a woman, which were the smaller moon and sun, hung in the sky. The stars that streaked across the almost black sky, making the scene very much like fire licking at a log, were now not just streaks of light but dragons and their riders.

Quinlan, in denial of what he was seeing, hastily rubbed his eyes. His brows furrowed. The figures were once again just the stars, suns, and moons.

In the commotion, Quinlan's blue-and-white Crystal dragon had landed behind him, the young dragon's trumpeting drowned out by the thunder. Quinlan clung to one of the beast's thick legs. His almost white blonde hair stung his face as the wind screamed around them.

Struggling to open his eyes, the young man squinted at the suns and the moons, not wanting to miss anything, despite knowing he was in danger.

The heavenly bodies had almost completely aligned now.

Quinlan could see the solar flares from the greater sun lashing around the greater moon. With the pattern of sun, moon, sun, moon, it truly was a magnificent sight of shadows fighting the flashing light.

Billows of fire raced across the sky. It was impossible to hear anything over the thunder's roar, which sounded more like a snarling beast than thunder. Lightning cracked and streaked across the sky, mingling with the light of the comets and shootings stars.

Then the suns and moons completely aligned.

The world was plunged into darkness. Quinlan couldn't see his dragon in front of him, let alone anything past the observatory. He felt himself yell, but couldn't hear even himself over the deafening noise.

Light flashed eerily over Duvarharia as the fire that had burned in the skies poured down onto the land. Wisps of light streaked through the dark, heavy air. Quinlan felt himself being pulled in different directions all at once, as if he were being dragged through a portal. Voices rose and fell around him. Figures which were shrouded in endless darkness and burning light raced past him toward Rasa. Before him, he could almost catch glimpses of a city made of stars with strange, foreign creatures moving inside it.

The gateway to Hanluurasa had been opened once more.

It was supposed to be scientifically impossible, and yet the path to the sky realm stretched out in front of him as real as the Dragon Palace behind him. The boy could barely grasp the significance of it all. His head throbbed. His heart slammed against his chest. Dread settled in him.

Quinlan clutched his head and groaned before sinking to the ground. Darkness settled around him. A nothingness consumed him. He could no longer feel his dragon beside him or the ground beneath him.

An explosion spilt the air. A swirling mass of gold, white, and red magic encased him in a great orb. He scrambled to his feet as he felt the presence of another person move past him. His voice finally broke through his paralyzing fear.

"What's happening? Tabor? Is that you? Where am I?" Quinlan could barely hear his own screams for help over the loud, crackling magic around him. His eyes burned from the glare.

"Quinlan," a voice rang out in the light. The teen froze. "Child of the Dragon Riders, rider of Krystallos, hear me and understand. I have chosen you to bear this message and its fate."

Everything around Quinlan was then silent and empty, except for the magic that still swirled and snapped around him.

Quinlan shook with fear. Who was this Being? Why was it here?

"Gods of all." His voice sounded so small compared to this Being. "Who are you? What is happening?"

"I have come for my people. I have come to begin and fulfill." The voice was deep and terrible but also somewhat sad.

Quinlan gasped as he felt the voice reverberate inside of him. Images flashed confusingly around Quinlan as the Being began to speak.

> *"Dragon folk now heed the call,*
> *from the wars of man's great fall.*
> *In your days of sloth and peace,*
> *the hands of death shall find release."*

A vision of the Dragon Palace came into focus, only it wasn't the Dragon Palace that Quinlan knew and loved. Only a few dragons flew through the skies. Crime riddled the streets. Beggars pleaded with the wealthy for money, the idea of magic was long forgotten, and people fought each other for fame and riches.

> *"But up from you, there shall rise,*
> *a keeper from this fear and demise.*
> *Features pale with dark blood hair,*
> *eyes of red beyond compare."*

The scene changed and Quinlan watched the hazy image of a woman as she picked up a young girl from a crib. He breathed in sharply when he saw the little girl's red hair and eyes.

> *"Guide this girl, whether to or fro,*

7

she must come to the Stone Plateau.
Raise her up, to love not hate,
never straying from her fate.
And to this girl, marked with my hand,
a helper too, both fierce and grand.
Beware her helper, though young and wise,
will need be steered from lust of prize."

The image of a handsome, black-haired, middle-aged man stood before the scholar apprentice as the man held a handful of gold coins, greed shinning in his eyes.

It only just now occurred to the Quinlan that he was seeing the future. He was being given a prophecy. His heart nearly stopped within him as he began to realize who this Being must be.

"Soon hard years, from death you cannot run,
for a traitor from your ranks will come.
A young boy, Quinlan's own dear son,
will bend to evil and then be won."

"Good gods." Quinlan's breath caught in his throat. He was staring at a very indistinct image of what looked much like a small family of four—two boys, a mother, and a father—a man who looked eerily like Quinlan himself. "No, no, no." Dread welled up inside of the boy. The Being couldn't possibly have meant him, could it have?

"Listen, riders, that all may know,
all this could be avoided so.
Turn back, my children, back to me.
I'll set you from the Dark Lord free.
But if my voice, you do not heed,
my urgent warning, I now plead.
Then know that I will then set forth,
destruction, terrible, from the North.
And if you turn away from me,

know this quite for certainty:
No rider will retell your lives,
no help for you shall then arise."

Swirling all around Quinlan was nothing but war; pictures of magic clashing against twisted creatures of evil, the rivers ran with blood, and mangled Duvarharian bodies littered the ground like a carpet.

Tears trickled then poured down Quinlan's face as he watched the carnage stretch out before him. The Dragon Palace lay in ruins. Fire burned down the beautiful buildings. Magic tore through the land and destroyed the bodies of all who came against the traitor. The magnificent Stone Plateau, on which the entire city of the Dragon Palace had once stood, was now only a bare, stone table; its ancient markings, which had been hidden by the city for so long, were exposed to the air and charred by fire. In the current Dragon Palace, only a small part of the Stone Plateau had been exposed, and that small bit had been used as a landing pad for the Dragons. Though his beloved home lay in ruin before his eyes, Quinlan couldn't help but feel awe at seeing the entirety of the Stone Plateau as it had been when originally built. However, the sight was grim, as if the bare stone lay as a monument to the destruction of Duvarharia.

Anger, hate, and horror flooded the young teen, and he so desperately wanted to destroy this Being who was foretelling all of this. However, dread quickly washed all other emotion away. He knew he couldn't, especially if this Being was who he thought it was—the Great Lord Himself.

"Lord, please do not do this. What must I do?" His hands shook and his voice faltered. Curiously, though, Quinlan could almost feel the sadness of the Lord. *He doesn't want this to happen,* the boy realized. *He wants something else.*

"So, Quinlan, stand near the Stone Plateau,
for in five years the moon will throw
the fate for all, written in stone,
knowledge to learn and skills to hone.
Follow its riddles, follow to know,
what the future then may show.
Go to your leaders, speak of this hope,
to fight the evil and to cope.

Remind the people to seek me out,
with a whisper or a shout.
For I, your Lord, am never far,
and know each one for who they are."

The images faded, and Quinlan gasped, trying to process all that was happening. He quickly found that even if he tried, he wasn't able to forget anything that the Being had spoken to him. The images and words that the Being had shown and spoken to him burned into his mind and obsessively repeated themselves.
The powerful magic now wasn't as bright as it had been, though it still snapped and swirled around the young man.

"You, you're the Great Lord." Trembling, he fell to his knees.

A figure stepped out of the magic in front of the boy. It was dressed in a long, simple cloak, which covered all his body and most of his face.

"Yes, I am the Great Lord, though not the one most think."

Quinlan frowned, his head swimming with questions.

The magic began to fade and the light became less bright, the darkness less dark.

"Wait! Then, who are you?"

"I am the Son of the Great Emperor."

Soon, only the figure's silhouette was left in the strange, gray void.

Quinlan had never heard of a Great Emperor, but he was struck with reverence before this Man. He could feel in his soul that whoever this Man was, He was truly who He claimed He was.

On his knees reverently before this Being, and not quite able to grasp everything that had just happened and still was happening to him, Quinlan couldn't stop the question that jumped out of his mouth.

"Lord, am I the Quinlan in the prophecy? Will it be," he choked on his words, "*my* son?"

The man bowed his head, and Quinlan watched as a golden tear rolled down the man's face.

"Surely, while cursed, you have been blessed too. Stay strong, Quinlan. I am never far from you."

A bright flash of warm light left Quinlan lying on the Dragon Palace observatory patio. The suns and moons were just coming out of their union. The sky was brightening back up, and the Moon-Shone, Sun-Flash, and Comet dragons were once again soaring through the sky.

"Quinlan!" A man grabbed the boy, and Quinlan screamed, flailing against the man. "Calm down, boy! It's me! Tabor! By the gods, what happened to you?"

When Quinlan caught sight of his mentor, he shamelessly threw his arms around the man, unable to hold back his relief at being back at the Dragon Palace and even more so at being back in his own time. He gasped with joy through his tears. The Dragon Palace was still here and not destroyed. His relief quickly turned to dismay as he remembered all he had seen. He swallowed hard, a knot forming in his stomach. "They're all going to die. We're all going to die. My son. My son. Oh gods, what happened? What's going to happen?" Words poured meaninglessly out of Quinlan's mouth.

Tabor wrestled the young man off him. "Quinlan!" The confused older man slapped the young man and shook him. "Pull yourself together! This is no way for a sixteen-year-old rider to be acting." His words fell on deaf ears.

"'Go to your leaders.' My leaders. My leaders." Quinlan repeated what the Great Lord had told him in the prophecy, continuing to rant incoherently.

Krystallos nudged his young rider, the Crystal dragon's mind filled with worry.

Quinlan, are you okay? The dragon's voice was finally able to find its way into his soul mate's mind, but Quinlan didn't pay much attention to him either.

"Go to my leaders." Wide-eyed, his skin pale and clammy, a cold sweat on his brow, Quinlan shoved Tabor away from himself, dizziness and shock temporarily paralyzing him from the sudden movement.

His legs trembled, threatening to buckle under him as he struggled to his feet and tried to stem the tears which poured down his cheeks. Gasping for breath, he attempted to mount his dragon, but Tabor quickly stopped the teen and restrained him.

"Where do you think you're going? You're in no condition to fly, and you have to tell us what happened to you. We've been looking all over for you."

Quinlan shook his head, trying to rid himself of the images of a solemn, red-haired girl, a laughing boy with purple eyes, and the scenes of death and destruction from his mind. The words of the prophecy pounded in his mind over and over again, echoing horribly.

"You've been looking for me?" he mumbled.

Tabor laughed incredulously. "Gods of all, kid. You've been gone for a whole

11

hour!"

Quinlan's mouth hung open. He had been gone for an hour. He had really been missing. *Where did I go? What happened?*

"Come on, Quinlan. I think you need to rest, and then you can tell me and the Council everything that happened to you. The Lord himself is even very worried, and I'm sure your parents are not going to be very happy with me."

Nodding, Quinlan stumbled along, mumbling, "Yes. The Council. The Lord. The leaders. They must know."

With Krystallos right behind them, Tabor led the dazed and fragile young man from the observatory's balcony and into the Dragon Palace.

He was quickly wrapped in a blanket and given a warm drink to sip on as the Council pestered him with questions. Little did he know, everyone and everything around him would one day fade into myth and the only rider who was alive on this day and would live to see the prophecy fulfilled would be himself.

PART ONE
Farloon

CHAPTER 1

Trans-Falls, Centaur Territory
One Day after the Battle of the Prophecy

ERON, FOR THE GODS' sake, stand still!" Jargon, medical chief of the Trans-Falls Centaur tribe scowled at his patient. "Honestly. You act like this is killing you."

"Maybe it is." Aeron shifted his weight uncomfortably.

Jargon was doctoring a large gash which ran across Aeron's back, shoulder to hip.

Jargon rubbed the healing salve particularly harshly on the wound, a good-natured sneer spreading across his rugged face. He wasn't the most handsome Centaur, but something about the strange twinkle in his eyes and the mysterious way he conducted himself was overall attractive. "I would have thought a big, tough warrior like you would be able to stand up to such a small bit of pain."

Aeron winced at the needles of pain that shot up his back, a slight smile almost crossing his face. "It was just a little scratch before you started wrenching on it, Jargon. I think you've only made it worse."

Jargon gasped and stamped his hooves, pretending to be offended. "With an insult like that, I think I'll just leave and take my practice to those who will appreciate what I do, thank you very much." He stuffed the jar of healing salve into his medical bag and made to walk away before Aeron humorously grabbed his arm.

"Jargon, I would never dream of you leaving. What would my tribe do without you?"

Amused, Jargon narrowed his eyes and turned up his nose at the leader. "Fine then, if you are sure. Now let me finish."

After just a few more painful moments spent in silence, Aeron's wound was liberally covered in the sweet-smelling salve and properly dressed. The dappled gray Centaur flexed his gray-skinned shoulders and nodded approvingly.

The salve, a special mixture of herbs and medicinal flowers along with a few spells, was specifically designed to rid a wound of Eta poison.

Aeron sighed in relief, the pain slowly subsiding. "Thank you, Jargon. I will always be in debt to you." He reached out his hand and Jargon grasped it.

"And don't you forget it, *fom*."

Aeron watched the medic trot off to his next patient before himself moving into the woods to look for Artigal. He hadn't seen the old Centaur since the battle started, and he was worried for the Igentis' well-being.

It was often that Artigal would have a secret agenda other than what he had ordered the troops or led Aeron to believe.

The Battle of the Prophecy had proved to be one of those times, and Aeron was desperate to find out if Artigal had been successful or was even still alive.

As he threaded his way through the forest, complimenting his people on their performance in battle or sharing in their sorrow of a lost loved one, he happened to overhear a very heated conversation between two young warriors. One was a palomino color and the other a bay.

"We shouldn't have retreated. The dragon men and their dragons had just arrived. The battle would have been won, and we would have been rid of Thaddeus once and for all. Sometimes I wonder if Artigal is just getting too old to be our leader. Besides, why would we even march out here in the first place? The Etas don't bother us in Trans-Falls and we have no concern with the rest of the Kinds of Ventronovia."

"I sometimes wonder that myself as well." The bay Centaur spit disrespectfully and stamped his hoof, an ugly sneer on his face.

In fury at these brash Centaurs, Aeron stepped out from behind the brush, about to land a punch on one of their faces and lecture them harshly when a disapproving, milky voice rang out from behind him.

"I'm afraid what exactly we were doing out here is above your ranking, *kodaazh*." Artigal's cold voice froze the young soldiers to the spot, their eyes wide in horror and their mouths hanging open.

Artigal limped past Aeron, who did a double take.

Cuts and burns lined Artigal's body, and he was trying to hide the fact that one of his arms seemed to be hanging lifelessly beside him. His pure white hair was marred with dirt and grass stains, and, most disturbingly, blood. His usually stern, emotionless face was ridden with pain, confusion, and exhaustion.

Though Aeron was disturbed and concerned for his leader and mentor, this rugged sight of the Igentis only struck more fear into the young Centaurs, who had only ever seen Artigal well composed and at a distance.

After a few moments of silence and Artigal staring viciously at the shocked soldiers, they bowed low. Their eyes stayed trained on the ground before them while they stuttered over each other.

"Please forgive us, Igentis! We were only upset about our untimely retreat. *Gubelœwur leñi rok!*"

Artigal didn't respond for a moment, his countenance only growing darker and fiercer.

The young Centaurs' foreheads beaded with sweat, their chests heaving.

His eyes wide, Aeron himself began to worry. This kind of slander toward the Igentis was considered a high form of treason. For this, Artigal could banish them; they would be marked by magic and shunned by all tribes of Centaurs, forever outcasts of their own kind.

"Perhaps so." Artigal's voice was chilling and merciless. "And only because we need every warrior in this time of need, I shall forgive you this one time."

The Centaurs panted in relief, but Artigal wasn't finished with them.

"Just remember, lowly warriors. I do not forget *anything*, and I have more eyes and ears than the *Fayum* itself. If this should happen again, I will not hesitate to banish you from all the Centaur tribes and Ventronovia itself. Understand?"

Both Centaurs, having been laid low by their leader, were nodding violently and muttering their thanks.

Artigal ignored them, waving his hand in dismissal.

"Get out of my sight."

In only a few seconds, the two Centaurs were nowhere to be seen.

So many questions were suddenly running through Aeron's mind as his eyes ran up and down the length of Artigal's abused body, but Artigal merely glanced at the leader and motioned for him to follow.

Now was not the time for questions.

They passed many other warriors on their way to the center of Trans-Falls, the capital of all the Centaur tribes. Each Centaur, male or female, young or old, wounded or not, bowed respectfully. Aeron was the High Chief of Trans-Falls and

Artigal's right-hand warrior. Only Artigal, as Igentis, held a rank higher than Aeron. To be in the presence of both great leaders was an honor only some had chanced upon.

Many individual tribes like Trans-Falls were scattered around Ventronovia, but they were all united under one leader—the Igentis. He oversaw the rulings of all the individual tribes and made the highest decisions.

Because of this high status, Artigal was free to live in any one of the individual tribes, but he had chosen to live in Trans-Falls. Rumor had it that Artigal was born here. Others believed a stronger spiritual power resided here in Trans-Falls. No one knew for sure though, seeing as no one really knew anything about Artigal.

It wasn't long before they found Jargon faithfully treating the wounded and the dying.

Artigal waited patiently for the black Centaur to finish whispering instructions about a cure to his patient.

"Artigal, I think—" The expression on Jargon's face melted into shock, and whatever he had been trying to say was lost in the wind. "Oh stars, what happened to you? *Zuru.*"

Artigal sighed heavily, as if he had been more defeated in the recent battle than he let on.

As trusted as Aeron was by Artigal, Jargon often got to hear more about Artigal's struggles because of his medical status. He was also the only Centaur who had the authority to give Artigal an order, as long as it was medically based.

"Jargon, I need you to heal me."

Jargon's eyebrows rose in shock and even Aeron couldn't help but stare at the Igentis in amazement. Artigal had always healed himself. He possessed the magic to do so and the knowledge of hundreds of years of being alive. He had even been able to heal his own nearly severed arm once. It was a rare occasion that Jargon knew something that Artigal didn't already.

"*Me* heal *you*? And might I ask why?"

Artigal hung his head, his eyes dark.

Panic gripped Aeron like an icy claw. Artigal had always been their rock, and to see him so defeated shook the High Chief more than he would have liked.

The Igentis' voice lowered to a whisper, and Jargon, who was quick to see how much this disturbed Artigal, quickly pulled him aside, away from other wounded Centaurs nearby.

Artigal shook his head and coughed violently.

Frowning in worry, Jargon handed him three small purple berries, which Artigal popped into his mouth. He sighed as he chewed on the berries, his eyes closed, before taking a deep breath and looking from Aeron to Jargon.

"It was Thaddeus."

Jargon's face went white, and he grasped Artigal's shoulders. He was one of the few who knew of the wound Artigal had dealt to Thaddeus many years ago. Because of that, he had been confident in Artigal's ability to fight and defeat Thaddeus. This was a disturbing turn of events. "Thaddeus? But what about the *Shushequmok?*"

Artigal's face drained of what little life it seemed to have left. He pulled the nearly mangled, dented armor from his chest.

"Emperor help us." Aeron couldn't tear his eyes away from what looked like a black shadow creeping through Artigal's chest, stark in contrast against the Centaur's white skin. The blight spread out into tiny little threads of inky blackness, traveling through his veins, his skin, and deep into his body.

Jargon ran his hand across Artigal's abdomen. The darkness squirmed under his touch. His eyes widened with disbelief. *"Kijaqumok?"* His voice was barely audible.

Aeron wondered if he had heard right.

Artigal nodded his head in assurance.

"Yes."

Aeron frowned, his heart pounding in his chest. This seemed to be like nothing he had ever encountered before, and it most certainly was not Thaddeus' own magic. It was something entirely different that was stronger than any of them here, especially if Artigal himself couldn't heal it.

"What is that?" Aeron moved in closer, and Artigal nodded to Jargon to explain.

Swallowing and shaking his head in incredulity, Jargon crossed his arms. "Corrupt Magic. Darkness straight from the depths of Susahu."

Aeron whistled. "So it can't be healed?"

Jargon nervously looked to Artigal. "Only by the Pure Magic—*Shushequmok.*"

Aeron ran his fingers through his dark hair. "Emperor help us." He quickly turned to Artigal. "But you should have some, right?"

A half-hearted chuckle parted the old Centaur's lips. "Oh yes, I should. But no longer. I am afraid that the *Kijaqumok* took its toll on me and I have temporarily lost connection with the *Shushequmok*."

Aeron felt dread grip him like an icy claw. "But that means that—"

Artigal nodded.

"You'll die." Jargon's eyes misted.

Artigal had, like many other Centaurs, been a mentor to Jargon, and in later life, a close friend.

The Igentis' face was grim as he nodded, his lips pursed and his jaw tight in frustration. He took a deep breath. "But no matter. I have lived my time on this world, and I long for peace. I thought perhaps, though—" He shook his head.

Aeron placed his hand on his friend's shoulder, and Artigal looked to the bright morning skies above him.

"I had only wished to see the Great Emperor's return, that's all." His voice was quiet and nostalgic, his eyes glazing over as if staring into the past before he shook his head and sighed heavily. "But it is of no matter. It was not meant to be."

A cloud hung over the three friends before Artigal suddenly clapped loudly. "But let us rejoice, for the Emperor has chosen to bless us and this land. All that has transpired has been in His will, and we must not tarry in our paths. Aeron, I want you to take your mate and son to the *Gauyuyáwa*."

Aeron, even though he was confused at this order, bowed low. "As you wish, Igentis."

Artigal nodded to him before turning to Jargon. "Jargon, if you could give me something to at least heal whatever can be healed, then I will see about covering this up." He gestured to the Corrupt Magic that was slowly spreading inside of him.

"Of course. I think I may even have a few things that can at least slow down the *Kijaqumok's* progress." Jargon quickly bowed, intending to go straight to his home to get the ingredients, but Artigal rested his hand on the medic's shoulder, halting him.

An odd smile spread across the Igentis' face. "Oh, and Jargon?"

"Igentis?" Jargon raised one of his dark eyebrows.

"I think there might be something of interest to you at your home. When you have healed it, bring it to the *Gauyuyáwa* as soon as possible, but let no one, absolutely no one, see or know of it."

Jargon's face wrinkled in confusion.

Aeron's eyes went wide before narrowing. *What was Artigal's second agenda?*

"I will do so, Igentis."

Artigal quickly dismissed Aeron before he and Jargon retreated from the prying eyes of the other Centaurs.

A puzzled look on his rugged face, Aeron quickly trotted through the forest in search of his wife. She too was a lead healer, second only to their friend, Jargon.

A small smile lifted his lips as he thought of his mate. While a fantastic warrior and archer, her heart had always been in healing. She would be toiling nonstop to help all she could.

Pushing a few branches out of his way, he came across a large gathering of Centaur warriors by one of the main medical buildings within the large, shrouded city-tribe of Trans-Falls.

It didn't take him long to spot his mate, and when he did, a broad grin spread across his tanned face, his heart skipping a few beats.

Frawnden was just finishing bandaging the wound on another Centaur's forehead. Her black hair was intricately braided down her back, a few soft curls framing her sweating, concentrated face. She had a perfect buckskin color: the flowing feathers of hair on her legs were black as night, and so was her tail, while the rest of her horse body was a warm, fiery brown.

His breath caught in his chest as his grin turned to a boyish smile He quietly walked over to her and encircled her in his arms. She sighed and laid her head back on his chest, feeling his warmth.

He kissed her forehead and smiled down into her light brown eyes. She smelled of sweet herbs and flowers—a certain bonus from being a healer.

"What has brought you to my humble little trade, mighty warrior?"

Aeron chuckled and kissed her lips. "Artigal wishes for your and Trojan's presence at the *Gauyuyáwa* ."

Her eyebrows rose in curiosity, but he shook his head.

"That's all I was told."

Nodding, Frawnden quickly disengaged herself from Aeron, and motioned for another healer to take her place before disappearing into the woods. When she returned, a young Centaur was trotting beside her, and once again Aeron's face broke out into a wide grin.

"Father!" Aeron's five-year-old son bucked with joy and ran to give his father a hug. "Mother said that Artigal wanted to see us. Why?" Trojan's eyes sparkled joyously and pleaded with his father to tell him more, but Aeron only shook his head and reminded his son how much Artigal hated anyone being late.

Trojan quickly ran ahead of them, and the proud mother and father watched their son, chuckling at his impatience. The young Centaur took after his mother in his desire for speed, his love of archery, and even his color—a beautiful, perfect buckskin. However, he had never been interested much in healing and preferred to train beside his father with a sword.

Frawnden linked her arm with Aeron's, and they quickly made their way along the roads of Trans-Falls.

Trans-Falls, the Centaur tribes' capital, was a city built as one with the forest. Parts of the magnificent city were on the forest floor, inside the trees themselves, and even high above in the branches. In fact, much of the city couldn't be seen except for what was directly in front of them because it was shrouded in vines and hidden by huge, towering trees, which blocked all but a very green glow from the sunlit leaves.

A ringing bugle caught the attention of all the Centaurs, and a loud murmur rose among them as they too began making their way to the middle of the city.

Because Aeron was their leader, the Centaurs quickly parted for them, and he and his mate were able to move swiftly through the crowd.

Frawnden observed the number of Centaurs that were gathering. "Must be important if he is calling all the tribe together."

"I believe it is." Aeron quickly filled her in on all the details he felt comfortable sharing from his earlier conversation with Artigal and Jargon. A nervous air hung about the two adults.

Aeron called after Trojan to slow down and wait for them, which the young Centaur did respectfully but with a hint of annoyance.

It didn't take them long to see the *Gauyuyáwa,* as it towered high over all the other buildings and trees around it. It was a massive Ravenwood tree, the last Ravenwood tree to exist in Ventronovia and possibly all of Rasa.

The tree was thousands of years old, and because of its age, had been completely hollowed out. Because it was so massive, the Centaurs had been able to craft it into their capitol, which boasted of multiple stories in the trunk of the tree and a fantastic, expansive basement in and amongst the massive root system that had once given the tree life many years ago.

It didn't take the family of three long to weave their way through the parted path of Centaurs and up to the tree.

Aeron nodded to one of the many guards that surrounded the tree. Usually, the tree was considered sacred and the creatures of Trans-Falls had enough respect to not approach it and guards weren't needed. However, big events, such as the aftermath of a battle, usually came a certain amount of unruly chaos, and the guards were an added precaution to both Igentis and the holy tree.

The guard, instantly recognizing his leader, stepped aside so Aeron and his family could gain entrance to the tree.

Pushing open the great, carved wooden door, Aeron quickly entered, followed by Frawnden, and then Trojan.

It was Trojan's first time ever in the great tree, and he was struck by sheer amazement, even at such a young age.

A winding, wooden staircase twined up the interior perimeter of the tree, climbing to higher floors; its railings were made from saplings which had once surrounded the holy tree. Lanterns hung from the twenty-foot-high ceiling, lighting the spacious dwelling with warm, golden glow which seemed almost magical itself. A large, circular table, nearly twenty-five feet smaller in circumference than the tree's interior perimeter, resided in the middle of the room and was covered in an array of maps, charts, furs, and the most delicate of rare sweet-smelling flowers, which filled the room with their pleasant aroma. Beautiful paintings depicting scenes of the more spectacular of Ventronovia's fair landscapes adorned the walls. Small relics with strange engravings only legible to the most learned Centaurs decorated small tables attractively arranged around the room.

Hearing the familiar sound of hoof-beats on wood, Aeron and Frawnden gazed up to see Artigal descending the spiral staircase. Both sighed in relief to see him healed and cleaned up.

He had cleverly hidden his untreatable wound, and other than the sadness that hung in his cold eyes, it would have been hard to tell he had fought so fiercely in battle.

Bowing low before the Igentis, the family awaited orders.

Trojan, who was too thrilled to remember much about courtesy, couldn't help but breathe out a "Woah" at the sight of the majestic Centaur leader, whom he had only ever seen from a distance.

A rare warm smile spread across the wise Centaur's face as he gazed down upon the small Centaur.

Bowing low, Artigal placed his hand underneath the child's chin and lifted Trojan's head up to meet his eyes. Though he had never made it apparent, he had always been especially fond of Trojan.

"You, my son, will grow up to be a fine young Centaur, and your days will be wonderfully filled with the best of purpose and intentions."

Trojan's eyes widened in wonder, and his parents shared a glance at each other that was filled with pride but also worry. It seemed to always be both a blessing and a curse when Artigal bestowed his favor upon someone. His blessings usually had double meaning, only known when it was too late.

"You have been blessed, child, to play a key role in the fate of our country. Never let anyone despise your youth and never stray from the one you will come to love."

Trojan's face shone with amazement and delight. Bowing his head respectfully, he murmured his gratitude, his face a rosy pink blush. Even after many years of toil and hardships, he would never forget those words.

Straightening, Artigal instantly resumed his usual, distant composure of strong leadership, though his eyes still shone with the unmistakable happiness that youth always brought him.

"I hope, Aeron, that you will accept my gift to you and your mate today, and will always cherish the joy, and perhaps the sorrow, that it will bring to you and your family."

Once again, another double-edged blessing. What could the Igentis mean by all this?

Confused, curious, and slightly disturbed, Aeron nodded. "I am positive I will, Artigal." He shared a quick glance with Frawnden, who was just as puzzled as him.

"Good. Now come with me, all of you. I shall present my gift to you and to all of Ventronovia!"

Just before Artigal opened the door to exit, the other three Centaurs close behind him, he quickly turned around and nearly smiled.

"I know that you are worried for my fate and the fate of our Country and the world, but do not fear. We are all in the hands, and under the will of the Emperor. All shall be revealed in the fullness of time." He stepped out of the tree, leaving them just as confused as they had been before.

Shrugging and having to nearly drag their son out of the wondrous place, they quickly followed Artigal outside.

RAISING HIS ARMS to the crowd around him, Artigal immediately acquired the undivided attention of all the individuals. A still silence spread across the city.

"I want to praise you all today for how valiantly you fought on this tragic day." With a bit of basic magic, Artigal was able to project his voice throughout the city so no one would have to repeat him or miss what he said. "If it were not for your courage and sacrifice, this world would be deeper into the hands of Thaddeus, Kyrell, and the Eta King Veltrix's army."

A cheer rose from the crowd, and Artigal paused to let them celebrate in their victory. It had not been clear whether the warriors' mission had been achieved, or even what that mission had been. They hadn't known whether to celebrate or mourn. It was also very seldom that they were openly praised by their strict leader.

A smile crept across Artigal's face before he silenced the people once more.

"I understand that it was hard for many of you to fight without quite knowing why. For those who saw the Duvarharians today, I want to give you closure, and for those of you who did not, I feel that you deserve to know."

Apprehension was thick in the air as each Centaur awaited the answers to their questions.

"The Lord and Lady of the Dragon Palace were indeed taking their child, the *Shelesuujao* spoken of in the Great Lord's Prophecy, to a human city for safety from Thaddeus."

Murmurs rang through the crowd.

"And it is also true that Thaddeus himself intercepted them."

The crowd gasped. Many who had fought Thaddeus before cursed the traitor openly.

Artigal had to wait to be heard.

"Thaddeus himself killed both Lord Drox and Lady Andromeda along with their dragons."

A shocked silence replaced the crowd's noise.

"It had been my hope that we could have prevented such a thing from happening while also saving Ventronovia's *Shelesuujao,* but this was not the case." He paused for a moment, his people hanging on to each of his words. "I understand that there have been rumors going around that the *Shelesuujao* of the Prophecy is dead, along with the Prophecy itself, and I have brought you all together to tell you the truth."

Aeron had to force himself to breathe. Millions of questions ran through his head, and by the look in Frawnden's eyes, he knew she was wondering the same thing. *What had really happened between Artigal and Thaddeus? What had happened to the child?*

Artigal nodded to a Centaur who was hidden by the *Gauyuyáwa's* shadow. Jargon moved into the light, and Aeron strained to see what was with him.

Trojan, who had a better view than his parents and the others in the crowd, gasped in excitement and pawed the dirt even as he did his best to stand still.

"Today, I bring to you a child that is to be adopted into the Tran-Falls Centaur tribe as our own.

"Into the hands of my second-in-command, and Trans-Falls' leader, Aeron, and his mate Frawnden, I present the child promised to us by the Great Emperor, the *Shelesuujao* of Ventronovia—Stephania Lavoisier!"

A gasp rippled through the crowd, and Aeron felt his heart skip. It seemed even the wind had gone silent.

Jargon laid down and whispered something behind him. A small child timidly slid off his back and hid behind his legs, slowly peeking to look out at the creatures before her. It was a small Duvarharian child with long, curly, red hair. No one could doubt it. It was Stephania.

A loud salvo of approval rose amongst the people. Though most were rejoicing to hear that the savior child had lived, others harbored more mixed emotions. Adopting someone of a different Kind into the Centaur tribes had never been done before. It was even more odd to give the child to the tribe's High Chief.

Artigal had to nearly yell to be heard over the excitement, but for once he didn't demand their silence, a broad smile spreading across his face instead. "Aeron and Frawnden are to raise the babe until she returns to where she belongs in New-Fars. Until then, she is a part of us and is the daughter of Aeron and Frawnden. Treat her as such and make her welcome!"

A unanimous cheer rose out across the valley as the message reached every Centaur in the tribe.

Stephania rubbed her dark red, glistening eyes and peered with wonder at the Centaur Aeron, who stood before her, and at Frawnden, who stood beside him, beaming.

Artigal motioned for Stephania to come to him, and she obeyed, standing silently in front of him, her eyes intelligently drinking in all there was to see. His face stern and solemn, he bent down to her and gazed into her large, wondering eyes. Mixed emotions flowed through him. When he stared into her eyes, he felt a deep connection with her, as if she were his own child. He suddenly wanted to take her into his own home and raise her as his own child but ... he sighed heavily and tried to ignore the wave of emotions that suddenly surfaced. He couldn't. Not after what had happened the first time. Tears glistened in his eyes.

Taking a deep breath to calm himself and detach from his emotions, he gently laid his hand on the side of Stephania's neck and spoke a few words in the forgotten Centaur language.

There formed, on the right side of the child's neck, special, red markings that proved her to be a member of the Centaur tribes for the rest of her life.

Just as Artigal was about to hand her over to her new family, Stephania suddenly reached out and placed her hand on the old Centaur's cheek, her face soft and worried. "*Nuse?*" She whispered in the Duvarharian Ancient language.

His eyes met hers, and he suddenly felt like he was no longer in the city of Trans-Falls but in a quiet woods, which now only existed in his memories.

A young Duvarharian girl of about four years old sat on a log in front of him, a large smile across her face. She used to call him '*nuse*' too. He could almost picture her perfectly in his mind as she had been all those years ago—long, silky brown hair, sparkling green eyes, a single dimple in her cheek, her chubby legs swinging as she sat on a fallen tree, a child's laugh barely parting her young lips.

A sad smile spread across his face, and his heart burned with pain. If only, if only. Clenching his jaw, he swallowed hard, trying to push these painful memories out of his mind.

When he opened his eyes, a tear drew a line down his cheek, and Stephania wiped it away in a sudden show of affection.

"*Mewa.*" He whispered to Stephania in the Centaur language.

She tilted her head, and a similar tear traced down her cheek. She could feel his pain and see his memories. She couldn't understand them, but she could understand the pain. Her instincts told her to fill his pain and the void of loneliness and loss within him, and she tried. She threw her arms around Artigal, and he, too shocked to stop himself, hugged her back.

Oh, how he wanted this again! To have a child of his own, even if she was adopted. Why had life treated him so cruelly? He clenched his jaw against the tears which threatened his composure. He had promised to never again have a child of his own. Being immortal had made him realize how hard it was to watch the people he loved die again and again, while he continued to live on. It had made him realize that hardening his heart to those around him was a mercy, but now, that resolution was being shaken to the core.

Gritting his teeth, he shut out the pleading supplications of his heart and suddenly pushed Stephania away from him and into the warm, welcoming arms of Aeron and Frawnden. She would be safe and loved by the High Chief and his mate. They could be the family Stephania needed; he could not.

Once Stephania looked into the eyes of her new family, Artigal felt the connection break and he sighed with relief. He quickly turned his head from them, his face suddenly cold and unloving, and he furiously buried his past—what was, and what could have been—deep within him once more.

Aeron and Frawnden's faces were bright with exhilaration as they held their new child. A roaring cheer rose from the crowd.

His heart no longer sharing in the joy of everyone around him, Artigal disappeared into the forest, leaving the festivities behind.

The child of the Prophecy was safe.

CHAPTER 2

W E SHOULD SEND A MESSAGE to the Dragon Palace to alert them that Stephania is alive and we are taking her to Dalton." Aeron quickly pulled out a blank scroll and hastily dipped his quill into the ink.

A gentle hand rested on his, and he looked up.

Artigal's shimmering, multicolored eyes stared sadly down into his.

"No."

Puzzlement shone clearly on Aeron's face. "Why not? I'm sure they are looking for her."

Artigal shook his head. "No. They are not looking for her. They believe that Stephania is in Thaddeus' control and that the prophecy is dead. They don't know who the helper is, making the last pieces of the prophecy they have impossible to fit together. They have given up."

"But surely they would do anything to get her back."

"What can they do?" The Igentis put his hands behind his back and sighed, averting his gaze from Aeron. "They are extremely outnumbered. They would never survive an attack against Thaddeus' castle in order to retrieve her. They don't know why he would want Stephania, other than that he would raise her to not hate him. They have no idea what really lies within her, what the prophecy really gave them."

Questions spun through Aeron's head, and he slowly placed his quill on the table, looking at the blank paper. "I don't understand."

"I'm afraid you don't have to, nor could you. You must trust me." Artigal barely glanced over his shoulder at Aeron. "And Duvarharia's military leader Syrus—he mustn't know we have her. He is not to be trusted."

"Not to be trusted? But he's leading them! He is Drox and Andromeda's ward! They trusted him."

Artigal thought back to the moments after the battle when he had spoken briefly with Duvarharia's military commander. It was then that he was told that Duvarharia's leaders had been killed, and it was then that he had realized the commander was holding something back. "Yes, but there is something he is hiding. I know he will not betray his people, but I fear that through his love and devotion to Stephania and the mystery he guards within him, he will inadvertently destroy them.

If he comes after her, he will leave the Dragon Palace defenseless. The Duvarharians, especially their military commander, cannot worry themselves over raising a child during war. He must neither be distracted nor tempted by her or Thaddeus. That is why Drox and Andromeda wanted her to be with Dalton in New-Fars to begin with."

Aeron ran his fingers through his thick hair, untangling a few knots along the way. "You're right, of course. And I don't understand, but I will trust you." He stood up from his couch and met Artigal's intense gaze.

A sigh of relief left the old Centaur's lips. "Good. Syrus must not know she is alive. We must keep her hidden from them as long as we can and then take her to Dalton. He is the only creature outside the Dragon Palace who can truly keep her safe."

§

"JARGON, DO YOU HAVE any more of that healing salve?" Frawnden wiped Stephania's warm brow. So far, the child hadn't shown any obvious signs of trauma pertaining to the loss of her parents. Even so, Frawnden, who had quickly grown quite attached to the red-haired girl, knew more was going on in the child's mind.

"Umm." Jargon rustled through his medicine bag and soon pulled out a simple jar with a small label on the lid. "Here. Just make sure you don't use too much of it. It can cause irritation to a child's skin."

Though Frawnden knew this basic information, Jargon still muttered it out of habit, causing his lifelong friend to smile.

They were both very tired from all the hard work over the last few days after the battle and both were ready for a break. Nevertheless, their work was one that never ended, and they were forced to press on. Scooping out a small fingertip of the salve, the Centaur woman smeared it on Stephania's fevered chest.

"Why do you think she has this magic burn on her chest?"

Jargon stopped what he was doing to look more intently at the burn. "I'm not sure," Jargon drawled carefully. "It definitely *is* magic, though."

Frawnden frowned. She knew that the only creature who could have used magic on her was Thaddeus, but it didn't make any sense that Stephania was alive if Thaddeus had really attacked her.

Jargon had his own theories. He instantly recognized the magic to be *Kijaqumok*, the Corrupt Magic, but here it was in a curable form, along with a bit of the *Fubeżersufa*, one of the gentlest but strongest manipulation spells. He began speculating what might have happened between Artigal and Thaddeus, but he didn't like the conclusion. Somehow, Stephania had been with Thaddeus and he hadn't wanted to kill her. For some reason, Thaddeus had wanted her alive.

Considering this and what he knew about spells and the Corrupt Magic in Stephania, Jargon thought the magic wound looked like it was a rebounded spell. Either that, or somehow part of the spell had been blocked by something else. That could possibly mean that Thaddeus himself had a wound similar to that of Artigal's. However, with Artigal's weakening control over the *Shushequmok*, the Pure Magic, it was more likely that Thaddeus' wound would only be temporarily crippling instead of fatal like Artigal's was.

Jargon looked up at Frawnden, who was tickling the solemn girl's feet. A small smile was almost forming on her young, stony face.

Shaking his head, a smile on his own face, he went back to sorting his medical bags and checking off what he needed more of. It wouldn't do any good to worry Frawnden or Aeron with his theories, and it wouldn't be worth it to try and worm the truth out of Artigal.

He felt a sharp tug on his mane and turned around to find Stephania with a fistful of his black hair, her eyes wide with wonder.

"Pretty," she giggled, gripping the hair tighter.

Smiling with shock and delight, the black-colored Centaur pulled her fist out of his hair, and he too tickled her feet, relishing in her light, trilling laugh.

"She is a smart little girl, that's for sure." Jargon shook his head with wonder as Stephania gazed silently at him, her eyes alluding that she completely understood all she saw and heard.

"Incredible, isn't it?" Frawnden sighed heavily. "She's growing up faster than the average Dragon Rider. At least, that's what I've heard from rumors." Her face darkened. "I feel bad having to give her over to Dalton to be raised in a human village. The human children progress so slowly." She shook her head in mourning, and Jargon readily agreed.

"Perhaps it will be soon after she arrives at New-Fars that she will be able to go back to her real home without much fuss from the humans." Jargon smiled, his voice bright and hopeful, though his eyes told a different story. The Dragon Palace was suffering from constant Eta attacks, and now, without parents or anyone else to devote much time to her, Stephania would have to stay with Dalton for an even longer span of time.

Frawnden placed Stephania on her back, the babe instantly threading her hands in the Centaur's soft mane.

"Where is Trojan, do you know?"

While Trojan had been extremely excited to meet his new sister, he had been rudely and accidentally pushed aside by the many high-ranking Centaurs, who wanted to see Ventronovia's savior for themselves, many of whom remembered their fathers and grandfathers telling them of the Prophecy.

Jargon frowned. "I think he got pushed away from the ceremony, and I feel like I recall Aeron telling him to play with the other young Centaurs at the youth training area until you could go and get him."

Frawnden laughed. "Of course he would."

Ever since one of the well-respected Centaurs had approached Artigal with the idea about sporting games for the youth, it was all that was talked about among the children, and was an excellent way for them to learn the ways of war, among other things. Trojan had become quite good at the games and was jumping at every opportunity to go.

As soon as Jargon had replaced all his remedies in his bag, they took off into the forest toward the games.

"Where are we going?"

Frawnden jumped at the light, trilling voice behind her. "Oh!"

She shared a quick, knowing look with Jargon. So Stephania *was* more developed than normal.

"We are going to find your brother, Trojan."

Stephania's little, dark eyebrows shot up before furrowing down into a frown, as if she were contemplating her options. Much to Jargon's surprise and delight, she threw up her chubby, little hands and let out a chuckle.

"Brother!"

A large smile instantly spread across the mother's face. "Yes, your brother!" Frawnden was thrilled with how well Stephania was appearing to adjust to the sudden change in family and lifestyle.

As they traveled through the camp, Centaurs swarmed over to the High Chief's mate and admired, with many blessings and questions, the new and strange addition to the tribe.

Finally, after many interruptions, the two medics arrived at the stream and lake which had been partially designated for the youths' activities.

There were many young Centaurs running around. Some were in organized groups, but many of them were simply running wildly, swinging fake swords and shooting harmless arrows at each other. Normally, it wouldn't be so chaotic, but the young Centaurs liked to celebrate just as much as their parents, even if they didn't quite know why they were celebrating.

After hollering for Trojan for what seemed like an unreasonable amount of time, Frawnden suddenly heard another voice calling Trojan's name as well; she and Jargon were both thrilled to see that it was Stephania who had joined in, having easily caught on to what they were doing. Finally, one of the older Centaurs realized that it was Frawnden herself, along with Chief Medic Jargon, who were calling for the High Chief's son, and it wasn't long before the news traveled and Trojan came bursting out of the crowd. He was grinning wildly with elation at seeing his mother, his breath coming in quick gasps from playing hard.

§

"MOTHER! WHAT ARE you doing here?" He was absolutely thrilled that his mother was finally done talking to the Elders of the tribe. His heart pounded in his chest. He had a new sister, and a Duvarharian one no less! That was something he alone would be able to boast about. His small chest broadened with pride.

His two young friends—a thin, dark-skinned, black Centaur and a golden one—quickly gathered around him, each straining to catch a glimpse of the Duvarharian.

Frawnden smiled softly at her son. "I was wondering if you wanted to spend the rest of the evening with your father and new sister back home."

Trojan's eyes lit up. "Yes, I would love to! Is Father here? I thought he had business to attend to." He danced around, kicking up his heels, before he caught sight of Stephania, who had poked her head around Frawnden's torso to see what was going on.

Trojan hadn't had the chance to see Stephania at great length or spend any time with her, and now he was held spellbound by deep curiosity and awe. It was the first time he had ever seen a creature with only two legs *and* one of the Duvarharian Kind. He and his friends watched her with amusement and wonder.

Stephania grasped hold of the long, braided hair in front of her and slid off Frawnden's tall back, landing with surprising grace on her two feet. After regaining her balance, she tottered over to Trojan and gazed up at him in similar wonder.

"Brother." Her face stern, she solemnly placed her right hand on Trojan's chest.

Both Jargon and Frawnden had to suppress their delighted laughter, though Stephania was extremely serious.

Trojan blinked several times, a surprised gasp leaping from his lips. She was nothing like what he had expected, and he was delighted at the surprise.

A broad grin spreading across his young, face, he grabbed Stephania's hand and pulled her over to his mother.

"Mother, *please* let her ride on my back!" His large, young eyes pleaded pathetically. "I promise I'll be extra careful, and I'll make sure she doesn't fall, and I won't run too fast, and—"

With a laugh and a wave of her hand, Frawnden cut him off, her light brown eyes sparkling at her son's eagerness to welcome Stephania into the family.

The little girl gazed deeply into her new mother's eyes with adoration. "Please?" Her eyes were also large and pleading—impossible to refuse.

"All right, you may!" Frawnden finally gave in.

Jargon roared with laughter, nudging his friend with his elbow.

"She has you wrapped around her little mane." His eyes sparkled jokingly, and she couldn't help but laugh in agreement.

Even before Frawnden's words of consent had finished coming out of her mouth, Trojan had laid down on his front legs and instructed Stephania to climb onto his back.

With a lopsided grin on the pretty girl's face, she straddled his back with ease, quiet chuckles coming from her open, red mouth, her eyes sparkling brightly.

"Are you ready?" Trojan inquired gently.

"Yup! Let's go!" Stephania tapped her heels against his sides, and Trojan started walking slowly after his mother, the two adults already in deep conversation.

"Faster." Stephania had quickly tired of the slow pace.

"No, Stephania," the new big brother gently chastised his sister. "We'll just walk for now."

Stephania pouted profusely, even though Trojan couldn't see it. "Please?"

With such manners, Trojan couldn't help but feel inclined to obey. The young Centaur boy quickly changed his gait from a slow walk to a trot and soon pulled ahead of the two grown-ups.

Stephania's firm grip around the boy's waist assured him that she wouldn't fall off too easily, and he skipped over a few logs here and there, relishing in the laughs and squeals of delight that emitted from his small passenger.

It would be a long walk through the winding wooded road up the mountain that their home had been built into, but Trojan was a long way from tiring.

The longer they walked and talked, the more Stephania got accustomed to her new brother and the more open she was as she spoke to him. Stephania was now deep in conversation with Trojan, and both adults were thoroughly shocked at how wonderfully the child was able to speak and how well she was able to comprehend everything Trojan said.

"Marvelous!" Jargon breathed in delight as they neared the spot where he would part with them. His home was located much closer to the center of the valley than Frawnden's so he could respond to medical emergencies in a timelier manner.

"I can't believe how well she speaks! And for only being about eighteen months old!" Jargon shook his head, his eyes sparkling in wonder at Stephania.

Frawnden was shocked speechless as they listened to snippets of the youngsters' conversation as they told each other about their lives up to this point.

"And he would visit me every day." Stephania was speaking of the times the Dragon Palace's *Susokxoch* had played with her. "He would bring me wittle swords to play with." Her memory was nearly impeccable, and even Trojan was astonished.

"Sword fighting!" Trojan breathed in awe. "I bet that was fun." His mind ran fast, already planning to get her a little sword so he could teach her.

Stephania tapped her heels against Trojan sides. "It was!"

After a few more turns in the road, they came to a simple but elegant log cabin type dwelling that Jargon called home.

While Trojan ran around with Stephania clinging to him happily, the two adults walked through the shady, blossoming trees that lined the walkway to Jargon's house. On either side of the walkway, a large garden sprawled though the cleared out section of woods. Many unique and rare plants grew here, for this was Jargon's medical garden.

"You have quite the special child with you, my friend." Jargon's voice was nearly inaudible so as to not attract the attention of the children.

Frawnden nodded thoughtfully. "Yes, I do, Jargon."

The black Centaur shook his head mournfully, his eyes sad. "I'm afraid though, that with such a good memory, every detail of her parent's death and all that went on there will stay with her forever." He shrugged, sighing heavily. "And who knows what that will do to her!" He speculated that the young girl would easily remember her encounter with Thaddeus and the Battle of the Prophecy, and he worried about how that would affect her mind as she grew. However, he didn't want to worry Frawnden with the extra details.

Frawnden frowned and kicked a rock. "Yes. I think you are right. I only hope that Aeron and I can do a sufficient job in raising her properly."

Jargon placed a reassuring hand on his friend's shoulder. "I know you will."

Bowing respectfully to her, he gently kissed her hand. "Until I see you again, dear friend." He paused before using the old courtesy, "May the suns smile upon your presence."

"As do the stars sing upon yours." The woman finished the saying with a smile and turned away before beckoning her children to her for their long journey home.

§

"FATHER! FATHER!" Trojan breathlessly burst through the doors of the large and stylish log cabin, which hugged the rocky side of the mountain.

Not hearing an answer, Trojan shrugged nonchalantly. He wasn't sure where his father was—his mother hadn't told him—but he knew that it would only be a while before the older Centaur came home.

Stephania, who had fallen asleep during the last few minutes of the journey, jerked awake at the noise. She blinked a few times before yawning and rubbing her eyes.

Gazing around at the new building she was in, the young girl was able to take in most of the beauty and appreciate it.

A large, *Gaikuzh* bear rug greeted them from the middle of the living space, its head facing toward the door with its mouth wide open, showing rows of sharp, terrifying teeth, as if silently protecting the house from any intruders. Mounted on the walls were the heads of many other wild animals, such as enormous wolves, bobcats, buck deer, moose, and other strange animals that lived in the mountain range around Trans-Falls.

Numerous pieces of comfortable and stylish Centaur furniture were arranged attractively around the room. Though the general color for the room was a dark brown, it was made cheery with the addition of intricate metal and glass lanterns, which hung from chains attached to the vaulted, wooden ceiling. The ceiling itself was cleverly adorned with flying buttresses, which were stained the same glossy, dark, red-brown color as the rest of the house.

Just past the living room was a large dining room, the rooms separated by sliding doors. On the left wall of the dining room, double-wide doors led to the spacious kitchen. Built into the wall that separated the living room and the kitchen was a lovely fireplace lined with rock from the surrounding mountainside.

Trotting through his home, Trojan searched for his father, but the adult Centaur was still nowhere to be found.

The youth had raced home ahead of his mother when they had been about half a mile away; it would take Frawnden at her slow walking pace much longer to arrive.

Gently sliding Stephania off his back, he placed her on one of the couches.

Yawning and rubbing her eyes, the babe gazed at her brother.

Trojan laid down, placing his elbows on the edge of the couch, and gazed in awe at the girl. It was still difficult for him to grasp that she only had two legs. He snuck a glance, feeling it almost intrusive to look. Her little feet with five small toes each were so odd and cute.

A broad grin swept across his face, and he stifled a chuckle.

"I'm going to teach you all sorts of things, Stephania." He smiled dreamily, pondering about all the fun they were going to have together. He had dearly wished for a sibling, and it seemed like his dream had come true.

"Archery, sword fighting, swimming, watching the stars, playing *Yu'jac* ..." The list went on and on until Stephania was slumbering quite happily on the comfortable couch.

Noticing this, Trojan abruptly stopped his banter and sneaked as quickly and quietly up the free-hanging spiral staircase as he could.

The staircase led to the upper rooms, which were actually built *in* the mountainside; these rooms consisted of guest bedrooms, game rooms, safety bunkers, libraries, studies, and much more. There was even a second kitchen, in case it was needed.

Once he had reached the loft-like balcony, he trotted quietly to the left and slipped through the large door, entering the cozy cave-like section of the mountain home where guests usually stayed. Continuing further, he came to another door and slid it open. Now he was in the rugged tunnels and rooms within the mountain.

Galloping along the corridors, the boy came to a storage room dedicated to extra pillows, blankets, sheets, and other such bedding items.

Selecting the softest of the smaller blankets that he could find, Trojan grabbed his small bundle and galloped back through the halls, only halting his pace when he came to the staircase in order to not wake Stephania up.

A relieved smile spread across his face at finding the child asleep right where he had left her. He quickly draped the blankets over her small body and tucked them carefully under her, watching with satisfaction as she sighed contently, and a small smile curved her little, red lips.

Then jumping up onto the longest couch, Trojan curled his legs underneath him and leaned against one of the armrests to patiently await the arrival of either one of his parents.

Just as his own eyes were beginning to droop low, a deep voice announced his father's presence behind the boy and near the staircase.

"Trojan! What are you doing here?"

Snapping wide awake and leaping off the couch, Trojan rushed to his father and gave the older Centaur a quick hug. It wasn't in the least bit odd to find his father coming from the interior of the home, for the home was ridden with secret escape routes in case of an attack.

"Oh, Father!" The boy, though bursting with excitement, tried to be as quiet as possible. "Mother said that we could stay here with you for a long time!"

It had been a while since the family had been able to stay together for a long period of time. Aeron was gone most of the time either doing important tasks for the tribe or leading them into battle. Frawnden was usually busy healing the members of her tribe. Because Frawnden was often needed daily at Trans-Falls, she and Trojan spent much of their time at Jargon's house. Sometimes neither adult Centaur got to see each other, or their own home, for months at a time.

"Did she really?" Aeron's deep, amused voice rang out loudly in the room, and Trojan was quick to respectfully quiet his father.

"Yes! Yes, she did!" Excitedly, he put his finger to his lips and "shhhhed" his father. "But, Father, please speak quietly. Stephania's asleep, and I don't want to wake her up. She looks so peaceful."

At the name of his new daughter, Aeron's handsome, battle-worn, and scarred face became solemn, though an unmistakable twinkle of elation sparked in his light blue eyes.

Aeron nodded and lowered his voice. "Thank you, son. I'll speak quietly. Where's your mother?" He was impatient to go and see his new child. He had always wished for a daughter, and the new addition to his family seemed to somehow make it complete. Ever since Roan ... he shook his head, banishing the unwanted memory from his mind. Ever since that day, their family had seemed so small.

"Oh, *Mother*." Trojan screwed up his face and waved his hand. "She should be here soon. She was going so *slowly*. I thought I was going to grow a beard in the time that it took to get home."

Aeron chuckled and ruffled up his son's hair. "Perhaps so, but remember, Trojan, fast and reckless doesn't always get you where you need to be. Sometimes, it can be the exact opposite of helpful. Don't ever criticize someone for their slow pace, lest you not pay attention to yourself and trip over your own path in life."

Trojan bowed his head in slight embarrassment and humility. "Yes, Father. I will remember."

"Good!" A broad grin spread across the father's face and his son's face reflected it.

Just then, the door opened and Frawnden quickly stepped inside, quietly shutting the door behind her. The basket on her right arm swung by her side, much the same as her sword that hung by her left hip. It was an odd combination to be both warrior and healer, but it was one Frawnden had always been fiercely proud of.

Aeron took the basket from her and placed it on a table, its contents of medicinal herbs and flowers adding to the home's pleasant decoration. "Trojan told me that we would be able to stay home."

Frawnden took her mate's hands in hers and nodded excitedly. "Artigal told me we could spend the next six months together, pardoned from our duties, to spend time with Stephania!"

41

"Thank goodness, I think we really need it." Aeron tenderly hugged Frawnden, and he could feel her nod against him.

After quickly kissing her mate, she carefully picked Stephania up. Cradling the small child in her arms, she walked to the rooms downstairs. "Trojan, why don't you pick out one of the rooms for her?"

Trojan quickly trotted back and forth between the two empty rooms that were near his own and his parents'.

After a minute, he picked the room right beside his own that had a door connecting them through the closet.

After he let his mother know of his decision, she handed his sister to him, and turned to her mate. Smiles bloomed across all their faces.

The rest of the evening was spent in a hustled flurry as they worked together to prepare the room for the young girl. The joy that Stephania was bringing was already apparent, but the sorrow Artigal mentioned when adopting her into the tribe still hung over Aeron like a dark cloud.

CHAPTER 3

RTIGAL SLID A HAND under his ceremonial armor and peeled it off his chest. The metal hit the ground with a resounding ring. He stared back at himself, solemn and unmoving in the reflective glass. His colorful eyes strayed to the reflection of his hand on his ribs, and slowly moved it away.

His jaw tightened.

A black spot about the size of his fist crept through his veins just under his skin on the left side of his abdomen, just under his heart. It was small, almost innocuous, but Artigal knew its power.

A string of curses left his lips. It was a fatal wound. It could take years for it to kill him, but nonetheless, his time on Rasa now had an end.

A strange flutter stirred in his heart. *My life is coming to an end. I am ... mortal.* Slowly, he turned away from the mirror, trying to wrap his head around the situation. How many lives had he lived on Rasa? Two thousand? Five thousand? He had stopped counting and stopped caring a thousand or more years ago. He had forgotten the thrills and joys of life. Each hundred years had only been as one. Seconds passed like rain—forgotten as soon as they landed on parched earth. But suddenly, he could count the years he had left. Suddenly, he was mortal again.

He staggered, leaning against the rough wood wall of the *Gauyuyáwa* for support. His heart pounded in his chest, and his head swam. *Free. I will be free. Free from this life, these burdens, all this sorrow. I will go home.* Tears sparkled in his shining eyes.

But a darkness settled as he remembered Stephania. He couldn't die. Not yet. Not before he saw her grow and fulfill her destiny. He had to protect her—it was his duty. Aeron, Frawnden, and Trojan's faces flashed before him, and his heart lurched. His teeth ground against each other. *My ... family.* The distant memory of a beautiful, dark Centaur woman surfaced.

Come on, Athysios!

He could almost hear her again, almost feel her as she pulled him along. *I want to see the falls! The Leño-zhego flowers will be in bloom.*

Fresh tears ran down his face as he reached his empty hand out, grasping at air. Her eyes remained fixed in his mind, but now he wasn't staring at her face; he was staring at Aeron's and Trojan's. They had her eyes. He clenched his fist and snarled. *Athysios.* The name rang in his head like an alarm bringing with it feelings and memories of a life he had buried thousands of years ago.

But through the thousands of years, *she* had come back to him in Aeron and Trojan, and he had taken them in as he never had with any Centaurs since that lifetime so long ago. Through them and Stephania, he had found something to live for again. Would he really have to let all that go?

"No more!" He slammed his fist on the table next to him, his eyes blazing a fiery red. Viciously, he banished the memories from his mind. He had no time to grieve—no time to remember. He had to focus on his duties. Though he himself had been wounded, there was a chance Thaddeus hadn't been and was now on his way to attack Trans-Falls to claim her.

Artigal straightened. Only one way would tell him for sure.

Searching through the many cabinets lining the thick walls, he found a small vial of what he was looking for—*Awowfeya.*

He popped open the container's cork cap and breathed in the thick, almost sugary scent. Letting a single drop of the milky substance within fall to his finger, he quickly capped the vial, returned it to the cabinet, and shut the cabinet door with his free hand.

He hesitated before saying the spell. Dabbling into memories was a low-level form of magic most creatures could easily accomplish. Many creatures used this kind of magic to bask in the good parts of their lives or lessen the hurt of lost loved ones. But Artigal had never been one of them. He had spent thousands of years alive, none of which he wanted to remember or relive, and he had spent too much time burying the few parts of life he had cherished. It had taken him years to perfect the magic that kept his memories at bay. It was dangerous to dabble into his past. He had sworn against it, but now it seemed like he had no other choice.

Before he could change his mind, he let the spell tumble off his lips. The liquid on his finger lifted, hanging over his hand—a droplet suspended in space—before it burst into a swirling orb of crackling, white sparks. The magic that had been trapped in the physical form of liquid pierced his mind, reaching far back into his memories.

Groaning, he sank to his knees. Faces, voices, smells, tastes, sounds, books, places, and homes he had pushed deep down exploded all around him, screaming at him, mocking him, and pushing forward from the depths of his soul. The pain was agonizing. But then a darkness spread through the memories—a single black thread permeating evil. He grasped it and let it drag him from the abyss of his mind to the one memory he had been looking for ...

Hooves thundered. Thorns tore into his skin. Red, blood-stained, white hair.

A tree disintegrated from acid crashed in front of him. He leapt over it, dodging the sizzling branches that fell around him.

Hot heavy breath stung his chest. His muscles burned with effort. Cries of mourning filled the air.

The pursuing dragon's wings were loud, his breath spraying droplets of acid into the air. Its shadow barely flickered through the trees above as purple magic lit up the sky and lit the path in front of him.

His gasping breaths mixed with blurry eyes, stinging cuts, and mumbled prayers.

A purple vine grew out of the ground and tied itself around his hoof.

He fell to the ground, bruised, dirtied, battered.

The dragon roared and began to land.

Artigal prayed. "If it is my time, then this is something worth dying for." He readied the Ancient Magic.

But something was wrong.

The dragon was no longer landing, but was instead rising higher in the sky.

A loud, maniacal laugh rang out from the rider.

Using the Pure Ancient Magic, he was able to hear the voices above him, and his blood froze in terror as he realized Thaddeus and Kyrell were no longer working alone. The traitor now had Corrupt Magic; he had been empowered by the evil and the Dark Lord. With the powerful magic's help, he had figured out that the child wasn't here and had traced her to her current location.

"*Zuru!*" He reversed his course, straining to keep up with the dragon as it sped toward where Stephania was being taken.

"*Zuru,*" he cursed. "I'm getting old." He gasped and shook his head. His muscles burned with the exertion, but the magic that flowed within him pushed him on, guiding him through the thick, dark forest.

Branches whipped his face and vines reached out to trip him.

He could hear the hair-raising screams grow louder ahead of him.

His blood ran cold.

Artigal galloped into a clearing. He ground to a halt, stumbling at the sight that lay before him.

Nearly all his guards lay brutally slain, their bodies butchered and mangled, some even unrecognizable. He stepped forward over a still form, unable to tear his eyes away from the carnage. His eyes wandered over the face of one of the warriors. His head spun. It was the Centaur who had been so happy to take Stephania, so happy to simply hold a child again. He must have been the first to die, and Artigal had been too late to stop it. He had failed the Centaur. If only he had been here sooner. He tore his eyes from the still Centaur's face. His fist tightened. He would avenge him—him and every other Centaur who had died here.

The blood that soaked the ground splattered up onto Artigal's white legs. He recoiled, tasting bile.

Stephania's soft cry jerked him back. He snapped his head around.

Thaddeus was cradling the child in his arms and softly speaking to her, his hands delicate and gentle on her as if she were his own child.

For a moment, Artigal was so struck by seeing this murderer and traitor handling a child so carefully, and almost lovingly, that he could only stare in awe.

Feeling Artigal's presence, Thaddeus' eyes snapped up from Stephania and met the gaze of the old Centaur, a slow grin spreading across his face.

"You are too late, Igentis. Stephania is mine."

Artigal slowly stepped toward Thaddeus, his eyes never leaving the traitor's. He did his best to ignore the moaning cries of the dying Centaurs around him, many of whom he had trained and mentored. They were his brethren; he even had the power to heal some of them, but he was forced to focus on Stephania. With a wave of his hand, he could use the bit of power he had to wash away their pains, but Thaddeus would still win. *Why? Why do I always have to make this choice?* He steeled himself and pushed his emotions aside. He had a duty to Ventronovia, his people, and Stephania's deceased parents. He couldn't let anything stand in his way.

Thaddeus drew a loving finger down Stephania's cheek; she was now merely staring solemnly into his purple eyes. The *Fubeżersufa*, the strongest of the manipulation spells, was slowly working its way into her young mind, calming her, soothing her, comforting her.

"Amusing how the most powerful Dragon Riders always start out as innocent children, isn't it, Artigal?"

Artigal narrowed his eyes and chose not to answer. He could feel the Pure Magic growing in him. However, he knew that if he released this much Ancient Magic, he, in his old age, might not be able to channel it well enough to keep himself or Stephania from being negatively affected. It was risky, but it was the only choice they had left.

"You know, I always wanted to have children, to be married, to have a family." Thaddeus' face softened, and he allowed a small smile to spread across his face. For a moment, a fleeting glimpse of something else surfaced—someone not consumed by evil, hate, and revenge, but someone who had been horribly wronged and denied love. However, it quickly disappeared. "But, you see, the woman whom I loved was never given the chance to love me before she was brutally slaughtered." A light mist covered his eyes. "I'm afraid I was never quite able to love after that. After she and my mother were murdered, I just never really had the heart."

Artigal paused his stalking to listen. No one knew much about Thaddeus' past.

"All I ever wanted was to be loved. To be understood, or at least to be accepted." Thaddeus' face drained of emotion, and he stared blandly down at Stephania, who was beginning to fall asleep. "To have a family and live among people who accepted me. I was robbed of that. It made me realize that I had to renew the corrupt Duvarharia and make it as it had been thousands of years ago, when every dragon and rider was free. Free from the corrupt authorities and toxic societies. Free from their worthless religion, which has done nothing but oppress them."

He gripped Stephania closer to him, his eyes staring off into the distance, past the mutilated Centaurs he had slaughtered. "And now, I have the power to do so. Do you even know what lies in this child, Artigal?" The blankness of his expression disappeared, an evil grin replacing it. "And after her, I only have the *Kvaźajo* to win over to my side before I shall really be able to finish what I started 800 years ago."

Artigal had just been about to release the Pure Magic, but now he hesitated. No one knew who the *Kvaźajo* was. Not even the stars mentioned the individual who was promised to help Stephania free the land from evil.

"Oh, yes," Thaddeus chuckled. "I forgot. You fools don't know who the *Kvaźajo* is, but I do." His voice faded into a whisper, and his eyes glazed, as if he were thinking of something very old or distant. "I think I always knew. I think I was always sure what my fate and his would be."

Artigal hoped pride would get the better of the traitor and that he would reveal the identity of the helper, so he waited, holding the magic within him.

Thaddeus roared with laughter.

As if he could read Artigal's mind—something Artigal begrudgingly realized might be possible with the Corrupt Magic—Thaddeus smirked. "You silly, old beast. You don't really think that I would tell you who it is, do you? Fool. I am not nearly as stupid as some would think. And while it will be hard to convince him to join me, I am confident in it. You see, I know more about the *Kvażajo* and the prophecy than anyone else, and now, thanks to the *Kijaqumok,* I know even more."

Artigal's face paled, his suspicions confirmed.

The Dark Lord was giving Thaddeus power and information now.

The End really was near.

"So you can sense it too. I am guessing that is why you haven't attacked me yet. Perhaps, you have come to the realization that your Lord is not as powerful as mine."

Silence filled the air as they tried to stare each other down.

Artigal was doing his best to channel the Pure Magic through him, but it didn't take him long to realize that Thaddeus had been doing the exact same; now they were simply waiting to see who made the first move.

Artigal knew it would be a disadvantage to release his magic first. Thaddeus, who apparently had more *Kijaqumok* at his disposal, would be able to perfectly counteract Artigal's attack and defeat him. However, the longer Artigal waited, the deeper Stephania would be lost in Thaddeus' manipulation spell. He had to release his own magic now or never.

He took a deep breath to clear his mind and gain as much control over the chaotic power as he could before letting go.

White magic exploded around them but was instantly dissolved by darkness. Artigal cried out as he struggled to channel the powerful magic.

Stephania started screaming, and Thaddeus cursed in his rage.

It all seemed to happen in a matter of seconds.

The darkness crashed down upon Artigal like a thousand knives, and he felt the magic run through his body like a spear, driving the evil deep into him, creating a wound that could never be healed.

Thaddeus laughed in triumph as Artigal slumped to the ground, the energy drained out of him.

Artigal grimaced against the pain and defeat. The dark magic lashed through his body and mind, causing excruciating pain. He tried to stand, to reach out and save Stephania, but he only fell to the ground again, writhing in pain.

Perhaps Thaddeus *had* won.

The traitor suddenly cursed and screamed before another blinding flash of light tore through his vision. The mark of the Great Lord flashed through the darkness in front of Artigal. The magic seemed to be coming from—seemed to be coming from—Stephania.

Thaddeus' and Stephania's screams mingled before the shrieks of the magic itself and of the battling demons and angels that suddenly surrounded them, drowning all else out.

A massive explosion of light knocked Artigal into unconsciousness, and the world around him was plunged into darkness...

With a violent gasp, Artigal lurched back into the present. Blood tickled his throat, and he coughed, the red liquid splattering on his white chest.

His head throbbed and every muscle in his body ached as if he had jumped off a cliff. A curse left his lips followed by a prayer of hope. He had missed something in the memory of when he had fought Thaddeus. It was at the end—that second blast of light. It hadn't come from him, which meant it could have only come from one other source—Stephania, and if that were true, then there was a possibility Thaddeus hadn't escaped unscathed. But he had to be sure.

With a shaking hand, he wiped the blood from his mouth and quickly muttered the spell for the memory-recalling magic, hoping it hadn't all been spent. Again, he was thrown into the raging storm of his memories, but this time, he called that thread of dark magic to him. Again, he let it drag him back to when the darkness had pierced him, and again, the memory from the battle replayed; but this time, he saw something else. A dark silhouette stood against the second explosion of light. A spear made from the light was sticking out of the dark silhouette's chest. A scream mingled with the roar of a dragon filled the air.

Artigal stumbled to the floor, unable to hold himself up. Pain clawed at his body and mind, but a triumphant smile spread slyly across his face. Taking a small towel from the table, he dabbed the blood off his chin and chest, and pulled himself to his feet, gripping the table for support. Slowly, he dragged himself out of the room, down a flight of stairs and into the library. It only took him a few seconds to find the book he was looking for: *A Study on the Ancient Magic, Sleshqumok*

The pages slipped from between his shaking fingers; the weight of the book felt colossal in his exhausted hand, but he patiently searched for what he was looking for.

A sigh of exhilaration parted his lips.

Ancient Magic could only be healed by the opposite pole of magic; a wound made from Pure Magic would only be healed by Cursed Magic, and vice versa.

He closed the book with a satisfying thud and slid it back onto the shelf. Somehow Stephania, even as a babe, had channeled the Pure Magic that had wounded Thaddeus. Artigal judged it would be a near identical wound to his own, which meant that even though he was incapacitated, so was Thaddeus. They would have no trouble from the Duvarharian traitor for a long while. Now it was only a race to see who could heal himself fast enough, or if he even could.

A dark cloud dimmed Artigal's hope. The Pure Magic had been failing him lately. It was unlikely that he would be able to summon enough of it to heal himself. Thaddeus, however, seemed to be at only the beginning of his power in the Cursed Magic. While Artigal would have to rely on magic stored in physical objects, mythical berries, and the protection of Trans-Falls' magic, Thaddeus might be able to gather the Cursed Magic to heal himself, and, even if it took years to do so, they were years that Artigal and Stephania might not have.

Gritting his teeth against a string of curses, Artigal dragged himself from the library and back up to his room.

The laughter of children caught his ear from the open window. The darkness hanging over him lifted with the sound, and he moved closer, peering down to the city in the trees. A curly, red-haired head bobbed next to a black haired-head— Stephania and Trojan.

A slip of a smile sneaked across his pale white lips as he watched them play at the base of the *Gauyuyáwa*. He knew they were waiting for Aeron and Frawnden to leave the meeting they were attending four stories below.

Family.

The word again caught him by surprise but continued to ring in his head. He frowned. He had not called anyone family since he had lost his own many, many years ago. And yet...

He looked back down at the two children playing with each other. Stephania looked up, and her eyes met his. Artigal was startled, but didn't look away. He felt the connection between them again and instead of red eyes, he found himself staring into green ones. Shaking his head, he blinked and broke the contact. He was looking down at her face again, but her eyes were her own—red and suspicious—and the connection was gone.

Aeron and Trojan—descendants of my mate. Stephania—a child like my child. They are ... family.

A frown tugged down his lips. He had let them all into his life, taken them under his wing, cared for them like he hadn't for anyone else in a long time, but he hadn't thought of them as family. Not until now.

His hand strayed to his chest, and his mortality struck him again. He couldn't think of them as family, not now—not when his death loomed near enough that it could cause them suffering.

His gaze shifted down to his hooves, wishing he could drown out the happy sounds of Stephania and Trojan playing below.

A splash of color caught his eye. A spark of dread clipped at his heart. *It is just the floor, nothing else.* But something in him whispered doubtfully. He looked closer. There! On his hoof—a brown spot.

Artigal recoiled in horror, stamping his hoof. The spot was not dirt. He scrubbed at it. It was not a stain.

"Emperor, help me."

It was coloration. His colors were returning to him. He held out his hands, unable to stop the trembling. A bit of pink was hinted in his palms. His heart slammed against his ribs, and he stood perfectly still. Color had left his skin thousands of years ago when he had left his first life behind.

Hastily, he spoke ancient words, and the brown spot and color in his hands were covered by the snow-white sheen he'd had for so long.

Staggering, he slammed the window shut and leaned against the wall. Perhaps his old life was surfacing again. Regardless of how hard he had tried to cover it, it was clawing its way back out.

Was it a gift? Or was it a curse? Whatever it was, Artigal was sure that his past was chasing him down like death now was, and he certainly didn't like being hunted.

CHAPTER 4

Aeron and Frawnden's House

Trans-Falls, Centaur Territory

Year: Rumi 6,098 Q.RJ.M.

Several Months later

A COLD SWEAT BROKE out on her skin. She whimpered, pulling the covers tighter over her head. The room was quiet, dark. A glint of moonlight shone in, striking a stone on her bedside table. Streaks of dim, purple light reflected around the room. The purple flashed through her mind. She felt herself being pulled down, down, down, staring into two purple eyes. The screams of battle reverberated through her ears.

"Fatta!" she wailed, tears pouring down her face. The eyes grew bigger, closer. She felt something warm and wet splash onto her. She screamed hysterically, recoiling.

The door slammed open, and the room flooded with light. Two strong arms pulled her out from under the covers.

She screamed, thrashing against the man until she heard his voice.

"Stephania, my child! It's okay! It's me!"

She stopped struggling, taking a moment to look into his fatherly gaze before burying her face into his shoulder, her sobs echoing around the room.

"It's okay, child. It's okay. I'm here. I'm here." Aeron smoothed her hair, whispering into her ear.

He heard Frawnden's hoofbeats at the door and turned around, nodding to show everything was okay.

She nodded back, her eyes dark with concern. She stayed a moment longer before moving to Trojan's room to assure him all was well.

He listened to her sobs slow down and then stop, her breathing evening out. He didn't need to ask her what had frightened her. It was the trauma of losing her parents. Almost on a weekly basis, he or Frawnden would hear her screams and come rushing to comfort her. The child had not yet been able to give words to these overwhelming, frightening emotions, so they were forced to let her cry herself to sleep.

His eyes slipped around the room as he tucked her back into bed, looking for something that might have triggered the flashback. His eyes landed on a purple gem she had found earlier that day and placed on her bedside table. The purple seemed so familiar. He closed his eyes, concentrating. A memory surfaced and he remembered seeing the flash of a purple dragon soaring overhead—Kryell. Gritting his teeth, he slid the covers over the girl, moving away as Frawnden slipped in next to him, kneeling beside the bed. She whispered something to their daughter that made her smile. Frawnden wiped the girl's tears away and sang a quiet song in *Sházuk*.

Aeron walked around the bed and picked up the stone, a burst of rage coursing through him. Stephania should be safe in their home, not haunted by the blood and gore of her past. She should be safe from that traitor, not haunted by his memory. His fingers wrapped around the gem, and it shattered. He felt the shards pierce his skin, felt the warm, sticky blood on his palm, but he only narrowed his eyes.

He looked down at his mate and adopted child, and felt pride, love, grief, and anger surging through him. The broken purple gem felt like a promise. At even the cost of his own life, he wouldn't let Thaddeus ruin his family. Not again.

§

"NOW PULL BACK. Slowly! Easy!" Trojan stood behind Stephania and instructed her on how to pull back the string on a bow. It was her third summer and her new family had deemed her old enough to learn archery.

The little girl had shown herself to be a quick learner of all the things that her now six-year-old brother was teaching her.

"Like this?" Stephania's voice wavered as she struggled to hold back the powerful string on the small bow that Aeron had made for her.

"Yes! Yes!" Trojan stamped his hoof, a smile tugging the edges of his lips before he slowly let go of her hand, allowing her to hold the string back with her own meager strength.

Grunting at the exertion, Stephania pointed the arrow, as best she could without wobbling too much, at the painted, red, wooden target that loomed before her, nearly fifteen feet away.

She suddenly let go; her arrow arched up and into the sky before soaring over the target and flying into the woods behind the target.

Pouting at her poor shot and disappointed that she hadn't hit the target after nearly an hour of practice, Stephania sighed and sat down, picking at bits of grass in frustration.

Trojan huffed and sighed. "Come on, Steph. Just a few more tries, and then you'll get it!"

The pretty little girl's face twisted. "I don't know, Tro. Maybe I'm just not cut out for this." She shrugged her little shoulders with regret. A few tears leaked out of her shimmering red eyes. She had been looking forward to archery the most, and it pained her to see that she failed miserably at it. She had been so excited to start learning when Frawnden had handcrafted a beautiful bow and surprised her with it. Stephania sniffed back tears. She didn't want her mother to be disappointed that she couldn't shoot, not after all the effort the archer Centaur had put into making the little bow just perfect for her.

Trojan held his hand out to her reassuringly. "Maybe you just need to practice a bunch more. I just *know* you're going to be great at archery."

She grasped his hand, and he helped pull her to her feet.

"You're just saying that to be nice." Her voice was hollow as she accused him.

"No, I'm not! Maybe you're just bad so you'll spend hours practicing, and then *talfindo*! After all that practice, you're a professional!"

She gazed at him skeptically but with a glint of hope. "You really think so?"

"Yes, of course!" He sighed with relief that she was willing to try again. "Come on. Let's go get your arrow. I'll give you a ride."

Her face lightening up, she jumped onto his back with a grace and ease that came from being a Dragon Rider.

Galloping as fast as he could to the woods just past Jargon's yard, Trojan suddenly spotted the arrow sticking straight up in the soft, fertile ground beneath the shade of an enormous oak tree.

"See look! There it is!"

After he came to a stop, Stephania slid off his back and ran over to the minia-

54

ture arrow before grasping it by its shaft and pulling out of the ground.

A sharp gasp parted her lips as she dropped the arrow.

Trojan instantly sensed something was wrong. He took a few steps toward her before the red-haired child screamed and ran over to him, hiding behind him.

Her face grew pale as she stood, paralyzed by fear.

"What is it? What is it, Steph?" Trojan panicked in worry and his own fear. He had never seen her afraid of anything.

Closing her eyes tightly, Stephania breathed through her tears, "A snake!"

Trojan's eyes widened in shock. Stephania had *never* been afraid of snakes or any other reptile for that manner. In fact, she seemed to be some sort of a snake or reptile charmer. Even the poisonous snakes, which were often seen around the valley and surrounding mountains, had been as tame in her hands as a snake raised by a Centaur since its very first day out of the egg.

Releasing her grip from his arm, Trojan took a deep breath and made up his mind to protect his sister no matter what, even if it meant death.

Slowly walking over to the spot where Stephania had been frightened, he cautiously began to search the ground until he spotted it.

It was a pitch-black snake that was nearly seven or eight feet long. It had strange, shimmering, red scales that weaved together into demonic symbols and writings. Its eyes were blood-red, a slim, black pupil in the middle. A dark blue, forked tongue slipped in and out of its mouth as it tasted the air. He had never seen anything like it. A darkness hung in the air around the snake and moved to envelope Trojan. He gasped as the air grew dark and cold.

Turning its head toward the young Centaur, the demonic snake slowly slithered closer to the frightened youth, its tongue mockingly flicking in and out of its mouth.

Licking his dry lips, Trojan carefully reached down to the ground, feeling for a rock, stick, anything that he could use to destroy the demonic beast. But before his fingers could wrap around a large stick that he had felt out, the snake struck at him.

Rearing up, the boy leapt back, dancing around the beast. As he evaded its attacks, he suddenly felt calm; adrenaline poured into his veins.

All around him, the world faded.

Stephania's sobs were the only other thing he heard besides the hissing and slithering of the snake. His focus singled out the snake. He saw every twitch of the creature's body and heard every breath it took.

Feeling out the beast's movements, Trojan reared up once more before he brought his hooves crashing directly on the beast, crushing the triangular shaped head beneath his hoof. This instantly killed it, though its death throes caused it to lash about in the most frightening manner.

The courage within him fleeing, Trojan galloped back to Stephania in a frenzy, his eyes wide with fear and his heart pounding in his chest.

Grasping her hand, Trojan dragged Stephania along beside him until she found the footing to launch herself onto his back and grasp his waist.

Neither spoke a word, each too frightened to say anything.

Trojan galloped past Jargon's house frantically, the cabin vanishing behind them in a blur.

Trees blended together as they tore their way through the woods, not bothering with the roads, which would only prolong their plight.

Galloping through the trees at a surprising pace, a trait he had inherited from his mother, Trojan held his hand out to the trees and traced the carvings he had painstakingly knifed into the bark. This gave him a path to follow. He had made it in order to travel between Jargon's house and the city quickly if necessary. It was much more efficient than the confusing, winding roads.

Finally, they broke through the trees and into the skirts of the tribe. From here, Trojan had no trouble finding his way through the bustling city.

As the two youngsters raced through the crowds, the Centaurs, who were going about their normal everyday duties, cast inquiring glances at the strange couple they had grown used to being among them. They never saw Stephania and Trojan apart. The duo was always seen together, like the moon and stars, or thunder and lightning.

After not finding his mother in any of the places where she usually used to be, Trojan began to panic.

Stephania instantly picked up on his emotions.

"What's wrong?" It was easy for her to sense the boy's worry.

"Nothing." He attempted to brush her off, but she persisted.

"Tell me. I know it's something. I can feel it from you."

He sighed, a small smile nearly making its way onto his face. He couldn't keep anything from her.

"I can't find Mother. She isn't anywhere she should be or where I thought she would be." Exasperated, he stopped to catch his breath and think.

Her heart pounded in her chest. The number of Centaurs in the city center bore down upon her. The clash of hooves on stone mixed with loud banter and the ring of metal hammers on weapons. The noise and chaos pulled her down, back to a memory not long ago, a memory of a battle between Centaur and Etas, between her parents and a traitor. Bile rose in her throat as her nightmares rushed forward, threatening to overcome her. She choked back the unwanted emotion. Now wasn't the time to snivel over nightmares and memory. They needed to find their mother, and right now, she needed the power she had begun to realize she held over the Centaurs.

Stephania slid off her brother's back, ignoring his pleas for her to stay with him and all the fear in her heart, she ran over to the closest Centaur: a large, burly dun male, who was hammering on a sword that he was making. She quickly tapped him as far up his leg as she could reach and waited patiently, her hands quivering from fear of the snake, and now the memories she held at bay.

Growling in frustration at being interrupted from his work, the intimidating Centaur flexed his huge muscles and turned to face the small child, who wasn't the least bit afraid of him.

Seeing who his caller was, his face softened as he bent one leg and bowed low before the child in reverence.

Not at all fazed by the gesture, though Trojan was shocked frozen, Stephania waited until he stood back up before speaking.

"Thank you for your time." Stephania smiled politely, her voice sweet as honey. With an immediate task on hand, it was easy to ignore terror and trauma in favor for a palatable personality that commanded respect.

"Of course, m' lady." His deep voice was gentle and soothing. "What do you ask of me?"

"I need to find Frawnden, my mother. Do you know where she is?"

"Hmm. What a coincidence. As a matter of fact, I do." He absently rubbed the recently changed bandage around his arm. "Come, child. Let me carry you upon my back." He nodded to Trojan. "Come along, son."

Picking the little girl up, who was as light as a feather to him, he placed her upon his broad back, and she immediately gripped his mane.

Trojan, though he was entirely shocked at the patience that had sprung from this short-tempered warrior, followed quickly behind. It was rare that a Centaur Warrior let anything be placed upon his back that would make him equal to a lowly horse, especially a rider.

Very soon, they came to *Gauyuyáwa*.

Gingerly lifting Stephania from his back and gently setting her on the ground, the warrior bowed to her once more. "You shall find her inside. May the suns smile upon your presence, Lady Stephania."

"As do the stars sing upon yours, warrior." Her politeness caused a rare smile to spread on the Centaur's face before he cantered back to his work.

Stephania smiled nervously at Trojan, and he laughed. "By my mane, Stephania! You had that warrior wrapped around your mane!"

A soft giggle parted her lips, and she blushed before mounting his back.

His hooves clopping against the pounded dirt, they slowly approached the elegantly carved door.

Trojan swallowed nervously. Surely, it hadn't been this large and intimidating the first time he entered it, had it?

With a shaking fist, Trojan knocked as loudly as he could and then stepped back.

Only seconds after announcing themselves at the door, Trojan and Stephania watched as the door opened and a young male Centaur with a gleaming, dark brown body poked his head out.

Smiling at the two youngsters, the Centaur turned his head and shouted as loud as he could.

"Frawnden! Your son and daughter are here!"

The air was abruptly filled with the roaring sound of hooves thundering through the hollow tree as Frawnden hurried to see her children.

When she had made it down the flights of stairs and outside, she cried out, "What's wrong? What happened? Are you both okay?" She had specifically instructed them to only come get her if it was an emergency.

Before Trojan could answer, attracted by Frawnden's sudden, anxious actions, Jargon appeared as well, along with Artigal.

Hastily, Trojan told them how they had gone to get Stephania's arrow, encountered the strange snake, and then how he had killed it and ran to get his mother.

Breathless at the end, Trojan panted as everyone soaked in the information before Frawnden spoke, her voice calm and filled with relief that neither had been hurt, though she was obviously disturbed by the story.

"Jargon, will you come with me to see this snake? Artigal, please forgive my sudden haste." She lowered her eyes to the ground out of respect to her leader.

Nodding, Artigal placed a hand on her shoulder. "Of course. In fact, I will come with you."

Turning to the Centaur who had answered the door, the Igentis addressed him. "Chartin. Come with us."

Chartin bowed, always willing to obey the orders of his Igentis.

"Lead the way, Trojan." Artigal motioned solemnly for Trojan to step ahead of him.

With great pride at leading some of the most noteworthy Centaurs, including the Igentis himself, Trojan started off at a canter, hearing and feeling the rumble of the hooves in the soft dirt behind him.

Ducking into the trees where they had exited not long before, Trojan began explaining what he was doing before questions were asked. "This is the way we came from Jargon's house; it's quicker than the road."

"It's fine. Keep going." Artigal was cantering just to the right and behind the young leader.

In silence, the Centaurs hurried on, but not without their own troubled thoughts.

Artigal naturally knew of the dangers of such a beast as Trojan described, especially one that Stephania was afraid of. He had come to trust the little girl's instincts; they were nearly always right.

He also knew that if the snake truly had such strange, demonic symbols on it, then that would mean that it could be a spy from, or at least a creature of, Thaddeus. If it was attracted to Stephania, then that could only mean that she was beginning to develop a magic trace and could be tracked anywhere she went by friends or enemies.

A dark frown creased Artigal's face. She was growing up faster than he had expected.

Jargon could only think that if there were more of these snakes, then he would have to collect this specimen's venom to make an anti-venom. He fumbled for a vial in his bag, wondering if it would be large enough to collect the venom if the snake was really as big as Trojan described.

Frawnden repeatedly kept thinking about how her two children could have been killed and how proud she was that Trojan was able to protect his sister. Silent prayers of thanks to the Emperor parted her lips.

Abruptly, the collection of Centaurs broke out of the trees and onto the road that passed in front of Jargon's house.

Jargon's eyebrows flew up in surprise at the accuracy of the path that led to his house. Subconsciously, he was brooding over whether to take that path to the city when he went to work or continue to take the road. He shook the thoughts from his mind; he would think about that later.

"Over here!" Trojan called out and galloped over into the woods where he had slain the threatening beast.

Artigal was the first to arrive on the scene.

Kneeling, the white Centaur stared long and hard at the cold body of the now still reptile before he picked it up.

Chartin stood at the ready, his dagger drawn in case he needed to strike out at the snake.

Trojan had done his job well, and the snake was stiffening in death.

Frawnden and Jargon gathered around Artigal, and the leader's face darkened.

A whispered name left the old Centaur's lips.

Jargon raised his eyebrows in question, wondering if he had heard the name right, but Artigal didn't explain.

Artigal decided to tell no one of his thoughts, choosing instead to keep them to himself.

Jargon reached out, the small vial in hand, and placed it under one of the four fangs that protruded from the snake's large mouth. Drip by drip the venom from the smashed head filled the bottle. Once it was full, he capped it before pulling out another bottle.

He filled the second bottle with the dark red blood that oozed from the beast's damaged head. He would use these as samples during his study of the creature's anatomy. He knew Artigal would oversee studying the magical aspects of the creature.

Chartin sheathed his weapon after determining the snake no longer posed a threat and carefully collected its body. The leaders mused among themselves for a moment longer before retreating to the cabin, periodically praising Trojan.

The little Centaur boy didn't hear more than a few words; he was already picking up the arrow he and Stephania had originally gone out to find.

With Stephania once more riding upon his back, he trotted over to the target and let her slide off.

"Now, we mustn't shirk your practices just because of failure and fright." Puffing his chest out proudly, he picked up her little bow and handed it to her.

"Try again, only this time, before you shoot, if you have to, point the bow down lower. Okay?"

Stephania nodded solemnly and took the bow from his hands. Notching the arrow to the string, she took a deep breath and pulled the string back as far as she could to her cheek.

"Good! Good! Good!" Trojan jumped up and down in excitement.

She pointed it at the target, her aim wavering, her muscles burning with the strain, before releasing the arrow and snapping her eyes shut at the last second.

The arrow streaked through the air and landed with a thud, the tip just barely embedded in the target and only a few inches from the edge. It was her first time landing the arrow on the target.

Trojan was yelling and dancing around her in elation, and the girl cracked her eyes open to see.

Her eyes widened, and she giggled with joy before running over to Trojan and hopping onto his back.

"Let's go show Mother before she leaves!" Stephania's heart raced in excitement, her face flush with pride.

Trojan, who readily agreed, galloped back to the quaint, little cabin, where the four adults were standing and talking grimly about the situation.

"Mother! Mother!" Stephania's shrill voice rent the air. "I hit the target, Mother!"

Frawnden turned her attention to her children and allowed Trojan to pull her to the target.

Artigal followed silently.

"I can shoot a bow, Mother!" Stephania danced around the target and waved her small bow around.

"I'm so proud of you, little dragon!" Frawnden quickly hugged Stephania and kissed her on the forehead before rubbing their noses together. Stephania giggled gleefully.

"Indeed, you can." Artigal's deep voice rang out from behind Frawnden, and everyone jumped in surprise.

Bending down, the white Centaur picked up another arrow and handed it to Stephania. "Shoot again, child."

She quietly took the arrow and walked away from the target as everyone cleared out of the way.

She inhaled deeply once more and pulled back the string. Pointing the arrow as close as she could to the center and holding it for as long as she could, she released it and closed her eyes in fear before she heard the satisfying thud of the arrow striking the target.

Opening her eyes, she turned her gaze from Artigal, whose face displayed pure, unshielded shock, to where her arrow stood, stuck in the target mere inches from the center.

Even she was amazed.

"Child," Artigal turned his face to her. "You truly have a gift for shooting a bow. I want you and Trojan to practice every day for a week and then exactly seven days from today, when the suns are high in their path of the skies, come find me behind the *Gauyuyáwa*."

With that, he turned from them and trotted back to the cabin where Jargon stood, with the snake in a bag he had gotten from his home.

Frawnden praised her children before reluctantly departing from them after a few minutes.

After the adults had gone, keeping their private talk from the children, Stephania and Trojan stood in silence before the older one's voice broke the still air. "Well! We must keep practicing if you are to be a master marksman by next week."

He picked the quiver up from the ground and pulled out another one of the red-feathered shafts. Bowing to his sister, he majestically held it out to her playfully. "Shall we?"

She laughed and took the arrow from him.

All the rest of that day, they both shot the bow and arrows until neither of them could lift their arms, and they resorted to staring at the smooth, blue sky while lying in the lush summer grass.

CHAPTER 5

North of Trans-Falls, Centaur Territory
Outskirts of the Cavos Desert

AERON HELD UP THE LETTER he had received from Artigal. His face was masked, so his closest advisor and second-in-command couldn't read his wave of emotions.

"Artigal sends for me, Flandor. Gather my armies and set yourself up to lead them into battle tomorrow against the human army in Nor. We still need to find proof that some of the humans are being led by Thaddeus. I will go alone back to the tribe. When you attack Nor, leave no survivors, and make sure there is nothing left for Thaddeus to take. We will rebuild the city later." Aeron's solemn, deep voice penetrated through the silent tent.

Flandor, a gleaming black Centaur with a cold but thoughtful and wise personality, bowed low. "It will be done, Aeron, though I do not advise you to go alone. Regardless of the reason Artigal sent for you, it can't be safe for you to travel alone, even if you think you could go faster that way."

Aeron nodded. "Thank you for your concern, Flandor. I will consider your argument. For now, go tell the leaders of the divisions of my departure. I will be gone by sundown." His harsh, commanding voice ended the conversation, and Flandor bowed once more before exiting the tent.

Standing at the table in the center of the room, Aeron laid out the letter and read it again.

Addressed to the First-in-command, Aeron, High Chief of Trans-Falls and right hand to Igentis.

I bring to you news of your family. Stephania was recently attacked by a young Susahu Viper. Thankfully, Trojan slayed the beast before it did your daughter any harm.

Her skills in weaponry are progressing rapidly with help from Trojan, and her Duvarharian powers are growing at an alarming rate.

Thaddeus' allies are already searching for her, and I fear it won't be long before the more dangerous followers catch wind of her. I only hope they haven't already.

As for you and your army, be prepared to leave your camp by tomorrow. When the moon starts waning, I am taking some of the Trans-Falls tribe to go with us to New-Fars for protection. If you do not arrive back in Trans-Falls by that time, we will be force to depart without you.

Give orders to Flandor to take over the mission against the human army at Nor. They are a threat to us and may be the source of the Susahu Viper. Take the city, find evidence of Thaddeus' leadership in the Human Domain, then leave nothing behind. We will rebuild the city at a later date.

After this, they are to travel to the Sankyz tribe with reinforcements. There have been five sightings of approximately 500 Etas outside of the Sankyz tribe of the Cavos desert. Their army has been weakened by a series of attacks from Veltrix and his Eta army over the last few months, and I fear for their demise.

Make haste to Trans-Falls. It is time.

The Igentis, Artigal

The letter left Aeron worried and empty. Secretly, he had hoped that they wouldn't have to take Stephania to New-Fars for quite some time, or if ever. He had hardly been able to spend any time with her, and this seemed so sudden. He had so much he wanted to teach her and so many memories he wanted to make.

It would take almost a year to reach New-Fars; with mountain ranges, skirmishes, and other detours and delays, it could take even longer.

Rolling up the letter carefully and tying it back in the silky ribbon it had arrived in, the gray-bodied Centaur placed it in his satchel before drawing out a fresh blank piece of paper.

Dipping his writing quill into the black ink, he then proceeded to carefully write out detailed orders for the battles at Nor and Sankyz along with directions for travel. He gingerly folded the letter and dabbed a bit of hot wax on it before pressing his signet ring into the wax, sealing the message.

He grabbed his satchel, which held all he had taken to war except for his armor and weapons, and took one last look around the large tent. A heavy sigh left his lips, and his shoulders sagged a bit.

Flandor would take care of everything, but Aeron hated to miss being in the heat of the battle. However, he was sure he would get to do plenty of fighting when he began his travels back to Trans-Falls and from there to New-Fars.

Trotting out of the leather tent, he proudly gazed out over the hill at his army, which resided in the valley and stretched across the hills of the grassy, sloping land.

Cantering down the side of the hill, he pondered the roads he would take, along with what short cuts would make his travels quicker and easier and those which would make it more dangerous. He also mused about who to take with him.

He mourned that he couldn't take Flandor; the black Centaur was his brother in war and had trained the hard and grueling war courses with Aeron, even since a very young age.

Just as Frawnden was with Jargon, Aeron and Flandor were inseparable. Aeron knew that it could be nearly five years before he could ever hope to see his friend again; a lot could happen in that span of time, especially when one's life was on the battlefield.

As he was reaching the bottom of the mountain, he made up his mind. He would take Landen, a young, light brown Centaur, who was beginning to display a talent for shooting the bow and who was quickly rising to the top of the best archers in Aeron's army. Not to mention, the younger Centaur was also proving to be a wonderful healer.

Landen reminded the High Chief of his mate, Frawnden.

Before Frawnden had gone into the schooling of medicine, she had top scores in the elite archery class; it was in that class that Aeron had met her, and they had fallen in love.

The battle-hardened Centaur smiled at the memory.

Although he relished the life of war, he deeply missed his small family, and readily awaited the day when he would be back with them.

Trotting amongst his troops, as all of them saluted their formidable leader, he searched until he came to the group of archers where he knew Landen would be.

All the Centaurs, male and female alike, came to attention.

"Landen! Come forth!" Aeron's deep voice echoed in the land, and the quiet but sharp-eyed Centaur stepped forward.

"Pack up your things and meet me at the edge of camp to the south. You and I will leave by sunset."

Though surprise lit the obedient Centaur's face, he bowed respectfully and answered in his quiet drawl. "Of course, commander. I will be there."

Aeron nodded, satisfied that the young soldier would indeed be there.

Trotting back through the camp, he came to a small tent that was pitched farther away from the rest and positioned next to another much like it. It wasn't the main meeting tent he had been in moments before; it was Flandor's personal tent. Aeron's was the one just beside it.

Ducking under the deerskin flap that covered the door, the commander began to pack up the rest of the things he needed, including his armor and weaponry, along with a short supply of food.

In only a few moments, he completed the packing of his meager supplies. He could only hope that Landen would be just as fast and thorough with his packing, not causing Aeron's pace to be any slower than needed.

He wasn't disappointed.

Landen was already waiting at the desired meeting place, and Aeron breathed a sigh of relief. He motioned to Landen that he would be a few minutes before trotting off again to find Flandor.

The black Centaur was inspecting the weaponry of a small blacksmithing division. Some sort of fight seemed to be ensuing between Flandor and another Centaur who apparently wasn't doing the best he could at sharpening the swords.

The barbaric growls of the two Centaurs quickly filled the small camp, and the other warriors backed off as the younger Centaur challenged his superior.

Aeron stifled a chuckle as he watched a sly smile spread across Flandor's scarred, chiseled face.

The two Centaurs locked together in a gripping fight, their hooves striking out viciously at each other, their muscles stretching and flexing, their skin shining in the bright sun as sweat collected on their sleek bodies.

In less than five minutes, the blacksmith was thrown and pinned to the ground.

"If your hand-to-hand combat is really this pathetic, solider," Flandor hissed through heavy breath, "then I expect those swords to be sharp enough to do *some* sort of damage."

Panting, his eyes wide with defeat, the bested Centaur nodded quickly, and after Flandor let him go, struggled to his feet before limping away and into the arms of his laughing friends.

Flandor only allowed himself a broad smile when he was beside Aeron.

"Such fire. I wish half our army had the spunk he did. We'd have Thaddeus' *elu* whipped in a matter of days."

Aeron roared with laughter and slapped his hand on his friend's back. "You old *fálaz!* You've still got it."

Flandor shrugged and brushed himself off as he drawled out in his thick, exotic accent, "Don't think I ever lost it, my friend."

Aeron shook his head. "No, of course you didn't."

They were suddenly both grave as their eyes met. There was so much to be said, but nothing they needed to speak out loud.

Flandor clasped Aeron's shoulder and they merely stared into each other's eyes for a moment. "Take care, *fom*. May the suns smile upon your presence."

Aeron nodded. "As do the stars sing upon yours. Take care of my army, will you?"

"On my honor."

"Until I see you again, *fom.*"

Flandor nodded slightly. "Until then, Aeron."

Each quickly clasped the other's forearms, small smiles lifting their lips before they parted, neither looking back.

Consumed by the heavy emotions that flowed through him, Aeron motioned to Landen. "Come, son. We must move quickly if we are to reach Trans-Falls in seven days." With a heavy sigh, Aeron traced the path of the setting suns with his hand to determine the time of day.

Landen nodded and shouldered his pack, his armor on him, his weapons across his back and around his waist.

They started off at a brisk trot, traveling in silence except when the sounds of the forest broke the quiet. Much to Aeron's gratitude, the lad never asked a single question but did exactly as he was told the instant he was ordered to, only giving input after he had completed the task or if he had seen a better way to proceed. Aeron observed that the young male had great potential to become a leader, and he knew he had picked an excellent companion for his long journey.

The High Chief hoped that the young Centaur would keep up the good work. It was a hard and long road ahead, and they had only just begun.

§

"**TROJAN HURRY!**" Frawnden's motherly voice rang out after her son as the excited youth galloped around the house, franticly gathering the things he needed to take into the city today.

It was exactly one week since the day the Susahu Viper had attacked, which meant it was the day that Artigal wanted to see Stephania shoot her bow and arrow.

They had been practicing every day from sunrise to sunset, and Stephania could now shoot the middle of the target three out of five times; Trojan was fiercely proud to be her teacher.

He knew he would be looked upon as a marvelous teacher—a revered position in the tribes. The Centaurs believed that the greatest warrior was he who braved the insolence of youth to pass his knowledge on. Therefore, Trojan also felt very responsible for how well Stephania would do today, and he was making sure everything would be perfect for her.

On the other hand, Stephania wasn't the least bit worried. She knew she would do just as well today as she had been doing, if not better. She mostly considered it amusing how seriously Trojan was taking this; she had yet to realize just how special this occasion was.

"I *know*, Mother! I'm just trying to find Stephania's armguard! I know I put it here somewhere!"

Frawnden chuckled at her son. She was proud of her children and knew they would do splendidly in the demonstration Artigal had requested.

"Tro, I have it already." Stephania's light, amused voice came from behind a doorway, and her head popped out around the corner.

"What?" Trojan exasperatedly raced to her, running his fingers frantically through his hair. "Why didn't you tell me that earlier? You know I've been looking for it!" he growled angrily at her, swiping the leather armguard from her outstretched hand before shoving it in the small bag he was carrying.

Stephania shrugged and smiled slyly. "It was funny to watch you run around for it." A giggle parted her delicate red lips and displayed twin dimples in each cheek.

Trojan groaned and shouldered his leather pack.

"Stephania, you mustn't tease your brother like that, even if you think it amusing to watch. He is working very hard to get you ready for this day, and the lessons he has given you are the reason Artigal was impressed enough to invite you. Do not treat your brother and mentor so lightly. Do not laugh casually at another's struggle." Frawnden placed her hands sternly on her waist.

Stephania bowed her curly, red-haired head. "Yes, Mother. I'm sorry for teasing you, Trojan. I should be more considerate of you. Please accept my apology." A nervous smile raised her lips. She hated doing anything that caused her mother to scold her.

Trojan smiled and placed a reassuring hand on her small shoulder. "I accept. Now are we ready to go?"

She lifted her face and smiled her bright, elated smile. "Yes!" She hopped astride his back, wrapping her thin arms around his waist.

Trojan galloped out of the house, knowing his mother would catch up later.

While they still had plenty of time before when Artigal had designated they meet, Trojan had projected a desired departure time so he and Stephania could stop by one of the streams. They were merely going to be late for their opportunity to take the small detour for a swim. He had figured it would be relaxing and help ease their stress over the demonstration, but he now realized that only he was anxious.

Trees flew by in a blur as they hastily made their way to the rushing stream which happily bubbled over smooth stones polished by its sparkling, blue waters.

When they reached their destination, Stephania swiftly jumped from her brother's strong, broad back and took off her boots and cloak, along with her top-shirt and small over-pants, leaving her in a simple brown undershirt and tight, black shorts.

Trojan threw off his belt and the knives with it, dropping his carrying bag at the edge of the stream before leaping over the ten-foot ledge and into the waters beneath him.

Stephania quickly followed suit, and they were both soon splashing and swimming around in the four-to-five-feet deep waters, cooling themselves off after the hot run. Though Stephania had proved to be a fairly decent swimmer, Trojan made sure he kept an eye on her at all times.

Soon the seasonal rains would slow and the waters would recede to their normal, more shallow depth, but until then the children took advantage of the cooling waters whenever they could. Both loved the solitude of the quiet, secluded stream.

After nearly half an hour of swimming, Trojan measured the path of the suns and realized that it was time for them to go or they would actually be late this time.

"Come on, Steph. We'd better get going." Though he knew they had to leave, he still let out a mournful sigh.

Hurrying out of the chilling water, they did their best to dry themselves off with the little they had. After stuffing Stephania's dry clothes in the bag, Trojan clipped his belt back on and slipped the quiver over her back.

She would put her dry clothes back on when they reached Jargon's house and the wind had sufficiently dried her off.

For most of the trip, they moved in silence—something that often reigned while they were together. They were so close, they hardly had to exchange words to be understood; they were most often simply content to be in each other's company.

Trojan persistently unbuckled and buckled the small piece of leather on his chest, his tail swishing erratically and nervously. Something that sounded like a whispered prayer hoping he had trained her well enough poured from his lips.

Stephania hardly paid any attention, however. She was brooding over something much deeper and pressing—something that troubled her young mind and haunted her thoughts continually—her real parents.

She often wondered about her birth parents, Andromeda and Drox. The night they died, she had seen more death than anyone should ever have to see. She had seen the disgusting bloodiness of war, had smelled the rankness of death and Etas, and had heard the screaming cries of the dying and the wounded.

Sometimes, she wanted to talk to someone about it, to tell someone what it felt like to wake up screaming, thinking she was in the mist of the battle once again, but she didn't know how. She had no way to properly process her emotions or feelings, let alone begin to understand the turmoil that festered within her.

Instead, it festered inside her, fueling fear and anger; it hung over her like a constant, rank cloud, driving her further and further into seclusion.

She knew Trojan had come close to understanding those few times she had let a thought slip out, but he never pushed her past what she was comfortable sharing. More often, he was simply quiet, letting the silence and the gentleness of their love sooth her pain.

She didn't fully understand the trauma that surrounded and followed her. She wasn't like the other children, like Trojan's friends. Their eyes were bright, youthful, happy—the opposite of the lurking darkness she could never seem to shake off. She didn't know how to talk to, or even see the Centaurs without the slaughter of that night overcoming her, drowning her in blood. The confusion it brought was too overwhelming to cope with and forced her to avoid the other Centaurs besides her adopted family and Jargon. Somehow, Trojan felt like home—the only place she felt safe. Without him, she felt estranged from everyone else, as if she didn't have a tether to the creatures and world around her. But even with his comforting presence, she always felt alone in her fear and anger.

Tears collected in her eyes, her little hands balling into fists.

"Stephania. Stephania!" Trojan yelled at his sister until he got her attention.

Jerked from her thoughts, Stephania tumbled from his back and rubbed her eyes.

She hadn't realized how long she had spaced out. She pushed her thoughts to the back of her mind, but they were never really gone, simply waiting for her later. As long as she remembered, she would never be rid of this shadow.

They were at Jargon's house, and Trojan was tossing her dry clothes to her, which collected in a pile at her feet.

"We're here? Already?" She stumbled around as she struggled to dress herself in her absentmindedness.

"Yes, we are." Trojan impatiently stamped his hooves. "Just hurry and let's go. We're going to be late. There's only five more minutes until noon!"

At this news, Stephania was wide awake and pulling on her clothes as fast as she could. After adorning her in the miniature archery armor Aeron had crafted for her, Trojan strung her bow and slid it across her shoulders along with her quiver.

In moments, after grabbing a quick snack from Jargon's house, they were once more rushing through the leafy boughs of the various trees that dotted the landscape and gave life to the valley.

Stephania was beginning to become anxious at the feat ahead of her, but she didn't have much time to think about it because all too soon, they arrived at the center of Trans-Falls.

Gauyuyáwa loomed above the two children as if challenging them. It made Trojan and Stephania feel very small and even more nervous.

Stephania quickly dismounted, and they shuffled up to the door.

Trojan hesitated. Biting his lip and fighting back the butterflies that took flight

71

in his stomach, he reached up and knocked against the mighty wooden door before stepping back to await an answer.

As always, they didn't have to wait long.

A Centaur, one whom neither child recognized, opened the door. When her eyes met the Centaur's Stephania took a step behind Trojan, her heart racing.

"What may I do for you, Stephania and Trojan, daughter and son of Aeron and Frawnden?" The Centaur's deep, gentle voice eased the boy and girl's fears slightly, but Stephania still found it difficult to meet his piercing, skeptical gaze.

Trojan cleared his throat. "We've come to see Artigal. He requested our presence at this time and day." The young buckskin shifted his weight and looked the older Centaur in the eye, his eyes never straying from those of the elder.

He nodded and smiled at the confident youth. "I will summon him, Trojan." The door shut heavily behind him.

Trojan breathed out a loud sigh of relief.

Just when the two children were beginning to think they had been forgotten, the door swung open and Artigal appeared, his black armor shimmering in the noon suns' shine—a stark contrast to his white skin and hair.

Trojan bowed, never ceasing to be awed at the sight of their leader's majesty, but Stephania remained still, her eyes locked with Artigal's as a suppressed memory rose, one of pain, magic, and purple eyes.

Trojan's confident voice snapped her back to reality. "Sir. I have trained Stephania Lavoisier, my sister, as you have instructed me to." His tail twitched nervously but his words never wavered. "She is ready to demonstrate her skill in archery for you here today."

Artigal nodded solemnly. "Very good. Come with me."

They followed him far into the woods behind *Gauyuyáwa*.

No one else followed, not even Frawnden, who had just arrived. She wouldn't know of the outcome until they came back.

They soon came to a pleasant clearing where a plethora of targets and obstacle courses dotted the landscape.

This is where Artigal personally oversaw the training of the top Centaur Warriors, including Trojan's own father, Aeron, and Jargon. It was where only the best were trained, and once again, only Trojan understood the significance of this. He sucked in a deep breath. "Wow."

"How far do you usually shoot away from the target, Stephania?" Artigal turned to her when they had reached a few large targets. His multicolored eyes portrayed nothing of what he was feeling.

"About fifteen paces, sir." She looked down at her feet and shifted her weight nervously.

Artigal narrowed his eyes. "Then shoot twenty paces away." He smiled slyly, almost daringly.

Stephania's eyes widened, and Trojan gulped before stepping out of the way.

"It's up to you now, Steph. Good luck."

Nodding, she took several deep breaths before she counted the distance away from the target to twenty paces.

Artigal's silence almost unnerved her, but she pushed her fear and memories aside, focusing instead on strapping the quiver to her back and drawing out her small but powerful bow.

Closing her eyes, she imagined herself alone, in the middle of a clearing, tall forest all around her, glowing red eyes peering out at her through the branches.

In her mind, she pictured an Eta. It was simple but terrifying all the same with its rotting flesh and oozing, black blood.

She let her hatred of those repulsive beasts fill her mind.

When she opened her eyes, her dark red irises were glowing a bright bloodred, which matched her hair—something neither Artigal nor Trojan could see.

A spirit moved inside of her—a spirit of fear and anger, of destruction and death. It consumed her and controlled her.

She pulled back her bow and aimed it at the center of the target. She no longer saw the wooden target with the red paint, only the image of the Eta she had created; its heart lay over the center of the bull's-eye.

She took a deep breath and closed her eyes. A few barely inaudible words in the Ancient Language subconsciously ran out of her mouth. She released the string. The arrow streaked through the air with a sinister hiss.

A loud thud marked the entrance of the arrow into the target.

Artigal gasped.

Trojan yelped in shock and elation.

Stephania's eyes opened. The spirit of fear and anger had left her, and her eyes had dimmed to their normal dark red. She gazed, perplexed, at the target.

Her arrow had struck the exact center of the target and had gone all the way through it, lodging itself into the solid piece of wood that held the target upright.

This, however, wasn't the cause of shock from Artigal and amazement from Trojan.

The arrow was covered in flames, and in seconds, the whole target was engulfed in them; its heat radiated all the way to the three Ventronovians nearly twenty feet away.

Stephania had created magic.

CHAPTER 6

Gauyuyáwa,

Trans-Falls, Centaur Territory

THIS IS SO MUCH WORSE than I had feared." Artigal's cold, worried voice echoed forebodingly throughout the hollow tree. "With her sudden easy and inexplicable knowledge of magic, I'm surprised we haven't had more visitors than just that little snake. With her magical footprint embedded more and more strongly here, even by the minute, we are putting us and her in extreme danger. I fear that New-Fars, with the power that she is channeling, may even be too close to the enemy, but that can't be helped. It is, however, the best place for now, and we must strive to do what her parents had in mind for her. We will have to think of something else in order to keep her safe from her magic trace. However, until we figure something out, it can't be helped.

"As much as I would have liked her to remain in the protection of Trans-Falls' magic until she was older and traveling wouldn't be so difficult, we cannot afford to wait any longer."

Artigal turned his piercing gaze from his commanding officers to Frawnden, who was standing a few feet away from the others, her face pale. She swallowed hard and fidgeted with a strand of her black mane.

Artigal's heart softened, and he allowed her a very small smile.

"I'm afraid that we can't wait for your mate either, Frawnden. Tomorrow, a third of us will break camp and leave. If Aeron is not back by then, we must leave without him."

Frawnden nodded miserably, tears misting in her eyes. Once again, her family would be divided and for a longer period of time than she had ever dreamed of.

"I'm sorry all this has fallen so heavily on your shoulders, Frawnden. I will do my best to ease your pain, but this will be hard on all of us. Remember, your family is not the only one that will be broken."

Frawnden stepped back into the shadows, the barely audible sounds of crying reaching Artigal as he shut her misery from himself.

He turned back to his commanding officers.

"I will need your most elite Centaurs on the job. Stephania must see as little of the skirmishes as possible. The more she knows of magical things, the more her trace will grow, putting not only her, but all of us in danger. Only Dalton, being a Dragon Rider, can teach her who she really is while keeping her undercover with his magic until she is ready to shield herself with her own. Please prepare as best as you can. Take only what you will need. You are dismissed."

The officers saluted their leader and hastened to ready their troops.

"Frawnden," Artigal whispered sadly.

She bowed in reverence to her leader, her teeth digging into her bottom lip. "Yes, Artigal?"

Though his heart ached to say more, he had to keep his words short. "Pack up only your most prized and needed belongings. Gather up Trojan and Stephania to you and keep them safe. Our lives depend on their safety. Take comfort in the Great Emperor. He shall preserve us."

§

"WOULD IT BE WISE for us to break camp here or to continue until midnight?" Landen shifted his pack onto his other shoulder.

"We have about another fifty miles to cover in two days." Aeron squinted into the sunset. "I think it would be wise to make camp here." He nodded at the youth, approving his sharp eye.

After the command to stop, Landen began to build a fire and soon declared that he was going off to gather water for the night.

With pride, Aeron watched as the capable soldier trotted off down the small cliff in front of him to a stream that parted the miniature valley beneath them.

They were just entering the mountain range that protected their homeland, and though they only had a mere fifty miles to go, it would be hard to cross the monstrous mountains and bear through the valley's treacherously unstable weather patterns.

So far, Aeron hadn't regretted his choice of the young soldier in the least.

The young adult's gift for hunting and scouting was just what Aeron had needed. Landen's expertise with the bow was incredible, and it would give an edge to the two travelers should the need arise for fighting in this wilderness.

As the land stretched out before Aeron—the purple mountain peaks looming in the near distance with clouds dancing around their snowy tops— he couldn't help but wonder how and why Thaddeus thought that he would be able to subjugate all of this wild land.

It wasn't anyone's land but its own. Not even the Centaurs had been able to tame it. Only the Dragon Riders had been able to bend the very earth to their will, and only because they had a shadow of the Creator's Magic.

From where they had camped at the top of the plateau, Aeron watched a stream slithering at its base. Bubbling happily, the clear water trickled slowly across the meadow in the carved-out valley it called home.

Aeron wished, for a fleeting moment, that life was more like the stream—gentle, happy, peaceful but as he thought of it, he realized that if he were a stream, he wouldn't be able to comprehend the beauty that he saw around him.

A smile drew across his face, and a chuckle left his lips.

It was with great fondness that Aeron looked out over this land. He remembered crossing this valley when he was a young teenager years ago, when his father had decided to move back to Trans-Falls after Aeron's mother had died. It was here that Aeron had shot his first bull elk with the bow his father had lovingly carved for him. Aeron had been hunting animals since he was Trojan's age, but the experience of shooting his first elk was momentous. He still had the grand antlers and even the bow.

By now, Aeron could see Landen crouching by the stream and filling up the water flasks.

Suddenly, the young Centaur jumped up and drew his bow, fitting an arrow onto the string and pointing it at his target in a mere fraction of a second.

Aeron held his breath and readied his sword; all his senses were on the alert in case whatever might be down there would also be up here.

Landen's eyes narrowed. His chest rose with a small breath and he released the string.

A sickening, unnatural scream rent the air.

Aeron kicked dirt into the fire before galloping down the side of the plateau cliff.

Landen shot a second arrow, and another scream echoed in the rocks of the nearby ledge.

Aeron dropped his burden at the base of the ledge and galloped to the young warrior's side.

All movement ceased.

Both Centaurs stood absolutely still, ready to spring at any second, their breath held fast in their chests.

A screech tore through the silence as another one of the mysterious creatures launched itself at Landen's back.

Aeron had no time to warn him. In one heart-stopping moment, Aeron's sword cut through the air. It seemed as if he would be too late, but the blade slid into the abdomen of the creature, and once again the air was rent with shrill shrieks. The creature fell, twitching in the throes of death.

They waited at the ready, but no more came out.

After wiping his sword on the grass, Aeron knelt beside the first creature that had been killed and surveyed it.

"Is it a mutant with mange?" Landen shifted his stance uneasily.

Aeron slowly shook his head.

After he kicked the body into the stream, the creature's identity became clear as a thick trail of black blood flowed into the current.

Landen's eye widened. "Etas."

§

AERON GALLOPED INTO the sprawling forest city; it was still dark out. It was the morning two days after Landen and he had fought the lone Etas.

Trans-Falls was deadly quiet. A gentle breeze brushed eerily through the trees. The sky was a light gray, the color it always was just before the suns began to flash their pink rays over Rasa. But the sight, usually so beautiful, now seemed dull.

Landen breathlessly caught up to his superior a few seconds later. Being an archer, he wasn't as conditioned to running as Aeron was.

Aeron had yet to check Jargon's house and his own, but the lack of early morning movement in the tribal city disturbed him greatly. The worst scenario filled his mind. What if the Etas had attacked and ... he violently slammed his hooves into the soft dirt. However, he saw none of the damage that Etas would have left in their wake. Instead, only silence reigned in the valley.

"Come on, Landen. I'm going to check Jargon's house."

Landen obeyed without question, instantly knowing the route to the medic's house. Anyone who had spent any amount of time at Trans-Falls, or had been around anyone who had, knew Jargon.

At a gallop, they reached the healer's house in only a few minutes.

A sniffing, snarling sound was coming from a couple of bushes to their right.

In a heartbeat, Landen had his bow drawn back to his cheek.

Aeron held his breath, his sword at the ready. It could be nothing, just a boar or badger.

The bushes parted. Double red eyes locked onto the Centaurs.

A scream rent the air but was abruptly cut off by a gurgle.

The Eta fell forward, an arrow protruding between its two glassy eyes.

Aeron snarled. More rouge Etas.

That explained why Trans-Falls was deserted. They must have evacuated, leaving for a nearby tribe. Stephania's magic trace must have been too powerful here, drawing in too many demonic creatures. It was one thing for the Centaurs to easily hold off an attack, but it was much harder to defend against small things—little deadly creatures that wouldn't be noticed as they slipped in and wreaked havoc. Better to lay low, saving their weaponry and soldiers for while living in the security of a neighboring tribe, waiting until it was safe to return.

But that would mean ... Aeron galloped up to Jargon's house, wishing and praying that someone was still here.

The home was dark. All the shades were drawn, and the front gate, which was always open for patients and visitors, was closed and locked.

Aeron's face hardened before he charged wordlessly down the road that led to his own home.

Landen followed at a slower pace. It was common knowledge where the Trans-Falls High Chief lived and so Aeron didn't wait for him.

When Aeron reached his home, he tried the doorknob. It was locked. Frawnden never left the door locked unless she and her family had to leave for a long time.

He sank to his knees and buried his head in his hands.

He was too late.

They had already left for New-Fars.

§

FRAWNDEN LOOKED BACK over the valley that she had lived in since birth. She had never left that peaceful valley for more than a few months at a time for war. She had never thought she would be leaving for the next five years.

She imagined Aeron rushing to the city only to find them all gone. Would he follow? Or would he go back to his army to lead them into battle?

A tear ran down her cheek. Either way, even if Aeron tried to follow them, he may not ever find them in this wild land. Artigal had left no message for Aeron of what road they would be taking. Some of the rouge Etas Trans-Falls had fought off in the last few months had been intelligent enough to read. Artigal wouldn't want precious information falling into the wrong hands.

Artigal was at her left, Jargon at her right, Stephania on her back, and Trojan just behind them. They neared a fork in the road. The way to the left was the common road to New-Fars. Artigal chose the right.

As the two males silently led the bit of the tribe they had taken with them, Frawnden paused at the fork in the road.

This split in the road marked the end of the path that would lead her to her mate and the beginning of their separation. The rest of the tribe who weren't on the road to New-Fars had either gone to reinforce a neighboring tribe, or had moved into the surrounding mountains to act as confusing deterrents to any rouge Etas looking to attack. It was the first time the entire tribe was well and truly split. Most of the Centaurs would move back into Trans-Falls after a few weeks or months. She realized with bitterness how much she envied them.

A sick uneasiness settled over her as she gazed at the valley.

"Frawnden?" Jargon's soft, comforting voice gently shook her from her thoughts, and she slowly turned to him. He reached out his hand and wiped away her tears. "Come, Frawnden. There is nothing we can do."

She dragged herself away from the cliffside and let Jargon lead her down the overgrown path.

CHAPTER 7

An Obscure Road to New-Fars, Human Domain

Year: Rumi 6,099 Q.RJ.M.

One Year Later

STEPHANIA KICKED A STONE and watched as it tumbled and rolled until it came to a stop. She kicked it again.

They had been traveling for about a year now, and Artigal was assuring them that they weren't far from the human village, even though it would still take a good long year to reach it. The path they had chosen had proved to be slow and difficult. It never would have taken this long if they had traveled on the main road. However, with an easier path came more danger.

All the constant walking had caused the young Centaur, and the Duvarharian to develop incredible endurance, and with it, strong character to bear the hard journey. Even so, Stephania always began to tire before the Centaurs.

Trojan paused and looked at his sister. Her curly, red hair bobbed as her head nodded; she was nearly falling asleep while walking.

A small smile lifted the corners of his lips. He paused until she had caught up to him. He gently tapped her shoulder, causing her to jerk awake and mutter something. When she saw it was Trojan who had tapped her, she sighed and returned his smile halfheartedly. He held out his hand to her, and she took it before mounting his broad back.

Wrapping her delicate fingers in his long mane, she leaned her head onto his shoulder and sighed, letting her eyes flutter shut.

"Tro, what do you think happens to us when we die?"

She felt him shift his shoulders. He didn't answer.

The silence dragged on, but she waited. She knew he was thinking.

"I'm not sure, Steph." His words were soft and well-considered. "But I think we get to go back to Hanluurasa. And there we will become a part of the stars we were born from. That is what the Emperor promises us, I think, that we get to go home."

A bird sang. A breeze moved the still air.

"You really believe that? Do you really think something like that could happen?" She sneaked a glance at the sky. The low-hanging suns shone back, offering no answers.

Again, he was quiet for a long time before he answered. "Yes. I believe it could and will."

"Why? How do you know?"

He turned his head to the sky, and she followed his gaze. A single star was bright enough to be seen, even through the light of the setting suns. "Because when I look at the stars, I feel like I'm looking into a mirror." His fingers trailed the air above him. "Because when I read the stars, it feels like listening to a mother. And when I listen to the stars, it feels something like hearing about home."

"Will I get to go to the stars?"

He frowned and hummed. "I don't know. Artigal and the scholars have only talked about the forest children being born from the stars, never the Dragon Riders. He's mentioned something about a Duvarharian Great Lord, I think. Perhaps that Lord is your way home."

Her bottom lip jutted out. "But if home for me is not in the stars, then where is it?"

He shook his head, his black mane rippling in the breeze. "I'm not sure, but somewhere. Somewhere with the Emperor."

Somewhere.

The word echoed in her mind again as it often did. Somewhere she had a home. Somewhere she fit in. But it wasn't here. No, it was never here. Memories of a mountain room, of a shining palace with a grand waterfall and polished stone flashed before her. Memories of a mother, a father, a friend—people she loved dearly—danced in her mind. The memories washed away with blood. Then there were memories of a cabin, a cottage, the smiling face of her Centaur father. But now even he was gone. And now the cabin home in Trans-Falls was too. She hadn't stayed there long. Had it really been home?

The air grew still around them once again. A bird tittered and then fell silent.

Trojan kicked a stone. It skipped a few times before stopping. The clatter of hooves echoed on the rock walls of the valley around them.

What is a home? Would she ever know?

Tired from the walk and from the heavy weight of wonder, she quickly fell asleep.

§

DURING THE LONG JOURNEY, Trojan had taught Stephania all he that he could, from archery, to strategy games like *Yu'jac*, and even reading the stars.

Because Aeron was still missing, Artigal had taken it upon himself to continue Trojan's training, teaching both young children all he could that Frawnden had not yet impressed upon them.

The majority of Trojan and Stephania's days were spent under the watchful and mentoring eye of Artigal. Even so, Artigal still remained cold and indifferent to them, as if he were simply mentoring them from memory.

As distant as he was from the children, Artigal always treated Stephania as an equal, walking and talking with her as if she were a seasoned adult, not a child of only four years. Even though the other Centaurs knew she was the rightful heir to the Dragon Palace's throne, they were still not able to grasp the idea that their strong, cold-hearted leader held someone like her with such esteem. He was never like this, even to leaders of other Kinds.

The young girl and the old Centaur spent many hours walking and talking together.

Most of the time, Stephania insisted on Trojan being with them. It pleased the young Centaur to be included in their private talks, and he had learned to listen and think very hard before saying what was on his mind.

They were a strange little trio to watch walking together, but soon it became a norm to see the three leading the tribe while Frawnden and Jargon walked together some ways behind.

Today, Artigal was testing Trojan and Stephania's knowledge about Etas. He fired questions at them, and they just as quickly answered.

Jargon trotted up beside them and quietly waited for an opportunity to speak.

"Artigal, may I speak to you?"

Artigal nodded. "Children, walk ahead of me."

The two young creatures obeyed quickly after bowing respectfully.

Stephania closed her eyes, focusing her hearing on the conversation behind her. Her hearing was far better than she let on, and this was only one of many conversations she had listened in on.

"What is it, friend?"

Jargon bowed his head.

"There is a small band of Etas approaching from the East. They are expected to reach here by dawn. I have already alerted only the elite warriors, but I have yet to alert the rest of the tribe, including Frawnden."

Artigal nodded, unfazed by the pending attack.

"Igentis," Jargon bowed his head respectfully.

Artigal eyed him coldly, waiting for the medic to continue.

"If I may interject, I'm not sure how helpful it is to continue to teach Stephania about her race, the Etas, Thaddeus, and everything else." He paused, trying to read his leader's face to see if it was wise to continue.

Artigal's face hadn't changed, and Jargon prayed the Igentis wasn't angry.

"Since you have begun these studies, I have noticed an increase in attacks. I think her magic trace is growing. I understand that, to an extent, it is important for her to understand the world around her, especially since she is the prophecy's savior. However, I am wondering if other studies, like battle strategy, literature, language, and mathematics would be a safer alternative." He kept his head bowed respectfully. The seconds of silence dragged into a minute. He swallowed.

"You did well not to alert the tribe." Though Artigal seemed to have ignored everything else Jargon had said, the medic knew the Igentis had heard him and was, at least, not angry. "Send the elite to intercept but leave a few here. Notify Frawnden, the blacksmith, and the other more reliable Centaurs. Order for them to be on the ready to defend should close combat issue. Stephania and Trojan will stay with me."

Jargon bowed.

Artigal slumped, a low moan escaping his mouth.

Jargon quickly supported his leader, his eyes worriedly searching the Igentis'.

"It's the *Kijaqumok,* isn't it?"

Artigal nodded, his eyes dull as his hand strayed to his chest. "It gets just a little worse every day. Not much, nothing too noticeable, but enough to cause some complications." He held his hand out in front of him. A few veins in his wrist had turned black.

Jargon took in a sharp breath. "It's definitely spreading." He pulled a few purple berries from his bag before giving them to Artigal. "I wish there was more that I could do but"—a heavy sigh left his lips—"there's not much I can do without being in Trans-Falls. The *Gauwu Zelauw* can keep the Corrupt Magic in check for a while, but I'm afraid we're just too far away."

Artigal's eyes darkened. "Will I be able to get Stephania to New-Fars?"

As Artigal titled his head back and swallowed the berries, Jargon was just about answer when his sharp eye caught a small brown spot just behind Artigal's ear. Instantly his medical instincts told him something was wrong. In all his years of knowing Artigal, he had never once seen a bit of color on the old Centaur.

Artigal took a deep breath and shook his head against what Jargon knew was the bitter flavor of the berries. As he did so, his hair shifted just slightly and Jargon took in a sharp breath. It wasn't just one small brown spot; nearly six inches of Artigal's milky white hair was brown.

"Is that—" Jargon pointed slowly to Artigal's shoulder.

For a moment, something like fear and horror flickered in Artigal's eyes, but it disappeared under red anger. In a heartbeat, a shimmering wave of nearly invisible magic washed over the Igentis, and the coloration disappeared.

"What are you asking, Jargon? Have the veins spread to my shoulder?" Artigal narrowed his eyes in challenge, daring Jargon to ask another question.

A cold shudder passed over the medic, and he decided to quickly drop the subject and simply answer Artigal's first question. "I think you should be able to reach New-Fars, but you must be careful. *Kijaqumok* is wild and unpredictable. Any contact with evil could cause its power to spike."

The white Centaur stamped his hooves. He turned his face away, but Jargon didn't miss the small flicker of relief on his old face. "Very well, then. I shall continue on my way and finish what I have started. If I die, then I die. It is all in His plan."

Jargon frowned but made sure Artigal didn't see. "Of course."

The Igentis smiled and clasped the black Centaur's shoulder. "Stay positive, Jargon. I'm not going to fall over dead any second."

Jargon grumbled. "Actually, you could."

"Just don't remind me, okay?

A small smile lifted Jargon's lips.

"Good. Now take care of those Etas."

Jargon bowed, his bright attitude having returned. "As you command." He quickly trotted down the path into the thick woods.

§

STEPHANIA FROWNED AS Jargon moved away from the Igentis and disappeared into the forest. So Artigal really was wounded. She had nursed her suspicions, but she wasn't sure if she liked being right. Artigal's condition seemed critical. How much longer would he be able to protect her? Was this why he was teaching her so much? To prepare her in case he died?

"Stephania, Trojan, come here."

Stephania and Trojan paused their gait and waited for the agile Centaur to catch up.

"Now, where were we?" Artigal stroked his narrow chin. A challenging look glinted in his eyes as if he knew exactly where he had left off but was testing if his pupils had been listening.

"You were questioning us about the Eta's reproduction, or really the lack of it," Stephania quipped in her beautiful, mystical voice, her red eyes shimmering in the light of the suns. Her soft, wavy trellises of hair moved off her face, brushed away by the cool, caressing breeze.

"Of course. I'm glad you were listening." Artigal allowed them a small smile, one that was rare and that the two children cherished.

Artigal quickly launched himself back into his teachings, rapidly questioning the young creatures, delighting in their quick and accurate answers.

After he had kept his thoughts to himself for a while, Trojan finally spoke in his quiet, deepening voice.

"The Etas can only split randomly, without the side-effects of becoming an El-core, once in hundreds of years. Otherwise, they can only reproduce by having a limb cut off and then re-growing a body. That would mean war only encourages the life cycle of the Eta, because, as far as we know, they don't seem to die of old age. Which is, of course, something similar to other magical creatures, especially the Duvarharians."

Artigal nodded with a deep appreciation for the young Centaur's sharp mind.

"Exactly, Trojan. But therein lies the catch. If we don't fight them when they attack for the purpose of reproduction, which they do, then we *all* get killed. Nothing stops Etas but death. The only way to rid the land of them is to completely eradicate them."

A long silence issued as they all brooded on the information, especially Stephania.

The more she heard about the Etas, the harder it was to push aside her memories of the Battle of the Prophecy. Embracing the Etas' existence and becoming equipped with knowledge against them had helped her be less afraid of them. Her nightmares had slowed, now only haunting her every few weeks. But in fear's place, hate took hold. A burning, consuming hatred against the creatures that had taken, and continued to take, everything she loved away from her. And, of course, Thaddeus was at the heart of it. Artigal was right: Thaddeus, Kyrell, and all the Etas needed to be eradicated. For Ventronovia's sake, and for the sake of all who lived here. There was no other choice. *She* had no other choice.

CHAPTER 8

A mountain pass

A few miles from the border of the Human Domain

Year: Rumi 6,100 Q.RJ.M.

EASY NOW, STEPHANIA," Artigal chastened the five-year-old girl as she practically strangled the sword she was holding.

She bit her lip and frowned. *Why does this always have to be so hard?*

"Treat the weapon like it is a friend, girl, and not your enemy."

Taking a deep breath to calm herself, Stephania loosened her grip, and her wrists stopped aching.

"Good." He turned to face the west.

The cool breeze blew softly through his mane and tail, pushing them to the side.

It was about noonday, and the two suns were high upon their course in the skies. The small group of traveling Centaurs had stopped for a quick rest to eat and maybe take a nap.

Artigal had left Trojan with Frawnden, but had taken Stephania with him up the side of the small canyon mountain pass they had been traveling through.

He shifted his weight uncomfortably, his hand subconsciously straying to the right side of his chest. A sharp pain stabbed through his chest, and he clenched his jaw, his hands balling into fists. The *Kijaqumok,* thanks to Jargon's diligence and skill, wasn't spreading as fast as it could, but he felt the effect it was taking. He would have random spiking pains throughout his body, which then led to his chest. He was more tired than usual, and it was slowly becoming harder to perform magic. And then, of course, there was the matter of the returning coloration. It hadn't spread as much as he had feared, but now his right hoof was almost half brown; keeping it white was just another task he had to focus his magic on, draining his strength bit by bit.

Banishing these unwanted thoughts and pains from his mind, he shifted his attention back to his young pupil. Noticing a mistake, he fixed her fighting stance and watched as she slowly made a faux slice to the side, making sure every detail of her body would be flawless.

"Do you know why I make you train in slow motion?"

Her brow crinkled. *Why indeed?* She finished the cut and returned to the resting stance. "So I develop strength instead of letting the sword's momentum do all the work?"

He grunted in approval. "Yes, and because it also forces you to perfect the smallest details in your stance. Then each important detail becomes muscle memory and effortless in battle. It is also the same reason we train our children from such young ages." He poked her arm.

Forcing back a grimace, she changed the position of her arms and legs, her muscles burning in protest.

"You are impressionable at this age, like soft clay. What you learn now, you will carry with you for the rest of your life, even if you think you have forgotten it."

She nodded, licking her sweat-lined lips.

"Will Trojan be sent off to war?" She didn't want to ask, but the words slipped out of her lips. There was no reason to teach children to fight if they would never be sent off to battle. One day or another, each Centaur would have to choose his path in life, to be a warrior or a city worker as a merchant, scholar, architect, or similar positions. She already knew that Trojan had chosen to be a warrior. He would have it no other way.

She could feel Artigal's cold, steely gaze on the back of her head, scrutinizing every twitch of her body, every mistake in her stance. "Yes, he will be. Though young, he has already chosen his path. After his thirteenth birthday, he will be assigned to a regiment and will train as a solider."

She bit her lip. Trojan—her brother, her only friend, only comfort, only home—marching off to war. It didn't sit well with her. What if he marched off and never came home? Where would she turn to? Tears sparkled in her red eyes, but she brushed them away. She wasn't one to cry. A warrior would never cry, never show weakness. If Trojan could be a warrior, then so could she. She would follow him to the ends of the earth.

A lump formed in her throat. Her shoulders sagged. But she couldn't follow him, could she? He would be sent off to war, to fight for his tribe as he wanted, and she would be sent off to Dalton in New-Fars and then later to the Dragon Palace to lead her people. Trojan had chosen his life's path and was content, but was she?

A sharp jab in her ribs reminded her she was still supposed to be practicing. She lifted her arms, but found she didn't have the heart to continue.

"Artigal?" Stephania's soft, musical voice impeded his anger over her dismissal of the training.

"Yes, child?"

"Why do I have to go to New-Fars?" Her eyes blandly followed his, gazing out over the land, but she felt as if she weren't really seeing anything before her.

She could feel his shock in the silence. She had never before questioned their motives for taking her farther and farther from her real home in Duvarharia and even Trans-Falls.

"Well," he stalled. "You have to be in New-Fars because that's where your parents wanted you to be, and we are obliged to obey their wishes regarding their only child. Wouldn't you agree?"

She nodded and stared at the ground, drawing little, meaningless symbols into the dirt with the tip of her small sword.

"Yes, I agree. But why did they want me to go to New-Fars? I've heard Jargon say many times that I am unusual for any child, even a Duvarharian, and that I learn quicker and more thoroughly. He has done several studies to figure out why, but all he's concluded is that I was blessed by the Great Emperor."

Artigal nodded. "Keep going, child."

She took a deep breath. She was surprised he was letting her state her opinion for so long. Usually, it was he who did the talking, and it was always to instruct her. "Well, then if this is true, then I must be capable of living with my fellow Dragon Riders and growing up amongst them. I'm not sure I can effectively learn the ways of the people I am supposed to protect if I am living with the ignorant humans."

Thoughts raced through the aged Centaur's mind at an alarming rate. Every conclusion he came to was always the same. She *was* growing up quickly. *Too* quickly. If her mind kept developing at this rate, she could have a sudden explosion of understanding, awakening powerful magic in her; it was possible that her young body or mind wouldn't be able to handle the stress and power, and she could be seriously injured. Besides that, her magic trace would be impossible to cover, and Thaddeus would have no problem finding her. Nothing he could do now could stop this. Unless ... a new thought formed in his mind. It was a horrible thought. He bit his lip and snarled. He hated himself for thinking of such an awful thing. *How could I do such a thing to someone and cause them so much pain? Could I really harm another Duvarharian like this again? Is it the only way?* He pushed the thoughts far from his mind. He would never let that happen again if he could prevent it. Somehow, he would find another way to keep Stephania safe. He had to find another way.

He took a deep breath. "Stephania, you are more than capable of living with your own people, and I do understand that you are different than other children. I don't need you to tell me that. If you weren't, I would not be risking my best Centaurs to keep you alive."

Stephania pointed her eyes at the ground, humbled. She hadn't wanted to overstep her boundaries. She wondered if he would send her back to Frawnden like he had when she had let her mouth get the best of her before.

She heard him sigh and sneaked a glance. He looked tired, as if he hadn't slept for a long time. His eyes stared absently into the distance. A relieved breath left her lips. Good. He wasn't upset, at least, not yet.

"There are many things right now that you cannot understand and that you are not meant to understand. If I told you all the things that would be wrong with taking you back to Duvarharia straightaway, it would cause the very thing we are trying to prevent."

Her shoulders slumped, and she sighed.

"However," the old Centaur suddenly added, and she lifted her eyes to him.

"There are a few things you can, and need to, understand." He waited for an answer, and she slowly nodded, ready to drink in the information.

"Duvarharia is swarming with Etas and only a few dragons and Dragon Riders remain at the Dragon Palace. They have their hands full with just staying alive. They are men and women of war, and caring for a child is the last thing on their minds. They would hardly have time to raise a child and teach her how to fight, use magic, cook, take care of herself and others, have manners, bond with a dragon, ride a dragon, and all the millions of things you need to learn to be anything of an intelligent creature."

Stephania twitched her lip to the side as she processed Artigal's words. He had a good point.

"Not that we are capable of teaching you all those things either," he added. "But we can teach you a few things like archery, potion making, swordsmanship, reading the stars, and being a part of a community. On top of that, Thaddeus doesn't want to kill you."

Her eyes widened like saucers. She became completely still, as if even a breath would cause him to change his mind about telling her more.

"He wants you alive. Why he does, I have a few theories, but you are much too young to understand them."

She couldn't hide the disappointment. *When will I be told? When will I step out of this shadow I live in?* He was right, of course, though. She was much too young to understand such things, but nevertheless, not knowing weighed on her like the sky against the mountains.

"As you know, there is a Dragon Rider living in New-Fars who was close to your parents and was their Chief Advisor. Although his dragon is long since dead, he can still teach you even more things than I or the other Duvarharians can, and he can keep you safe while doing so—something we cannot."

She scowled. "Artigal, you have kept me safe thus far, and we are far from the Etas' stronghold. Why could you not continue to keep me safe?"

A small frown formed on his lips, and he sighed.

She sensed he was withholding other reasons too, as to why he couldn't keep her here with them, but she suspected they were personal.

He ground his jaw. Jargon was right. Perhaps she knew too much. Even now, with how smart she was, she was quickly processing all she had been told. Her magic trace was already stronger than when they left Trans-Falls, and he was regretting having disclosed anything. What else could he say without jeopardizing her and all the Centaurs with them?

"There are things not even I can protect you from, and there will be things that Dalton will not be able to protect you from either, but at least he will be able to instruct you on how you can protect yourself."

Artigal shifted his weight from hoof to hoof and pawed at the ground, eager for the conversation to end. The bond that he felt forming between them was making him uncomfortable.

Stephania let out a hot sigh and pushed a lock of blood-red hair out of her face. She knew she was pushing his tolerance right now, and she also understood that for him to put up with her ravings for this long meant that what he wanted to tell her was very important. Sensing his discomfort and a strange emotional pain, she knew it was time to stop questioning him.

She looked down at her sword. *I suppose I have been told enough. For now.* She didn't want to take advantage of his good mood, ruining her chance of learning more later.

"Teach me, Artigal." She held her sword up to him.

A rare smile spread across his face as he turned to her. "And what do you want to learn?"

She bowed low. "Anything I can, Igentis. Anything I can."

§

"COME ON! BREAK UP CAMP! Let's move!" A commander's voice rang out over the traveling Centaur tribe. Those Centaurs who had been asleep shook themselves awake and stumbled around, helping to pack any provisions needed.

Stephania tried to stifle a giggle as she watched a lean Centaur guard stretch. It never ceased to amuse her how the Centaurs would stretch: bowing low on extended front legs and then stepping forward on extended back legs, all while stretching their arms above their heads and yawing extensively.

"Hey, don't laugh. I do that too." Trojan tried to sound offended, but he could do nothing to mask the lift of his lips.

Her small hand covered her mouth before a snicker could escape. "I know," she gasped with stifled mirth, "and it's funny too."

Shaking his head, he scowled at her but in only a few seconds, they fell into suppressed laughter, telling each other to be quiet or else they would be noticed in their hiding spot behind a thick berry bush.

"Stephania! Trojan! Come on. We're leaving." Frawnden's motherly call reached them, and Trojan instantly sobered.

Standing, he brushed the leaves and dirt from his sleek hair and extended a hand to his sister. "Come along, Stephania. We have to pack too, you know."

She frowned and shook her head. "Just a moment longer." Her eyes strayed back to the Centaur guard. He had donned his shield and sword, his hands quickly tying his long hair into a knot away from his face.

Trojan shrugged and trotted away, calling after their mother that he was on his way.

In low tones, the guard discussed something with his partner. The other guard nodded his head, his face solemn.

Stephania's red eyes narrowed before she closed them and took a deep breath. *Focus. Focus.* Slowly, their words sharpened as all the other sounds around her dulled.

"... captured. It said their forces were gathering ... possibly just ... cursed rouges ... could be an ambush ..."

Stephania's eyes snapped open, and she gasped. Startled by what she had heard, she fled from her hiding spot and rushed back to their family tent, her heart slamming in her chest.

Trojan mussed her hair and muttered something about leaving him to do all the work, but she barely heard it.

As if in a haze, she went about the packing before quickly slipping away from her brother and mother.

"Into an ambush," Stephania echoed hesitantly, the words sending a shiver down her spine. *They have kept the attacks secret from me for so long.* She had stayed up nearly all night thinking about what Artigal had told her, and now she felt like she had broken their trust. *What have I done?*

She moodily kicked a stone, cursing the sudden complexity of life, before pulling her bow off her back, along with an arrow from her quiver.

Placing the arrow on the string, she pulled it back to her cheek. The bow's weight was no longer a strain to her. She could hold it here all day.

Aiming the weapon at a knot in a tree, she subconsciously drew an imaginary pattern on the tree trunk with the tip of her arrow; after she had thought long about what she had heard, she aimed, once more, at the knot.

Pulling her string back a bit more, she let loose the string, and her arrow streaked toward the target.

Just as the arrow hit its mark exactly where she had been aiming, the arrow caught fire and a glowing trail of the shimmering magic swirled across the trunk in the playful pattern she had drawn earlier.

As she gazed at it in wonder, a beast about the size of a panther lunged out from behind the tree, its bloodthirsty stare directed straight at her.

Stephania turned around too late.

With a piercing screech, the catlike creature slammed into her, knocking her to the ground as she screamed from the pain and fear. The world went black around her.

A horrible, gut-wrenching pain tore through her leg, dragging her from the blissful darkness. She thrashed against the beast, screaming.

"Stephania!" her mother screamed in horror.

The sound of swords sliding from their sheaths rang and mingled with the pained cries of the girl and the shrieking yowls of the creature.

The beast's body was suffocatingly heavy. One of its claws sank into her arm, and she screamed as the arm went numb. She fumbled for her knife. Tears poured down her face. Her heart pounded, her mind blank with stark fear. *Please, no. I don't want to die.*

Finally, her fingers brushed the deer antler handle of her knife. She grasped it firmly and stabbed wildly. She felt the blade pierce flesh. The animal let out a pained scream and leapt off her.

The beast screamed and howled, trying to claw out the blade protruding from its shoulder.

Stephania scrambled to her feet, clutching her arm, her leg bleeding profusely, and tears streaming down her pale cheeks as she stumbled away from the beast.

The beast screeched, sniffed the air, and turned back toward her. With a snarl, it lunged. She screamed, clenching her eyes closed.

It never hit her.

The beast yelped and fell to the ground, thrashing wildly.

Trojan leapt around it, swung Stephania onto his back and galloped to his mother.

§

ARTIGAL SHOVED HIS WAY through the Centaur warriors, who rushed to the beast, thrusting it with their weapons until its screams fell silent and its body fell still. They then fanned out, scouting to discover if more were nearby.

"Stephania! Trojan!" Artigal could hardly make himself heard over the chaos, which ruled the camp. He had barely seen what had gone on and wasn't sure if the children had made it to safety.

Within seconds, Artigal reached the family's tent.

They were all, including Jargon, bent over Stephania's small body, which they had laid down on a mat. Trojan was the closest to her. His face was pale; his small chest rose and fell with his shaking breath.

"Is she okay?" Artigal's voice was strained with panic, and they quickly made room for him. His dark, concerned gaze moved from Centaur to Centaur and then back to Stephania. Though his face was impassive, his eyes rapidly changed colors, betraying his worry.

Stephania turned her wide eyes to him.

Her blood stained the furs as it ran down her arm and leg. A dark green liquid mingled with the blood and filled the air with a rank odor.

Even though Frawnden and Trojan stepped back, Jargon stayed hovering over Stephania, doing the best he could to clean and bandage her wounds without it being too painful.

"Is it—" Stephania swallowed, dragging her eyes from Trojan to Artigal, pleading with him to help her. Her skin was cold and clammy, and she was nearly about to faint. "Is it gone?" A sharp bark left her lips and fresh tears welled up in her eyes.

Jargon winced. "Sorry, child. This will hurt a bit."

She could only nod and bite her lip.

Artigal nodded his reassurance, wanting so badly to take her in his arms, cradle her small, fragile body, and assure her everything was going to be fine, but he had to restrain himself.

"It hurts, Artigal. It burns inside!" she moaned and Artigal's heart lurched. Eta poison was specifically tailored for the Duvarharians and was designed to destroy every bit of them—physically and mentally.

As his eyes locked on hers, he felt something reach out to touch his mind. He instinctively recoiled. He'd never had something touch his mind before. It persisted, and he probed it with a bit of magic. It was *her*—Stephania. Duvarharians were supposed to have lost the ability to connect minds with another rider thousands of years ago, and he hadn't ever heard of any other race being able to touch minds with a different Kind entirely.

After taking a deep breath, he let himself open to her thoughts.

It's dark, Artigal. I'm scared. My soul hurts, Artigal. Why? Why does it hurt so much?

Only the darkness of her mind consumed him. Memories flashed here and there, but they were vague and filled with death. They grasped at him, and he had to push them away. Her pain suffocated him, and he could feel the poison tearing through her mind and body.

He gasped as he felt a darkness creep into him. A hopeless, bottomless darkness where there was no love. It ate at him and consumed him, but it wasn't from him—it was from her. It was at the very essence of her being, something that fed off her hate and anger for the Etas. The poison was feeding on this hate. It was destroying her from the inside out.

Artigal felt the breath taken away from him as he desperately tried to banish this death from his mind. But even though he tried, he failed. It was too powerful, too all-consuming.

His chest exploded in gut-wrenching pain, and he cried out. The *Kijaqumok* inside him was spreading. It was trying to take hold of her through the path the poison had created. He pushed her mind away from his, but she held onto him, desperate to be saved.

Please help me! I don't understand! Her weak little voice echoed in the darkness as he felt her consciousness slip away from him and the Light, and further into death.

He knew he had to do something, but he didn't know what. The *Kijaqumok* was killing the Pure Magic within him, and he was sinking deeper into the pain along with her. He couldn't do this on his own.

Just when he felt he couldn't take the anguish and the impending darkness anymore, he felt a warm hand on his shoulder. Not physically, but spiritually.

I Am! A strong, pure voice rang out in the darkness. He could hardly believe what he had heard, but he recognized the voice; he had been spoken to like this before. He had heard the same voice long ago when it had instructed him to be Igentis, when he had predicted that the Great Lord's prophecy was coming true, and when it had instructed him to bless the chosen girl of that prophecy. He also heard an echo of it every time he read the stars, for the stars spoke of the very voice and will of Him; it was the Creator.

Confusion now flooded through Stephania. She didn't know this Being. Part of her recoiled from it, but part of her reached out, eager to learn, eager to know more.

Look at me, Stephania. Fight the evil within you. Think of your Creator.

The name of the Creator was new to her. The message was new to her, but even so, it sent a ray of Light piercing through the darkness.

A healing hand reached through him and touched the girl. Then the pain started to wash away from the depths inside her.

Abruptly, his mind was wrenched away from hers and he was once more kneeling in front of her, Jargon by his side.

Jargon was gazing at Artigal intensely. "What just happened?"

Artigal scowled. "What do you mean?"

Frawnden and Jargon shared a strange look

"I mean: what just happened, Artigal? You just went into a coma. Your breathing and heart rate slowed, and that,"—he pointed to Artigal's armored chest, implying the wound underneath— "got darker and looked like it was spreading. Then you suddenly jerked awake, and Stephania's condition is abruptly more stable. Don't tell me you had nothing to do with it."

Artigal's scowled deepened. "I don't know."

Frawnden opened her mouth to press, but he shot her a look that instantly had her fumbling with medical supplies.

Knowing that Artigal didn't like to be pressed for information, Jargon placed his hand on the Igentis' shoulder and searched the leader's tired but oddly excited eyes.

"Are you well?"

Artigal's hand strayed to his chest, and he nodded. "I think so, Jargon." He gave him a half-smile, hoping it would calm the healer's fears, but it didn't. "Just focus on Stephania."

The black Centaur stared for a long time at Artigal, but Artigal only shook his head, implying that Jargon should drop it.

Jargon, however, wasn't so easily dissuaded, but just as he opened his mouth to protest, Stephania groaned, and all their attentions snapped back to her.

Jargon pressed a glass of a clear liquid to her lips, and she drank it before coughing. "I want—" She gasped in pain as Jargon dabbed the wound on her arm with a cold cloth. "I want my knife back." Her little face hardened, instantly expecting someone to fulfill her demand.

Jargon pushed Artigal aside. "She's going to be fine, and I don't think I'll need any help. Frawnden is more than capable of taking care of her daughter from here."

Artigal stood and turned to leave, but Jargon stopped him again.

"Unless you want to tell me what happened between you both just then."

Artigal paused before turning around slowly, his eyes cold. He had been inside Stephania's mind, and it was a destructive place to be, not just because of the Eta poison, but because of the sheer amount of hate and anger she held inside her. He couldn't say he was surprised by what he had found, but he had been overwhelmed with the intensity of her hatred and turmoil. He felt responsible for the chaos inside her. He was, after all, the one who continued to teach her about the Etas, causing her to internalize her vengeance. He felt selfish for filling her with such malice in order to make sure she never joined Thaddeus. Was he really doing the right thing? He didn't want to think about it, and Jargon was only making him even more irritable.

"I'm afraid I don't even truly understand what happened, Jargon. Since I am not much help here, I shall leave." Before Jargon could plague him further, he trotted out of the tent.

§

JARGON SHOOK HIS HEAD and grunted in frustration before turning to Frawnden. She was clearly just as worried and curious.

She drew her hand across Stephania's feverish forehead. "How is she?" When her own emotions were involved, as it always was when tending to those she loved, she found it comforting to leave the healing to someone else.

"She's going to be fine. Just a couple of small flesh wounds. She's in too much pain though for me to clean her up while she's awake. I'm going to sedate her."

Frawnden nodded, and she and Trojan quickly left the tent so Jargon could concentrate. In only a few minutes, he came out, a smile on his rugged, plain face. "All done. Just make sure she doesn't do anything too strenuous."

"Thank you."

"Of course."

The mother and son quickly disappeared back into the tent, and Jargon searched the crowd for Artigal.

The Igentis was standing a distance from the other Centaurs, his hands behind his back and his gaze trained on nothing in particular.

Jargon's voice jerked him out of his thoughts and back into the present.

"Her knife is what pushed back the animal the first time. And Trojan's sword is what stopped it the second."

Artigal barely nodded his head at Jargon. "Thank you for letting me know, Jargon."

Sighing in annoyance that he was now obviously dismissed, Jargon stalked away.

He could, of course, order Artigal to disclose information because whatever happened had affected Artigal medically, but it was always a better idea to leave the leader alone if he was this chafed by something.

§

ONCE HE KNEW that Jargon was far behind him, Artigal allowed himself a long sigh and a small smile. So Stephania and Trojan had used their training to protect themselves. He was bursting with pride that the young creatures had been brave enough to fight against the demonic beast, but he didn't let his pride show; he wanted to see how Trojan would react.

"Trojan." Artigal called loudly.

Trojan ducked out of his tent and cantered over to Artigal. Bowing before his leader, the young boy held his breath. "Yes, Igentis?"

"Go. Retrieve your sword and your sister's knife and bring them to me."

"Yes, Igentis." Trojan hurried over to the carcass of the beast and pulled his sword out of its side.

Black blood ran out of the wound.

Trojan's eyes narrowed in hatred as he realized it was an Eta. He retrieved Stephania's knife as well and carried the two weapons back to his leader.

Laying them in front of the Centaur, Trojan stepped back, his hands clasped behind his back and his eyes fastened respectfully on the ground.

Just as Artigal began to speak, one of his personal guards approached him and whispered something in his ear.

Smiling broadly, the aged Igentis nodded and turned his attention back to Trojan as the warrior left.

"Trojan, you fought well today, and I understand that your sword dealt the beast a critical wound, one that it would have eventually died from."

Trojan nearly smiled with pride but kept his composure.

"We will no longer be breaking camp due to this accident. I request that I see you before sunset when I call for you. Until then, you may return to your mother and sister and be in their company for the rest of the day."

Sucking in a sharp breath, his cheeks flushed with pride, Trojan reached for the sword and knife, but Artigal held up his hand, stopping him.

"I will keep those for now."

Cocking his head and frowning, Trojan bowed and mumbled his gratitude.

§

AT HIS FAMILY'S TENT, Trojan was paid no more attention than a bug. Taking a long dagger in place of his sword and his bow and arrow set, he wandered off into the woods.

Cheerfully, he began to trot as his spirits began to soar again. But only too soon, his joyful mood began to sink as the forest got quieter and quieter, and seemingly darker. For a moment, he thought he might be lost, but he spotted a little stream ahead. Their company had stopped by it before proceeding to where they were currently camped. A nervous sigh left his lips. He wasn't lost, but he had wandered farther away from camp than he had thought. Even despite the acoustics of the canyon, he could no longer hear the echoing of the camp's sounds.

Nervously, he slowed to a walk, his footsteps crashing through the fallen leaves and snapping numerous twigs, despite how hard he tried to move silently.

Pulling out his dagger, he held it in front of himself and slowly made his way out of the thick trees and into the clearing adjacent to the stream.

Just as he decided to retreat to the safety of the Centaur camp, some movement further down the mountain pass caught his attention.

Narrowing his eyes, he waited motionless, trying to catch a glimpse of the movement again. He noted how it was becoming increasingly difficult to see. The clouds were suffocating any bit of sunlight that made it through the trees, and the heavy fog hung thick in the low canyon. Taking a deep breath, he assessed his surroundings. If it came to a fight, he would be at a disadvantage because of the low visibility. His best chance would be to attack first with his bow.

He cocked his head to the side, spotting a hiding place behind a large boulder. He drew his bow and fixed an arrow to the string, another in his mouth and ready to fire.

A voice, which seemed so familiar, cut through the fog. "Trojan?" The voice was deep and rough, obviously belonging to an older male.

Chills ran up and down his spine. *How does this creature know my name?*

He was fairly sure that it was a Centaur, or at least an equine-like creature; he could hear the clop of the creature's hooves on the rocks. It could've been a human riding a horse, but he had never met a human and doubted one would know his name. Though he knew many Etas were intelligent and evolved enough to under-

101

stand language, he wasn't sure rogue Etas had ever been known to talk this well. *Unless it isn't a rouge.*

He swallowed, taking deep breaths to steady himself. *How did this creature get past the perimeter warriors and the scouts?* Dread filled him as another thought occurred to him.

"Trojan! Trojan, where are you?"

Even though the voice, which belonged to whoever was moving quickly toward him, had called his name, Trojan dared not come out from behind his vantage point.

His breath was quick and panicked. What if the warriors simply hadn't been able to see this creature? Too many times he had heard legends about ancient demons that could morph into your worst fears by simply reading your mind without you even realizing they had tapped into your thoughts. Only the person they were targeting could see them, and it eventually turned them insane. Sometimes, though they might be exaggerated, rare stories came back that these creatures were still alive and walked the land further north.

He waited and waited, the creature continuing to call him. Now he could make out a silhouette through the fog.

Yes! It was a Centaur!

Trojan was just about to reveal himself when he realized that this Centaur wasn't wearing the armor of a Trans-Falls Centaur. Its chest was completely bare, except the straps for its quiver and belt.

The Centaur was limping; if it came to a fight, Trojan would at least have the advantage of mobility.

Suddenly, taking a risk just as the Centaur called his name once more, the young boy leapt out from the behind the rock and quickly galloped down the small side of the ravine. His arrow was ready to be fired at the slightest movement.

"Stop." Trojan's voice was deep and carried well through the pass. He sounded much older and much more confident than he was. Though his eyesight was poor in the dark fog, it was just good enough to see that the Centaur had stopped.

"Under command of the Igentis, I order you to state your name and business, Centaur." Trojan kept his arrow trained on the Centaur's chest.

"Trojan, my boy, haven't you grown up to be such a fine warrior!" The Centaur stepped closer until he was only about twenty feet from Trojan and almost clearly visible. His voice was hoarse and beaten, as if he had been yelling for a long time and hadn't drunk enough water, and yet there was something about it that was familiar and comforting. "I thought I would never be able to find you." He smiled warmly, tears pouring down his face. He

Trojan gasped, slowly letting down his bow as he finally recognized Centaur. "Father?"

CHAPTER 9

S HE'S DOING JUST FINE." Jargon stood up from Stephania, who was still sleeping soundly. He had come back to Frawnden's tent under the pretense that he was checking on Stephania, but he knew Frawnden was just as capable at taking care of her daughter. Covertly, he had come to see if he could get any information from Stephania on what had happened to her and Artigal. He had found out nothing so far. Apparently, she had no recollection or knowledge of anything strange happening.

"Do you think the Eta poison had a worse effect on her than most?" Frawnden lightly covered her daughter with a blanket.

Jargon took in a deep breath. "It appears it did. I don't think I've ever seen any creature react to the poison that way. Thankfully, its spread was stopped before it could do more serious damage; not by anything I did, however. As you know, she'll be very sore and possibly cranky for the next few days."

Frawnden nodded. Eta poison was nothing to laugh at, but something Jargon had said didn't make any sense. She narrowed her eyes. "What do you mean by 'nothing you did?' What stopped it?" She had a feeling the cure had something to do with Artigal, but wanted more solid answers.

Jargon quickly surveyed the opening of the tent to see if anyone else was near before moving closer to her, their foreheads almost touching, and lowering his voice to where even she could barely hear it.

"Did you see what happened between Artigal and Stephania?"

She nodded grimly. "Of course. But in all my years of healing, I've never seen anything remotely like it. Healing without physical cures? It doesn't make sense. What do you think happened?"

He shrugged and shook his head. "I haven't the faintest idea, but if I were to guess, I think their minds connected, and somehow—" He bit his lip. It was inconceivable, but there seemed to be no other explanation. "It healed her."

Frawnden frowned. "But that's not possible. How could you even know that? Duvarharians can't connect minds with each other, let alone a Centaur."

The black Centaur ran his fingers through his hair impatiently. "But they could do it a long time ago."

"Who did what?"

"The Duvarharians. They could connect minds with each other a long time ago. At least, that's the myth."

Her mouth parted but no words came out for a moment.

Jargon nodded, and she shook her head, a smile of disbelief crossing her face. "Okay, maybe, but that doesn't explain anything. They can't anymore, and definitely not with a Centaur. And how could Artigal heal her that way? It doesn't make any sense."

Jargon stamped his hoof excitedly, and his whisper became even more conspiratorial. "I know, I know. But the legends speak of a time—an end time, mind you—when the powers of the world will flow together and act as one, channeling forces in ways we cannot even imagine."

"So you think—"

He shook his head. "I don't know. I can't be sure. Artigal won't tell me anything about what happened, and I can only assume." He nervously shifted his weight and clenched his jaw. "I could give him an order to tell me what happened since it affected Stephania's health but—"

"That wouldn't go over well."

"No, it would not."

Silence filled the tent for a while before Frawnden broke it, her voice a low, quivering whisper. "Aeron mentioned something about an End."

Jargon's eyes snapped upwards from his hooves and fixed themselves steadily on hers. "What. What did he say?"

She shook her head. "It was a long, long time ago. Just after Aeron and I became mates. He said something that Artigal had mentioned to him as a child. Something about the stars and the End or something."

Jargon's face paled. "The stars. The legends." His mouth hung open. "The Prophecy. Of course." A lopsided grin spread across his face. "Yes. It all makes sense. Thaddeus is channeling *Kijaqumok*, and the *Shushequmok* is shifting strangely.

The powers *are* moving." He began furiously pacing the tent. "Surely Artigal can feel it. The whole balance of the world is swinging, as if it were on a pendulum, and there has to be some sort of mediator to balance it, Stephania of course, and a helper—the one mentioned in the prophecy—to help her channel it! By the Emperor!"

Frawnden placed her hand on his shoulder to try and calm him down, but he merely grasped her hand in his, crushing it in his excitement.

"Stephania and the helper! They must be able to channel both kinds of *Sleshqumok*, the Ancient Magic. Good gods." He stumbled, feeling lightheaded with shock, completely ignoring whatever Frawnden was trying to say to him at the moment. "Others must be able to as well, we just don't know about it. What else shall happen, then, if this is truly the End? Who else would be given this power? It could be anyone."

"Jargon, what in the world are you talking about?" Frawnden lightly shook her friend's shoulders. He sagged heavily against the table.

He turned his slightly glazed eyes up to hers, a strange smile spreading across his face. "The End, Frawnden. The return of the Great Emperor. *'And there shall be, in that time, a great shift. Forces shall be awakened and shall move once again among the creatures of the earth. The realms shall become one under the Ruler. The great beasts who shaped the land shall arise again and create a new world, one that shall be as it had in the beginning. The serpents of the deep shall move and part the oceans and shape the waters of the land. Magic will flow freely among the creatures of the world, and none shall be devoid of understanding. And they will know by this, that the last battle and the end of time draws near'.*"

Frawnden's heart raced in her chest. "The legend of the end of the world. But that's just myth. You don't think—" She swallowed. "You don't think it's actually, you know, real, do you?"

Jargon's eyes were bright with joy and hope. "I don't know, Frawnden, but maybe. Just maybe."

A loud, desperate voice suddenly pierced the air and shattered the thoughtful atmosphere in the small tent. "Mother! Mother! Come outside! Quick!"

Alarmed, Frawnden quickly stepped around Stephania and rushed outside to Trojan, who was hopping from hoof to hoof in agonizing anxiety.

"What's wrong? What is it?"

Too excited to give her an answer, he simply grasped her hand in his and dragged her along with him until she was galloping beside him.

"You are never going to believe this!" He squealed with excitement, their hooves pounding into the ground at an incredible pace. It never ceased to amaze her how fast her son was.

It was obvious to Frawnden that whatever Trojan wanted to show her was very important; usually he was extremely quiet and controlled in everything he did, but now it was as if he was once again only three years old, pulling her along to watch the adult Centaurs train.

Just as they broke out of the woods and into the small open land in front of the small stream, Trojan ground to a stop, his eyes misting with tears.

Frawnden was alarmed. "What is it, Trojan? Are you okay?" She cupped his young face in her hands.

He merely grinned through his tears, his eyes straying to his right.

Her gaze followed his, and her eyes landed on the burly gray Centaur that was standing only fifteen feet from them.

"*Da me koyuwuk.*"

Tears clouded her vision, and her hand flew to her mouth, words escaping her.

The Centaur opened his arms, his own tears spilling down his face and onto his chest. "Frawnden."

"Aeron." She galloped into his arms, their tears mingling in their kiss. "You're alive." She brushed his long, unkempt hair from his face and cupped his cheeks in her hands, her eyes searching his face as if trying to remember every detail. "I thought—thought maybe—" She bit her lip and shook her head, tears flowing thickly down her face.

Aeron buried his face in her shoulder, breathing in her flowery, herbal scent. "I know. I know. I missed you so much."

She could only kiss his neck and cheeks in response.

From the shadows, a large Centaur, one of Artigal's personal guards, stepped into the clearing and knelt before his leader. The other four did the same. "*Da rañ ñidauz yarazai zi fezh.*"

Aeron nodded his head and placed his fist across his chest. "Thank you."

"You knew. That's why the outer guards and scouts didn't raise an alarm." Trojan's eyes were shining as he gazed up into the still faces of the guardian Centaurs.

The leader allowed Trojan a small smile and his eyes softened. "Yes, child. We knew. The Igentis wanted it to be a surprise."

"Wow."

The large warrior turned once more to Aeron and bowed his head respectfully. "My lord, I suggest that we move back to the safety of the camp. Artigal wants to see you."

His arm wrapped around his mate, Aeron nodded gravely. "Of course. I have word to give him."

Frawnden, for the first time, noticed that Aeron was hurt.

"By the Emperor! Your back!" She gasped as she spotted multiple two-foot-long semi-infected gashes running from the shoulders of his horse body all the way to his hindquarters.

"It's nothing," he murmured, but he was obviously in pain.

It only took her a quick glance to assess the rest of his physical condition, and she didn't like what she saw.

He was mildly malnourished, and many more injuries lined his gray body, a good number of them infected.

She grunted and shook her head. "What else would I expect? It's so like you to forget to take care of yourself while you're busy fighting." Though her voice was stern and chastening, a twinkle in her eyes betrayed her amusement.

"Why would I want to take care of myself if I could have you do it, love?" His eyes burned passionately into hers.

A blush raged across her cheeks. Oh, how she had missed him!

"Trojan, why don't you go on ahead to fix your father a place in our tent?"

Trojan needed no second plea, and with one more sparkling glance at his father, he galloped into the woods. Grudgingly, because Aeron was telling them of his journey, and yet with a light step, Trojan rushed to obey.

"I have been following your tracks for months now, but gods was it hard to find them."

She nodded. "Artigal recruited some of the spell casters to cover them."

He grunted, amusement sparkling in his eyes. "I wouldn't expect any less." His gaze drifted off into the trees, and his demeanor darkened.

"I can guess that the very day I reached Trans-Falls was the day of, or the day after, you left. I just barely missed you, but it took me three years to correct that simple mistake."

Frawnden shook her head mournfully, the years seeming to melt away before her.

"I knew Artigal wouldn't travel on the road that went straight to New-Fars because it has frequent human traffic. I also didn't think he would take the southern route because it's so much longer and difficult to travel. So, I took the path going farther north."

His mate groaned. "And we took the southern."

This explained so much.

"I traveled for months taking every back road I could, hoping I could catch a glimpse of your tracks. I found nothing. I knew that I had been traveling faster than even this small group of Centaurs and should have caught up to you by then."

"I had the choice of either following the road until it met up at New-Fars and arriving nearly a year ahead of you, or I could've backtracked and been nearly two years behind. Of course, had I picked the latter option, I might never have known where you would have gone after New-Fars. So, instead, I chose to travel between all the roads and maybe catch up with you before you reached the city. Even so, I should have reached you about one and a half years ago, but there was one other problem."

Though Aeron's overall attitude was light and joyful, it suddenly darkened, and his strong-featured face became grave.

"What?" Frawnden nervously grasped her mate's hand in her own.

"I'm afraid it is something I must discuss with Artigal first, and then he will tell you."

She frowned but knew that it was always wisest to consult Artigal before anyone else.

"But, until then, I'm absolutely starving and aching. So, where's this alleged camp of yours that has so perfectly hid itself all these years?"

"Just right past those trees, sir." The leader of the five Centaurs pointed, and Aeron followed his gesture. His heart burst with joy. He had been alone for so long, he had forgotten what it was like to be with his own people. Tears glistened in his eyes, and the ache of his travels slipped away.

As they entered the camp, everyone fell silent. Not a sound was heard.

Everyone was in complete shock. Was it really him? Did the tribe of Trans-Falls really have their High Chief back?

Nearly all at once, all the Centaurs dropped to one knee and held their right fist over their heart.

Then, as Aeron walked through them, they leapt up and cheered, giving their leader a hero's welcome.

The Centaurs that Aeron was closest to came up to him in joyous throngs. Many embraced him, but all were careful not to touch his wounds.

As they pushed their way through the crowd, the five escorting Centaur guards broke away silently.

Aeron and Frawnden spotted Artigal standing by his large tent in the middle of the camp with Trojan by his side.

Taking a deep breath, his eyes shining contently and proudly, Aeron knelt before the Igentis.

Artigal placed his hand on the High Chief's shoulder. "Well done, Aeron, and welcome back."

At these words, the entire camp once more erupted in celebration.

Trojan hugged his father, squeezing him as hard as he could, his little eyes shining gleefully. Aeron hugged him back, tears glistening in his eyes before Trojan stepped back to stand beside Artigal. For a moment, Aeron's eyes darkened. "Where's Stephania?"

Frawnden and Trojan both filled the High Chief in on all that had happened.

A scowl wrinkled his face. He wanted nothing more than to rush to his daughter's side and see if she was well, but he had other duties, duties that painfully came first. "Thank you for telling me. I will come back with you as soon as possible."

His small family nodded and turned away, leaving the leaders to their duties.

The Trans-Falls Chief and the Igentis chatted like old friends, as if not a day had gone by.

Artigal led him into his tent, filling him in on all the events, especially concerning his family, that had transpired.

Trojan sighed as his father disappeared into the large tent, his eyes shining brighter than the stars on a clear spring night. "I can't believe it! He's home. Father's finally home."

Frawnden wiped away tears from her eyes. All she could whisper was, "I know, I know."

§

"STEPHANIA! STEPHANIA, wake up!" Trojan shook his sister, and she groaned before rolling over onto her other side.

"Stephania, get up! Father's here."

The little girl sat straight up, her eyes wide open in surprised disbelief.

"Father?" She rubbed her shining red eyes and tried to wake up. The anesthesia that Jargon had given her still making her a bit groggy.

"Yes! He came back! He found us, and he's talking to Artigal right now." Trojan began to tug on Stephania's arm.

"Ow! Watch it!" She winced against the pain and wrenched her arm from him, her little, chubby face twisting into a scowl.

"Oh, I'm sorry." Trojan meekly looked at his hooves. "I forgot about your wounds. Please forgive me."

Stephania nodded her head almost pridefully. "Thank you. I do."

Standing up, she grimaced and tottered over to where their mother kept food.

Grabbing herself a piece of bread, she split it with Trojan and listened as he, in very good detail, told her of all the things that had passed by while she had slept.

"When will I see him?" She was upset he wasn't here now. *Why does everyone else get to see him but me?*

"A little later, I think." Trojan snorted and crossed his arms. He too was a bit annoyed. "He's talking to Artigal about something very important."

Stephania grunted and tore a piece of bread off the loaf, chewing it violently. *How could those matters be more important than seeing my father?* She frowned, looking down at her food. *They aren't.* She jumped to her feet, teetering from the sudden dizziness. "I'm going to see him." Before Trojan could stop her, she ran out of the tent.

§

"A TWO-THOUSAND COUNT Eta army!" Artigal shook his head in pure disbelief.

Aeron nodded gravely. "On top of that, the leaders I overheard deliberating said they didn't even know how many more rouge Etas were attracted to Stephania's magic trace."

Artigal shook his head. "We would not be able to hold up to such an army. Though, I am glad that Thaddeus will not be present."

"I am too, sir." This, however, did nothing to raise their spirits.

"Where is Thaddeus? Why haven't we seen more of him in the last few years, especially with Stephania being away from the Trans-Falls forest? Surely he hasn't given up, has he?"

Artigal's hand subconsciously rose to his chest. "I think—" A heavy sigh left his lips. The memory of the Great Lord's mark flashing out in the darkness and of Thaddeus' screams of pain replayed in his mind. He, like Jargon, suspected Thaddeus had been wounded, much like himself, and was recovering. "I don't think Thaddeus will be able to come after Stephania for a little while. Something happened—" He shook his head, not quite knowing how to explain the millions of thoughts running through his mind. "I think Stephania might have channeled—"

"Father!"

Aeron felt a small body slam into his legs. Jumping in surprise and then grinning with joy, he swept the little girl off her feet.

"Daughter!" Tears collected in his eyes as he beheld the young girl, memorizing every detail of her face. She had grown up so much in two years. Her hair was longer, and she was definitely heavier.

"I missed you, little dragon." He held her close to him, her soft hair tickling as it caught the scratchy stubble on his face.

"I missed you too." She clung to his neck tightly, and he had to loosen her hold.

"Stephania!" Trojan burst into the tent, his face beet red. "Forgive me, Igentis. I was unable to catch up to her." His embarrassed eyes stayed fixed on the ground.

Aeron heard his son mutter something about how he hadn't expected that something with only two legs could be so fast and agile.

"Stephania, best you go back with your brother, okay? I will be with you all shortly." Aeron pulled her away, his stern, smiling eyes gazing warmly into hers.

She nodded, and he placed her down.

Tottering over to Trojan, she quickly hopped onto his back. With Trojan still muttering his apologies, they ducked out of the door.

Aeron sighed. The air seemed sad after the children left. He had missed his family, but he hadn't realized just how much until now.

"And what were you saying?" Aeron turned back to the Igentis just in time to see the leader wash the tender smile off his face, tucking his emotions once more behind his mask. Aeron shook his head and sighed. He liked to think he knew Artigal better than most, but in reality, he knew hardly anything, especially with the way the Igentis preferred to hide away his true feelings.

Artigal shifted his weight and cleared his throat, his eyes distant. "Nothing, I suppose. It isn't pressing."

Aeron frowned. He desperately wanted to know about what had happened between Thaddeus, Stephania, and Artigal, besides just Artigal being wounded, but he had the feeling that the Igentis was keeping this, and many other things, secret for a reason.

Artigal's voice was quiet and distant, as if his thoughts were on some distant shore. "I'm afraid that it is too late to call for reinforcements, but nonetheless, I will send a message right now. There is always the chance they can help in some way."

Aeron stood up from the comfortable mat he had been resting on and placed his hand on the white Centaur's shoulder.

"There is no need for that, sir." He stood a little straighter, his eyes glinting slyly.

Artigal looked at him quizzically and raised an eyebrow. His undivided attention was upon the Trans-Falls' Chief.

"If you remember, you know from the letter I sent ahead of me by falcon that I had taken a soldier, Landen, with me."

Artigal nodded. "Yes, I was beginning to wonder where he had gone as you were telling me of your journeys."

He nodded. "When we reached Trans-Falls and there was no one present, I instructed Landen to return to my army and that I would continue alone. He protested so relentlessly that we started arguing and got into a fight, and he lashed me across the hip with his knife." He pointed to a silver scar etched into his dapple-grey hair, and a boyish grin spread across his face.

Artigal chuckled and shook his head. Typical.

"Seeing as he wasn't going to leave me alone, I agreed to let him come along. However, I ordered that if I needed him to, he would leave immediately for the other Trans-Falls Centaurs."

Aeron shook his head. "Too soon that day came. Only a few months into our journey, after we had split ways for a few days to cover more ground in our search, I stumbled upon this Eta army. After meeting up with Landen a few days later, I ordered him to leave and take a message to Trans-Falls' neighboring tribe, Psithur. In the long run, he did more than that. Now, we have both a section of my army, a part that is no longer needed at Sankyz, and a section of Psithur's army that will meet us by New-Fars."

When Aeron paused, Artigal gazed at him expectantly, drinking all the information and instantly analyzing it.

"From what I have heard through messengers, they are going to make themselves a blockade between the Etas and New-Fars, but we have to get there before they do or we will be caught between nearly 4,000 Centaurs and an army of 2,000 Etas seems to be growing by the day."

Silence enveloped the tent as his words hung in the air.

Artigal's thoughtful, soft-spoken words broke the ill silence as he changed the subject.

"I know Frawnden will take plenty good care of you regarding your injuries, but I want you to tell her that I don't want her sedating you. I will be holding a small celebration to celebrate your return as well as another important occasion, and I want you to be wide awake. I trust that you will be there?"

Aeron bowed. "Of course, Artigal. What is one more day in the land of fatigue?" His jesting put a slight smile on the leader's lips, though neither of them was feeling quite cheery.

After a slight pause, Aeron let his eyes linger on the map that Artigal had spread out on the table. One last question remained. "Artigal?"

"Hmm?"

"Why did you pick this route?" He pointed to the dotted red line that Artigal had traced over the unused road he had chosen.

The road from Trans-Falls swung sharply to the south, rounding the west side of a large collection of mountains before skimming the coast of the *Salcon Miw,* or Salcon Bay, before curving back northward, and turning east, meaning they would be entering New-Fars from its direct western side.

It was the longest possible route that Artigal could have taken, besides venturing dangerously into the Cavos desert. Even so, it was a route that shouldn't take two years to travel, yet that was how much time Artigal had taken.

A deep sigh escaped Artigal's lips, and his eyes darkened. "I wanted to train her as much as possible. There is so much that our Kind can offer such a child, and I hoped that one day she could do more for our tribes than just be the fulfillment of a Duvarharian prophecy."

Aeron narrowed his eyes. He sensed that this wasn't Artigal's only reason for traveling so slowly.

"A year or slightly more would have been sufficient with how intelligent the child is. Why have you chosen to take longer?" He knew he was treading on fragile grounds with the Igentis, but he felt that it was his right to know.

Something that could have been akin to tears glistened in Artigal's eyes. "I fear that the humans will not want to take her in. I fear that she will not be welcome. I fear that she will not be safe because she knows who she is. I am to respect her parents' wish, which they gave their lives for, that she be with Dalton. I fear it was wrong of me to give her a family here when I knew she could never stay."

"And you care?"

Artigal didn't respond. He opened his mouth, his eyes a strange and confusing color, but merely turned away, crossing his arms. The discussion was clearly closed.

Respectful of his leader and mentor, though curious and a little frustrated, Aeron bowed his head before turning to leave.

Before he reached the tent's door, Artigal's deep voice caught him.

"Aeron, we are still nearly three to four months away from New-Fars at our current pace. How much time do we have before the blockade is to be in full force and we are trapped?"

Aeron took a deep breath and whispered very quietly, "Two and a half months."

Artigal's eyes darkened, his voice low. "Send home every Centaur who may slow us down."

"That will compromise the safety of Stephania."

Artigal's jaw clenched, and fists tightened. "Then so be it. We must move without dely. May the Emperor protect us now."

CHAPTER 10

THE JOYOUS CELEBRATION to commemorate the return of Trans-Falls' High Chief had been going on nearly four hours now. To everyone's delight and relief, the storm had held off, and the skies didn't show any signs of letting down rain anytime soon.

Standing by the small bonfire they had made, Artigal gathered his people before him, Trojan's sword in hand.

"My people!"

Silence instantly followed, and Aeron quickly moved to Artigal's right side—his rightful place.

"I have called you together today for the obvious reason that your High Chief has returned!"

A subdued cheer rose from the crowd. Artigal waited only a moment before hushing them. He wanted them to be able to celebrate, but with the Etas closer than ever, it was still imperative to not draw attention to their presence.

"But tonight, I also bring you together to present to you a new *Synoliki* warrior!"

The crowd murmured, and silence fell over them.

Synoliki warriors were the most elite band of Centaur warriors; it was a great honor to be a part of them. Thousands of years ago, when the Centaurs had their own Country—Ravenwood—an enormous, silent network of them had ensured the safety and peace of the tribes. Now, however, their numbers had trickled into near extinction, with only about four to five *Synoliki* per tribe.

Aeron's eyebrows rose at the news and questioning murmurs ran through the crowd.

"Would you please come to me, Trojan, son of Aeron?"

Gasps of shock rippled through the crowd as they parted a path starting at Artigal and leading all the way to Trojan, who had been listening at the edge of the crowd.

His heart throbbed in his chest, and his limbs became paralyzed. Him? A *Synoliki*? Only the very best were chosen to become a *Synoliki*, and they had to prove themselves worthy first. How had he done that?

Thinking this was some horrific joke, or even just a dream, Trojan took a deep breath, lifted his chin high, and delicately trotted up to Artigal.

Bowing before the leader, Trojan proudly whispered out in the old Centaur language *"Me koshoawázh, Igentis."*

Frawnden pushed her way through the crowd to gain a better view of her son, glistening tears of happiness streaming down her proud face.

Artigal placed his hand on the boy's shoulder, and Trojan stood up.

"Trojan, not only today, but for your whole life, I have watched you grow and learn the ways of life. You are still very young. Nine years a few months ago, correct?"

"Yes, Igentis." Trojan, though his voice was quiet, stared back fearlessly, a thrilled gleam in his dark blue eyes. Subconsciously, his long, black tail swished softly from side to side, betraying his inner excitement.

His eyes landed on his sword, which Artigal was holding. A small gasp left the boy's lips. The sword had been enhanced with a spell to make it a true weapon of a *Synoliki*. The sword was now bigger than it had been and was shining with strange blue markings. The boy turned his attention back to Artigal, his hands twitching in excitement and the anticipation of holding this new weapon.

The curve of Artigal's lips betrayed his own joy. He gently caressed the sword's shining blade. "I took the liberty of enhancing your sword, should you agree to become *Synoliki*. With intense training, you will be able to use the bit of magic within you, along with the magic you will gain as *Synoliki*, to turn this sword into any weapon you might have need of."

Trojan was unable to mask his shock and excitement. He had only heard about such weapons in legends.

"Additionally, if you are ever parted from it, you will be able to teleport the weapon to yourself.

"I have found much pleasure in instructing you, and today you have shown yourself worthy of becoming a *Synoliki*."

Once more, Trojan's heart raced in his chest.

"So, I ask you, Trojan, son of Aeron the High Chief of Trans-Falls: do you accept my offer? It is a hard and dangerous life, but a life filled with meaning and purpose. There will be times that it may not seem worth it, and times when there is no need for you, but there will also be times when our existence lies solely in your hands. Knowing the requirements, the expectations, and regulations of such a title, will you defend the weak and the poor, promise to destroy evil, and swear to protect the Centaur tribes with your life? Will you promise to seek only after Pure Magic and never waver into temptation of the darkness? Will you become a *Synoliki* warrior?"

Trojan took a deep breath and turned to face his father.

Tears glistened in the older Centaur's kind eyes, and he gave a small nod to show his son his consent and pride.

The young buckskin could see his mother out of the corner of his eye. A warmth from the overwhelming feeling of being so loved filled him, and he was unable to contain the sweet smile that spread across his face. As he turned his head back to Artigal, his eye caught something red.

Stephania slowly walked down the path that led up to Artigal and proceeded to stand on Artigal's left side. Though it was rare that anyone ever stood on Artigal's left side, unless it was Jargon or Frawnden, no one move to take Stephania away or scold her. It seemed right that she was standing where she was, as if it had been her place all along.

Trojan smiled at her, and as sleepy as she was, she smiled back and nodded.

Without any regrets, Trojan lifted his voice making sure it was loud enough for all to hear. "I swear on the Great Emperor, I will!"

The crowd stomped their hooves in a quiet rumble of celebration.

Artigal placed his right hand upon the boy's forehead, and closing his eyes, he chanted a spell. Intricate, glowing blue markings began to swirl across the right side of Trojan's face, down his neck, and onto his chest and arms.

Trojan opened his eyes when the process was complete, his eyes now shining a bright, daring blue—the mark of a true *Synoliki* warrior.

§

ARTIGAL STARTLED OUT of his sleep at the sound of a soft voice. He held his breath, waiting to hear it again. The party had gone on late into the night and some Centaurs were still singing softly outside where he knew they were staring up at the stars.

"Artigal?"

He frowned. It was Stephania. "Come in, child." *What is she doing in my tent this late at night?*

Her curly, red hair poked through the tent flap. Her gaze locked with his, and when he nodded, she stepped in, her eyes fixed on the ground. He couldn't help but notice she appeared more timid than usual.

"What do you have to say, that made you think it is acceptable for you to sneak away from your family and bother me at such a late hour?"

A blush rose on her little cheeks, and she played with the hem of her shirt. "I was just wondering, Artigal, if, um ..." Her eyes met his again. They were unusually soft and gentle, almost doe-like. "If you had a family."

Her question hit him like a brick wall. *A family?*

"Why do you ask, child?" His voice was harsher than he had intended.

She shifted uncomfortably, and he knew her nervousness was a mirror of his own at the moment.

"I don't know. I was dreaming and saw you with a child. A Duvarharian child. Like me. And a Centaur woman."

Artigal's eyes widened, and the air left his lungs. She had seen them—his family. *But how?* Had the connection between them really been that strong? Strong enough to give her his hidden memories? He had heard such things happening—of memories being passed from ancestors to their descendants, and from conscious connections made between creatures with Ancient Magic, but he hadn't channeled any of that magic when their minds connected. At least, not knowingly. Was their connection not just a strange coincidence or fluke of common magic but something more?

"I did have a family," he drawled slowly. "Once, a long time ago."

She frowned. "You don't have a family anymore?"

He scowled, not sure if he liked how intrusive she had suddenly become, or how sweet and gentle. It was as if a different girl were standing before him—a girl who had not experienced the horrors of life she had. "Not anymore, no."

"Aren't Mother and Father and Trojan your family?"

He didn't know why, but a rage washed over him. "Of course they aren't! Why would they be?" He instantly regretted his harsh tone when he saw how she flinched.

"I—I don't know. I just see how you treat them differently than everyone else." Her eyes filled with tears, and his heart lurched. "I just thought, maybe they were ... special to you."

They are, was what he wanted to say, but he forced the words back down. "Why do you care, child? What does this mean to you?"

"You're always alone. You're always so distant, as if you are a star, shining brightly and sadly with no other stars around you. The stars told me families are like constellations. No star is ever alone. But you are alone, Artigal, always. And the stars say it isn't right." The tears that had brimmed in her eyes spilled over, and she sniffed loudly.

Her words stabbed at him like cold knives. She had taken their star reading lessons closer to heart than he had thought, and she could now read them as well as any trained Centaur. But what she told him didn't bode well. He knew he was alone, and he knew it wasn't right, but that had been his allotment in life. In exchange for the Pure Magic, he had sacrificed all else. It was a choice he would never go back on, but that didn't make it any easier to live with.

"The stars never lie, child. You are right to listen to them."

"Then you shouldn't be alone. You should have a constellation." A scowl creased her forehead.

His eyebrows rose. *Why is she so persistent? What had she seen in that dream that made her so afraid?*

"No, Stephania. I am a star no longer."

Her sharp eyes bore into his, and he almost smiled. Here was the stubborn, fiery girl he was used to.

"Yes, you are. You even said, 'we are all children of the stars'."

"No, child. Not all. Only the Centaurs and forest children are. Duvarharians are the children of different Beings."

She winced as if she had been hit. "But you are still a star."

"No. I am a star no longer."

"But—"

"Be gone, child." His patience had run out. Her persistence and ill-timed questions had chipped away at places inside of him he wished to remain hidden. "Return to your family at once and leave me in peace."

Tears shamelessly poured down her face. "I just wanted—"

"Leave!" he barked despite the stinging in his throat. He met her teary, pleading gaze once more, holding it with power and indifference, before she fled from the tent crying.

Regret filled him, but he instantly shoved it away, an unease settling in its place. But then another sensation settled on him—remembrance and duty.

The words that had brought him comfort so many years ago rang in his mind once again: *You are a star no longer. Go forth and shine like the suns, as a shadow of Light.*

He was alone, but Stephania didn't have to be. She had her family from Trans-Falls; he had made sure of that. Though he could never be part of it, he had done his best to ensure the happiness of that little family, *his* little family, and though it brought him only sorrow now, he knew it would be the only legacy he would be proud of once his soul finally left Rasa.

CHAPTER 11

A Few Months Since Aeron's Return

AERON, HOW MANY more days until the barricade is in place?"
Artigal's voice was tense with concentration as he and Aeron pored over
every map of this part of Ventronovia that they could.

Aeron didn't even look up as he traced his finger over the road they were taking.
"I calculate only seven more days, Igentis." His eye twitched. What they were trying
to accomplish just wasn't possible.

"*Zuru fuñofufe!*" Artigal threw down the compass in fury and ran his hands
through his silky mane. Many other curses quickly followed as he passionately
paced the tent.

"How many days out are we still?" A thoughtful look suddenly crossed Aeron's
ruggedly handsome face. Artigal's fits of anger were nothing new to him, and they
hardly fazed him anymore, though they usually sent most people scurrying for safety. Even so, Aeron got the impression that Artigal was disturbed by more than just
the problems they faced. In fact, it seemed that the Igentis had been unnerved by
something private for the few short months since Aeron had returned. Aeron knew
his leader and friend well enough to know that unless it had something to do with
the Tribe, he would never learn of it.

Artigal stalked away from the table. "Still nearly two and a half weeks, no matter
what *zuru* way I draw it."

Aeron shook his head. "The only thing that can travel two and a half weeks of
land in seven days would be a galloping Centaur ... with only a small burden, of
course."

Artigal nodded before his whole face suddenly lit up. "Yes. A galloping Centaur
with a small burden." The white Centaur began to once again pace the room anx-

iously. "Yes. Of course. This could work."

Without another word, Artigal raced to the maps and furiously began crunching the numbers, days, and distance.

"The Eta army is approximately three days behind us. If we leave now, we could make it. I would only take a few. No, actually, just two—and the boy. The boy, of course. He needs to see this. And if I leave *them* behind, they could buy us some time."

Artigal's chaotic scheming didn't faze Aeron. The younger Centaur knew that the random rambling was the result of a crazy yet brilliant plan.

"Aeron, find Frawnden and Trojan. Oh, and Aeron, don't bring anything you absolutely can't live without. We'll travel as fast as we can. It'll be more dangerous without the rest of the warriors, but it is necessary. We might, might, just make it in time."

Aeron bowed his head, knowing better than to ask any questions just yet.

"Stephania!" Artigal turned to a flap in the tent, and Stephania instantly stepped out of an extra room in the tent where she had been reading a scroll explaining the art of reading and listening to the stars.

"Yes, Artigal?" Her young voice was smooth and dripped with grace and honey, her red eyes glistening in the light. A lock of her soft, red hair fell delicately into her eyes, and Artigal nearly smiled at her as a warm feeling of pride and love filled him at the sight of the Duvarharian child he almost considered to be his own. Almost.

"Go with your father and be very quick about it."

Stephania obeyed without hesitation.

Aeron helped her onto his back. "Did you learn a lot?"

She nodded, her eyes sparkling. "Some of it was hard to read, but Mother's been teaching me. I learned more about reading the stars."

Aeron's eyes glinted with pride for his daughter and mate.

Taking a deep breath and popping his back, Artigal began to furiously write instructions on a parchment, which he would leave for the next-in-command and Jargon.

When he was finished, he hastily strapped on his sword, a few knives, and his bow and arrow.

A heavy sigh left his lips as he stood still for a moment. He could feel the *Kijaqumok* throbbing in his chest, and he tried to ignore the constant, searing pain that raced through his body.

"Just let me live long enough to get her to safety, Emperor. Please." He began packing as minimally as possible, unsure of what he would need most. In the end, he settled on a few maps, light rations, and a small jar that contained a branch from Trans-Falls.

He hesitated before putting the jar into his satchel. The branch was from the *Gauwu Zelauw*—the forest that grew around the edge of Trans-Falls. As he held the jar, his chest felt a little lighter and he breathed a little easier. The Magic in the leafy twig had done well at staving off the evil's power up until now, but how much longer before it wore out?

Shaking his head, he quickly stuffed it into his bag.

They were in a race against time, and it seemed only death had the advantage.

§

THE TREES BENT and sighed around them as the wind tossed and turned in the branches. The stars were bright overhead tonight, along with the greater moon. Trickles of light fell from the heavens and scattered across the dark forest floor. The wilderness seemed so much bigger, so much more consuming when traveling in a small group.

Aeron, Frawnden, and Trojan were all stretched out across the ground in various positions, fast asleep.

Stephania, however, was lying on her back, her hands behind her head and her eyes fixed on the stars, which glistened and winked at her through the treetops.

Artigal had been poring over his maps, sleep having abandoned him hours before. "Just two more days!" Artigal let the scroll slide together.

They had been traveling for five days now, just the small family and Igentis, at full gallop nonstop all day; the Centaurs were extremely tired, and Artigal had been struggling to keep up. The *Kijaquomok* was spreading further through him, and every day it seemed harder and harder to do anything.

They were almost on time—just a half a day late.

Chuckling softly to himself, Artigal trotted over to Stephania and followed her gaze to the stars above them.

"I think," she whispered softly, pausing to shift her weight and cast a moment's glance at the white Centaur, "I think that they're singing." She smiled, and lifting her hand, she traced a few constellations.

"Oh." She frowned. "But now they're sad."

Artigal focused on the stars. He couldn't feel the stars the same way she could; he could only read what they told him. She, on the other hand, could *hear* them. He had heard of this being possible, but no one he had known, himself included, had ever been able to.

"What are they mourning about?"

She sighed heavily. "Something about someone they know and love that will be leaving. Of a sad parting of one knowing one loved and the other not knowing. Or maybe they mean not remembering." Her frown deepened. "I don't understand it, Artigal. It really doesn't make any sense. What does it mean?"

He swallowed and turned away from her, strange tears glistening in his eyes. He knew exactly what the stars sang of tonight, but he didn't have the heart to tell the child. He knew what he had to do to keep her safe. He had hoped against it, prayed against it, wished there was another way, but that horrible, perfect idea always came back. Would he be able to hurt another like this again? A brown-haired Duvarharian girl smiled back at him. He bit his lip and shoved the memory away. It didn't matter. This was the only way she would be safe. It had to be done.

"I don't know, Stephania, my child," he lied quietly and turned away from her, unable to look into her sweet, innocent, red eyes. "I really don't know."

§

"AERON?" FRAWNDEN CLIPPED her sword sheath onto her belt.

"Yes, my love?" Stringing his bow, Aeron slipped it over his shoulder.

Their gaze strayed to their children who were just waking up. Every morning before this had been a rush to get moving as quickly as possible, but this morning was different. It seemed no one wanted to be in a hurry. Both child were very solemn and quiet. They knew that this was their last day together, but neither wanted to mention it. It was hard for them to understand why Stephania had to leave them.

"Do you think, um ..." Frawnden looked down at her knife, tracing its sharp edge with her finger. "Do you think we have to leave her? Maybe we could stay or—" She broke off suddenly, her eyes wide. "Did you hear that?" Her heart thumped frantically, and dread filled her.

Before Aeron could answer, a horrific screech rent the air.

Stephania screamed as a large, dark bird dove out of the air toward her.

Trojan drew out his shining sword and sliced the bird clean in two, its black blood glistening on the blue blade.

The air was rent with the eerie screeches of thousands of Etas, most of them large, mutated birds.

"Trojan!" Artigal quickly shot an arrow into the heart of another diving bird, the next arrow fixed on his string in a matter of seconds. "Take Stephania and run east! I'm right behind you!"

Trojan swept the young Duvarharian up onto his back and charged further into the forest, quickly disappearing.

Grimacing with the pain that coursed through his chest and body, Artigal shot down two Etas with one arrow before collapsing to his knees. Black veins spread from his chest up to his face.

Aeron was by his side in a second, shaking Artigal's shoulders.

"Artigal, look at me! Focus!"

Artigal coughed, trying to draw a breath. His eyes were dull and rolled into the back of his head.

"*Shaif zuru!*" Aeron slapped the Igentis' face, but the old Centaur was unresponsive.

"What's wrong?" Frawnden was frantically digging through her medical bag.

"Dark magic. Find something for dark magic."

Frawnden's face went white. "Dark magic?"

He could only nod. His eyes landed on Artigal's pack. Surely Artigal would bring something in case this happened. He tore open the satchel and pulled out the branch. He shook his head. The magic he was sensing from the branch was very depleted. Of course Artigal would put his faith in something so small and simple. A smile almost spread across Aeron's face; those who didn't understand Pure Magic might think the Igentis was superstitious. But he wasted no time in tearing the seal from the jar's lid and stuffing the branch into Artigal's hand. The white magic from the leaves seeped into Artigal's arm, and he shuddered. Aeron prayed it would at least be enough to buy Frawnden some time.

The healer, confused and terrified, was frantically searching through her bag. "I don't have anything for dark magic." She started to panic, until her fingers wrapped around a very small vial. She pulled it out, and both she and Aeron stared at the simple red bottle. In it were two small berries—*Negluu* berries, sometimes known as fire mountain berries or even *Jok Kukeb,* meaning instant death.

They were the most powerful ingredient known to healers and were known for killing people instantly if not used correctly. They seemed to jump and bite with their own powerful energy, as if made entirely out of magic.

"I can't do it." She swallowed hard. She held the bottle to him, her hand shaking. Though the *Negluu* berries could banish the dark magic, they could also kill Artigal. This was the best they had. It seemed hopeless.

Aeron's face was dark and emotionless. He could feel Artigal's breath slowing down, and he knew they didn't have much time. Most of the Etas had followed Stephania's magic trace, and he feared for his children's lives.

"Frawnden, you have to."

She shook her head. "I don't have any of the other ingredients! I could kill him, Aeron."

He clenched his jaw. "Frawnden, he's *dying*. It doesn't matter anymore. We have to try. He'll die anyway if we do nothing."

She paused for a moment before quickly opening the bottle and dumping one of the berries out into her hand. An angry hissing filled the air from the berry's powerful energy. Before she could change her mind, she quickly opened Artigal's mouth and forced the berry in.

Seconds went by. Nothing happened.

Aeron bowed his head, his jaw clenched hard. They couldn't do this without Artigal. "Emperor," he whispered. "Heal him."

Artigal coughed, his eyes snapping open. "The children." He pushed Aeron and Frawnden away from him, struggling to his feet. The world spun around him. His entire body ached, and his head throbbed horribly. He brushed their protests aside. They wanted him to retreat to safety.

"No." He gritted his teeth against the pain. The dizziness wore off.

"Artigal, let us do this. You don't need to risk your life just to be there. Let Aeron and I go ahead. You stay out of the danger. We can't risk losing you." Frawnden's gentle voice was firm and demanding, but Artigal merely shook his head.

"You've never been one for goodbyes, anyway." A small smile almost lifted Aeron's face.

"No. I will go. I have to do this. There is something that remains to be finished, and only I can do it." Mist collected in the old Centaur's eyes, and Aeron and Frawnden shared a look of worry. Could they do nothing to convince him otherwise?

When it became apparent that he wasn't going to do as they asked, they galloped through the woods together, following the dark cloud of Etas that flew after Trojan and Stephania.

All around them rose the horrifying crackling of Etas shape-shifting. Snarls and screams soon filled the forest as the Etas began to swarm across the ground. The majority of the Etas, blind to anything but Stephania's magic trace, ignored the three Centaurs. However, a couple were drawn to Artigal's trace.

"Artigal!" Frawnden screamed and threw herself in front of the old Centaur.

A second scream parted her lips as her body twisted and crumpled to the ground.

"Oh, stars of old." Aeron collapsed beside her as she futilely struggled to stand. A long, knurled spear was lodged deep into the flesh around the back hip of her horse body.

For a moment, Artigal was frozen with disbelief at what she had done for him.

The Eta whose attack on Artigal had failed stumbled in confusion.

Rage clearing his mind, Artigal released a vicious spell, taking advantage of the Eta's distraction.

The Eta's body began twitching miserably. Its bones slowly dis-integrated and it melted to the ground in a puddle of flesh.

A sharp pain tore through the Igentis' chest, and he snarled. He shouldn't have released that much magic in the spell. He had once again let his emotions get the best of him. *How much magic do I have left? Will I have enough for what is ahead of me?*

"Can you walk?" Aeron's panicked voice tore through Artigal's thoughts.

A sharp cry of pain answered the leader. "I don't know."

Artigal's eyes quickly flickered over to Frawnden. He had many guards whose sole job was to put themselves in harm's way for him, and he knew that any one of his tribe members would die for him but could have never imagined it would be Frawnden.

A huge laceration decorated Frawnden's right back leg, the torn, bleeding flesh bubbling with poison.

Artigal had seen many wounds in battle but seeing the pain on Frawnden's face and the worry in Aeron's eyes caused him to blanch. Was his life really worth the life of someone like her? He had never before thought twice about a Centaur giving his life for him. He had never realized the true worth of sacrifice until now. He didn't like the guilt and pain that took up residence deep within him.

"You have to walk. We have to make it to Stephania." Tears filled Aeron's eyes. If they couldn't get to safety, he would have no choice but to either leave his mate to die, or to die with her.

She tested her leg again, but once more it collapsed under her, a low groan leaving her lips.

Artigal knew he had to continue. Stephania and Trojan needed him. Something was stopping him, something that hadn't stopped him from making decisions for a long time—love. He couldn't bear to watch Frawnden suffer, and Aeron mourn. It was painful to remember what it felt like to really care about others. A wave of nausea crashed over him, and he was violently reminded of why he had stopped loving others—it was too hard to watch them die.

He didn't want to leave them, but he had to choose: Trojan and Stephania or Frawnden and Aeron.

CHAPTER 12

TREES RACED PAST and the wind screamed in their ears. Brush snagged at Trojan's legs and tore into his skin, but he didn't feel it.

His breath was hot and fevered as he struggled to keep ahead of the dark cloud of Etas that soared overhead, some diving down to attack them.

He had to jump over several large fallen trees, but most of the time he had to quickly weave his way through the thick forest, praying he wasn't just running in circles.

Wielding her small knife, Stephania had already slain as many Etas as she could from his back, but it hadn't been enough.

A trail of black blood and mangled bodies followed them, becoming thicker as the Etas closed in.

It was hard for her to fight with just her knife. Soon, she began using her rudimentary knowledge of magic and Duvarharian instincts to fight them off. Unfortunately, though it was effective, her magic only attracted the Etas all the more.

Stephania's face went pale as she looked behind her. The trees had fallen black, not because of shadows, but because of Etas. Snarling, mangled, mutated beasts charged after them, growing closer and closer.

"Trojan," she whispered hoarsely. "Trojan, faster!" she screamed as a small cat-like Eta jumped at her, suddenly massing into a ball of red sparks before it emerged as a huge bat-like reptile. She buried her face into Trojan's long, blood-splattered mane.

An arrow pierced the Eta's chest, and its lifeless body hit Stephania's back before tumbling to the ground.

From the direction in which they were running, crashed a thunderous wave of hooves, a blood-curdling battle cry filling the forest.

Gasping in fear and awe, Stephania clung to Trojan as he dove behind a five-foot-wide fallen tree trunk for protection.

A wave of mighty Centaurs leapt over them and the tree as effortlessly as a bird could fly.

The ground shook. Screams filled the air. The clash of metal mingled with battle cries. Hooves, tails, and bodies flashed passed them in a blur as hundreds of Warriors rushed into the battle.

Just as the amount of the Centaurs began to thin, Artigal came galloping toward them and pulled them out from behind the log. "Come! We are almost to the falls."

Barely missing being trampled, Artigal galloped through the oncoming wave of fighters with Trojan and Stephania close behind.

Soon, the last of the warriors rushed by, the sounds of battle faded behind them, but they didn't stop galloping. The air burned in Trojan's lungs, and Stephania now felt heavy on his back. After what felt like forever, they broke out into a peaceful clearing. A large waterfall drowned out the distant noises of battle and death.

Gasping for breath, the two children dropped down beside the water and quenched their thirst.

Artigal gasped and stuttered, the world spinning wildly around him and his breath struggling to fill his lungs. He could feel the magic rapidly draining out of him as the *Kijaqumok* fed off his own energy.

"Where are mother and father?" Trojan's worried voice twisted a knot in Artigal's stomach.

Despite his own worry and pain, Artigal pulled a mask of confidence and indifference across his face. "They're coming. They'll be here soon."

Trojan nodded and moved away, but Stephania stared at Artigal, her eyes narrowing. The Igentis found it too hard to look into her eyes and turned his back to her in dismissal. She huffed and walked to where Trojan was settling down in the soft grass.

The two children laid down, their eyes sliding shut.

Trying to keep his mind off the things pressing against his heart, Artigal surveyed his surroundings. Through the treetops he could see the peak of Shadow Mountain rising into the clouds. The vegetation then took his attention and he observed apple tree saplings growing around the edge of the clearing. They would produce fruit in a year if taken care of properly. As he admired the sturdy wild fruit trees, his gaze fell on a hawk. The brown bird of prey was perched peacefully on a branch nearby; while it appeared to be sleeping, Artigal could feel its gaze on him, and he whistled lowly.

Cocking its head from side to side, the bird suddenly left its perch and soared down to Artigal before landing on the Centaur's white arm, gently pecking at him in hopes of food.

A small smile gently lifted Artigal's lips, and he sighed with relief. A note was fastened to one of the hawk's talons.

He read it. It was a note from Dalton saying that he was ready for Stephania and all Artigal had to do was send the hawk back with a note saying he had arrived.

Taking a quill out of his small pack, Artigal scrawled a note before tying it to the hawk's leg and watching as the bird took to the skies.

He observed the sleeping children, hoping that their parents would arrive in time to say goodbye.

Now they could only wait until Dalton arrived.

§

NEARLY AN HOUR had passed, and it was impossible for Artigal to continue to brush aside the illness that rose inside of him.

The worried and pained faces of Aeron and Frawnden kept flashing through his mind. *Did I do the right thing?* They had assured him that he should go after their children, but now he was regretting his choice, the guilt of leaving the wounded Centaur who had saved his life driving him mad.

"Artigal?" The voice was faint, as if it was far, far away.

One of Artigal's color-changing eyes opened, and he scowled. Was it one of the children?

"Artigal?"

He breathed faster, his eyes wide with disbelief. Stephania and Trojan were still sound asleep. No, it was someone else.

It sounded like—"Frawnden!" Artigal jumped to his feet and whirled around.

"Artigal, thank goodness we found you. I'm afraid I can't walk for much longer." Frawnden smiled, most of her weight supported by Aeron, who while he looked relieved, seemed ready to drop to the ground with exhaustion.

"Mother? Mother, Father!"

The parents laughed as Stephania and Trojan rushed to them and clung to them. The worry that had weighed upon them all quickly melted away.

Through the joy, a dread hung in the air. A solemn silence fell upon the small family.

"Stephania?" Artigal's eyes turned downward. He couldn't bear to meet the eyes of any one of the four Ventronovians. He could feel Stephania's pain and sadness. He could feel her pleading with him to let her stay with her family. He could feel her fear. And mostly, he could feel her magic trace—the beacon to evil.

Tears collected in his eyes. Could he bear to do this *again*? He had sworn that he would never hurt another like this, and yet he was back where he had started, as if he couldn't ever really escape from his past. It would always drag after him and haunt him.

Images, memories, emotions flashed through him. A Duvarharian girl with long brown hair, sparkling, wide eyes, a bright smile, and so much love and trust. It all washed away, and was replaced with pain.

"Yes, Artigal?" Stephania's light, scared voice pierced through his thoughts, and he was quick to banish the tears from his eyes.

"Walk with me."

They slowly ambled away from her family until they were out of hearing distance. The waterfall roared next to them, a rainbow shimmering in the mist.

Artigal took a deep breath, his eyes dark with grief. "This is the end of our journey together, as you know. There is a chance that we will meet again, but there is a chance we may not. I have taught you all that I can, and now it is time for you to continue on the path that the Great Lord has laid out for you."

"But Artigal, I really think that—"

He held up his hand and silenced her, doing his best not to look into her eyes and be sucked once more into her pain, anger, and hate.

"No, child. You cannot stay. This is not your life anymore. This is not your home anymore. You must continue to push on. You must put all of this behind you and become what you were meant to be."

Tears formed in her eyes, and she choked on a sob. "What does it matter to have family if they always leave?"

Artigal's eyes widened, and his heart lurched. "They don't leave you."

"My parents left, and now you are too." Her tear-filled eyes pierced into his soul, shattering his heart.

Curse how intelligent this innocent child is. Emperor keep me strong. Artigal closed his eyes and took in a deep breath. "We will always be with you, no matter where you are or what you may face. But that brings me to one last gift I will entrust with you. This will make sure you remain a part of us forever."

After sniffing loudly and wiping her nose on her sleeve, she turned her teary eyes and looked into his as she bit her lip.

Reaching into a small pouch that he had by his side, he pulled out an extremely old silver pendent that was decorated with a single, milk white stone in the center of the cold metal. Carefully woven around the cylindrical stone was a small silver wire, which twisted and turned to create a small tree, its roots and branches wrapped around the gem. A word in the Centaur language was carved above the crystal into one side—*Kofuz*. And on the other side, also above the stone, was a word in the ancient Duvarharian language—*Sleo*. Both words she knew to mean "Protector." Underneath the stone on both sides, the word "Farloon" was engraved in the metal.

Stephania's eyes widened. The word "Farloon" meant a connector, a mediator, and an equal of two Kinds. To be the Farloon—the protector of all the tribes of the Centaurs, equal to Artigal himself—was the highest honor that a Dragon Rider could even dream of obtaining. It was also laden with difficult responsibilities, for it was the Farloon's job to ensure the two Kinds acted as one people and were never divided. It was a sacred bond and a sacred title and responsibility.

"Artigal. Farloon." Her bright red eyes were wide. She bowed her head reverently. "It would be my honor, *Yelar*, to serve you and your people."

Holding open the necklace just in front of her, Artigal took a deep breath and whispered a spell as he placed the pendent around her neck.

Just like it had on Trojan when he became *Synoliki*, Artigal's words became magic and twined into the other small swirls on the right side of her neck and jaw. At first, the markings were a bright red, but as he finished the spell, they faded until they were just barely visible; the white stone that was inlaid in the pendant had changed to red and still shone brightly.

Artigal bowed to her, and she did the same.

Walking back to her family, she watched, without any embarrassment, as all three of the Centaurs knelt before her.

They rose, their faces shining happily and decorated with broad smiles, and their eyes glistening with tears of joy.

Stephania embraced her family. Tears streamed down their cheeks. Last whispers of "I love you" and "goodbye" lingered on their lips for what might be the last time.

The clop of hooves captured their attention, and they watched as a man rode into the quiet clearing.

The rider dismounted, tied his dark brown horse to a tree, and threw back the hood on the brown cloak he was wearing.

His face, though it had a youthful appearance, looked worn and tired. His light brown eyes sparkled deviously. Only a few gray hairs peeked out from his tousled dark brown hair. A shady stubble decorated his strong jawline. He was the perfect image of an ageless man. Though he didn't look a day over forty, his eyes betrayed a soul much, much older.

After letting his dark gaze sweep silently over the Centaurs and linger on Stephania, who stared back at him with as little expression as he showed to her, the man strode over to them with long, sure strides.

Holding his forearm out to Artigal, the man spoke out in a ringing tenor voice. "May the suns smile upon your presence, Artigal."

The white Centaur gripped the man's arm back with equal strength.

"As do the stars sing upon yours, Dalton." He quickly turned around and motioned to the other Ventronovians for introductions.

"I'd like you to meet Aeron, High Chief of Trans-Falls." Artigal paused as Dalton and Aeron gripped each other's forearms and exchanged warm courtesies.

"Frawnden, Aeron's mate and second High Medic of Trans-Falls."

The dragon-less Rider bowed to the buckskin Centaur and kissed the back of her hand.

"Trojan, their son and newly appointed *Synoliki* warrior."

The man then ruffled the young boy's hair, and Trojan smiled broadly.

"And of course, Stephania, daughter of Lord Drox and Lady Andromeda Lavoisier, rightful heir to the Duvarharian throne, and Farloon of the Centaurs."

Dalton turned to the little girl, who was now standing reclusively beside Artigal and gripping one of his white forelegs.

Her eyes bright and wide, Stephania stepped forward and nodded her head. "May the suns smile upon your presence, Dalton."

The Duvarharian bowed his head to her. "As do the stars sing upon yours, blessed child."

He stooped down on his knees in front of her and held her little hands in his.

"I am so honored, Stephania, to finally meet you. You look so much like your mother, and you have your father's stern eyes. Oh! And such lovely little dimples when you smile!" He laughed, praising her, and she giggled, revealing a small dimple in each blushing cheek.

Dalton loved children and had always had a way with them. Aeron and Frawnden, though brokenhearted to give up their child, felt a measure of ease when they saw how gentle, kind, and familiar Dalton was.

Standing back up, Dalton turned his attention back to Artigal, his face grave once more.

"I already have made up stories so the humans don't ask too many questions and have prepared a place for her to stay." Dalton spoke quietly so only the adults could hear. "I have been waiting for her for a long time, ever since I heard that Drox and Andromeda had—" His jaw suddenly clenched, and tears lined his eyes.

Artigal knowingly placed his hand on the man's shoulder, and Dalton stood taller, determination in his sad eyes.

"She is the child of my only friends. I will guard her with more than my life and will raise her as if she were my own child. It is the least I can do for Drox and Andromeda, and Ventronovia as well." His voice, though it held a hidden pain, didn't waver once, and Artigal felt sure that the Duvarharian would be true to his word.

"Good. However, there is one more thing we need to do." Artigal's voice was dark, and a mournful glint dulled his soft, multicolored eyes.

Dalton looked at him questioningly. Artigal merely motioned for the adults to follow as he walked toward the waterfall, his steps unusually slow and hesitant.

As her parents walked away, Stephania could hear Frawnden plead, "Artigal. What if we stayed here? Trojan, Aeron, and I?"

Aeron stepped forward and gripped his mate's arm. Stephania thought he might try to say something against the idea, but he nodded fervently, his eyes sparkling as he too pleaded. "Stephania could visit us, she wouldn't feel so alone and scared and—"

Artigal's shoulders sagged. "Actually, Frawnden, there is something else I fear we must do—" His eyes traveled to Stephania, and they locked gazes.

She thought he would be angry that she was listening, but he merely sighed and motioned for the adults to follow him farther away.

Stephania turned her attention back to Trojan. His bottom lip was wobbling, his eyes red. It was quite unbecoming, she thought, of a *Synoliki* warrior and all of his nine years, but she swallowed, jealous of his tears. She wished she too could cry, could mourn the loss of her family. But she couldn't. As she clung to Trojan and felt his tears splash on her neck, her eyes remained dry. Something about this was all too familiar, as if this was what family was all about. You love them, and then they leave you.

Frawnden's wailing and Aeron's angry shouts drew their attention to the adults. Frawnden stumbled away from Artigal, who was trying to calm her down. Aeron moved between his mate and leader.

"I will not let you do this!" Aeron's fury echoed off the rocks around the waterfall. "Should we make ourselves monsters to fight monsters? Do you feel nothing?"

Artigal flinched, seeming so small in front of the furious High Chief. He muttered something, and Aeron took a menacing step forward.

Dalton quickly moved between the Centaurs, his voice low. Stephania couldn't hear what he was saying. After a few minutes, Aeron stepped down, covering his face in his hands. Frawnden cried out, shaking her head as if she were trying to wake from a bad dream.

The adults moved slowly back to the children. Stephania eyed Artigal with suspicion. Aeron's face was stoic, a mask to hide the desolation she saw in his eyes. Frawnden only bit her lip and gasped through her tears. Dalton and Artigal's faces were emotionless as stone, but she sensed something amiss behind the cold stares—hearts in pain.

A lump rose in her throat. This grief was something she recognized. Whatever they had planned, she knew she had to trust them—her Centaur parents and brother, Dalton, her Duvarharian parents, and Artigal.

Artigal drew the little girl near to him. "Stephania, I—"

Before he knew what was happening, she threw her arms around his neck and kissed his cheeks.

"I'm going to miss you, Artigal," she whispered into his ear and gripped him tightly; her eyes squeezed shut.

Memories flashed before him—the brown-haired girl hugging him—his adopted child.

"Don't leave me, Dase!" She clung to him, tears streaming down her face, her eyes red and puffy.

His heart raced. The other Centaurs were getting closer. Any second now, he and his daughter would be dead. He had to get her away again. He had to save her somehow.

"I have to, yulu fe. I have to." Tears poured down his own youthful face. He loved her.

He had raised her, but he had to give her back. 'Help me, Emperor. Help me show them your power to overcome everything'.

"No! Not again!" Her scream echoed in the forest. Her arms tightened around his neck. He could feel her hot tears on his shoulder. "Please don't leave me again, Dase!"

He tried to pry her from him. They could run no longer; no place was left in Ventronovia where they could be safe. He thought of the spell that would teleport her to the Duvarharian city and back to her lawful guardians. But he couldn't–she would only escape again. And, if she came back here, he knew the Igentis wouldn't let either of them live.

He heard their shouts, their cries for blood, as they followed the young girl's crying.

Suddenly, he knew what he had to do. His stomach turned with the thought. He bit back bile. It was horrible, wretched, and he hated himself for thinking of it. There would be no turning back, but there was no other way.

The words for the spell formed on his lips and rushed out on the wind of his voice before he could change his mind.

Tears streamed down his face. He felt her go limp in his arms as she entered a deep sleep.

Time had run out for them. None was left to explain what he had done, or to tell her how much he loved her, or to tell her how much he would miss her although she wouldn't miss him ...

Suddenly, Artigal couldn't hold back his fear and pain anymore. He crushed Stephania in his fatherly embrace, tears shamelessly pouring down his face.

Her face portrayed shock only for a moment. She hugged him harder, threading her fingers through his soft mane. Finally, finally, the tears fell from her eyes.

"I'm going to miss you too, Stephania." He shut his eyes tightly. His thoughts and emotions flowed wildly as he held this small child whom he had helped to raise. All those days spent with him, with Jargon, with her family, all of it would just fade away because of him. Everything they had worked so hard for—all those days spent training, studying, discussing, laughing, hurting—it had all been a waste. In the end, it had amounted to nothing. Gods of all, could he do this again?

His confidence wavered. Horrible memories flashed in front of his mind. He had to. He had to do it again if he wanted to protect this child.

He felt her small, fragile body against him, and he felt the overwhelming urge to hide her from the world and never let anything near her, but he knew from experience, that never worked. He had to let her live her life, and to do that, he had to take something away. He knew there was no other way, so why did it hurt so much?

Letting the foreign tears trickle down his face, he gently pulled Stephania away from him, his heart lurching at the sight of her tear-stained face and her scared, pleading eyes.

Now he had the time—the time he needed to do it right, the time to say what he wanted.

He placed his forehead on hers in the traditional Centaur show of affection. "*Me yuwuk fezh*, Stephania." He whispered it so quietly she did a double take to make sure she had heard him properly.

His tears blinding him, a radiant though sad smile spread across his face, and he nodded slowly.

She threw her arms around him again, her warm tears falling down his shoulder. "*Rilar że dachek*, Artigal."

A small smile lifted his lips again, and he pulled away, his hands on her shoulders, her shining eyes staring into his. He could feel the wondering and shocked gazes of the Centaurs behind him, but right now, at least, he didn't care that they had seen his vulnerability.

He could only bear Stephania's gaze for a moment before he had to look away, his eyes growing dark.

"Stephania, there is something we have to do, and—" Artigal broke off, unable to tell her, unable to share his darkest action with her, unable to break the heart of the one person he had come to love the most.

She gazed at him expectantly. Yes, she would trust him.

"I just need you to know that there's one more thing we have to do, but you'll be even more safe this way." He bit his lip against his self-hate. He couldn't turn back. Not now. He forced himself to look into her red eyes.

Though she appeared confused, she nodded. "Of course, Artigal. Whatever we need to do."

Trojan had been slowly making his way closer to Stephania. He was almost beside Artigal, his face crinkled in apprehension. "No." Trojan's normally confident voice wavered. "Wait. What are you doing?" He looked up into Artigal's face with horror.

Artigal turned from him, focusing all his attention on Stephania. He forced down his emotions, swallowing against the lump that rose in his throat. "I'll give them back to you some day. I promise." Before he could change his mind, he began to clearly speak out the spell.

Stephania's head began to hurt tremendously, and everything around her blurred.

Trojan raced over to her and embraced her, a cold sweat on his forehead. His eyes burned toward Artigal with pure hatred.

The pain was horrendous, and she groaned, clutching her head.

Artigal almost stumbled over the words, almost stopped. Hesitation filled him as he gazed into Trojan's eyes, and horror began to consume him when his mind reached out to Stephania. He could feel her slipping away. He could feel her bond, magic, and memories disappearing into the darkness. He resisted the urge to cry out in her pain and end his own life. He was destined to be the leader everyone needed but never the father, brother, or friend. He felt the ice grow over his heart once more. He would do what needed to be done. Even if he didn't have all the magic he needed, he would have to find a way. He would finish this.

§

THE WORLD FLASHED VIOLENTLY around Stephania. Her memories repeated themselves over and over before fading. She could barely hear Trojan's words or feel his tears on her cheek.

"I love you, Stephania! I will always be waiting here for you! Please don't forget me!"

"Of course, Tro. I won't ... forget." Then everything went silent around her.

Gazing around, she frowned in confusion as Trojan's mouth continued to move but she didn't hear the words. He shook her shoulders, begging her for something. She watched Artigal raise his head to the sky and groan in desperation. Magic exploded in a ring of fire around him, and he fell to his knees, the fire extinguishing, his head in his hands. Frawnden screamed, resisting all comfort; Aeron's face was ashen with horror and regret. Dalton was saying something, but she couldn't hear him. The Dragon Rider tried to move Trojan away from her. The young Centaur kicked and screamed against him, and Dalton stepped away.

Slowly, more than just the sound faded. Soon, the familiarity washed away and nothing but strangers in a strange place surrounded her.

The designs on her neck, face, and hands marking her as Duvarharian and Centaur, faded from sight. Her magic trace slowly disappeared.

Her eyes locked on an almost familiar, emotionless moon-white face. The creature said nothing nor moved to comfort her before simply turning away.

Then everything went dark, and of the first five years of her life, she remembered nothing.

PART TWO
New-Fars

CHAPTER 13

Dalton's Swordsman Arena
New-Fars, Human Domain
Year: Rumi 6,112 Q.RJ.M.

THE CLASH OF METAL on metal rang through the brisk autumn air and echoed across the fertile valley.

A small village, appearing as a collection of assorted dots that represented houses, barns, and other buildings, was nestled in the wide valley between the two mother mountains, Leguows Mountain and Yufloy Mountain.

This almost forgotten haven was the village of New-Fars.

It was peaceful. Farm animals grazed in the lush pastures. Small children played in the distance. Some men worked in the fields. Young women gossiped and sang softly while they washed clothes in the bubbling Rose River. The occasional clanking of a hammer on a sword or shovel rang out in the blacksmith shops.

The sun beat down on the two swordsmen and warmed them, despite the cold breeze that blew from the small, surrounding mountains. Falling from the trees, red, yellow, and orange leaves swirled around the opponents as the man and girl masterfully sparred with their shining swords.

The male swordfighter was tall, had mid-length, dark brown hair, bright brown eyes, and a short, scratchy beard. Though he was muscular, his body showed many years of hard work and toil.

The other swordfighter was an unlikely fighter, with a strikingly attractive figure. She was a young woman of seventeen years, boasting a strong but petite, curvy figure, a cold personality, and bright flaming red hair. Her eyes were narrowed with concentration, her lips pursed with annoyance.

She was very much unlike the man she was fighting; his eyes sparkled with amusement and tenderness, and his lips casually tugged into a smile.

"Lift up your arms, girl! It's a dance. Poise!" The man gently poked her in the ribs with the tip of his sword before quickly whacking her thigh with the flat of his blade.

Sweat poured down her face, and a fierce snarl twisted her otherwise gentle face. She renewed her efforts and landed a sharp rap on his shoulder.

"That's it, that's it. Now you're getting it!" The instructor licked the sweat off his lips and squinted into the sun. "Come on." He feinted a thrust at her side, wheeled around, and brought the flat of his blade crashing into her stomach, completely winding her. "Oh, that must have hurt."

She coughed and wheezed as she tried to regain her posture, struggling to not fall to her knees. *By the gods, when will we be finished?* They had been sparring since the ninth shadow on the sundial of this morning, and now it was almost noon. Her head throbbed, her muscles burned, and her eyes stung, blinded by the suns and her sweat.

"Stephania, Stephania." Her mentor shook his head, resting for the moment. "You can't look at the person's appendages; you must consider their eyes. I could have easily killed you. You have to look *into* your opponent, not *at* them. Try to become one with them. Feel what they feel, know what they know, see what they see. Become one with them, and you can conquer them."

Stephania nodded wordlessly. She understood. *I know,* she thought in defeat. *But why must it be so hard?* She longed for the city hall bells to ring, signaling noon. Today's exercise seemed unusually long and difficult.

"Alright, prepare yourself. It's not noon yet."

Another nod.

Stephania reluctantly lifted her sword and firmly planted her feet on the loose dust. An annoyed grunt left her lips. She was tired of doing the same thing over and over and over again. It was the same every day. They would spar, and she would lose. They practiced the same moves over and over again. If only she could do something new. Something unexpected. An excited feeling fluttered through her. A memory of sorts tickled the edge of her mind. It was familiar, but so far away, like the name of an old friend that sat perched on the tip of your tongue. She closed her eyes and took a deep breath. Too often she had this feeling—nostalgia and déjà vu all rolled into one fleeting image. But this time ... she felt different, as if this was not memory but instinct.

She let the familiarity wash over her and surrendered herself to something primal within her. A small smile spread across her face, and her eyes fluttered open.

They circled each other again, both waiting for the other to strike. *This time, I'll let him make the first move.*

Her instructor lunged at her. She expertly blocked his attack. They moved in the same set of blocks and attacks, over and over again.

She feinted to the left and watched as he prepared himself for a hit toward his shoulder as she usually did.

Her body moved on its own in accordance with the instinct.

She twirled her sword in an intricate arch around her.

Confusion flashed over the man's face.

She took advantage of his distraction and struck.

His blade matched hers, but he had been caught off guard. He was put on the defense.

A wild grin flashed across her face, a strange glint in her eyes. She followed up the attack. The volley of complex blows she rained on him came as naturally to her as if she were breathing. She didn't have to think.

Her style had changed. She no longer felt like a one-handed broadsword fighter. She was something more. Something wild, agile, and delicate.

Finally, with a quick motion of her wrist, she flicked her opponent's sword out of his hands, sending the weapon sliding across the floor of the arena.

He raised his hands in defeat, and she pressed the tip of her sword under his chin. Though she was exhausted earlier, her breath was steady in her chest now, and her body felt light, as if delighted by this new way of fighting. It felt like coming back home.

Their eyes burned deeply into each other's. The air was tense and electric.

She stepped back, a broad grin sweeping across her face.

She had accomplished what she had always thought impossible—defeating Dalton.

She threw back her head and whooped in victory. Her clear, trilling laugh rang out across the valley. She danced around him, kicking the loose sand.

Dalton responded with a sheepish smile, his hands held out in admittance to his defeat.

"Well, old man. It's been done. You can't deny it."

"You're right, I am defeated, but I can always regain my title as best swordsman in New-Fars tomorrow!"

She smirked and brandished her sword elaborately. "We'll see if you can."

"Huh. Sure." Retrieving his sword, he wiped the dust off the blade with his shirt. He shook his head in wonder and awe. "Wherever did you learn such advanced moves? I barely know half of what you just pulled on me! And the style. It's almost like—" He frowned, and his face suddenly paled as if something horrible had occurred to him.

Stephania shrugged as she pondered that same question herself. Where had she learned it from? She frowned too. The more she thought about it, the stranger it seemed. Even now, she could hardly remember a single technique she had just employed.

Pulling herself from her thoughts, she caught Dalton staring intensely at her, and she quickly and brashly returned his glare.

He shook himself and looked at the two blazing suns above them.

"Well, it's still not noon."

However, just as he lifted his sword, the city hall's twin bells began clanging loudly across the valley.

Stephania grinned wildly, sighing in relief. The sound of the bells was like the call of freedom. She quickly sheathed her sword in the scabbard strapped across her back and sprinted out of the arena, her feet pounding in the dirt.

"Race you home, old man!"

Laughing after the eager young woman, Dalton sheathed his sword as well and started after her. In seconds, even with her head start, he was right beside her.

She grunted in annoyance. Dalton could run faster, jump higher, and sword fight better than every other man in New-Fars—something that was widely known and well respected in the city. That was what made the nickname 'old-man' so ironically fitting.

Panting, her muscles screaming in protest again, Stephania reached a shaking hand to her face and swatted a sweaty strand of her unruly hair. She struggled to keep pace.

Their fighting arena was nearly a mile away from the house. Stephania wondered if he had it built so far away just for the added exercise.

In only a few minutes, Dalton pulled ahead of her and reached the house long before her. She may have been the only person in New-Fars to beat him in a sword fight, but she was confident she would never beat him in a foot race.

When she finally stumbled into their small blacksmith shop behind the house, she was exasperated to find that he was, like every other day, lounging casually in one of the chairs in the large, hot room. His sword had already been polished and was hanging up in its place. Not a remnant of the brutal exercise hung about him.

"Show off," she muttered ill-temperedly.

"Nothing a little magic can't do," he chuckled under his breath. A dancing sliver of brown energy disappeared above his palm.

Stephania whirled around. "What did you say?" She eyed him intently.

He merely shook his head, failing to hide his amusement. "Oh, nothing. Nothing at all."

She grunted and stomped through the room, collecting the materials needed to take care of her weapon. She quickly polished and sharpened her blade, downing almost a gallon of water in the process.

"Uncle Dalton?" She slid into a chair after chores were complete and she had caught her breath again. She stared into the distance.

Dalton's eyes were half closed. He had propped his feet up on the table, his hands behind his head, his chair leaning on the two back legs. "Hmm?"

"Jackson mocked me again yesterday." A frown flickered across her face. Her eyes sparkled with the beginning of tears.

"Did he now?" Dalton hid a smile. He wasn't worried about Stephania getting into a fight with Jackson; he was worried about the boy getting into a fight with Stephania.

Her gut twisted uncomfortably, and she picked at a hangnail. She wanted to cry, to curl up into a ball on Dalton's lap. Jackson's hateful, stinging insults rang fresh in her mind. She wanted to disappear, to be free from the hate she endured. But she was seventeen now. She wasn't a child. She couldn't keep burdening Dalton will all her troubles. She needed to be strong.

"I told him that if he did it again, I would ground him into a pulp and leave him for the vultures to eat." Her eyes were dull as she gently set her glass of water down. Her voice was cold and emotionless as if she had pulled a mask down over her feelings.

"And are you going to?" He barely opened one of his eyes to see her reaction.

Stephania looked at him and responded so blandly that it sent shivers down his spine. "I don't make idle threats, Uncle."

He watched her carefully. She clenched and unclenched her jaw. Her fingers fidgeted in her lap. Her voice sounded calculated and cold-blooded, but she knew her body and eyes told a different story.

A darkness settled across his face, and she cringed. *Can he see through this act?* she wondered. She had started putting on this mask after turning thirteen. After that, she had stopped talking to him about the bullying and had stopped confiding in him.

"Stephania," he paused and searched her face. She felt exposed and vulnerable. She wanted to run into his arms and let him hold her, but she resisted. "If there's anything you want to talk about, you know I will listen, right?"

She nodded curtly. A sense of dread welled up inside her, but she couldn't tell if it was due to the fear that he wouldn't persist in questioning her or that he would. Finally, she could bear his gaze no longer and quickly busied herself with retying her bootlace. A dark, unwelcome silence hung in the air.

She felt his eyes on her but refused to meet his gaze. She thought if she did, she wouldn't be able to hold up her façade and she would break under her twisted emotions. When she heard him humming, she straightened up and forced a smile on her face. Perhaps he would let it drop now.

She twirled a lock of hair around her pale finger, directing her mind to other matters in an effort to look innocent and without lies. She frowned as she peered down at her hand. Despite how much time she spent outside in the sun, her skin refused to either burn or tan, usually staying a ghostly white. Her curly, red hair cascaded down past her shoulders, and a shorter lock of hair persistently covered her right eye. She let it fall across her face now, shielding her from Dalton's intense, questioning gaze.

Dalton let his chair fall back on its four legs. He grunted and poured himself a glass of water, downing it in seconds. He wiped his mouth and sighed. "Well, just don't kill the boy. He has the mind of a fly. Show the brute some mercy."

She snorted, her dark eyes glinting red in the light. "Okay, I might." A ghost of a smile flickered over her face. The knot loosened ever so slightly in her stomach, but the fear remained.

The air grew awkward and tense. They avoided each other's gaze, hiding behind their water glasses. Dalton finally broke the silence. "We should get changed."

She met his gaze. Her eyes flickered in confusion, and he frowned.

For a fleeting moment, relief washed over her. Her mask had worked once again. But the relief was quickly replaced with disappointment and crushing loneliness. Why was it so hard to keep these things bottled up inside of her? She gripped the glass tighter in her hands. *No. It is better this way. I have to learn to be strong. I have to learn to stand on my own two feet.*

"Yes, of course."

Before he could say anything, she was in the house, her hasty footsteps thundering up the stairs.

He sighed, feeling as if he had failed at something before slowly going to his own room.

I hate my clothes. She frowned in disgust at the simple, common clothes that sparingly dotted her closet. Most of them were the kind of dresses she was expected to wear. Though it was societal law in New-Fars that women wear skirts and dresses, she rebelled against this daily and most of her clothes consisted of tight pants, sleek shirts, and fighting clothes, most of which were in dark or glaring colors. Dalton had stopped trying to make her conform to society years ago when they both realized that no matter what she wore, she would be hated and feared by the humans. She didn't mind wearing dresses; she actually enjoyed them. She just hated the ones the women of New-Fars wore. They were plain, ugly, and uncomfortable things.

Dalton had gone out of his way to buy tasteful clothing, dresses and pants alike, from expensive traders who had traveled to New-Fars from the bigger cites in the Domain. He had even spent a large sum on her compound bow. They had seen it at a weapons shop traveling from the Domain capitol. She had never seen anything like it with its strange pulleys and knobs. Dalton said it was designed to have more power with less draw poundage; she didn't know if that was true, but much preferred the modern bow to the difficult horse bows or long bows she always had trouble firing.

She'd never found out how Dalton managed to make that kind of money; he didn't work the fields or sell anything. They weren't wealthy, but they always seemed to have just enough.

She finally picked one of the less detestable outfits and slammed her closet door shut. With a sneer, she tossed a dress onto her bed, trying not to look at it too long lest she change her mind.

Muttering curses against the small village mentality she had to live amidst, she quickly washed in her bath. She knew the cities in the Domain didn't have such conservative rules for women, and she wondered if Dalton would ever consider moving. A frown crossed her face as she thought what it would be like to live in a bigger city. Sure, culture would be more prominent, but she would also be so far away from the countryside and forests she felt so at home in. Maybe it wasn't worth the trade. She forced the thoughts from her mind, slid the dress over her head, and tightened the strings as much as she could. She wouldn't be able to reach the rest.

"Uncle Dalton!"

"Yes, my lady?" he teased.

She blushed at the formal nickname he used to call her when she was younger.

"I see you decided to act the part of the 'lady' today. To what honor does the village owe this rarity?"

She muttered something foul under her breath. "Just get over here and do this up for me."

He chuckled. Wrapping the long lacings around his hands, he pulled hard.

A gasp and a half-hearted curse tumbled from her lips. "By the gods, that's enough." She wheezed, shrugging her shoulders to loosen the fabric around her torso.

"Dragon Riders never have to wear *suluj* clothes like this. *Suluj* humans," he cursed under his breath.

She had barely caught the words. *Did he just say, 'Dragon Riders'? Whatever in Susahu did he mean?*

"What did you say?" She turned her face to him. He looked shocked that she had heard it.

His eyes found something interesting through the window behind her. "Oh, nothing. Nothing." He smiled disarmingly, but she merely huffed.

Why does he always have to be so secretive and confusing? He had been speaking under his breath more and more recently. She would let it drop—for now. "Thank you, old man."

His shoulders sagged as if in relief that she hadn't pressed the matter. "Of course."

Once she had finished dressing and her hair was brushed, Dalton twirled her around, admiring how graceful she was. A warm smile of pride spread across his face, and he chuckled. "You could dress in a feed sack and still put the gods to shame with your beauty. You have grown into such a fine young woman, Stephania. I couldn't be more proud of you."

Stephania played with a loose string on her bodice, innocently tucking a lock of hair behind her ear. "Thank you, Uncle Dalton." She gave him a quick hug and kissed his cheek.

Before he could stop the words from his mouth, he took her face in his hands and gazed into her eyes, whispering gently, "You know, you are the spitting image of your parents. I can see them in your eyes."

Her mind reeled. Her parents. Her mouth had dropped open, her eyes wide with curiosity. They rarely talked about her birth parents.

Tears misted in his light brown eyes.

"What did they look like?

"Dalton?" She waved a hand in front of him. He had gone completely still, not even blinking, for nearly three minutes. Her heart pounded with curiosity and worry.

He shook his head. Tears had traced paths down his cheeks.

"Never mind, Stephania. Let's just go get our shopping done."

Spurned, Stephania watched as her much loved guardian once more evaded her questions about her deceased parents and somberly walked down the steps. Her heart twisted within her. He had talked about her parents so much more when she was little, but now she could hardly remember what he had told her. She knew their names—Andromeda and Drox—such beautiful, uncommon names, she thought. She knew they had died in an ambush. She assumed she had been an only child. But that was all she knew. She didn't know if they had been a happy family, if they had lived in a city or the country, what gods they worshipped, if any, what kinds of games they liked to play, or even what they looked like. Would she ever know?

A stinging lump rose in her throat. She hissed, struggling to box up her feelings. Crying over it would change nothing.

She followed Dalton down the stairs; together they stepped out of their home and strolled down the dirt road. Neither spoke a word about what all had passed in the last hour.

Though they lived a fair distance into the countryside, they were immediately swept away by the bustle of noon time.

In the morning, almost all the people who lived in New-Fars worked on their daily chores: washing clothes, tending to the harvest, making tools, cleaning house, or preparing food for the week. Noon had always signaled a time of merriment, and usually, for the rest of the afternoon, people abandoned work and went into town. Most went to the market, though for many different reasons. Some went to buy a pair of shoes which were presented in a stately manner across the tables, or perhaps to buy new pots, which, as they hung on the racks in the market, clanked together as they swayed in the wind. By the big fountain in the village square, while their parents were browsing through the market or perhaps selling their own wares or visiting relatives and friends, children played Ventronovian games, listened to stories, or mimicked sword fights.

After about half an hour's walk, they ambled into the outskirts of the small but lively village. The last month of autumn was upon them, and it would soon be winter. The town buzzed with the special energy that only came with final harvests and hasty winter preparations.

Two women chased after their laughing children as they tried to bring them in to wash their small, chubby faces off for lunch. Several men quickly paced down the street, arguing about how much a year-old bull was worth. One young woman was speaking in quiet tones to a young man, blushing furiously, while another lady was yelling at an older woman about how much of an old croon she thought the older one was because of "the ridiculous price" of her herbs. A young couple strolled down the road. The wife was far along in her pregnancy; by the way they talked about all the "adorable baby things" they could buy, Stephania assumed it was their first child. Two bachelors stood by a house and were discussing how much money it cost to buy and sell crops. Another pair of younger men had started a fight and were rolling around in the dusty road.

Stephania merely turned her head up at all of them.

By now, Dalton and Stephania could start to smell the fresh meat, herbs, and wheat, along with the tantalizing smell of baked bread and cooked potatoes. They could also detect the fresh spring-like aroma of the assorted flowers, including roses, lilies, and buttercups.

They strolled nonchalantly through the bustling market, taking samples of the food and feeling the fine clothes and other products.

Stephania wilted under the judging, hateful gazes she drew from all the townsfolk. She wished she had brought her hood so she could pull it over her face and disappear. Instead, she pulled her hair down around her face, peeking out every now and then. She took a few deep breaths. *You don't need to hide. There is nothing for you to dislike about yourself, no matter what other people say. Nothing.* She repeated the words Dalton had said over and over to her while growing up. *I have nothing to hide.* She closed her eyes and imagined putting on her mask. She shouldn't fear them.

They should fear her. The strength of anger flooded through her, and she threw her head back, banishing her hair from her face. A few people spat at her feet, but she only sneered and, again, turned her head up at them.

As she and Dalton entered the middle of the market, the whole bazaar fell silent, except for those few who pointed and whispered at her. All eyes turned to her. A dog whined at one of the booths.

Her eyes narrowed, sparkling red in the suns' bright light. She glared at a few people until they could no longer hold her gaze, moving from person to person until she had made it clear she was finished being stared at. A few of the townspeople scurried away, wanting to put as much distance between her and them as they could.

Slowly, the market shuddered back to life as the people continued their duties, although less energetically; whatever positive energy the market had possessed earlier now seemed forced and superficial. Though the villagers appeared to be ignoring her, they always had one eye on her, watching, as if she were a snake about to strike.

A wave of confidence washing over her, she smirked and strode proudly through the booths and small stores as she and Dalton purchased the necessities for the week. Though Stephania was quiet when they were purchasing their goods, and Dalton was always the one doing the negotiating, the sellers never ceased to become very nervous when she walked up. Usually, they wouldn't look at her for more than a brief second, hurrying the buying process as much as they could so she would leave.

When the last of their products had been bought and they turned to make their way home, a loud, obnoxiously egotistic voice rang out over the crowd.

"I see that you had the guts to show your repulsive face, spark head."

Her stomach twisted. She knew that voice. She remembered it whispering, *Go die in a hole. I bet no one would even notice you missing.* She could hear it ringing in her mind as loudly as the first time he had said it. Tears stung her eyes. Yes, she knew that voice well. It was Jackson. Her first instinct was to run—to run all the way home, lock the doors behind her, and hide. But she had done that before. He had caught up to her. Her breath caught in her throat, and she shoved the memory away. She could beg. Beg that he forgive what she had said to him last time. A tear escaped her eye.

Her skin crawled. Her hands balled into fists. She hated him. Oh, she hated every inch of him to Susahu and back. *I told him that if he did it again, I would ground him into a pulp and leave him for the vultures to eat.* If only she could! If only she had a sword. She wouldn't have to run away. A streak of light blinded her eye, and she found its source—a blacksmithing shop. Two brand new swords were hanging out front. Anger heated her blood. A smile flickered across her face before being washed away in cold-blooded hate. Today she wouldn't run.

Her eyes blazing, she whirled around to face him.

He was tall, and rather muscular for his age, only a year older than Stephania herself. As if in a bid to constantly mock her, his medium-length brown hair was the most common type of hair color, and he loved to remind Stephania of this.

"Jackson," Stephania replied coldly, her voice dripping with near seduction. "Do you remember what I said would happen to you if you mocked me again?" Her eyes batted almost childishly, as if she were begging him to pick a fight. Her heart slammed against her ribs. Her head throbbed. *Come on, you brute. Take the bait.*

Jackson spread his hands wide, a lazy, self-absorbed smile spreading across his face. "Oh, *sure* I do. After all, it was so terrifying of you to say such a gruesome, violent thing, and I just quake with the fear of what you might do to me." He made a show of being scared stupid of her. His cronies guffawed loudly from where they had gathered behind him.

She rolled her eyes and placed her fists on her hips.

"Look, little girl." He was dead serious now.

A flicker of fear flashed through her at his tone.

In only a few strides, he was standing inches from her, his hot breath on her face. She was unable to move—unable to step back, to run away, or push him away. Her head spun nauseously.

"I'd appreciate it if you would just realize that no matter what little 'threat' you throw at me, you're just going to be a helpless little demon baby like you've always been." His lips almost touched her ear, his whisper like nails on glass.

The boundaries between present and past faded. *Demon baby,* she remembered him whispering to her; remembered when he had thrown her to the ground. Again, she felt his hot breath on her skin and his hand and knees pinning her to the dirt. She was unable to scream, unable to move when he raised his fist. Pain exploded in her head. Darkness, then blood covered her vision. Her ears rang. She tasted blood in her mouth. She screamed, kicked, and struggled, but she was too weak to stop the beating. She was alone, so alone. It was dark. The pain was unbearable.

A barking dog wrenched her from her memories. She licked her sweaty lips. Jackson's eyes still stared challengingly down into hers.

She wasn't on the ground, beaten, bleeding, and bruised. Not yet. Not this time. Her breathing steadied as she shoved the memory aside, focusing on the present. The knot of fear loosened. Rage coursed through her. She pushed back her shoulders and met his gaze with pride. *There is nothing for you to dislike about yourself, no matter what other people say. Nothing.* Enough was enough.

"What're going to do, spell-weaver?"

She wanted to punch out his toothy grin.

"Helpless baby!" Jackson's friends joined in jeeringly. "Yeah, little demon!" "Spell-weaver!"

She glanced just slightly to her right, locking eyes with Dalton. He was still, poised like a wolf before striking. She knew he was ready to protect her. She turned back to Jackson. *Don't worry, Dalton. I'm not weak anymore.*

People began to back away as the tense atmosphere grew violent around them; a vicious energy emitted from Stephania.

Stephania spat on the ground by Jackson's feet. "You think I make idle threats, boy?"

He opened his arms mockingly and stepped back, taunting her. His eyes glinted. He relished that she wasn't backing down. He wanted a fight. "Who are you calling 'boy'? I'm older than you, and you're nothing but a wuss. A weak, little *girl.*"

Dalton melted into the shadows to wait, his eyes shining proudly. Subconsciously, she felt him watching her and she knew that while he wanted to protect her, he knew this was her fight. He wouldn't intervene unless he absolutely had to, and this time, she would make sure he wouldn't need to.

Stephania whirled around, her hands balling into fists and her eyes flashing angrily. *Little demon baby.* She turned to the blacksmith shop and pulled the two swords from the rack. A sly grin spread across her face. The cliff before the unknown in her mind was just under her feet; beyond the edge was instinct—the one that felt like home. She took a deep breath and stepped out. *Perhaps I'll show him just what a demon can do.*

Without warning, she threw one at Jackson. He caught it and laughed. "You wish to fight me, girl? To pretend that somehow having the best swordsman in New-Fars as your guardian makes you worth something?"

Stephania adopted a ready stance and flexed her muscles, popping her neck and back. She was already sore and exhausted from the morning, but she could feel the adrenaline pumping through her veins. She was Stephania, demon of New-Fars, and she wasn't going to let fatigue get in the way of revenge. She closed her eyes and rolled her head in a circle to loosen her muscles. Images sporadically flashed before her. She couldn't tell if they were memories or a message or both. She strove to reach for them, but they fled from her. They felt like the instinct, as if the instinct was one with the images, and they were all a part of something deeper within her.

She remembered every hateful thing Jackson and his friends had shouted at her. She remembered every time his skin had bruised hers. And she remembered how it had made her feel—angry, bitter, humiliated, alone, despised, fearful. It was time he felt it too.

A new strength flowed through her. Her eyes snapped open, glowing like pits of bright, gleaming red; fire dancing in them. The pendent on her neck seemed to be alive with a similar energy, pulsating, and burning like a heart of fire. She directed her raging hate toward him, willing it to somehow reach him.

Jackson's eyes widened. A grimace twisted his face as if he were in pain. He spat on the dust road and rolled his shoulders as if he were trying to rid himself of an unwanted plague.

A victorious sneer decorated her lips, and she raised her sword. "On guard, commoner."

He quickly collected himself. "What could you possibly do to me, girl? I'm the best in New-Fars." A chuckle parted his lips. "But if it's a fight you want, I can't deny a *lady*, now could I?" His goons howled with laughter. "On guard, spark head." He returned the insult with a flourish of his sword. "Perhaps you'll finally learn your place, demon."

Lunging at him, she swung her sword in an arc and hit his with the flat of her blade. The move seemed childish, but if one had looked at her sure, flawless stance, and the ease which she had swung the heavy weapon, one would have instantly known that she was merely testing the strength and reflexes of her opponent.

Jackson was a very strong young man, and the sword she had provided him was well-made. However, neither of these were a match for her. She smirked.

"This is child's play. What are you going to do? Bang on my sword all day until you exhaust your anger and yourself?" Though he jeered loudly, the confidence was draining out of his voice and eyes.

His friends laughed, but Stephania was no longer affected by the mockery. Now she had a way to fight back. She smiled a heartless smile that, despite how full of himself Jackson was, made his arrogant sneer falter and fear dull his eyes.

"No. No, child's play today, boy. Today you learn to fight like a man." She smiled seductively and motioned in front of herself, half bowing in respect. "Now, we fight."

Jackson was fuming. He rolled his eyes, his bullish confidence and anger oozing from him again as his cronies goaded them on.

Stephania's mocking laugher rang throughout the market and drew more spectators to the fight.

"First, I will go over the basics." Her voice was gentle, as if she were talking to a very young child. She then quickly proceeded to perform some very basic sword thrusts. It took all her self-control not to defeat him right away. *I will, but only after he tastes humiliation. Just a little longer.*

At first, he tried to brush it off with mockery and laughter, but his joviality was fading as a wretched realization settled over his face. He aimed a few intricate swipes at her, his footwork quick and fancy.

She blocked his attacks as if they were flies. His elaborate show of skill appeared silly next to her casual, calculated steps.

"Very good, Jackson," A honeyed grin spread across her face, the smile failing to travel to her eyes. She lost focus of people around her; they began to fade until all she saw was Jackson in excruciating detail. She could almost feel his heavy, nervous breath and clearly see the cold sweat that collected on his brow. "Not bad for a commoner. Now I'm going to give you a few things to work on."

"Like what?" He spat at her feet. "Like how to block a child holding a stick?" He laughed, but it was nervous.

"Not quite, boy. More like this."

She feigned a strike to the left and then whacked him sharply on the shoulder. Taking advantage of his pain, she followed up with gently jabbing him in the ribs. Masterfully, she blocked a thrust from him. She looped her sword around his, batting it out of the way, before slapping him on the thighs, just like Dalton had done so many times to her.

By now, his face was as red as the tomatoes in one of the many farmers' booths. He was trying desperately to gain the upper hand, but to no avail. His sword had not even touched her skin, though hers had given him some nasty bruises, which would most likely show for a couple weeks, along with a few minor cuts.

"Now that you have something to practice, I'm going to show how a real swordsman fights." Stephania's smile was cold and unfeeling with no mercy. Whatever playfulness had been in her stance, words, and face was gone, replaced with a burning hate and a lust for revenge. *No longer will I cower. Feel my pride. Feel my hate!*

Before he could prepare himself, she spun around, bringing her sword in an arc around her head, her red hair flying everywhere and her skirt swirling around her ankles. The bright shining blade crashed into Jackson's, creating a shower of sparks; the sheer force of the strike nearly knocked him off his feet.

Effortlessly, she unleashed the same volley of thrusts and cuts with which she had defeated Dalton. Her feet danced on the packed dirt, light as a feather, barely touching the ground. She looked gentle and delicate, but her sword hissed through the air, its keen edge begging for death.

Jackson's eyes were wide with terror. Rivers of sweat darkened his brow and soaked his shirt.

Her eyes pierced into his soul.

Now he realized that she wasn't human. She was something more—something much more powerful. She was something he hated and feared deep down, but something that also brought him a strange peace and awe, as if his very soul were content with this new knowledge.

Blow after blow she laid on him until, with a powerful strike, she threw him to the ground. His sword flew through the air. The crowd around them screamed and scattered, afraid that they would be impaled.

The sword speared one of the blacksmith's posts, vibrating as it wobbled back and forth.

A snarl decorated her face as her eyes burned into his. He couldn't look away. He whimpered. She pressed her sword tip under his quivering chin and drew a drop of blood. As gasp of pain parted his lips, she said, "Today, you have my mercy, boy, but next time, my threat *will* prevail."

Turning, she stalked away from the defeated man and nearly shoved her way through the parting crowd, though most of the people jumped out of her way, making a path through their crowded bodies. She didn't look back once at Jackson as he struggled to his feet, sliding in the dust, before he slunk into the crowd, trying desperately to hide his shame.

CHAPTER 14

Dalton's Home

New-Fars, Human Domain

Nearly 13 Years Earlier

FATHER?" A LITTLE red head peeked around the corner.

Dalton looked up from the drawing at his fingertips, carefully putting down his pen. "Stephania?"

The dark eyes, barely visible from around the door, blinked slowly. "May I come in?"

A smile crept across his face. He chuckled and carefully rolled up the half-finished map, sliding it into a drawer in the desk.

"Of course. Come here."

Timidly, she opened the door wider and stepped through, her footsteps soft on the heavy carpet. Her eyes roamed for a moment over the tall shelves full of books, some big, some small, some covered in dust.

A single stream of light poured in from the lone circular window high above the shelves and bounced off the dusty air.

Dalton patted his lap, and Stephania struggled up, pulling herself onto his knee. His strong, gentle hands steadied her. "Stephania, I'm not actually your father."

She frowned. "I don't understand." She played with one of the drawstrings of his thick, warm shirt.

"Your parents, Stephania, were killed in ambush while they were traveling to the Domain."

Her frown deepened. "Why did they leave me here?"

The corner of his lip twitched. "They knew it would be safer if you stayed with me."

"Then, who are you?" Her innocent eyes pierced into his soul.

He looked away. Emotion rose in his throat. *Who am I?* Even he no longer knew. It had been a long time since he had known, since he had cared.

"I'm a good friend of your parents. Your father was like a brother to me, and your mother was ... like a sister. I'm kind of like your uncle."

"Uncle." She wrapped the string around her finger and pulled.

The shirt tightened around his neck.

A heavy sigh left her ruby lips. "Can I call you Uncle?"

"Yes, of course. You may call me Uncle Dalton, or whatever you would like."

A small smile flickered across her face. "Friends. Will I have friends, Uncle Dalton?"

His mind wandered to the other children in the city. *Will they accept her?* He looked at her red hair, her dark, sparkling red eyes. *I doubt it.* A frown tugged down his lips.

"Yes, I'm sure you will, Stephania. I'm sure you will."

CHAPTER 15

Present Day

THE CROWD FINALLY dispersed from around her, and those who hadn't fled shuffled back to what they had been doing before the fight. Stephania meandered around, looking for Dalton. She had seen him just before the fight but had lost track of him.

Her heart was still pounding against her ribs. Her ears buzzed. Her hands shook. A new confidence flushed through her. She had stood up to Jackson and all his years of bullying. And, this time, she had won.

A new spring in her step, she strode proudly through the scared villagers. She didn't know how good it would feel to be feared instead of mocked.

It didn't take long to find him. "Hey there, old man."

He stepped out of the shadows, his eyes shining proudly. "Hello, my lady. Finished?"

She blushed and muttered something under her breath. She seemed calm and composed, prideful even, but on the inside, she was buzzing with an unexplainable energy and countless unanswered questions. She felt like she had begun to wake up from a deep sleep, somewhere between dreaming and being truly alive.

"While you were enjoying yourself," he chuckled, a bright sparkle in his eyes, "I was able to get some great deals on these. Seems fear has an excellent way of making a man forget about money." He held up his parcels, and she caught a glimpse of silky fabric and fresh bread.

"I'm just going to drop them off at the holding room. You don't have to come. I think you can fend for yourself now, eh?" He winked at her, and she couldn't stop the unsure grin that adorned her fair face.

Watching as Dalton made his way through the streets, she nonchalantly leaned against the post of a tanner's booth; an evil smirk spread across her face as the tanner nervously abandoned his tasks. She barely heard him mutter that he needed to purchase something for his wife before he disappeared into the back of his shop, clearly relieved to be rid of Stephania's toxic presence.

Now that the adrenaline and anger had dissipated, she felt small and empty. A deep sigh escaped her ruby lips, and she visibly deflated. *Toxic. Am I toxic?* Her lips tugged downward.

She ran her hand across the sharp sword, her reflection frowning back at her in the shining blade. Her finger came to a small drop of blood on the almost immaculate metal, and she gently rubbed it off. She looked at the sword and then at her finger, her eyes lingering on the red, sticky liquid. Was this really what she wanted? To have blood on her hands? Flashbacks surfaced of Jackson hitting her; her blood was on his hands; her blood dripped onto her own hands. Was this her fate? To have another's blood on her to keep her own from spilling? Bile rose in her throat, and a wave of nausea crashed over her. Her eyes swam with tears as she hastily rubbed the blood onto her pants. She felt dirty.

Gods. What is wrong with me? Her hands curled into fists. Her eyes shadily roamed around her and slowly took it all in. She noticed how people cast their eyes at the ground around her, how they shuffled quickly to get past her, the mutterings under their breath—old mutterings to ward off bad spirits—the way they held their children closer to them though the children didn't understand. She knew New-Fars hated her. She had always known. But *why* did they hate her?

In a sudden spike of rage, she thrust the sword into the dirt road. Her strength was more than she knew, and she ended up driving the blade halfway to the hilt in the packed earth. She groaned, running her fingers through her hair. She could feel the villagers' fearful gaze on her, heard them as they whispered and quickly shuffled away.

She was no one. She never had been anyone as long as she could remember. Regarded as a demon, a spell-weaver with no parents, a curse, a mistake—she didn't belong. She had no one to turn to.

Except Uncle Dalton.

Hot, angry tears clouded her vision, and her fists tightened, her knuckles turned white, her eyes churned a sad, burning red.

Dalton. The man who had raised her, who had taken care of her since she could remember, and who had taught her everything she knew.

She sniffed and wiped the tears from her eyes before it became apparent that she was crying. She didn't want anyone to think she was weak. Her mask would only work if she kept it on all the time. It had been so much harder of late though. She found herself letting down her façade more and more, as if all the years of enduring the hate and pain were finally catching up to her. Fear gripped her. If she let her guard down, she would once again be as helpless as she had been all those years ago; she didn't want to be scared of going outside alone; she didn't want to go back to jumping at every shadow or coming home covered in bruises.

She bit her lip; melancholy mixed with anger roiled inside her.

She had always relied on Dalton for everything. He had fed her, clothed her, schooled her, comforted her, scolded her, disciplined her, and loved her. But there was something that bothered her. Why didn't he talk about her parents? It was clear that it hurt him more than her to talk about them, but didn't she deserve to know?

With all the hate she had endured here, along with never fitting in, living as an outcast in her own town, never having any friends, why didn't he have them move? Why couldn't they have gone somewhere else and made a fresh start? What was so special about New-Fars that they were forced to stay here no matter how bad it was?

A deep sigh escaped her lips. The bustling and persistent noise of the town was making her head throb and her skin crawl. She wanted to slide down the pole she was leaning against, crumple up into a ball and disappear. *I need time alone. I have to get away from this.*

She wiped her eyes and looked into the suns. She could see Dalton walking back to her. He stopped to greet some of the merchants and villagers. Somehow, despite raising Stephania, whom everyone hated, Dalton remained in good standing with a many of the citizens.

With a bit of concentration, she was able to pick up some of their conversation, even though she was a distance away.

"Good noon, Lacey. How is William faring?"

"Fine, Dalton, but what about—" Her eyes shifted nervously as if speaking Dalton's niece's name would call up demons. "Stephania?" Lacey leaned closer toward Dalton, her voice barely a whisper. "I can't believe you let her do that to Jackson! She's a beast! A real liability. Dalton, she's *dangerous!*"

Dalton laughed, waving his hand in a dismissing manner. His eyes flashed dangerously with fury, but neither Stephania nor Lacey saw it. "Oh not really. She's more of just a tyke, don't you think?"

Stephania angrily turned her back to her guardian and stared blindly down the other side of the road, tears filling her eyes once again. *Thank you, Dalton, for standing up for me as always.* Her arms tightened across her chest, her teeth viciously tearing into her bottom lip. *Gods! Why does everyone have to mock me? Even Dalton.*

She had heard many times: "Dalton, I can't see how you can put up with her!"; "She's a demon. You must take her to the town's council. They'll put her up on trial for black magic, and you won't have to live with her"; "She's a hopeless cause, Dalton. No young man will ever want her. I mean, she's got red hair!"; "You should just take her to the orphanage, they'll give her discipline"; "She's dangerous!" Stephania had heard it almost every day of her life, but it never seemed to get any easier to hear or any less painful. It didn't even matter how far she tried to bury herself behind an air of false confidence or indifference; the pain, the rejection, and depression were always lurking in the shadows.

All these stinging insults had been whispered behind her back, thought to be inaudible or even incomprehensible to the red-haired lass—some thought she was born disabled. However, with her extraordinary hearing and intelligence, she had fully understood these derogatory comments even since she was six.

But that's why she had to be strong. If she could just wait it out a few more years, she would be old enough to live on her own and she could leave this god-forsaken place.

But until then, she had to find some sort of peace elsewhere.

Quickly banishing her tears, she composed herself. She didn't want Dalton thinking that she was a wuss after all. She had just proved her worth against Jackson. She didn't want that accomplishment to be tainted by her emotional vulnerability.

When they were finished in town, she would tell Dalton that she was going to spend some time alone in the woods. If he was worried about her, she would simply say that she wanted to make her own lyre. He had wanted her to make one, but she hadn't had the time with studies and sword fighting. It was, in her mind, the perfect cover.

A sly grin spread across her face as she thought of what a week of being away from all these idiotic, rude villagers would be like. Finally, she would be able to be on her own for a while and figure out what she wanted to do with her life.

Barely making eye contact with her, Dalton nodded, and she joined him as he slowly made his way to the city square.

As they walked toward the fountain and the granite benches in the center of

New Fars, children from toddlers to tweens poked their heads out of all sorts of nooks and crannies, which only they could find, and watched the two adults. When Dalton gave them warm smiles, they rushed out laughing. Pulling on his clothes and her skirt, they dragged them to the edge of the fountain. The children were never afraid of Stephania, despite the fear and hate their parents worked so hard to instill in them. They thought her to be something out of the stories that Dalton told them, and they looked up to her in awe.

As soon as Dalton sat down, the children climbed onto his lap and several fought over who got to sit on his shoulders. Stephania laughed at the sight of the hardened warrior covered in kids. The sight never ceased to please her.

He plucked one of the two kids off his shoulders and lightly scolded him.

"Now, Freddy, you know you got a turn last time."

The three-year-old crossed his arms and pouted. "No, I didn't!"

"Nice try, young man! Here, you sit on my lap, and you too, Grace."

He quickly scooped up a little girl who happened to be Freddy's cousin. She was five years old with long, curly, blond hair, and a sweet, dimpled smile.

"Now, everybody be quiet and sit down." Instantly, the children who filled the square quieted and sat down, their eyes fixed eagerly on the man.

"Today I'm going to tell you guys a legend about the Dragon Riders of Duvarharia."

This statement drew excited squeaks from the children. Stephania noticed that the stories of the dragon riding men were their favorites.

They were wonderful stories, at least to tell children, but Dalton also told them to Stephania, over and over and over again, and made her read and study them until she knew them forwards and backwards. She could never understand why Dalton drilled her about these legends. For hours every day, he made her write the stories from heart and take tests on them repeatedly.

When he told the legends to the kids, he told them in a way that the young children would understand, like fairy tales should be told. However, when he told them to Stephania, he always seemed so sincere, like he actually believed them to be true. That's what really worried her. Perhaps his mind was failing him as he grew older.

A wave of guilt crashed over her, and she awkwardly shuffled her feet, her eyes straying everywhere but to her Uncle. *If that really is the case, then maybe I shouldn't be so eager to move away. What if he needs me?*

167

She drew herself back to the present.

"Dragons!" a little girl yipped out happily, clapping her hands as Dalton answered: "Yes big dragons!"

One of the kids had raised his hand. " 'Ow big?"

Dalton spread his hands out and replied glamorously. "Huge! Bigger than four of your houses put together!"

"Woah." The kid fell back on his rear end as if shell-shocked.

"Now, this is one of the most important legends of all, so listen closely."

The children's eyes widened as he began.

"Thousands of years ago, the dragon men were going about their normal duties, patrolling, learning about magic, and tending to the wild lands of Duvarharia, when the Etas struck! There were thousands of them! Then, the big dragons and their riders took off into the skies and fought the beasts! It was a magnificent sight! Blue, green, purple, and orange, red, yellow, and brown. The colors flashed in the sky, and you could hear the roaring and the calls of the mighty beasts. Magic flew through the air in amazing shapes, colors, and with incredible power. The riders yelled out their battle cries as the battle grew in intensity. The fight raged on, and the Duvarharians fought bravely, but the Etas gained the upper hand."

The children gasped. Dalton's eyes sparkled joyously.

"Yes. Alas, many good riders and dragons were slain, but what happened next was something no one would forget."

Dalton paused and looked expectantly at the youngsters.

A small girl inquired as if on cue. "What?"

Dalton grinned mischievously. "Why don't I tell you?"

He launched into the story, describing it so vividly that Stephania felt as if he had taken her back in time.

§

THE STORY WENT ON for a few hours, resulting in an epic win for the Dragon Riders when the Duvarharian Lord of the Golden Age arose and fought off the Etas for good, saving the Cavos Hatching grounds and bringing all of Duvarharia into the greatest age it had ever seen. By the time Dalton had finished, the shoppers were just finishing up their purchases.

Now that the story was over, the children began to yawn and nod off to sleep in their parents' arms.

Some of the parents thanked Dalton for entertaining their children while they were shopping. Many of them simply snatched up their kids, doing their best to not make eye contact with Dalton or Stephania, and left with a muttered thanks whispered under their breath.

When the last of the kids had run off, Stephania approached Dalton. She couldn't explain the twisted knot in her stomach. Perhaps she was scared that he wouldn't let her go.

"Dalton," Stephania twirled a lock of her hair nervously, her eyes darting everywhere but to her uncle.

"Hmm?"

"I was wondering, could I—if you wouldn't mind of course—I was just thinking I could, uh, spend about a week out in the forest? By myself?"

Dalton turned, a mildly surprised look on his ruggedly handsome face. "Why yes, it's okay with me. I knew it was only time before you wanted to be alone from *them*." He jerked his head toward the village.

Her eyebrows furrowed, and he quickly turned back to the road. He swung his foot, kicking a stone a few paces ahead. "Most of us do, you know. Crazy as it is, even I want to be back."

A frown pulled down her lips and creased her forehead. Once again, he was spouting nonsense. "What?"

"Mmfm. Nothing." He stuffed his hands in his pockets.

She gave him a puzzled look, trying to process what she thought he said. *What does he mean he wants to 'be back'? Back where?*

Before she could press him to repeat himself, he shook his shoulders, as if dislodging himself from an unwanted memory, and continued talking.

"Although, I would prefer if you went tomorrow morning instead of tonight, if that was what you were planning."

Her eyes widened. *So soon? I was thinking next week, but this is much better.* She couldn't help but wonder why he seemed so eager for her to leave. *Maybe he's sick of me and the insults he has to endure because of me.* She fiddled with a loose thread on her dress. *Surely he doesn't want me gone?* The dark thought pushed her shoulders down under its weight. She tried to shove the unwanted thoughts away, but they lingered, filling her with an empty pit of rejection.

"The morning is usually the best time to find oneself." Dalton kicked the rock again when he reached it.

They both watched it bounce down the road until it came to a rest, blending in with the thousands of other rocks along the road.

He sighed heavily. His mouth opened, then closed, then opened again, as if he were unsure if he wanted to say what was on his mind. Finally, he spoke. "I have another assignment for you when we get back to the house. I need you to finish it before you leave." His tenor voice was hard to hear through his partially closed lips and over the gravely crunch as he dragged his feet across the rocky, dirt road. He avoided looking at her.

Stephania's frown deepened, puzzled at this change in his attitude. She hadn't known him to go from exuberant one minute to quiet and reflective the next. Something was wrong. Something she had said had disturbed him.

"Dalton?" Her thin, long fingers softly squeezed his arm reassuringly, her eyes tender and worried.

He absentmindedly jumped at her touch.

"Huh? Oh, yes, I'm fine, of course. Just uh, a little tired, that's all."

He quickly gave her a weak smile and needlessly began shifting through his bags, once more mumbling incomprehensibly.

She stuffed her free hand into one of the dress' small pockets. Her other hand was weighed down heavily with her nearly stolen sword, trying and struggling to keep the tip from dragging through the dust and gravel. Dalton had bought it for her, but now she wished she wasn't carrying the weapon that had drawn the blood of another human. She snuck a glance at Dalton, a new knot tying in her stomach.

Whatever he had thought of mere moments before had radically changed this man of many secrets. She knew him well enough to assume that whatever it was, he would never tell her about it. At least, not for a long time.

CHAPTER 16

New-Fars, Human Domain

Nearly 8 Years Earlier

STEPHANIA! STEPHANIA!" Dalton's worn hands were cupped around his mouth. "Stephania!" His hair was disheveled, his eyes wide and dark with worry.

Curse the gods. Where is she?

He rubbed his temples, closed his eyes, and listened.

He heard ... sobbing.

His eyes snapped open, and he ran farther down the dirt road before veering off into the woods.

The crying grew louder. He heard her sniff.

"Stephania?" Cautiously, he brushed aside the thick undergrowth and peered into the base of a tree.

Stephania's curly, red head hung between her legs. Her shoulders shook with her tears.

"Stephania?" His voice was quiet, asking her if she wanted him near.

Her head lifted, her eyes peering out at him through a veil of tears and tangled hair. Sticks and leaves clung into the mass of curls; cuts lined her arms and legs.

She sniffed and wiped her nose.

"Why do they hate me?" She bit her lip against the tears, hardly able to speak around the emotion choking her.

His heart lurched at the desolation in her eyes. Dread sank into his stomach. An illness rose in his throat. He crouched to the ground, sitting on his heels.

"Because they are small-minded, scared people."

She bit her lip, wondering what he meant. *Small-minded? What is there to be small-minded about? Am I not one of them?*

"They called me ugly." New tears collected in her stinging, swollen eyes. She gripped her knees tighter to her chest.

"Who, child?"

Her face twisted into a miserable scowl. Their faces flashed before her. They were girls her age. She had been ever so carefully trying to include herself in their game at the town square. She had gathered up all her courage to say "hello", to ask if she could join them.

"Ew! I would never let you play with us!" The girl spat on Stephania.

"My parents say she's a demon. I believe it!"

"Get away, dog! You're so ugly! I bet your mother left you here because she couldn't stand the sight of you!"

"Your mother must have been married to a devil for you to look so wretched!"

"Ugly dog"

"Demon!"

Tears spilled down Stephania's cheeks, and she shut her eyes tightly, trying to block out their insults, their laughing faces, and to hide from her sight: her bright, red hair.

"The other girls." She whispered so quietly anyone else would've missed it.

"Fools!" Dalton spat on the ground, his hands balled into fists.

She jumped with surprise at his sudden anger.

He ground his teeth. *Fools.* He thought to himself. *They don't know a dragon scale's worth about beauty. If they did, they would see Stephania is the daughter of a goddess, nay, is a goddess herself!*

"Stephania, they are fools. They know nothing about beauty. They are jealous. You have something they will never have."

She frowned, wondering to herself. *What do I have that they don't? They have mothers, I do not. They have friends, I do not. They are normal, I am not.*

"I don't understand."

"A good heart, Stephania. You have a caring, kind, loving heart and true beauty on the inside."

She frowned. "I do?"

"Yes, child. And, while outside beauty is only fleeting in life, you are also truly a beautiful young lady. And I'm not saying that just because I'm your Uncle, child. I mean every word."

Her tears slowed. She cocked her head, thinking hard on his words. "Really?"

"Of course! Stephania, would I—" He abruptly stopped, the words unable to come out of his mouth. He thought of what he had been about to say. *Would I ever lie to you?* Nausea arose in him. Bile filled his throat. It was a lie in and of itself. He had never outright lied to Stephania, but all the same, her whole life was a lie, and he was at the center of it.

"Uncle Dalton?" Her eyes were filled with worry.

He snapped back into the present. "Huh? Sorry, child. Do you think I would lie to you, my little lady?" He smiled broadly to dispel any questions about his abruptly odd mood.

A smile spread across her lips, and she almost giggled. "No, you wouldn't."

"Good." He motioned for her to come to him. "Come on, enough sitting in the dark."

Gods of all, I hate myself. He pushed his loathing deep within him, telling himself it was all for her. Everything was always for Stephania.

"Ow." She snagged her shoulder on a thorny vine, biting her lip against the pain. And yet, as she looked at the prick of blood on her pale skin, she almost thought that perhaps she deserved the pain. At least it was better than the humiliation of rejection, insults, and being hated.

She grasped Dalton's hand, feeling his warm, strong grip pull her out into the sunlit forest. She squinted against the light. A thought moved through her mind. *I have red hair.* She remembered reading something about uncommon hair colors. *That is one way to describe my hair,* she thought. *Uncommon.* And then she remembered.

"Uncle Dalton?" She peered up into the silhouette of his face against the sunrays.

"Yes, child?"

"Am I a Dragon Rider?"

Everything in Dalton's mind shut down. Panic grasped hold of him in its cold iron grip. *Dragon Rider? Gods of all ...*

"W-why, uh, w-what makes you, made you, uh, think of that?"

She frowned at his odd question. "Because I have red hair. Don't the legends you read me say the riders have uncommon hair colors? And my eyes. They look different than the other people's eyes. And my ears," her hands strayed to her small ears. "They're kind of pointy."

No, no, no. Not now, oh gods, please not now. A million thoughts raced through his mind. *She is too young! What should I tell her?* He wet his lips. If he told her the truth now, they would be in serious danger. Her magic trace would grow, and any creature with any amount of training would know exactly where she was. She couldn't defend herself well enough yet, let alone cover her magic trace. Thaddeus would be here and gone within the week, Stephania forever lost in his grasp. Unless ...

"Stephania, child." He knelt to her level, holding her hands in his, looking up into her face. "Dragon Riders are legends. They are myths and stories we tell. Some don't believe that they existed, and some do, but no human has ever seen a dragon in all his lifetime, or even lifetimes before that.

"And, Stephania, you don't have all the characteristics of a Duvarharian. They have magic, you know. And their ears are much longer and pointier than yours. They also have slit pupils, like a reptile, much more so than you, and strong skin like a dragon's. And other things too."

She bowed her head and sighed. "I know, Uncle Dalton. I just thought—" Tears welled up in her eyes again. "Maybe if I was, then—" She sniffed and shrugged, giving up what she had been trying to say. *Maybe if I was, then I would belong somewhere,* she finished to herself.

His heart broke for her. "Oh, child." He gathered her into his embrace, smoothing her hair.

She clung to him, her warm tears quietly spilling onto his shirt.

"Stephania, you are beautiful, and unique, and smart, and kind, and caring, and so talented. There is nothing for you to dislike about yourself, no matter what other people say. Nothing. Do you understand that?"

She nodded against his shoulder, holding him tighter.

"And there is nothing wrong with you. Absolutely nothing. You are perfect. Okay?"

She nodded again and cried once more until the tears slowed. She hiccupped and took several deep breaths to calm her racing heart.

Dalton gently pulled her away and tucked a strand of her hair behind her ear, wiping away the tears from her cheeks.

"But, Stephania—" He hesitated. Should he say it? What consequences would it have? He pushed those thoughts aside and looked her straight in the eyes. "If you want to think you are a Dragon Rider, then there is no reason why you shouldn't. If it will help you combat the cruel hearts of others, then you tell yourself that you are strong, you are mighty, and that you are a Dragon Rider."

She blushed. "Really?" A smile threatened her face, but she tried to conceal it in vain.

"Yes, really."

"Thank you, Uncle Dalton." She quickly wrapped her arms around his neck and kissed his cheek.

He smiled. "Of course, child. I love you."

"I love you."

"Now, shall we go home? I will carry you if you want."

A bright smile leapt across her face, and her eyes sparkled. Lithely, she jumped onto his back, wrapping her legs around his waist and her arms around his neck. She rested her cheek on his broad shoulder.

Easily, though she was nearly twelve years old, Dalton carried her out of the woods and onto the dusty road, taking them home.

Stephania hummed a light tune, a smile on her face. Her eyes were still red and swollen, and tears still traced paths down her cheeks, but she was happier now. Thoughts of what it would be like to fly high above the clouds tickled her imagination.

I wonder ... Dalton closed his eyes and carefully reached out to the young girl with magic. Nothing. He let out a heavy breath he had been holding. Nothing had yet awoken inside of her. They were still safe.

"Stephania?"

"Hmm?"

"Do you know, even if you weren't beautiful, and talented, and caring, I would still love you?"

He could almost feel her blush. She smiled sweetly. "I know, Uncle Dalton."

He chuckled and leaned his head against hers. He had told her that many times. "Good, because I would."

A breeze flittered through his hair, bringing with it the smell of lavender.

Lavender. That's what she always smelled like—lavender and cedarwood. A memory of Andromeda laughing at something Dalton had said flashed before him. Tears collected in his eyes, but he forced himself to smile.

She's beautiful, An. He thought to himself. *I wish you could see her. She's an amazing young girl, your daughter is.* He chuckled. *You would be so proud of her.* His smile turned sad. *I'm sure she misses you.* He bit his lip. *We both do ...*

CHAPTER 17

Present Day

STEPHANIA GROANED and banged her head against the table top. "So ... many ... questions." She resisted the urge to spit on the open book in front of her before throwing it at Dalton.

He, thankfully, neither saw her slacking in her studies nor heard her complaints; he was too busy poring over a strange, old map that he had become obsessed with since they had arrived home.

Lifting her head back up, she groaned quietly and popped her neck and fingers. Her hand hovered over her writing quill, hesitating. Her eyes scanned the paper. It was full of questions. The top read *Abilities of the Duvarharians*. Of all the assignments he could give her now, why this one? She could have sworn she had done it over a hundred times.

So far, she had been able to fill out the ability to speak to their dragons through mental telepathy, hypnotize or control the non-magical creatures of the land, levitating, the ability to speed grow some small plants. They could also create basic spells like one to keep you warm or dry, one to purify water, one to light fires, and even one to recall all your memories and relive them.

By the gods. Whoever wrote up all these ridiculous details for the legends had way too much time on their hands.

She pondered on all the minute details. One of the most famous magical powers which were only present in the really old legends, was the ability to take over someone else's mind by breaking down their mental barriers and fighting them only with your consciousness.

Wouldn't that be nice. She pictured herself forcing Dalton to do this ridiculous homework or making Jackson dance like a drunken fool. An evil smirk had spread across her face, and she quickly wiped it off before Dalton saw it.

All the powers, of course, were determined by how much the Dragon Rider had been taught and how much skill and energy he had.

This all seemed so pointless to her, though. Why couldn't she just have gone to the school the people had set up in town? Maybe she would have been able to make some friends or possibly learn something she could actually use in her life, not fairy tales. Of course, she knew as well as Dalton did that it would have never worked. She had gone to the school in New-Fars a long time ago, and only for a month. She pushed back the unwanted slew of memories and emotions. It had been excruciating. Dalton was right to school her himself. Even if she was all the more ostracized for it, it had saved her from most of the bullying.

Even so, Dalton was now training her on things she wouldn't and couldn't even begin to use in her life. She rolled her eyes. *I can't believe I actually* want *to learn mathematics right now.*

Just as she got to the bottom of the page, and before she could sneak off, Dalton expertly slid another to her from across the table, not once looking up from whatever he was reading.

Gods of all, he's good.

She couldn't help but stare at the paper in front of her with disgust and exasperation.

Another? She rubbed her hands on her face and read the title. *How to characterize a Duvarharian.*

She hit her fist hard against the table. Instantly regretting her childish display of temper, she cringed, waiting for the lecture. There was only silence. She opened her eyes. Dalton sighed but did nothing more. She narrowed her eyes suspiciously, but he didn't scold her or even look up. He seemed far too engrossed in his map. She leaned over to sneak a peek, catching an elaborate sketch of a compass in the top right corner.

Even more questions rattled around in her brain. He hadn't touched his precious hand drawn map collection for a long time. What was the reason for the sudden interest?

She grunted, shaking her head. Maybe he really was going crazy.

Silent anger still simmering inside of her, she started filling out the questions once more, her quill pen splintering on the paper, her knuckles white from pressing so hard on the pen.

Cat-like pupils; slightly pointed ears for better hearing; unusual hair colors such as white and auburn along with colored hair streaks; higher cheek bones than humans; strange connection with animals, especially reptiles; colored swirls or other strange markings on the palm of one hand and sometimes on the forearm; high rate of healing, extreme tolerance to pain; and incredible strength, endurance, and stamina.

As Stephania read over her answers, she couldn't help but think, *sounds like a bunch of creepy lunatics to me.*

She took a quick look at Dalton. *Too bad.* A sneer crawled onto her face. *If it weren't for the fact that Dalton doesn't have little tattoos on his hands or slitted pupils, and that he has brown hair, I'd say he could be crazy enough to be a dragon man.*

Hiding her laughter as she comically fantasized Dalton being a dragon man, she turned her attention back to the crinkled page in front of her. A frown replaced her smirk. *Well, maybe me too, even.* She remembered playing pretend that she was a Dragon Rider after Dalton had said she could, but she hadn't for a long time. Perhaps it was because she didn't need an escape anymore. Her mask of cold indifference provided that now. *Or, perhaps I've learned it's more painful to chase after things of impossibility.* With her heart bound by a new depressive weight, she quickly finished filling out the other answers and pushed the pages back over to her uncle.

"Done." She leaned her chair back on two feet, her arms stretched in front of her, her fingers drumming on the wood.

He slid the parchment off the table, a deep sigh escaping his mumbling lips. "Do you understand everything on the test?" His eyes never left the page, not even bothering to look up at her.

She rolled her eyes disrespectfully. She had done this "test" more times than she could count. Of course she understood everything. "Yes, Uncle Dalton." Her arms crossed her chest, and she grunted with annoyance. The chair nearly slipped out from under her. She yipped and slapped her hands on the table to steady herself, a blush raging across her cheeks.

A chuckle parted his lips, and he shook his head. Brushing a small bit of hair out of his eyes, he nodded his head. "Good. You may go and pack your things. I will have an early dinner made, if you want it, and you can go to bed early, seeing as you'll most likely be leaving long before suns' rise."

The beautiful young woman shoved her chair away from the table and stood up glaring at him. Guilt crept up behind her annoyance.

She knew he was just trying to be helpful, but she couldn't help but feel rebellious against it. He didn't have to treat her like she was two years old, always micro-managing her life down to the exact second she would do everything.

Scowling against her confusing emotions, she flicked her hair off her shoulders, not bothering to answer him, before storming to the old staircase. Her heavy footsteps echoed painfully as she pounded up the stairs.

Slamming the door of her room behind her with unnecessary force, she threw herself onto her bed and groaned. Her eyes stared intently at the ceiling.

The bland, white ceiling which offered no answers, consolation, or surprises, chose to stare back silently. *The same way Dalton always does.* She cursed and rolled over onto her side. Tomorrow morning couldn't come fast enough.

Crawling off her chaotically mussed bed, she began to pack a few things she thought she would need. It took her a while. Dalton had never taken her out into the woods any longer than three days. He always said the forest would do strange things to her mind. She had never thought him to be superstitious, but he always seemed adamant that she never spend too long in the supposedly haunted forest. With a short temper, she realized she wasn't well prepared for this at all. Though she knew Dalton would be more than happy to assist her in packing, she stubbornly plowed on, more willing to struggle alone than ask for help.

At last, she was packed, making sure not to forget her lyre strings. Though making a lyre had started as just a cover-up for needing some alone time, she was actually looking forward to making her own instrument.

When she was younger, Dalton had toiled for hours trying to teach her to play the piano. Even though she had excelled at it, she had never liked sitting in one place for long, and getting her to finish even one song was harder than freezing fire. She had preferred the mobility that small harps had offered, and often played outside, singing with the birds.

A heavy sigh left her lips, and she rubbed her arms, not feeling chilly but somehow cold anyway. Her eyes strayed to the small piano in the corner of her room. It wasn't kept up. Cobwebs decorated its legs and danced across the keys more than fingers ever had. She couldn't bear to look at it. Not because it wasn't cared for and looked forlorn, abandoned in her fairly clean room, but because it gave her bad ... memories.

She couldn't pull her eyes away from it. It dragged her in. Darkness crept over her vision, but she didn't want to look away. Someone was sitting on the bench. The cobwebs vanished from the instrument; the color faded from its keys. The dust drifted off it like fog on a cold morning. The man's hands moved across the keys. A beautiful sound came out faintly, like she was hearing it through a veil. A voice whispered to her through the fog, singing to her. She could almost see the music in the air, almost feel the loving emotion with which he played, but it was too far for her to reach. She felt herself walking toward it. It was familiar to her, the music, that piano, the strange, dark room it was in, and mostly the man who sat at its bench and played its keys so perfectly. She cried out to it, to the man. She wanted to reach out, to pass through the veil.

The air screamed around her; pain raced through her mind. The image cracked, as if somehow ruined. Black shards shattered across the image. The air turned dark, rank. The man turned, but he had no face. A dark hole was where his head should have been. Cold surrounded her. The darkness of the face engulfed her.

Stephania's eyes violently snapped open as she gasped for air, her body shaking uncontrollably. A cold sweat suddenly chilled her, and she slid to the ground, her chest struggling to find air. She wrapped her arms around herself, ignoring the tears that streamed down her cheeks and soaked the collar of her dress. She could barely see the piano through the ocean in her eyes. Nothing had changed. It was still just a piano sitting in her bedroom corner.

She buried her face in the bed, letting her tears overcome her. Daily she had these and other nightmares and strange visions, but they never got any better. In fact, the older she got, the more horrifying and real they became. Some had once been sweet hallucinations; now they were nightmares that left her struggling to find reality. When she was younger, Dalton had tried all kinds of herbs to stop the visions, but they never worked. Eventually, she had lied to him that they did work just so she wouldn't have to deal with the panic, worry, and pain that perpetually gripped her guardian when he knew of her hallucinations.

The suns began to hang low in the sky, seeming to have stopped in their daily journey. She wiped her eyes and stood up, trying to pull herself back together. Still shivering, she pulled a blanket around her thin shoulders, busying herself with reorganizing her packed saddle bag before tossing it beside her door alongside her bow and arrows.

Her sword was in its usual place downstairs. She would pick it up on her way out in the morning.

Lying back down on her bed, not bothering to change into sleeping wear, Stephania closed her eyes and let the silence overcome her. Sometimes, if she was still enough, she could almost remember her parents, could almost see their faces, but the memories always faded before she could grasp a hold of them.

Grumbling, she turned over and propped herself up on her elbow. She stared out of her east-facing window. The setting suns were bathing the land in their golden rays, changing all the colors from brilliant shades of green and blue to bright shining gold, with the clouds deep red, orange, pink, and purple.

Sighing, she let the beauty calm her and entrance her. She knew Dalton was right. If she was going to leave early tomorrow, then she had better get some sleep.

After a while of studying nature's beauty, she reluctantly crawled off her bed and changed into her night clothes. She snuggled back under the thick fur covers. Tired and sore from the day's sword fighting, she succumbed quickly to slumber, though her dreams were shadowed by faceless people and sour notes from a singing piano.

CHAPTER 18

Dalton's Home
Nearly 12 Years earlier

U NCLE DALTON!"
Dalton's warm, brown eyes snapped open. Darkness welcomed him. Not even the moon was shining tonight. He listened. His room was unusually silent. Not even the usual cricket was playing its song.

"Uncle Dalton!"

His covers decorated the floor as he abandoned his bed and ran down the hall. Stephania's bedroom door banged open, and he rushed to the side of her bed.

"Stephania, Stephania, what's wrong, child?" He quickly pulled her to him.

Her arms wrapped tightly around his neck, her warm tears adorned his shoulder.

"I had a bad dream." Her sobs echoed heartbreakingly in the dark room.

"Oh, my child." His arms tightened around her. "It's alright now. You're alright. What happened?"

She choked on her tears. "There was ... there was a big purple lizard. And it—it killed a bunch of little people and ... and ..."

"It's alright, you don't have to talk about it—"

She pulled away from him, her little hands tightly squeezed his broad shoulders, his shirt gripped in her small fingers.

"It said it was coming for me. It said that ..." She hiccupped. "It said that it would find me!" She screamed and sobbed, burying her small face once more in his chest.

His heart lurched. Bile rose to the back of his throat. *A big, purple lizard ... that could only be one creature ...* Fear grappled with him. He sensed for the girl's magic.

Nothing. She had nothing that Thaddeus could find her with. She remembered naught of who she was. The magic still slumbered in her.

He sighed, his shoulders sinking. His hand slowly ran through her tangled, soft hair, and he let her cry onto him. As much as he hated it, Artigal's spell was working. Stephania would be safe.

"It's alright, Stephania. It was only a dream."

"Don't let it get me, Uncle Dalton. Don't let it find me." She hiccupped again, snuggling her face against his warm chest.

"I won't Stephania, I promise. I won't let him find you. You are safe here, with me."

He opened his mouth to sing, but something stopped him. *Andromeda* ... Tears rose in his eyes; in the darkness, he let them fall. *I suppose you would have sung it to her ... I will too. For you, my* rilar.

"Sleep my child, just close your eyes." He swallowed his tears and pushed back the memories.

"And wait for the morning of the suns' rise. A light will come and lead your life and wash you from your strife." He stopped wondering if he would be able to continue.

The seconds dragged on.

"Keep singing." Stephania's muffled, sleepy voice could barely be heard. "Please."

A sad smile raised his lips. "Of course, Stephania."

He cleared his throat and bit his lip. "Um ... always now in dark and fear, we will know that He is near."

He felt her fall asleep against him, and he laid her back under her covers, tucking the furs around her. He pressed his lips to her soft forehead.

"So, sleep, my child, just close your eyes, and wait for that morning of the suns' rise."

CHAPTER 19

Present Day

STEPHANIA JERKED AWAKE, panting claustrophobically, sweat running down her face. The sheets stuck to her clammy skin. It was pitch dark out. Her imagination formed shapes out of the darkness. Her breath fast in her chest, she rubbed her eyes and jumped out of bed, pacing back and forth, pushing the shadows out of her mind. She had that nightmare again. It was the same every time—dragons, half-horse half-human creatures, and black, mutilated animals.

She rubbed her shoulders, unexplainably chill, her blood pounding in her ears. A ringing noise in her ears filled the silent, cool air.

Why? Why do I keep having this nightmare? What does it mean?

Perhaps it was all the things Dalton was pouring into her brain, or perhaps it was memory.

She violently shook her head. "No, no, no. Impossible. That's never happened and never could happen. None of that exists."

Disturbed, but now more curious than frightened, she was about to crawl back into bed when she remembered that she was supposed to be leaving this morning.

A broad grin swept across her face. She pumped her fist and danced around for a few minutes in sheer excitement and glee.

For one glorious week, she would be able to ignore the ridiculous corsets, dresses, rules, and mockery of the city. She would be able to do whatever she wanted, regardless of what anyone thought.

Dressed in a matter of seconds, not ever bothering to run a brush through her wild, curly hair, she grabbed her pack and quietly tiptoed down the hall. Masterfully, she danced down the stairs making sure to not step on a single creaky board lest she wake Dalton. She was still convinced that he would try to stop her. Ready to sprint to the door without having to say goodbye, she came to a grinding stop.

One of the living room candles suddenly lit aflame. Dalton was relaxed across one of the couches, fully dressed, a mug of warm drink at his side, and that same old map in his hand.

"Good morning, Stephania." he drawled out absentmindedly, his eyes barely flickering up from the map, a curious twinkle in them. His voice was bright, as if he had already been awake for a while.

She frowned in confusion. *What was he doing up so early? And what was with that map?*

Flicking her hair off her shoulders, unable to hide her excitement, she twirled a lock around her finger. "Good morning, Uncle Dalton." Remembering her sword, she abandoned all stealth and bounded loudly through the house to the blacksmith room.

"I already have your horse, Braken, saddled up for you," Dalton called after her and took a sip of his drink, a satisfied sigh parting his lips.

Her mind and her feet came to a screeching stop but only for a second. He was really helping her leave. "Thanks!" she shouted over her shoulder before adding under her breath, "I guess."

Finding her sword, she lovingly clipped it to her belt before heading to the kitchen to grab a snack. Anxiously, she searched the kitchen until she found a chunk of bread from the night before. She took a few quick bites before stuffing the rest in her pocket.

Hurrying over to Dalton, she awkwardly paused and shifted her weight uncomfortably, knowing she should say something. She struggled with how she should act around him. Should she let her guard down? Be vulnerable? Or was it better to stay hidden behind her coldhearted mask of indifference? She was sure Dalton saw right through her act, but if so, why didn't he say anything? Did he just not care?

She twirled a lock of curly hair around her finger, took a deep breath and banished the turmoil from her mind. It wasn't like he was kicking her out. He was actually being very helpful. "Thank you, Uncle Dalton. I guess I'll see you in a bit. Or really more like a week." A rare, sheepish smile spread across her face, dimpling her cheeks. She looked up from the loose string in her pants she had traded her lock of hair to toy with.

He glanced up from his map, a strange expression on his face but an unmistakably elated twinkle in his eyes. "Of course. It's my pleasure to help you, Stephania, you know that. And, good luck, I shall say. I love you."

A warm feeling rose within her. "I love you too." She turned to the door.

"Oh, and Stephania."

The unusual note in his voice called her back.

"Don't do anything stupid once you figure it out. Okay?"

Once again, her mind drew a blank. *Uh, what? Since when does Dalton tell me not to do anything stupid? Not when I challenge Jackson to fight, oh no. But when I take a trip out into the woods? Gods of all, he's frustrating sometimes.* She knew just as well as him that she was head-strong and impulsive, but why would he remind her now?

"Okay, yeah, sure, whatever." Shaking her head, his words ringing in her mind, she quietly closed the door behind her. Knowing she would be haunted by his words and would overthink their hidden meaning, she forced them out of her mind as soon as possible and took a deep breath of the moist, cold night air.

Nothing but clear, open sky stretched above her, and she took a moment to appreciate it. The stars were bright, and the moon was barely a sliver on the edge of the night sky. Not even the suns' rays had pierced the sky yet. It was just her and the secrets of the night.

When she reached the barn, she found that just as Dalton had said, her buckskin stallion, Braken, was already saddled up and ready to go. One of his saddle packs had even been filled with enough rations for a week.

Gratitude filling her, and wishing she had done more to thank Dalton, she sighed before quickly loading her packs onto the horse's broad, sleek back. Perhaps she would make something for Dalton; she wasn't sure what, but something. Her mind drifted for a second, thinking back to his words of warning. Braken's whinny and impatient stamp brought her back to the present.

"You're right, boy. No more riddles, at least, not for a week." Her fingers trailed through his soft mane, feeling the ridges and ripples in his muscles and the sleekness of his hair. "Nothing but silence, peace, and truth, eh?"

As if he could understand her, the stallion whinnied and bobbed his head, nudging her chest.

"No, no treats, you big pig."

He dutifully snorted in her face.

She rolled her eyes. "I bet you could out-eat a dragon." Unable to help herself, she gave him a sugar cube and laughed as he fairly inhaled it. While he crunched loudly on the treat, she whispered in his ear where they were going and why. She knew he couldn't understand her, but sometimes she felt that, somehow, he could.

She led him out of the barn, careful to lock the door behind her, knowing Dalton would have her hide if she didn't. She quickly mounted the buckskin and once more breathed in the night air, her eyes closed. Her face tilted to the sky, letting the moon bathe her in blue light. She could feel Braken's breath under her, the life in his body, the pumping of his heart as he snorted, stamping the ground, anticipating the thrill of the ride. She swelled with pride at how unique he was, smiling fondly at the memory of the day she got him.

Not sure of where to go, she pointed the stallion west toward the forest that the townspeople were afraid of and spurred the horse into a gallop. Streaking across the valley, Stephania felt that she was finally free, and as the ground rushed beneath her, she couldn't help but feel like she was flying, and that just felt so right.

§

IT WAS NEARLY FOUR days since Stephania left on her expedition, but she had hardly spent a single one of those days working on her lyre. She had easily gotten distracted by all the unique plants and animals this forest protected. They were different than the other forests around New-Fars. She had quickly lost track of time and had yet to find a sturdy branch with which to make her lyre. She was becoming discouraged. Of course nothing would be wrong with using a young, bendable limb, but she had hoped for something a little more majestic.

Experiencing the odd sensation that she had been walking in circles, she tied Braken to a tree and plopped down on a rock, supporting her head between her hands, surveying the woods around her.

When she had entered these "cursed" woods, they had seemed just like a normal forest. However, the deeper into the forest she ventured, the stranger it grew. The trees grew closer together but never lost their age nor size. In fact, it seemed that the trees here were even bigger and older than the ones closer to the village. They stopped growing as straight too. Warps in the trunks began to look like faces and bodies if stared at long enough, and she even thought that sometimes she could make out words as the wind whispered through the leaves and branches. One night, when she had been drifting to sleep, she swore she even heard drums in the distance, but not any normal drums from the human villages. They were wild, almost animalistic. Along with the steady pounding of drums, a flute or pan pipe had whistled mystically and odd voices weaved in and out of the wild, frightening, chaotic music. She remembered folk lore speaking of a horrible force that once came out of this forest and destroyed New-Fars long ago. She was beginning to wonder if there was more to it than just myth.

Though she felt uneasy in the odd forest, instead of being scared back to the village, she felt entranced, as if it were calling to her.

Forcing herself not to stare at the haunting trees any longer, she pulled herself back to her feet, stretching to wake up her arms and legs.

"Gods of all, this is harder than I thought. I just wish I could find a good branch already!" Her words echoed strangely in the forest. The wind whispered in her ear as if responding to her. She narrowed her eyes challengingly at the still woods. Nothing moved. It seemed even the wind had stopped. An unusual bird song rang out for a few seconds before fading into the silence. Braken stamped his hoof in unease.

Almost in a trance, Stephania took a few steps forward. She thought she could see something in the forest in front of her—movement or a shadow. A voice called to her, whispered to her, beckoned to her. Braken whinnied, and she reached out absentmindedly to calm him. The horse instantly fell silent and stood perfectly still, as if understanding her need for silence.

She squinted, peering into the suddenly dark forest. *By the gods, it got dark fast.* In the abnormal shadows, she could barely make out the trees around her. In fact, it seemed that the trees were shifting, but perhaps it was only the shadows playing tricks on her.

Just when she was ready to turn around and get as far away from here as possible, something stepped out into the woods in front of her.

It looked like a man, a short man, the top of his curly hair coming up to about her neck. Two large yellow eyes stared at her, almost glowing with their own light, their black pupils small rectangles instead of circles.

She cocked her head, transfixed by the mesmerizing, sparkling eyes, her mouth open in shock.

It was too dark to make out a definite shape of his body, shrouded as it was by brush, but something about the way he stood seemed much different than it should have been.

Slowly, she neared, but stopped when she was still a few feet from him.

She could just barely make out his teeth, stark white against his dark skin, as he smiled gently, reaching out his hand to beckon her.

She stepped closer.

"Stephania. So you have finally come into the forest. I have been waiting for you for a long time." His voice was musical, magical even. It rang in the air like a crisply plucked string, the sound golden, warm, but also dangerous. She felt like she had heard this strange type of voice before, but a fog covered her mind. "Your awakening nears." His accent was thick and very hard to understand. "The forest has slept for a long time, but we are ready to be awoken as well."

He looked down at his side, and gently, almost as if it took no effort for him to move, he reached for something on his belt. A bright, glowing green jewel hung around his neck on a thick chain. Its strange symbols seemed somehow familiar, but her mind was slow and foggy, and she was unable to recall where she might have seen them before.

Unable to concentrate on any one thing, Stephania's eyes strayed to the forest around her. The trees circled them, their shadows bending down around them. Strange dots of glowing light gently floated from the trees to the ground like fireflies, but stranger.

As the light grew, she got a better glimpse of the man in front of her.

He had an extremely thick head of curly, dark brown hair, which looked as if it might have grown from his shoulders as well. His bare chest was also covered in the same dark curly hair, though it failed to fully cover his lean, fit build. As he bent over ever so slightly to unclip something from his belt, a belt which was holding up a pair of odd fur pants, she was shocked to see something besides just hair growing from his small head: horns. Two small points jutted out of his messy hair and curved backwards. She blinked several times to see if they went away. They didn't.

"You must take this, Stephania, as a token of our allegiance. Release this spell, which has grown over the fathers, and bring us back to life."

She looked down at his hands.

Held out in front of him was the most beautiful lyre she had ever seen. It was shaped and masterfully carved like a snake; the strings of all different sizes were strung between the curves in its 's'-shaped body.

"It will never go out of tune, nor will the sweetness of its strings fail you through decay or wear. Play it and remember that the fathers yearn to feel the warmth of their brothers again."

Convinced that she was dreaming, she reached out and ran her fingers along the instrument. It started to glow with a greenish hue under her touch.

"Yes." The man's eyes widened in excitement. "It is time."

The lights in the forest began to dim and the little floating lights began disappearing. The trees and shadows moved in on them and Stephania felt herself slipping into emptiness.

"Play it, Stephania, and do not forsake it. Do not forsake us."

Before she could say anything or ask any of the numerous questions that raced through her head, the man turned away.

"Farewell, Dragon Child."

Effortlessly, he leapt over the brush in front of him.

Shock paralyzed her when she caught a fleeting glimpse of his two goat legs.

Before she could ponder what she had just witnessed, she fell to the ground, surrounded by darkness.

Sweet forest, sweet woods,
Where have you gone?
Children of the forest, children of the stars,
Where are your dance and songs?
Deep within you we took refuge.
Deep within you, you took us to fantasy.
When I was a child, you held my hand,
When I was a child, you moved my feet.
Sing to me again, forest.
Sing a song again, children of the woods.
Play your music, frolic in dance.
Awaken from your slumber,
Lift your hearts from this trance.
Come home.
The fathers miss the warmth of their brothers.

CHAPTER 20

Nemeth's Home

New-Fars, Human Domain

Nearly 7 Years Earlier

WOULD YOU LIKE a scone, love?"

Stephania clasped her hands in her lap, shyly swinging her legs, which dangled down from the oversized chair. "Yes please, Ms. Nemeth."

The elderly woman gracefully turned back into her small kitchen and swiped one of the fresh pastries from the hot metal sheet. She grabbed a napkin on her way back to the sitting room and tucked the scone into it before handing the bundle to the young girl.

"Now, what do you want to hear about today?"

Stephania slowly bit into the delicious scone, her eyes narrowing. A crumb fell from her delicate lips into her lap. "Um, could you sing the Ballad of Condemned Love?"

Nemeth's wrinkled lips thinned into a smile. "Of course, sweetheart." The aged woman moved with an odd bounce in her step as she plucked her lyre off the fireplace mantle and brought it to her large rocking chair across from Stephania. She took extra time to adjust around her feet the long billowing skirts she always wore.

Stephania pushed herself back into her own chair, closed her eyes, and let the soft duck feather stuffed cushions envelop her. *Surely,* she wondered, *this is what it must be like to sit on a cloud.*

"Hmm, let us see, now."

A chord sang quietly from the lyre. And then another in a different key. A musical chuckle floated through the air.

"It would seem, my dear, that I have forgotten the notes." A sadness hung in her sweet, old voice.

Stephania opened her sleepy eyes. "Forgotten? How could you forget?" she asked, frowning.

Nemeth sighed. "That is simply what happens when you get old, love. Some things just aren't as clear as they once were."

Stephania wiggled until she was once more sitting on the edge of the chair. "How old are you, Ms. Nemeth?"

The woman's eyes grew distant, and the ghost of a smile decorated her face. A sigh left her lips. "Very, very old, love. Very, very old."

Stephania's question went unanswered, but she decided to let it go. The air was simply too soft to wonder too long about such strange things.

"I remember the notes."

"Oh? Do you now?"

The little girl bobbed her fiery head. "Yes. Uncle Dalton has been teaching me the lyre. I think I could play the song if I tried." Her cheeks grew rosy. "But I don't remember the words."

Nemeth handed Stephania the small instrument, which now looked large in the young girl's hands.

"Don't worry, dear. I could never forget this story."

Instead of sitting on the chair, Stephania sat on the floor, resting the heavy, wood, stringed instrument on her small thighs. She plucked a string and then another. She played a chord. A smile spread on her face, dimpling her cheeks.

"Okay. I'm ready."

"Wonderful. Now, let's see. Where did it all begin? Ah, yes, with a love that transcended Kinds, laws, and hate. A love between a Faun and a Human. A love, my dear, that was condemned the moment they set eyes on each other ..."

The sweet and sour notes of the lyre blissfully trailed out of the open window and onto the still air of the quiet countryside. Every so often, Stephania's inexperienced hands would pick a wrong note, but somehow Nemeth's mystical voice would softly sweep away the discord, making it seem like part of something bigger, as if it hadn't really been a mistake after all.

The notes turned into seconds. The phrases into minutes. The stanzas into hours. The suns sank low, hanging over the hilltops, hesitant to go to sleep.

Stephania's dark eyes blinked slowly as the song trailed off. An emptiness hung inside of her as the last notes faded into silence. The desolation, the utter lack of hope, the condemning loss of love hung over her like a dark but quiet cloud.

Neither spoke, and it seemed like neither breathed as well. A bird chirped outside. The wind whispered, just once, through the window.

Tears quietly streamed down Nemeth's soft, dark, wrinkled cheeks, down her neck, across her chest.

"Too often, Stephania, love is never given a chance to live. And, too often, love ends with the spilling of blood, and the desolation of lives. It would seem, more often, that love in our world is followed by the fires of destruction rather than cleansing water. This love was like that. And when she stood in the ashes of the city that mocked her and her lover, and when she stood on the bones of those who hated and tortured her and her beloved, the Faun realized that her lover was still gone, and that not even the power of revenge could bring him back. She realized that her wrath had only caused more to suffer and to feel the same hurt she herself had been dealt. After that, she was broken."

Nemeth's hands turned to fists in her lap. She bowed her head, her shoulders slumped. "Never, Stephania little love, never let hate consume you. Even if you think the hate is righteous for the ones you love. You will turn into the monster that so deeply tortured you in the first place."

Stephania nodded. The air was too heavy to speak. The emotion was too heavy to think.

"Come, love. It is time for you to go home. Dalton will wonder what became of you."

Slowly, as if moving through a dream, Stephania stood up, handed the lyre back to Nemeth, and let the old woman walk her to the door.

When they stepped outside, a cardinal took flight from an old stone under the large tree that often shaded Nemeth's house.

Stephania's eyes strayed to the stone. It was covered in moss. Water had beaten all of its once sharp edges into soft curves. Shallow curves were all but faded away from the stone's face. Something caught her eye. *Are those ... words?* she wondered.

"Ms. Nemeth?"

"Yes, love?"

"Is that a tombstone?" Stephania's slender finger pointed at the stone under the tree.

"Yes, dear. It is." New tears collected in Nemeth's thin, mystical eyes. She bit her lip, clearly fighting back unwanted emotion.

"Of whom?"

Nemeth shook her head, unable to speak through her tears.

Stephania squeezed her friend's hand in hers. "It's okay, Ms. Nemeth. You don't have to say."

Nemeth's smile wavered. "No, dearie. It's okay." Her chest rose with a deep breath. "It is the grave of a man I once loved more than life itself."

Red, soft curls bounced around Stephania's face as she nodded, satisfied with her answer. Though she was curious, she respected Nemeth's privacy and remained quiet.

"Thank you for the scones, Ms. Nemeth, and for letting me play your lyre."

The woman wiped her eyes. "Of course, Stephania. Please visit me anytime."

Bouncing lightly in a way only the innocent can, Stephania stepped quickly down the stone walkway.

"And, love, one more thing ..." Nemeth's shaking voice stopped the young girl.

Stephania turned around and cocked her head. "Yes?"

"The Faun, in the song we sang, her horns were taken from her. They were cut off to shame her. If you ever see a Faun without any horns, remember her story, remember how she loved, and remembered how she raged."

A light frown tugged Stephania's lips. *If I ever see a Faun?* she thought. *Are they not mythical?* She shrugged her small shoulders. "Of course, Ms. Nemeth. I promise I will remember."

Nemeth sighed in relief, a broad smile lighting up her face. "Thank you, Stephania."

As the young girl turned once more to the setting suns, skipping along the flat stones, a breeze blew softly through her hair. For a moment, just a moment, she thought to turn around, to see Ms. Nemeth just once more before heading home. But the wind tugged her homeward and the thoughts of dinner quickly smothered out all other thoughts; instead of turning, she continued down the path, forgetting what lay behind her.

CHAPTER 21

Present Day

YAWNING, STEPHANIA PUSHED something from her face and groaned. The warm, wet object pressed back against her face. Her eyes snapped open, and Braken whinnied, his lips tickling her nose.

"Ugh." She pushed him away again and watched as he nudged her saddle bags until a carrot fell out. Content to eat his snack, he wandered off while she sat up and rubbed the sleep from her eyes. She reached for her water skin, and quickly unscrewed the lid. She drained the last sip into her mouth and grumbled in disappointment. That was the last of her water. Now she needed to find a stream. Not too keen on getting up just yet, she frowned at the trees above her. She didn't remember going to sleep. Or making camp, for that matter. The lyre and the faun flashed before her.

"What a strange dream." Her eyes gazed skeptically at the still, quiet trees around her.

As she went to stand up, her hands brushed against something, and a sweet, perfect note rang out. The branches in the trees shifted above her.

"Oh gods." Her face paled. She licked her dry lips. She looked beside her.

An intricately carved, black lyre lay beside her, the painted green eyes of the carved snake stared at her.

She jumped to her feet screaming. It took all her will power to resist the urge to throw the instrument deep into the woods.

"Gods of all. That wasn't a dream. That wasn't a dream." Her chest rose and fell rapidly, and her hands trembled. She wiped her brow and began pacing in front of the lyre. As her eyes strayed around her, she spotted things she didn't want to see: hoof prints. But not horse prints, goat prints. In pairs. Only one thing could have made such tracks and they existed only in legends and dreams: Fauns.

Wringing her clammy hands, she slowly knelt beside the instrument, nervously tucking her persistently annoying, wild hair behind her ear, though it only fell back down into her eyes.

Gently, she ran her fingers along the perfectly carved scales of the snake and watched with fear and awe as the wood glowed the same way it had in her "dream".

Not sure what to do or think, she picked up the lyre, careful not to strike any of the strings. She was too afraid of what would happen if she were to play it.

Braken trotted back to her and nudged her arm, as if he too were curious about the instrument.

"What would happen if I played it?"

The faun's words haunted her from before. *"Play it and remember that the fathers yearn to feel the warmth of their brothers again ... . Play it, Stephania, and do not forsake it. Do not forsake us."*

"Play it. Play it. Play it." The wind seemed to speak to her, and she felt lost in the mystery of the lyre.

What would happen? She was afraid to play it in case something terrible happened, but she wanted to. It called her. The woods called her. The wind called her. But she was afraid that if she did, she would be disappointed if nothing happened.

Almost slapping herself, she jerked back to reality, a nervous chuckle parting her bloodred lips. "It was just a dream. I must have found it late in the night and then dreamt about it later at night." She wiped off the unwelcome sweat that beaded on her pale, clammy face. But she had not had the "dream" at night—it was the middle of the day. It was only just now evening. She had only been asleep a few hours.

Shaking, she stuffed the lyre deep into her satchel after wrapping it in a blanket, and mounted Braken. He seemed as nervous as her. Wanting to be away from this haunting place in the woods, she pointed the stallion in a random direction and spurred him into a canter.

Fauns were only something you heard of in legends and bedtime stories. Not as a sighting report or in records of recent incidents. The only person she could remember who loved telling those stories more than Dalton was Nemeth.

A smile bloomed across Stephania's face. Nemeth. She was the only civilian of New-Fars to ever truly take Stephania in and make her feel welcome. Stephania had often spent long afternoons sitting in the sun with her friend as the older woman sang ballads of myths—a far more interesting way to hear stories than just Dalton's reading.

Nemeth loved telling one particular story the most and Stephania loved hearing it. And she could remember one specific, strange day when they had played the ballad together. Though it was nearly ten years ago, Stephania could still hear the beloved woman's hearty voice as if it were yesterday—the Ballad of Condemned Love.

After riding for a while, the steady drumming of Braken's hooves hypnotically soothing her, she soon heard the miraculous sound of a bubbling stream. Elated, she licked her dry lips and guided the stallion toward the refreshing noise.

A gasp escaped her lips at the sight that she beheld after they broke out into a clearing.

"By the gods."

The stream she had heard bubbled directly in front of her. All across the clearing, waves of green grass rolled in the breeze. Little pink, white, yellow, and purple flowers dotted the small pasture and collected thickly around the stream. Most spectacular of all though, was the stream's origin.

A roaring waterfall about fifty feet tall poured over the edge of the small rock cliff and washed into a quaint pond beneath it. A mist rose into the air, and the suns' light caught on the water droplets, creating a shimmering rainbow. Toward the pond's edge, hundreds of little lily plants thrived, their small green leaves and white and pink flowers glistening in the water spray.

Birds twittered in the trees, as if they knew this was the perfect sanctuary from the dark and strange forest the humans so openly despised. A squirrel bounded out into the field, until it saw Stephania; it then stood perfectly still before very slowly and cautiously hopping back toward the tree it had come from. Another more courageous squirrel threw a couple of bark pieces at Stephania and Braken, chuckling angrily from his perch high on a tree.

Through the hole in the forest's canopy above her, she could clearly see the sparkling blue sky, along with Shadow Mountain as it loomed about a day's ride north.

Convinced she was dreaming again, Stephania slowly nudged Braken into a walk, and the horse gladly ambled into the tall, thick, green grass.

Overwhelmed by the feeling that she had certainly been here before, she slowly dismounted her horse, letting him walk freely in the pasture, her eyes fixed unwaveringly on the scene in front of her. Something like a memory almost flashed through her mind.

She could almost see four more horses in the field along with a man. One of the horses was ... she strained to remember. Was it a buckskin? The vision faded as quickly as it had come, just like all the others.

Disappointed that the strange vision remained a mystery, she sighed, shaking her head. *Curse these visions.* She grabbed her meager pack and carried it with her over to the pond. Her heart racing, she hurried to find a large, warm rock to sit on so she could drink in the stunning scenery around her.

"I know this place."

She closed her eyes and let the silence consume her. Faint voices whispered in her ear, but not from the wind or the trees this time.

"Not ... life ... your home anymore ... part ... us forever."

Her eyes snapped open, and everything faded. Sighing heavily, she slapped the rock with her hand. "Gods of all, this is frustrating. Why can't I remember?"

Seeing that it was getting late, she hurriedly washed in the refreshing waters of the falls and clear pond. When she had finished her bath and dried herself off to watch the suns set, she couldn't help but think about building a home right here and never leaving. It would be so much more enjoyable than living in the village. The falls weren't terribly far from New-Fars; she could still be close to Dalton. *Actually, he could live with me if he wanted.* But she doubted he would want to leave his cozy home in the country. She frowned.

A chill ran through her, and she shivered. Climbing down from her perch on the boulder, she went to retrieve her blanket from her satchel. As she pulled the rough patch of fabric out of the bag, something fell out and crashed onto her foot.

"Ow!" Biting her lip to quell the stinging pain, she bent down to pick up whatever it was that had fallen. When she saw what it was, she recoiled as if it were poisonous. It was the lyre.

Once again her heart raced in her chest. The instrument's magical pull was like a noose around her neck—unwanted but impossible to ignore. Slowly, she picked it up and stumbled over to the large, warm rock.

Dread settled in her. She realized that she either had to keep the lyre and play it or she had to, in only two days, find a branch and make her own lyre.

Wildly, she jumped to her feet, lyre in hand, ready to cast the instrument into the center of the pond.

Just as she was about to release it, every molecule in her body froze.

"Do not forsake it. Do not forsake us."

Shaking, shocked that she would have thrown it away, she sank to the ground, cradling the lyre in her hands. Tears streamed down her cheeks. It was heavy to hold, not in her hands, but in her heart. She could feel something from it; it emitted a strong sense of death, loss, loneliness, and evil.

She had forced herself to forget the vision of when she had received it, but the vision resurfaced. A sense of duty settled over her.

She raised the lyre and laid her long, slender fingers across it. Her teeth dug into her lip, her jaw grinding against itself. Whispers tickled her ear. The lyre became heavier. The forest darkened around her.

Taking a deep breath, she pulled her fingers across the strings. A clear, sour note rang eerily through the forest.

CHAPTER 22

A Quiet Cabin

Mountains of Trans-Falls, Centaur Territory

HIS BRILLIANT, BLUE EYES snapped open, and he gasped, his heart pounding in his chest. He leapt to his feet and galloped out of his home, not slowing until he had reached the center of the large, partially hidden city. The refurbished shell of an enormous tree loomed above him. A light shone out of a window at the top of the tree. He hesitated at the large, carved door that led inside, his fist inches from the door, ready to knock but hesitant.

"He's not here." His voice was barely even a whisper, as if he were afraid that his voice would startle away what was happening. His senses, he quickly noted, were heightened. He could feel all the life around him. He could sense the sleeping creatures nearby, and he could sense the creatures struggling to awaken from their slumber.

Looking down at the markings on his hands and arms, he gasped sharply. They were glowing brightly, but more than that, they were burning. Shaking his head, he tried to rid his mind of the muffled, wailing voices. He couldn't tell if they were coming from his mind or the forest. He broke back into a gallop, the trees passing by him in a blur. Through the trees ahead of him, he spotted who he was searching for. Vines trailing from the trees crept across the ground, emitting their own strange light. A heavy fog covered the ground.

Slowing down, the majesty of this forest filling his being, he gently picked his way through the vines so as to not damage a single plant.

A white figure stood in the center of a large circle of strange, old trees.

"The forest—"

The white Centaur raised his hand, turning to face the younger Centaur, who quickly kneeled before his leader. "I know." The white Centaur's voice was nearly inaudible. His gaze drifted across the thick forest as if he were looking at something other than what was visible around him. "It is awakening once more. The lyre has escaped the curse, and its strings have been played once again."

The handsome youth's face beamed, his unnaturally blue eyes glimmering with hope. "Does this mean that ... the forest will awaken? Does this mean it is the end?"

The white Centaur, a rare smile on his sullen face, shrugged his shoulders and turned his face to the trees.

They could both feel it—the life that poured from the forest. The stars faintly danced across the heavens, and the trees matched their movements, as if in the arms of the sky itself.

"Or, perhaps, my son, it is just the beginning!"

CHAPTER 23

The Waterfall

Base of Shadow Mountain

New-Fars, Human Domain

AGAIN, STEPHANIA PLUCKED a string and listened as the note rang through the silent forest. Anticipation: that was the only word she could put on the oppressing feeling she was experiencing from the air around her.

Braken nervously stamped his hooves, but he didn't seem scared, only excited.

Slowly and skeptically, she began to play the simple lullaby Dalton had always sung to her when she was little.

The suns had already slipped past the horizon, and the shadows once more began to play tricks on her mind. The moon rose behind her, shedding a bit of light on the meadow around her.

As she lifted her voice in song, she realized with unease that she wasn't the only one singing.

Voices rose from around her.

She tried to concentrate on them, because when she did, they sounded like nothing more than the wind.

The lyre became a little less heavy the more she played, and its unearthly green glow increased, filling the meadow with its powerful, beautiful light.

Braken stopped whinnying and pawing and now stood perfectly still and quiet, as if in a trance.

Something scurried over her foot, and she looked down. It was a small lizard, a kind she had never seen before. Another ran up onto the rock, its eyes trained steadily on her. Mystified by this strange behavior, she continued to watch, amazed as a third then a fourth crawled out onto the ground.

Having loved reptiles all her life, she was rather pleased with this turn of events.

A few snakes slithered up as well, their colorful tongues flickering in and out of their mouths.

She spotted movement up ahead in the grass.

Cautiously, she continued to sing, though a trifle quieter.

Her eyes widened. Her hands began to tremble. She could see the path the creature was making through the grass. It was enormous.

As it moved up onto the rock and into the light of the lyre, she gasped, nearly dropping the instrument. "Gods of all."

It was the largest serpent she had ever seen, with its head about the size of her hand. It had a large, green tongue, which flickered in and out of its mouth, its eyes trained on her.

Now she began to panic. She felt the strange peace from the lyre slip away, and fear gripped her instead.

Her eyes roamed around her, focused no longer on the beautiful music. The trees were swaying, their leaves rattling to the beat of the music, and strange shadows that almost looked like people flitted through the trees.

Words echoed loudly in her mind, and memories and years of training flashed before her eyes.

"How do you know if they're Duvarharian?" Dalton narrowed his eyes.

She tried not to groan. *"Because they look freaky."*

"No, girl, think." He rolled his eyes.

"Strange hair, pointy ears, colored swirls, reclusive."

"And their capabilities?"

"Fast healing, better hearing, better eyesight, entrancing animals, and sometimes humans."

Stephania staggered, nearly falling off the rock. The world spun around her. "Oh gods, no. This can't be happening."

She backed up, shaking her head in denial and disbelief. The reptiles in front of her swayed, their eyes glazed and staring at her, some advancing after her.

Dalton's warning mocked her loudly. *"Don't do anything stupid once you figure it out. Okay?"*

"No." She lowered the lyre to her side. A fog covered her mind as if trying to shield her from reality. As the clear, sour notes faded into the night air, the illusions of the forest disappeared.

The snakes and lizards lay passively at her feet; the large serpent stared at her intently, following her movements carefully.

"Those people don't exist anymore. They never even have. There has to be some other explanation."

Who didn't exist? A foreign voice in her head asked.

Them.

Who? Say it!

Panicking, sweat dripping off her brow, Stephania stumbled off the rock, falling to the ground, her breath hot and heavy as she forced air into her lungs. "The Duvarharians!"

Her hand burned as if it had burst into flames. Crying out, she dropped the lyre. As soon as the instrument left her hands, it stopped glowing.

She groaned, gripping her burning hand to her chest, before her other hand began to burn from the heat as well, along with her neck.

Panting through agonizing pain, she unclenched her left fist and brought it toward her face. Rivers of tears rand down her pale cheeks. Now it wasn't just her hand and neck that hurt, her head throbbed and so did all her muscles. Unfamiliar, debilitating pain filled her. She could only conclude it was her very soul burning.

"What in the bloody realm of Susahu is happening?" she screamed to the silent sky. A flock of birds scattered into the air. "Gods it hurts," she groaned, her eyes rolling.

Bringing her hand close to her eyes, cries of pain parting her wet lips, she strained to see what was causing the pain.

Choking on her tears, she gasped in disbelief. If she looked hard enough, she could make out little swirls and symbols just a shade darker than her skin tone twining themselves across her skin.

As the pain became almost unbearable, it stopped abruptly, and she found herself staring at very real, very clear legendary markings on her hands and forearms.

"Gods of all."

§

THUNDERING HOOVES HIT the dirt, throwing leaves and chunks of earth into the air. The wind screamed in the young woman's ears as it ripped and pulled at her red hair and the black mane of her horse.

The waterfall disappeared behind her as she fled from the haunting scene. Though she tried to forget, every time she closed her eyes, she could see those staring, glazed reptile eyes piercing into her soul.

After she had calmed down enough to stop hyperventilating, she followed the blubbing sounds of a stream. She soon came upon it and bent to drink ravenously from its clear water.

Unsure if she wanted to see what was on her neck, she peered into her reflection. Tears filled her eyes. The right side of her neck and jaw were also decorated in the cursed swirls, though they were of a much different design.

Thankfully, the bright red of the markings had faded, and they were now only slightly redder than the surrounding skin.

She scrubbed at them until her skin was raw and swollen. They didn't come off.

After crying beside the stream, the tears eventually dried, and her mind cleared. She mounted Braken and spurred him into a slow walk as she pondered the legends Dalton had taught her. Now something more than horror and fear began to grow inside her—excitement.

She tried to bite away the smile that crept onto her face. *What if I am a Dragon Rider? Could something be as wonderful as that?*

That would mean that all those legends were true. That meant that magic was real, and she could control it. Her eyes glinted mischievously, but then faded into a frown. At least, she only could in theory.

After much hesitation, she pulled out the lyre and played it. Much to her shock and delight, the birds around her sang along, doing whatever she bid them to.

"Come sit on my hand," she whispered unsurely to one of the birds after she caught its attention. It felt silly to be talking to wild animals, but it cocked its head and hopped closer. "Come to me." She put as much of her will into the words. Shock paralyzed her as the bird flew to her and perched contently on her hand. *It's too good to be true.* Her stomach turned with excitement. She gazed deep into the eyes of the songbird that sat gripping her finger, gazing at her expectantly. *Perhaps I am only dreaming. And when I wake, all will be dull again.*

She wanted it to be true, but she also didn't want to be let down.

She had to know for sure.

A wonderful, horrible idea formed in her mind, and she smiled uneasily.

Releasing the bird, she kicked Braken into a gallop, guiding him through the trees, and leading him back to the village.

She was going to control a human.

§

STEPHANIA WRAPPED HER cloak tighter around her, resisting the urge to simply go home and sit in front of the warm fire. It was just barely dawn in New-Fars and only a few people were already out of their homes. Most were just beginning to wake up.

Hopefully, it's too early for me to be recognized or spotted. She tugged her cloak tighter around her, the hood covering most of her face. She had left Braken tied up in a small patch of trees just outside the town. He would be much too recognizable if she were to bring him here.

Easily picking the lock of the back storeroom that belonged to a man named Grey, she slid behind one of the main shelves and waited.

There was a reason she had chosen this particular man to prey upon. She wanted revenge.

It had happened a long time ago, in his quiet, beautiful meadow, when she was just a girl.

Everyone loved his meadow. It had the perfect combination of sunshine and shade, along with a wonderful fishing pond, boat, and dock, which he let the whole town freely use—except Stephania. He had never liked how intelligent Stephania had proven to be at such a young age, but mostly, as she had overhead from the villagers on many occasions, he was wildly superstitious and truly believed Stephania was a demon from Shadow Mountain's haunted woods.

On the edge of the meadow, a lovely rose bush had grown. That fateful day, Stephania had decided that she wanted a few of the flowers to decorate her room with and to give to Dalton.

It was a terrible idea.

Grey had never withheld flowers from his bushes to any of the villagers, but Stephania, of course, was different. When he caught her taking some that day, he took the rope he was carrying and beat her.

She never forgot that.

That day, she had on her mother's ring that Dalton had given her on her tenth birthday. Grey had ripped it from her finger, claiming it as payment for her now trampled bouquet. Thankfully, Grey had been too wary of the foreign engraved words on the white crystal and tree pendant to steal those as well.

The creaking of the door opening startled her from her memory and jerked her back into the present.

Grey quietly stepped through the door and into the storeroom. The door banged shut behind him. His hands fumbled on the shelves as he searched for something to eat.

Stephania slid out behind him silently.

"Hello, Grey McGull." Her voice, low and seductive, sent shivers down the man's back, and he slowly turned around.

A gurgled gasp parted his lips, and he dropped the small slice of cheese he was holding. A cold sweat collected on his forehead and his face was drained of all color.

"W—who are you? A demon?" His eyes were wide as he stumbled backwards, his hands fiddling with the small knife on his belt.

A sly smile of satisfaction spread across her face. She was thoroughly loving every second of this. She could feel her eyes glowing red and saw their steady, dark light upon Grey's frightened face. Her new markings shone eerily.

"You know who I am, Grey," she smirked, reaching out one of her gloved hands. "Give back to me what is mine, and I will let you go alive." She knew he wouldn't comply, which is what she was counting on; after all, he could only guess who she was and what he had of hers. Her disguise was working perfectly.

He mindlessly fingered the ring on his smallest finger. "I—I don't know what you're talking about!" His voice wasn't shaking as much. Clearly, he wasn't as intimidated when he saw her small figure.

Raw, torrential rage suddenly tore through her, and she spat in his face, practically screaming in her fury. "You know full well what I'm talking about, you spineless thief!"

Before she could show any self-restraint, even before she knew what she was doing, her hand flew to his throat, clamping viciously around his neck. A foreign strength surged through her.

He gasped and clawed at her hands, trying desperately to pry them away from his throat. He was a big man, standing a head taller than her, and he was strong, but somehow, nothing he did could release her grasp. Somehow, she was stronger.

Her hand tightened around his throat. He could suck in just enough air to stay conscious.

She smirked, her mind cloudy, as if something else were controlling her.

Her left hand and her neck burned as if on fire, but she ignored the pain. She felt the magic within her squirm alive.

The man struggled harder, his face blooming red and his lips blue.

She began to sing. "A small stone, of one you don, nearly every day. A stolen treasure, one beyond measure, taken from a child. Give back to me what is rightfully mine, for though you don't think so, I tell you, you know me just fine." The song was crude, with sour, bitter notes sung with it, a mirror to her hurt. However, it wasn't the beauty of it that mattered—it was the result.

The man's eyes dimmed, and he sagged. She let go of his neck, and he dropped to his knees, massaging his throat and gasping on the air that flooded his lungs.

Her cloaked figure blending into the darkness of the room, she leaned toward him, her face inches from his. Her eyes and markings burned brighter than before, and new shadows loomed in the room. "Now, give to me what is mine." Her voice was barely a whisper, her lips close to his ear.

He whimpered. "Yes. Of course. Now I remember." He slowly slipped the ring off his finger. Though he stared forward blankly, agonizing pain could be seen just behind the fog.

A red haze covered his eyes, and Stephania knew he was fully in her power.

Licking her lips greedily, she watched as he dropped the small ring into her outstretched hands. He sank to his knees, bowing before her, and quivering at her feet.

"Please. Just have mercy!" His dull, glazed eyes turned pitifully toward her, but she merely scowled, feeling as if she were looking down at a lesser creature. He was weak, easy to control. While she reveled in this power, something revolted inside of her when she realized she could shatter his mind.

Pushing away nausea and snarling in disgust, she slipped the ring onto her finger, relishing in his whimpers and the way that he clawed at his head in pain, unable to rid her influence from his mind.

"Please, my lady." Foam collected at his mouth, and she snarled with repugnance.

"You worthless, weak creature." She spat on his face. "Fine, you shall have my mercy." In one liquid movement, she took the knife from his belt and hit him hard over the head with the handle. The resounding crack rang hollowly through the room. He fell to the ground, unconscious and released from her spell.

Hastily, she returned the knife to his sheath, and after searching the storage room, found a cheap wine bottle filled with the intoxicating liquid. She opened the bottle and poured some on the front of his clothes before dropping it beside his hand. Most everyone in the village knew Grey drank, and it wouldn't be unusual to find him with a splitting headache and a bottle of wine nearby.

Satisfied, her heart racing violently, she slipped out of the room and slunk into what was left of the shadows. As she masterfully weaved her way through the streets and houses, greed and pride flooded her, shoving away the revulsion of what she had just done. She could be a god or even a demon. After all, they already thought she was the latter. She could subjugate all these mindless wretches and make them do or give her whatever she wanted. Finally, she could have revenge.

She heard a twig snap behind her, but before she could turn around, a hand grasped her hood and pulled it off her face.

Gasping in rage, her hand flew to the handle of her sword. She began to turn around, but a heavy hand landed across her mouth, and another, in one quick motion, had her arm pinned painfully behind her back, rendering her motionless and weaponless.

A familiar voice grated harshly in her ears. "Oh, you are in so much trouble."

§

"WHAT IN THE BLOODY realm of Susahu do you think you were doing?" Dalton threw her into the house and slammed the door behind them, his face red with rage and his hair a ragged mess.

"I was getting something back that he *stole* from me!" Stephania caught her footing, making sure there was plenty of space separating her and Dalton, and rubbed her wrist where it stung from him nearly dragging her all the way to their house, Braken in shameful tow behind them.

"You can't just walk into someone's house and nearly murder him just for something so trifle!" He violently threw the ring onto the table and slammed his fist against the wood surface.

"Murder?" she scoffed. "I wasn't even close to murdering him!" Grey's pleading, deathly face flashed before her, and she blanched. Could she have killed him? Would his mind really have broken under her influence? She pushed these thoughts aside. "Dalton, he beat me that day. With a rope." Her hot breath heaved in her chest, her anger making it hard to form words. "As if I were one of his dogs!" she spat at him, her cheeks red as the suns setting on an autumn day. Humiliation mingled with rage.

"Yes, and he was a fool to do that. Don't forget the lengths I went through to punish him."

Her face flushed in remembrance. It had taken Dalton three long months, but eventually he had gotten Grey ruled guilty of abuse and the man had been punished with twenty lashes.

Dalton planted his fists and furiously shook his head. "But for the love of dragons! You never told me about him stealing your ring! You merely told me you lost it! If you had told me, I would have demanded it back and none of this would have happened!"

Knowing she was wrong, but stubbornly refusing to admit it, she hit the air, panting and cursing with rage and on the verge of tears. "Gods!"

The gleam of Dalton's polished lyre on the table caught her eye. If only she could put him into a trance ... Lunging for the instrument, she hastily began to pluck at the strings, singing orders to him.

Something like a mocking laugh parted his lips as he stormed over to her.

Gasping, she stumbled backwards.

He wrenched the lyre from her hands and threw it onto the couch before roughly pinning her down on the furniture as well, making sure her hands were immobile. Foreign words tumbled out of his mouth. A heavy fog settled over her mind. She could no longer sense the magic.

He released her and stepped back, unable to look into her eyes. Tears clouded his own eyes, and his teeth ground against themselves.

Her ears rang with fear, and her eyes began to water, her body hot and agitated, her breath shaking in her chest. "It didn't work." Her voice was barely audible.

He sneered and grunted, shaking his head. "No. That little trick doesn't work on me."

Her eyes fixed on his, and she melted into the couch. "B—but how did you know?"

Dalton stepped back and wrenched the glove off his right hand. He paused, his anger evaporating into depression. Whispering a few indistinct words, he watched with passive indifference as faint brown sparks hovered over his palm.

Unable to look at her, he held out his palm to her, and with a heavy sigh, he said, "Because I'm a Duvarharian."

She gasped, her hand gripping her chest, her heart freezing. "No. It's impossible."

Yet on his hand were numerous dark brown swirls of a kind she instantly recognized as Duvarharian. He must have used magic to keep the markings hidden from her all these years.

From a side table, he picked up a hand mirror and slowly handed it to her as if he were afraid she would take it and throw it across the room. She almost did.

Forcing herself to grip the mirror in her trembling hands, her eyes locked onto his. She shook her head, unable to look at her reflection. She had seen them once in the stream when it had all felt like a dream. She thought, if she saw them now, she would have to wake up to this new reality.

Dalton gazed at her mournfully, a hollow gap of sadness, disappointment, anger, and pain opening in his eyes.

Trying and failing to calm her rapid breath, she held up the mirror.

A stifled cry left her lips, and her hand flew to her mouth as she gazed in horror and almost wonder at the bright red swirls on her neck and left hand.

"And so are you." Dalton choked out, a catch in his throat, his eyes misting mournfully.

"I am—" She swallowed, as realization took over her and shock dulled her senses. "I am a Dragon Rider."

PART THREE
Awakening

CHAPTER 24

Nemeth's Home
Nearly 3 Years Earlier

S TEPHANIA'S HEART POUNDED in her chest. Her hands were slick with sweat. She licked her dry lips. Her ears rang with fear. *Oh gods. What happened?*

"Get out, girl! Get off my property!"

Stephania shrank back in horror, her foot snagging on the corner of the old, thick rug. "But, Ms. Nemeth, you said I can come anytime!"

"Bah! Liar! You little thief! How could I have said such an outlandish thing when I have never met you?" The old woman raised the heavy broom she was sweeping with. Her white hair was uncombed and disheveled. Her thick skirts, usually so clean despite being so long, were filthy from dragging in the dirt. Dark circles hung under her eyes like a bad memory.

"But Ms. Nemeth! It's me, Stephania!" Stephania's scream echoed in the small cabin as she tried to dodge the heavy broom handle. She was too slow. The thick wood smacked into her arm. Tears welled up in her eyes and spilled down her cheeks as she scrambled up from the ground. She clutched her throbbing arm where a large welt had begun to show. "Ms. Nemeth, please, I—"

"Get out, girl. And pray I don't report you as a thief." She raised the broom again, menacingly stepping toward the young girl.

"Please, Ms. Nemeth, it's me, Stephania," she choked through her tears. *Why does Ms. Nemeth not recognize me? What is wrong with the her? Why does she look so ill? Does she really not remember me?*

"Don't you remember? We are friends, and I—"

"I remember no such thing." She shook her head and snarled. "Friends." The old woman's eyes shone out hauntingly from her shadowed face. "I've never even seen you before, girl. Now get out!"

Sobbing uncontrollably, Stephania picked herself up and ran out of the house, hearing the old woman behind her screaming hateful and nasty things.

Blindly, she ran home.

"Stephania! By gods, child, what's wrong?" Dalton gathered the young woman into his arms, crushing her in his embrace.

For a few minutes, she did nothing but sob into Dalton's shoulder.

He looked down and spotted the red welt on her arm. Rage rose in him.

"Who did that to you?" his voice was harsher than he had intended, and he felt her flinch against him.

He heard her choke something out through her tears. It sounded like "Nemeth". He blanched, disbelieving his ears. How could the old woman have done such a brutal thing to her favorite youngster in New-Fars?

"Stephania," he whispered softly. "What happened?"

Stephania, through her tears and snotty nose, told him how she had gone to Nemeth's house. How she had welcomed herself into the home as always and stolen into the kitchen to find something to eat. How the old woman had yelled at her, denied knowing her, and had chased her out of the house with her broom.

Nausea rose in Dalton's throat as he shook his head. "I don't know why she did that, Stephania. Sometimes when people get old, they forget things."

The young girl only sobbed louder. "She was my only friend! How could she have forgotten me?"

Dalton smoothed her hair. "I don't know, Stephania. I just don't know."

§

DALTON SLOWLY STEPPED out of his home, latching the door quietly behind him. It had taken him a few hours to get Stephania to calm down, even though he had resorted to using magic to soothe her troubled mind. While she slept, he had healed her arm, unable to bear to see the angry welt on her.

He knew something was wrong. If his suspicions were correct, he knew who Nemeth was, and what she was. She wasn't some human prone to memory loss. No. She was so much more. And yet, only one reason could force her to forget Stephania. Sometimes for magical creatures, when their time ran out, it ran backwards.

He looked up at the moon—the crescent-shaped heavenly body was shining a thin sliver of light on the land.

If what he suspected was true, then he would have to hurry.

Not bothering to take the time to saddle his old, slow mare, he jogged down the road, cutting across fields to Nemeth's house.

Only too soon, he was standing in front of her small cabin. He paused, feeling the weight of where he stood. His eyes roved over to the stone under the tree. If the legends were true, then the man in that grave had once caused all of New-Fars to be destroyed. Dalton shivered, his eyes glowing warmly in the dark, his heart pounding with excitement and fear in his chest.

He stepped up onto the porch, hesitating. A chill came from the cabin, not from the night air, but from the feeling and presence of death. Shuddering, he placed his hand on the cold doorknob and slowly turned. The door shuddered open with a creak.

A dark figure lay on the floor.

Dalton rushed over. Dropping to his knees, he rolled the body over.

Nemeth's dark face was pale, her eyes staring back at him. A ragged breath rattled her chest.

"Tyrion?" She reached out and grabbed Dalton's shoulders, her grip surprisingly strong.

Dread sank in Dalton. He was right. Nemeth's time on Rasa was coming to a close. She was now only living in her past until it all faded away.

"Yes, Nemeth. I am here." He brushed the hair out of her face, playing along, wondering if his lie helped ease her pain, or if it was only cruel.

A thin smile spread across her face. "My love. I gave him the amulet."

Dalton frowned. "What amulet? To whom?"

She chuckled, but then coughed violently, blood trickling out of the corner of her lips. "To my son, of course. It saved him from the Sleeping. He's still awake. I found him!" Her eyes shone brightly, and her grip relaxed from Dalton's shoulders, her hands sliding down his arms.

He took her cold hands in his, willing them to be warmer.

"The amulet protected us both. It gave me strength. I escaped the Sleeping. I gave him the Zelauwgugey."

Dalton's eyes shot up. The Zelauwgugey? Could she really be talking about the famous Lyre of legends, the very essence of the forest? It had been supposedly destroyed long ago. Was it possible this old woman had possessed it all this time? He had to be sure.

"What is the Zelauwgugey?" He was almost scared to hear the answer.

She shook her head, her eyes sliding out of focus. "Oh, Tyrion. So silly of you to pretend like you have forgotten. It is the forest lyre, of course. The last pure artifact of my people. It contains the life of the forest, the forest's essence. Silly, don't you remember how it claimed vengeance for you? And now," she coughed violently again, spraying Dalton's face and chest with blood. "And now,"—it seemed her words pained her—"it is the only thing that can save them."

"Nemeth, what do you mean?"

He squeezed her hands, searching her face.

"Don't worry, Tyrion. He will give it to the Dragon Girl, the one from the prophecy. And she will wake us." A small smile spread across her lips, and then her face was still.

"Nemeth?" He gripped her wrinkly, bony fingers tightly in his own. "Nemeth!" Dalton clenched his teeth and bowed his head, letting her still hands slide out of his. A heavy sigh left his lips. She was gone. Gently, he brushed her eyelids down over her glassy eyes.

Seconds passed away into minutes as he sat, kneeling beside her lifeless body. Questions swirled in his head, only a few of which he had answers to.

His eyes traveled down to the dirty hem of Nemeth's dress. His heart pounded in his chest. If everything she had said was true, and if what he had believed all along was correct, then ...

His hand reached out. He wanted to stop himself, almost scared of what he would find, but his thirst for knowledge, for all things secret and unknown, drove him forward.

He grasped the soiled fabric between his fingers and moved it aside.

His breath caught in his throat.

Instead of normal legs and feet, he was staring at the hind legs of a goat.

Nemeth was a Faun.

His head spun, and he collapsed from his knees onto the ground, steadying himself. "By gods."

If Nemeth was a Faun, and if the tombstone was really that of Tyrion, then she must be Tyrion's lover—the Faun without horns—the destructor of New-Fars. If that was who she really was, then the lyre had been in her possession, not destroyed or lost as thought, and somehow, she had escaped the Sleeping. That would mean that one day Stephania would be given the lyre, and she would be the one to break the curse.

CHAPTER 25

Dalton's and Stephania's Home
Year: Rumi 6,112 Q.RJ.M.
Present Day

IT HAD BEEN A FEW DAYS since Stephania had learned she was a Dragon Rider. A few *long* days. Neither Dalton nor Stephania had said a single word to each other, and neither had left Dalton's property.

Now the young woman was sitting on her bed, her knees pulled tightly against her chest, as the last couple of days' events flashed through her mind over and over again.

She still couldn't believe it.

All her life she had known she was different, but it had never made sense why. She had deeply despised the villagers for fearing and hating her so much, but now she understood why they had. She possessed the power to control them. *All* of them. Whether they realized it or not, they instinctively knew she could; that's why they were so hateful and afraid. She was the predator and they, the prey.

She was afraid of accepting the truth, but eventually, she had gathered all of Dalton's major legend books and leafed through them, trying to wrap her mind around this new reality. She had done nothing but read them one after the other since she had found out her origin. Instead of seeing them as fairy tales, she was forced to interpret them as reality. The world seemed to make a little more sense now that she understood that magical creatures really did exist, even if they couldn't be seen.

But even so, she felt an empty hole inside of her. So much was missing. Who were her parents really? Where were all these magical creatures? What about the pagan sprites? The Fauns? The Centaurs? The great winged cats? Phoenixes?

Wyriders? Nymphs? What had happened to magic? And then the biggest, most dangerous question: *Who am I?*

A sickening feeling grew in her. She felt a new connection with Dalton. He knew what it was like to be an outcast, to be something totally different than what you hide behind. However, a bitterness rose within her.

All her life, he had told her nothing about who she was, where she came from, or even who her parents were. And though he had never outright said it, he had led her to think with all her heart that she was a human.

It was to protect her from something, she knew that much. But what? And why wouldn't he tell her? What was he trying to hide? The muttered excuses he had always offered to her questions led her to think maybe even he didn't fully know what he was protecting her from.

A new life had opened to her, but she didn't even know what to do about it, or if anything could be done about it at all. She obviously couldn't stay here with the humans. Even now they already seemed like bugs to her. But she couldn't just walk to Duvarharia and demand to be allowed to live there either. After all, she was a complete stranger to the culture of Dragon Riders. Did they even know who she was? Were her parents outcasts? Why was she living here with Dalton and not with the Dragon Riders? Why would Dalton, a Duvarharian, be living with humans in the first place? A horrible thought raced through her mind. What if magic really *was* dead and she and Dalton were the last Duvarharians? Was everything over before it had even begun?

A knock softly vibrated through her door, jarring her from her thoughts.

"Come in." Her voice was muffled by her knees. She shifted her weight uncomfortably.

The sound of the door opening and closing softly behind her seemed loud in the silence. She was acutely aware of his soft footsteps across the floor.

She didn't turn around.

A pregnant silence ensued, and she could feel the awkward tension. Everything had been oddly heightened since she had become aware that she was Duvarharian. She could feel everything now; from the smallest sense of life in a bug, to the emotions of her horse, it was a constant assault. It was a wave of confusion. It was a clanging noise. She jumped at every sound, startled. Her head spun, clouded with sensory overload. She ground her teeth and dug her nails into her skin.

"May I speak?" he asked cautiously, as he sat beside her on the soft bed.

"Yes, but I can't guarantee I'll listen." She scowled, but instantly regretted her rude response. A heavy sigh escaped her lips; she was surprised he hadn't reprimanded her for her attitude. "I'm sorry, Dalton. I just don't feel like it right now." She scrunched her knees closer to her body as if she could shield herself from her feelings inside.

"I know, but sometimes the best time to talk is when we don't want to at all."

She could feel his intense gaze on her, but even now she didn't look at him. If she looked at him, she thought surely all of the emotions would explode inside of her and she wouldn't be able to control herself.

She nodded instead.

"What's on your mind, Stephania?"

The red-haired girl rested her head on her knees, letting her soft, glossy hair fall over her legs. Perhaps, if she just sat here long enough and ignored him, he would simply disappear. Of course, he didn't, and after a few minutes, she looked up, biting back the tears that filled her eyes.

"Who am I, Dalton? I mean, am I really a Dragon Rider?" She paused and looked at her left hand. "Which I guess I am, then why am I *here* and not in Duvarharia where I belong? And why are *you* here with the humans? Who were my parents? Who am I?" She stared miserably out of her window. Her chest ached. Her heart sank within her.

For a moment, silence permeated the room until Dalton shook his head and chuckled.

"All those assignments, and it still took you this long to figure it out. I thought you would be a little smarter than that."

Stephania blushed. She did feel pretty ridiculous about it. After all, she had been drilled in Duvarharian characteristics all her life. Though she didn't have many of the main features, she had been blind not to see herself as one.

"Yeah." She let herself breathe out a soft laugh. "Guess you were wrong. But why don't we have the main characteristics?" Her hand strayed to her ears. Her tongue ran over her dull teeth.

Dalton grunted, a sad smile passing over his face. "Because neither of us is bonded with dragons."

"Oh."

They smiled awkwardly at each other before quickly looking away. The air was heavy around them.

Dalton shifted his weight and followed her gaze out of the window and across the land, which lay peacefully under the light of the late afternoon suns.

"You are the Farloon, or Chosen Protector, of the Centaurs."

"What's that?" Her hand strayed to the pendant around her neck. She had always wondered what the word "Farloon", which was engraved on it, meant.

"It is a sacred position, one that puts you as high in the Centaurs' tribal order as Igentis, the leader of all Centaurs. It is an oath made between the Dragon Riders and the Centaurs that binds their two Kinds together."

She shook her head. "But what if I don't want to be? I don't even remember swearing an oath. How does that count? That's not fair."

Only silence answered.

Taking a deep breath, Dalton continued, his voice quiet and meek. "You are the only child of Lord Drox and Lady Andromeda Lavoisier. And you are the chosen and prophesied protector of Duvarharia—a warrior called to rid Ventronovia of Thaddeus, his dragon Kyrell, and Veltrix once and for all. You are the *Shelesuujao* of the Duvarharians, the child of the Dragon Prophecy." His tenor voice echoed in the quiet room, his last words barely audible, emotion thick in his voice.

Who is Thaddeus? she wanted to ask. She opened her mouth. The words fell silent on her lips. Something felt so wrong about that name. A memory of piercing purple eyes surfaced, gleaming back at her. A wave of conflicting emotions ran through her, and she shivered, a confusing lump rising in her throat. *Later. I'll ask him later.* She tried to shove away the nauseous feeling, but it lingered, along with a dread of something creeping up on her. *Chosen prophesied protector. A warrior. Such foreign words. All words I don't want to describe me.* She chose to ignore those last words, too confused and too overwhelmed to want to think about them at the moment. "A Lord and Lady." Her eyes widened in awe and a small smile once more bloomed on her youthful face. "Drox and Andromeda Lavoisier. I suppose that makes me Stephania Lavoisier, doesn't it?"

She turned her head back slightly to him. For the first time in nearly four days, their eyes met. She saw tears in his.

He nodded, his eyes quickly straying from hers.

"You aren't in Duvarharia because you are the protector chosen by the Great Lord himself to save Ventronovia; it was foretold in a prophecy long ago. For a long time, Thaddeus didn't make any major attacks on the Dragon Palace, save for a skirmish here or there. They were doing quite well, the riders and dragons, I mean.

But something happened after you were born. It was like ..." His eyes grew distant. "It was like something woke up. The attacks were suddenly frequent and on larger scales. It became too dangerous for you to live in Duvarharia, so your mother and father decided it would be best to send you away for a few years until either the Dragon Palace became a more suitable place to raise you, or you would be able to handle war." He paused, his hands clenched into fists, and his teeth grinding against each other.

So how did my parents really die? Her brow furrowed. She began to ask but stopped when she saw how upset he was. Her heart twisted within her. She had a right to know, but she also didn't want to upset him. Perhaps it would hurt him more than her to tell the truth. Her nails dug into her palms. She resisted the urge to comfort him.

"Your parents and their dragons, um–" He laughed shortly, shaking his head. "When your parents tried to bring you here, they were, uh ..." He bit his lip. His eyes lifted to the ceiling, tears sparkling in the brown irises. "They were ambushed. By Thaddeus, Kyrell, and Veltrix's Eta army. The Centaurs tried to fight off the Etas, but there were too many of them." The tears rolled down his face. His mouth opened and closed several times before he barked a wet laugh. "They didn't stand a chance." His eyes clenched shut. She slid her hand over his. They sat still like that for a few minutes before she pulled away.

He took a deep breath, and his tears cleared. "It's called the Battle of the Dragon Prophecy, to those who believe in magic anyways. They all died protecting you. You were all they cared about." He turned his face to her. She saw a bitterness in his eyes. "You were everything to them. Everything."

Her heart lurched. A new wave of nausea swept over her. Her parents had died for her, to save her. She wondered if she should feel happy, grateful that she was alive, but an empty, aching hole opened inside her. Her parents were dead. They were really, truly gone. She had hoped that maybe, just maybe, they weren't dead. That they were out there waiting for her. But they weren't. She was never going to meet them. Tears rose in her eyes, but she didn't let Dalton see them. It was just one destructive piece of information after another. Maybe she didn't want to know the truth.

"This, of course, was not in your parents' plans. No one really knows how, but Artigal, the old white Centaur in the legends–"

She cut him off abruptly, "Yes, I know of him. Continue." She hated that Centaur. Everything she read about him, she hated. The name gave rise to such fury and pain in her, even when she was younger, that Dalton forced himself to cut any mention of the Centaurs' leader from all the texts he let her read.

Nodding slowly, breathing out a heavy sigh, he continued, "Yes, somehow, he saved you from Thaddeus and found you after the battle with a magic burn on your chest, something which was obviously done by Thaddeus. Then they brought you here, and I have raised you since."

Her head was spinning. She had been attacked with magic. Why hadn't she died? Who were "they"? By the gods, then that meant Artigal really could be thousands of years old! How was that even possible? She rubbed her head, unable to process any of this. It was all so sudden. She couldn't help but notice how much detail Dalton had left out. She was just about to press him for information, to pelt him with questions, when she remembered this was hurting him as much as it did her. She felt the overwhelming sensation that he had wanted to tell her all this a long, long time ago, but had been forced to keep it bottled up. Her heart skipped within her. Why had he needed to keep it a secret? What was he hiding from her?

"It's kind of strange, isn't it?" he chuckled lightly.

She raised an eyebrow at him.

"One day, you feel like nobody. Like the whole world hates you for no reason, like you are nothing but scum, dirt, a freak. And then the next day, you're suddenly special. Still a freak, still the world hates you, but now you are special and above it all."

Stephania grunted. "Yeah, it is, isn't it?" She glanced at him. "How did you know?"

"I too felt that way once, only under much different circumstances than you now."

She frowned, unable to think how Dalton, the famous and loved storyteller of the village and the so called "child whisperer", could be considered a freak like she had been and was.

"I know that you may think that's hard to believe, Stephania, but there was a time when all the city of New-Fars was leery of me. They knew I was different. It took a long time for me to gain their trust."

Her black eyebrows furrowed, nasty thoughts racing through her mind. "Why would you want to earn their trust?"

He didn't offer an answer for a long time. Unsettled by his lack of response, she chanced another look at him.

His face was completely emotionless, as if he were thinking of something unwanted. It was the same expression he had about a week ago after she had fought Jackson.

"Dalton?" Her honeyed voice gently shook him back to the present.

"What? Oh, yes. Well, at the time, I just really needed someone's trust." He smiled uncertainly before becoming occupied with something on his thumb.

She didn't press the topic.

Embarrassed to ask her question, Stephania shifted her weight a couple of times, her mouth opening, then closing, then opening again. "So, Dalton ..."

"Hmm?"

"How, um. How did you find me after I, uh ..." Her hand ran through her hair, and she chuckled nervously. "After I controlled Grey?"

He scratched his head and shrugged, a sheepish smile spreading across his face. "Well, it's not hard to follow a magic trace. Especially yours."

"A what?"

"Magic trace. It's what's left behind after magic is used."

Her eyebrows shot upwards. "So I really did use magic?"

"Yeah."

"Incredible." She couldn't help but glance at her hand. The markings were glowing bright red. She imagined they were smiling back at her innocently.

He laughed at her amazement. "Pretty incredible, isn't it?"

"Yeah."

Silence once more reigned for a few minutes before something Dalton mentioned flashed back through her mind. "So, what about this prophecy you mentioned?"

Dalton frowned. "I don't actually know a lot about it. I was never into such spiritual things. Never really had an interest in the Great Lord."

"How come?"

He shrugged, folding his hands in his lap. "Just never really believed in Him, I guess."

She too frowned. "But what about the prophecy? I mean, you said that I was some sort of protector. And, obviously, my parents believed in it, or they wouldn't have died for it."

The corners of his lips rose. "Yeah, so I guess it might be more true than I had thought. Even so, not many really know what the prophecy was originally about, only that you are to banish evil from the land."

"What evil?"

"Thaddeus and Kyrell, of course, and Veltrix the Eta King. At least, that's what they always said, the Duvarharians, I mean."

Stephania rested her chin on her knees and took a deep breath. None of this seemed real at all. It just seemed like Dalton was once more teaching her about all the old legends. She couldn't even begin to feel the weight of her part in all of this.

She was still too uneasy about Thaddeus to ask, but the question slipped out of her lips before she could stop it. "Who are they—the ones who brought me to you?" She couldn't hide the fear in her voice, and Dalton smiled sadly at her. She was relieved when he dodged the question.

"You will learn in time. I think that would be too much for you to understand right now. Besides, you don't have to worry about it. At least, not right now."

She was going to worry about it though. She didn't want to save the world. She had just found out that she wasn't human, and that the world was nothing like she had always thought it to be. She felt so pressured into all of this, like she was being forced into someone else's life.

"You don't have to do it alone, though, Stephania." His reassuring hand rested across her shoulders, and she leaned into his fatherly touch. "Of course I will be with you for as long as I can be, and there are others that want to help you."

She looked up at him, a smile on her face.

"You aren't the only person the prophecy talked about."

"Really?"

He nodded. "It also promised you a helper, or as the Duvar—harians call him, the *Kvażajo*."

Her eyes widened. "A helper?" She tried to repeat the foreign name but was unable to, making Dalton laugh.

"Mm-hm. Something like that." He squinted as if trying to look into the past or maybe the future. "It wasn't as clear who this helper is to be as it was about who you are, but it did promise one, so perhaps, he is at the Dragon Palace, waiting for you to return."

"We get to go to the Dragon Palace?" She bounced childishly in excitement. She could have only dreamed of going to the famous home of the greatest Dragon Riders, and its beauty lived only in her imagination.

"Well, yes, of course you get to go. It's your home, and you *are* the heir to the throne."

"Heir to the throne!" She uncurled herself, her face soft with awe. She turned to him, her eyes wide, her mouth hanging open.

He nodded, grinning at her amazement. "It'll be a long, hard journey, but yes. You get to go."

"I don't even know what to say!" A lopsided grin swept across her face. This was all such a shock. It was just like what Dalton said. A freak one day but part of the village, and then the next day, she was an exotic heir to a magical Kind's throne. Incredible.

"I know this is a lot for you to take in, but due to your growing magic trace—" he started, but she interrupted.

"What exactly is a magic trace?"

He merely shook his head. "I'm not sure how safe it is for you to learn about magic. I'll tell you about it later. But, anyhow, your magic trace is putting you and this town in danger, and the sooner we leave, the better."

"Leave for the Dragon Palace." She nodded, her mind flying through all this new information. It made her head swim and birth new questions. Now she had to abruptly leave the only home she had known since she was just a little girl. *How do I feel about this?* She wasn't really sure. Excited? Mournful? Angry? Sad? Maybe a little bit of everything? Maybe she was just in denial.

"Uncle Dalton?"

"Hm?"

"Why don't I remember any of this? Surely I would remember something." Her eyes flamed, and her hands balled into fists. She felt so helpless. She didn't remember the last time everything felt so out of control. If only she could remember, Dalton wouldn't have to tell her any of this and they wouldn't have to struggle with any secrets or misunderstandings.

Another deep sigh left his lips. "Because." His teeth dug into his lip. Something like anger crept into his voice. "Artigal decided it would be best if you didn't remember any of it."

The world went quiet around her. Her body felt cold. The room grew stale. "What? What do you mean?"

His eyes grew soft with empathy. "He took them away, Stephania. Your memories. Being with the Centaurs, using magic, fighting Etas, it awoke the magic within you too soon. It's dangerous for a child to awaken to their magic so young. And besides that: the Etas had already found you. It was only a matter of time before Thaddeus did too."

Disbelief, shock, and dread crashed down around her. This couldn't be true. "No. No."

"I'm sorry, Stephania. It was the only way. Even your family agreed it would have to be done to keep you safe. There didn't seem to be any way around it. It worked, Stephania. It really did. It has kept you safe this long. It was necessary."

She choked. "I had a family?" Her eyes brimmed with new tears, tears which shone through dead eyes. "And he took that from me?" Her heart pounded in her chest, but she felt as if a rot had taken its place. Maybe she should forgive him. After all, what if it had been the only way? But the more she learned, the more she was convinced Artigal had no right to do that to her. Her memories were her own. They were the only things that kept her tied to her parents, her home, and her family. Now she had nothing because of him. "Who were they?" The pain in her voice mingled with rage as the words hissed through her teeth.

He shook his head. "Aeron, High Chief of Trans-Falls, his mate Frawnden, Second High Medic, and Trojan, their son and your brother." Tears once more filled his eyes. She could sense jealousy and regret from him. "You were a very close family, very happy. I was loath to tear you from them."

"Aeron. Frawnden. Trojan," she repeated their names in a whisper. They were familiar, comforting names, but they felt so strange on her tongue. Grief mixed violently with her confusing emotions. She wanted to throw something, to hit someone, but she could do no more than sit perfectly still, sinking lower into the overwhelming pit that gaped open within her. *I had another mother, another father, a brother. We were happy. I was happy. And it was taken from me.* She cursed Artigal under her breath. A vengeful power rose within her. Her markings burned. *How dare he.*

"Curse that arrogant Centaur."

Dalton was quiet for a moment before he sighed. "Show him compassion, child. He cared a great deal about you. He did what was needed."

She sneered. "No, he didn't. You don't take away someone's joy if you love them. And you most certainly do not take away their family."

Dalton looked away. "He promised to give them back to you. Your memories, I mean. I'll hold him to it, Stephania. Believe me. You'll get them back. I promise." His fist tightened. "Or by the gods, I'll dying trying to get them back."

The pregnant silence grew again.

A war waged within her. She wished she could fight against all those who had hurt her—Thaddeus, Kyrell, Artigal, all the people in New-Fars—to feel their pain and seek her revenge. But she also wanted to cry and curl up in Dalton's arms and for him to tell her it was all just a sick joke. Neither happened. She was only left with the cold, numbing shock of reality.

The suns sank lower. The room grew darker.

Dalton shifted his weight and cleared his throat. "I'm so sorry, Stephania. For everything. Especially keeping these secrets from you. I never wanted you to be unhappy. I didn't want to take your memories away. Everything I did—" He choked on the emotion lodged in his throat. His eyes were red. "I did because I love you. Because your parents loved you. Because your Centaur family loved you. I wanted you safe. I wanted you happy. And I did the best I could to make it so."

She bit her lip. Her throat and ears stung as she struggled to hold back her sobs. She didn't know if she could forgive him. At least, not yet.

"You don't have to forgive me. Just please don't ... please don't hate me."

A few tears broke loose and danced down her cheeks. "Uncle Dalton, I don't hate you. I just—" She rubbed her nose on her wrist and clenched her jaw. "I just don't know what to think or feel anymore."

His shoulders sagged. "I know. I know." He hugged her, smoothing her soft, red hair. "I'm sorry."

She nodded against him and melted into his embrace. *If only ... if only we could stay like this forever. If only the world would fade away and I would feel safe. And loved.*

But time moved on.

Dalton pulled away, and she instantly felt the cold creep back in.

"I know this is a lot to take in. You can come down to eat dinner when you want. I'll have something made."

She did her best to smile at him. "Thanks."

The corners of his lips lifted, but the light failed to reach his dull eyes. "Of course, my child. Or should I say, my Liege?" He winked and mock bowed to her, attempting to lift her spirits.

A blush rose to her cheeks in embarrassment. An awkward laugh jumped off her lips. She wasn't sure how she was going to get used to people calling her 'my Liege', or 'Your Majesty'. She wasn't sure she liked it at all.

As he left the room and shut the door behind him, she forced herself to push aside her emotions. Crying over what she couldn't remember wouldn't change any-thing. She might not remember her two families or homes, but she had Dalton, and she had this house she called home.

Her mind wandered to the prophecy. She was promised a helper. To occupy herself, she dreamed of who her helper might be.

Man or woman? What would he look like? Would he be kind or cold-hearted? Would he fight with magic or weapons, or did Duvarharians fight with both at once? What kind of dragon was he bonded with? Or would he have a dragon? I assume the Duvarharians would all have dragons, but then why doesn't Dalton? She frowned, forcing that intrusive, controversial question out of her mind.

Just as she had devised who she assumed to be her perfect helper, she disgust-edly banished the thoughts from her mind. She knew well enough that as soon as she created expectations, she would be disappointed with reality. *I hope they're at least nice. I would hate to have to work with someone who's cruel or stupid.*

Her thoughts wandered from there to her future. It seemed so far away, so unreal, and yet she knew it was closer than she could believe.

Soon she, a Dragon Rider, would be going to Duvarharia and the Dragon Palace. She would be going *home*.

CHAPTER 26

Dalton's Home

Nearly 7 Years Earlier

STEPHANIA'S HAND BRUSHED against an old, rolled up piece of paper, knocking it to the floor, as she reached for a book. Her eyes followed the roll of parchment as it bounced on the carpet before coming to stop. The paper had unrolled only a little; years of being rolled up had warped its flat integrity, and it loathed to lie level.

It was yellowed, old, and had a recently broken seal on its edge. *It must have broken when it fell,* she summarized. *Surely, I remember it being sealed before I bumped it. Wasn't it?*

It was a seal she had only seen on two other documents and one small chest—a seal only used on her guardian's most private possessions.

Just visible on the corner of the parchment was what seemed like the end of a very intricate and prestigious signature.

Stephania forgot all about the book she had been reaching for and walked over to the unfamiliar parchment, peering down at it.

Why have I never seen this one before? Her ankles popped as she crouched down. Her hand paused over the paper, hesitant. *Should I–*

"Stephania?"

She snatched back her hand and jumped to her feet. "Yes, Uncle Dalton?"

"Where are you?" His head appeared around the doorway and a bright smile spread across his face. "Ah, I wondered if you'd be in here." His eyes quickly scanned the large library, stopping at the parchment at her feet. His smile faded. "Where did you get that?" Swiftly, he strode into the room and swiped up the parchment, hastily rolling it back up tightly. He held it close, protectively, to his chest.

"I didn't." Her hair waved as she quickly shook her head. "I was grabbing a book, and it fell off the shelf. I promise. It was just on the shelf."

He didn't seem convinced. "The seal is broken."

"Uncle, I swear, it must have broken when it dropped. I didn't open it." Her eyes were wide, her face flushed, her hands in fists. *Please believe me.* She cringed.

His eyes pierced down into hers before traveling back to the scroll. The frown deepened on his face, and he seemed to be struggling with something. His eyes reached hers again, searching her face. She tried to put all her honesty and innocence into her gaze, silently pleading with him to believe her. Finally, his eyes softened.

His heavy sigh of relief hummed through the air. "Of course, Stephania. I'm sure you didn't. The seal is very old; it was destined to break soon anyway. Thank you for not looking at it. That means a lot to me."

She let out a breath she didn't think she had been holding. *Thank the gods I didn't look at it. He seems so upset.*

"Of course, Uncle."

The man quickly grabbed a ribbon from the messy desk behind him, tied a bow securely around the rolled paper, and inserted the parchment into the middle drawer of the writing table.

"Now!" He clapped his hands together. "Today is a very special day, as you must know."

Her eyes sparkled brightly, and a blush rose on her high cheeks. She couldn't contain the smile that pulled her ruby lips over her perfect, white teeth.

"So, I wanted to give you something very special." Dramatically, he pulled a small, wrapped box out from the pocket of his pants. "It was your mother's. She gave it to me some time before she died. I think—" He paused and played with the string wrapped around the box. "I think you are old enough to have it, and I think she would have wanted you to have it."

My mother's. The young girl's dark eyes widened; she was at a loss for words. Solemnly, she reached for the wrapped box he handed her. Slowly, she pulled the strings of the bow, the wrapping paper falling open. A plain brown box was inside. She placed the wrapping on the overflowing desk. A still, expectant silence hung in the air.

The top half slid off easily from the bottom half, as if the box had been opened many times.

A small gasp parted her lips.

In the box was a ring—a beautiful silver ring with a red stone in the middle. Oddly, the stone matched almost perfectly with the mysterious pendant Stephania always wore around her neck. *Coincidence? Was the pendant my mother's too?* She looked down at her neck. No, the two pieces of jewelry were too different. The necklace had symbols from a language she knew nothing of. The ring was more plain. And yet the two pieces seemed to vibrate with the same energy. Something was still so oddly familiar about the ring, as if the two adornments were not so different as they seemed.

"Happy tenth birthday, Stephania!" Dalton smiled broadly.

She snapped awake from her thoughts, grinning happily back at Dalton, forgetting the deeper musings that weighed on her mind, the sealed scroll quickly forgotten. "Thank you, Uncle." She daintily slid the ring onto her thumb—the only finger it would fit on her small hand. "It's beautiful."

"But not as beautiful as you, child." He winked at her.

She laughed before throwing her arms around him and kissing his cheek.

"I love you, Uncle Dalton," her soft voice tickled his ear.

"I love you too, Stephania." He gently pulled away from her embrace and planted his hands on her shoulders. "Now then, today calls for a big celebration! Why don't you find something nice to wear, and we will go have dinner in the village tonight?"

Before her bright smile had finished blossoming on her face, she had already taken off to her room to prepare for their dinner. It was so very rare that they treated themselves to dinner in New-Fars, seeing as Dalton wasn't wealthy in currency.

§

DALTON STOOD FOR a while, smiling after her, before his joy faded and his gaze was drawn to the middle drawer of the desk.

Dare I look at it? His hands shook and sweat beaded on his forehead. An illness rose within him. He wanted to walk away, to forget what lay written on the paper, to forget what he had worked so hard to erase.

His hand moved on its own. The drawer opened. The parchment now rested in his hands.

He rubbed his mouth, his heart pounding in his chest. He had not once opened and beheld it since it had been sealed all those years ago.

He pulled back the paper, uncurling its secrets.

The print glared harshly back at him. Tears glistened in his eyes as the words stabbed him like a cold stone knife.

"Official Command and Terms of Banishment from Duvarharia Regarding Dalton Lefone, the once and no longer rider of Saorise."

CHAPTER 27

Present Day

DAWN APPROACHED the quiet valley and sprinkled the dew-covered land with the warming rays of the suns.

The muffled beats of a horse's hooves thudded on the soft, cold soil as its rider guided the beast along the narrow dirt path.

The rider gently halted the horse and gazed over the land, her pale face covered by a dark brown cloak that wrapped around her. A wisp of her bloodred hair, unhindered by the hood, blew with the soft wind.

After spending so many days in their home, left with nothing but her own thoughts, Stephania had finally found the strength within her to break out of the mental cage and get fresh air.

Despite their heart-to-heart conversation, the thought of Dalton withholding so much from her and never doing anything to help her fit in, caused her to harbor a bitterness she had previously been a stranger to. Her grip tightened on the leather reins. She knew she was just taking her anger out on him, and she hated that. Of course he wasn't the one at fault. He didn't deserve her anger. No. That would be saved for Thaddeus, Kyrell, the Etas, Artigal, and New-Fars.

Urging the buckskin stallion once more into a slow walk, she took her time riding back to the stables after she had galloped away from the barn hours ago. She was in no rush to get back.

She found herself not riding back home, but into town. She frowned. *Why did I choose this way?* She wasn't sure why she wanted to go to New-Fars all the sudden, but something in her heart whispered revenge.

On his own will, the horse began to trot, and she quickly settled into the rhythmic beat.

Her thoughts began to drift once again, even though she wanted dearly to be left with a blank mind.

If Dalton had lied to me about my real identity, then what else was he lying about now? And what about himself? She had always known he was hiding something. The sealed scrolls he was so protective of, the dodged questions—it was obvious he had not told all the truth. Her thoughts ran rampant with disturbing questions that had no answers. *Who is he really? Where is his dragon? Why is he halfway across Ventronovia instead of where he belonged in Duvarharia? How old is he really? And why would he rather live with the thickheaded humans? And what about all the other magical creatures? If Centaurs existed, why haven't I seen them or signs of them? And what about Fauns? Why did I only see a Faun when I obtained the lyre? And what about the Wyriders?*

Her fingers subconsciously brushed against the half-hidden instrument strapped to the horse's saddle. It was the lyre she had been given. Slowly, she had begun to accept the fact that she hadn't been dreaming. She had seen a Faun, and he had given her a strange magical instrument. Too afraid and too naïve in the ways of Fauns, she had resisted the urge to play the lyre. Even so, a strange dread gripped her when it wasn't with her, and so she felt compelled to carry it constantly.

Why hadn't Dalton asked her about it? Surely he had seen it—she knew he had!

Gods of all, Stephania, she cursed to herself, forcefully stopping her wild thoughts. This wasn't helping anything. It only brought up more questions.

She had reached the edge of town. The village was just stirring to life.

As she guided her horse through the streets, the square fell silent. Taking a deep breath, she lifted the hood off her face, adjusting so the markings on her neck were concealed. Trying as hard as she could to be polite, she spoke out in a delicate voice. However, her tone carried a hint of danger, as if daring them. "Well, there's no need to be afraid."

The silence only grew as everyone stared at her, some in fear, some in anger. Finally, a man stepped forward.

His eyes were narrow, though his nose was rather large.

She instantly recognized him to be the blacksmith whose swords she had used when fighting Jackson. She felt a blush rise to her cheeks, glad, at least, that Dalton had paid the man.

"You're alone." His glare deepened.

She was disarmed by his statement. "Why, yes. Is that so illegal?" Though she put on an air of indifference, an unease settled in her. Now that she thought about it, she had never before come into town alone. Dalton had always made sure to come with her.

The blacksmith's gaze skittered over her and her horse before he huffed and slid back into the crowd, murmuring something under his breath.

Impatience crept into her when no one responded, smiled, or stopped staring. *Perhaps there was a reason Dalton never let me come alone.*

"Well? What are you all looking at?" Her eyes flashed dangerously. Braken stomped with shared unease.

Most of the citizens recoiled from her gaze.

"What is it about me that you find so shocking that you must rudely stare at me like a slave on auction?"

The crowd stepped back, and a middle-aged man stepped out from everyone else.

"Your hair is like that of a demon!" he shouted out, his fist held high as he shook it menacingly at her, and everyone else readily agreed.

She rolled her eyes.

"I have no more control over what my hair color looks like than you do. If you're so put out about it, you should really talk to my parents." She eyed them coldly. "I thought you were a kind, accepting people. Why am I so different?"

"Because you have no parents!" An old lady's raspy voice cut through the air as she forced her way to the front of the crowd.

"I do have parents!" Stephania tightened her hold on her horse's reigns. *By the gods. Are they stupid? Everyone has parents!*

"Then where are they? Perhaps they dumped you off, unable to stand how much of a disgrace you are." The old woman deviously rubbed her hands together, her cackle ringing loudly through the murmuring crowd.

"How dare you?" Stephania's breath was hot in her chest, and her cheeks burned from anger and embarrassment. "My parents died to save me. They loved me."

"Yes, fine, but *who* were they?"

Stephania blanched. The only thing she knew about her parents was that they were Duvarharian. Her memories were gone. She didn't know who they really were.

Braken nervously shifted his weight under her.

"Only spell-weavers and demons have no parents!" Someone shouted out from the back of the gathering. The crowd erupted in shouts and accusations.

"No!" Her hands were shaking. Sweat beaded on her forehead. She tried hard to be heard, tried desperately to be cordial with these hardheaded people. *If I could just get them to understand, to see past my appearance and past the rumors.* "No, listen! I am not a demon or a spell-weaver!" She dismounted and stepped forward to the opposing crowd. She held her hands out, as if trying to show she wasn't a threat.

"Look! I am just like you!" Her eyes pleaded with them. She was desperate to try one last time to be a part of the people that she had lived with all her life. The desperation overruled her lust for revenge. Dalton had always been right. She had what they did not—a kind heart. Her want to be loved trumped her want to be feared.

Braken reared as the people lunged for Stephania. His reins slipped out of her grip. Hands from all around grasped and yanked at her. The dark cloak was torn from her body and the gloves from her hands.

The crowd roared with anger.

Someone screamed. "She has the mark of the devil! She has the mark of Susahu!"

Hands seized her as she fought her way to her horse. Her sword was strapped to the buckskin's saddle. It was the only defense she had. She didn't want to hurt any of them, but she would if it meant saving her life. A wild thought formed recklessly. *What if I used magic? Could I control them?* It had been easy enough to control Grey, but so many more surrounded her now, and she couldn't sense the magic within her.

Someone wrapped his hand around her neck and pulled her toward him. It was the militia leader of the town—a man who had always been open about how much of a danger he thought her to be. Worse, though, he was Jackson's father.

She gasped, futilely kicking against him. In her panic, her strength had left her. Sweat dripped into her eyes, and she could barely see him. His hand tightened around her throat, and she choked, black spots replacing the world around her.

"Hag." His lips were inches from her face, and she could smell the sweat and dirt on his skin, his breath hot on her face. "Too long I have watched you freely walk our streets, cursing those you came across, terrifying all who live here. Too long Dalton has defended you, even almost to his death. But no longer. My boy was unable to put you in your place, and you'll pay for his humiliation. It was foolish of you to come alone. Dalton can't protect you now. I don't care what excuse he has for you, or how much he coddles you, or that he raised you. You'll get what you deserve. I'll see to it myself."

Tears clouded what was left of her vision as she struggled to pry his hand from her throat. *Dalton would have died for me? He pleaded for my life? He really did protect me all those years. He really did care.* Overwhelming love poured over her. She wanted to see Dalton again, talk to him, eat with him, sing with him again. She didn't want to die. Not now. Not when she realized how much she had to live for.

She felt the sharp point of a knife prick her skin just under her breast, directly under her heart.

"No more shall we be forced to live with the scum of Susahu! This demon will get what she deserves one and for all!"

The crowd screamed in frenzy around her, calling for justice, for blood.

Rage filled her. A fiery lust for revenge washed over her. She was reminded of their insults, their bullying, their abuse, their hate. Was she to die at the hands of these pathetic humans? Would she let them have their way after all these years of Dalton protecting her? Would she let his life work be for naught? Would she let them have the final word?

A power rose within her, a terrible, dark power fueled by rage. Her magic markings began to burn, and the militia leader gasped at her in shock and pain. The smell of burning flesh filled her nose.

"What the—" He clenched his fist tighter.

The world fell black around her. Her lungs screamed for air. With her last bit of strength, she gripped his arm with her left hand.

He struggled against her before screaming in pain. She felt his skin burn under her hands, the sickening smell making her stomach turn, before he dropped her, and she fell to the ground.

The mob's shouting brought her back to consciousness as they began to drag her. She flailed, screaming and kicking against them. She couldn't get up.

No. Tears streamed down her face. *No, I will not die.*

Fury burned inside her, and she felt the power again, only it was stronger. She grasped onto it, felt as its tainted power filled her, feeding off her hate and anger.

Her eyes flashed open, but they were no longer normal. They were raging orbs of fire.

Only one man looked down into her eyes before she leapt to her feet, lunging at him, and breaking his arm with one effortless move.

Red haze covered her vision. She couldn't stop herself. She was no longer in control of the magic or herself. Her consciousness had been batted aside like a speck of dust. Men—trained warriors with swords, maces, and spears—fell around her like wheat at harvest, their weapons no match for her strength.

A cry left her lips. The magic tore through her body, exploding around her. A shock wave the color of blood rushed out of her and knocked down nearly twenty more men.

Stale, horrified silence gripped the town. They gazed at what had been their demon slaying gathering. It was now a small battlefield. Most of the men were only wounded, but nearly six stared up at the sky with glassy eyes, their bodies in unnatural positions.

The power had abandoned her, and she was left to gaze upon what her hands had wreaked. She bent over and threw up. A strangled cry left her lips as she staggered away. She coughed, and a spray off blood decorated her hand. Her head spun nauseously. Her heart slammed against her chest. Her gaze strayed to the unseeing eyes of the dead men. "Gods, no. No. That's not what I wanted. I never wanted to hurt you." Tears streaked down her cheeks, and she sobbed, covering her mouth against the horror.

"Murderer." The word started on whispered lips before it began to be wailed, screamed by the people.

"No! I never wanted to hurt you!"

They kept their distance as she stumbled to her horse, the stallion's eyes white with panic. "You attacked me! I didn't mean to. Oh, gods. It wasn't me. It wasn't me!"

"You sickly, barbaric people!" A familiar voice pierced the violent air.

Stephania snapped her head around, her mouth hanging open in shock.

"Stephania never meant us any harm! She only wanted to live among us like a normal person, but you denied her that! You made her what she is!"

"Jackson?"

She met eyes with her former tormentor, and he grimaced. "I'm sorry for everything, Stephania. I really am. I just never knew what you were until last week."

The townspeople, equally shocked, stood still and quiet.

Awkwardly, Jackson stood in front of Stephania before slowly kneeling before her, tears pouring down his face. "I had a vision a few nights ago. A man told me who you were. He said this would happen. I am ashamed of my conduct. I should have never treated you the way I did. I'm sorry."

"I—I don't understand." She shook her head, her heart sinking inside her. Was this really the same man who had persistently mocked her all her life? What had changed him? Who was the man he spoke of?

"Go, Stephania. You have to go, before you kill them, or they kill you. You don't belong here. Go home."

She backed up to her horse, her eyes locked on the sad brown eyes of the young man. She could sense from him that he was sincere.

She mounted Braken, instantly soothing the horse, just as the crowd spurred back to life.

The militia leader shoved his way to the front of the crowd, his eyes wide, his mouth agape. "Jackson? You *defend* her? After all she has done to you, to us? How could you?"

Jackson stepped forward. The crowd hissed in warning. "Father, this isn't right. Stephania never did anything to harm us. She is neither a monster nor demon. Her hate is of our own making. Please, father, I—"

His father spat on the ground. "No. I am not your father, and you are no son of mine."

Jackson's eyes swam with tears. "No. Please. You have to see the truth."

"Traitor!" Someone screamed, pointing at Jackson. "He is in league with the spell-weaver."

Stephania turned the horse but couldn't force herself to ride away. She knew how this would end. They called for blood, and because they were unable to have hers, they would have his.

"Jackson!" She screamed as he stood between her and the people of New-Fars, pleading with them to have compassion on her. His tears fell fast down his face, but he hardly looked afraid. He never once raised his hand against them in anger or defense. The crowd swallowed him up. His screams erupted through the air before abruptly stopping. The people grabbed his body and threw it outside of their gathering, screaming insults at his motionless, bloodied, broken form.

Stephania choked as his still eyes stared up at her, unseeing. She watched his bright red blood run from his body and into the hard packed dirt. The world slowed around her. Bile rose in her throat. Her body shook uncontrollably. Her ears buzzed with noise. Her own screams of horror were silent to her.

The crowd surged forward.

Four men appeared in front of the people, but they weren't real men. They seemed to be men made of pure light. They stretched out their hands, blocking the townspeople from reaching her. They were invisible to all but her.

One locked eyes with her. She could barely see him through her tears as she pushed away unconsciousness.

"Go, Stephania."

Braken burst into a gallop, and within a few minutes, the cries of the murderous riot faded behind her.

The air was dark and rank. A new sound filled the air—bloodcurdling, animalistic shrieks. Black shapes chased her. Crackling red magic flashed through the forest around her. The trees swayed and shifted.

Though the suns were rising over the horizon, she only saw darkness around her as she faded in and out of consciousness. She thought she could feel someone behind her, holding her on her horse, but when she tried to look, nothing could be seen.

The blackness surrounded her again.

"Oh gods, Stephania." Dalton's panicking voice reached her, and she felt his strong hands pull her from her horse and lay her gently on the ground.

"Too late. Oh, gods. I was too late."

A cold washcloth was pressed to her face, and she felt him place his hand on her chest, foreign, ancient words pouring from his mouth.

The animal shrieks grew louder. The flashing red sparks lit up the forest. Then everything went dark once again.

§

FUNNY HOW THE MOST *powerful Dragon Riders always start out as innocent children, isn't it, Artigal?*

Do you even know what lies in this child, Artigal?

You see, I know more about the Kvažajo than anyone else does, and now, thanks to the Kijaqumok, I know even more.

So you can sense it too. I am guessing that that is why you haven't attacked me yet. Perhaps, you have come to the realization that your Lord is not as powerful as mine.

§

"STEPHANIA. STEPHANIA, please wake up."

A cold, smooth cup was pressed to her lips. The visions that had haunted her fled her mind and were replaced with memories of the slain villagers. Their glassy eyes stared back into hers.

She sat up violently, gasping and spilling the liquid all over herself.

"Dead. Dead. I killed them. They killed him!" Her eyes ached miserably and watered due to the painful ringing in her ears. Her stomach churned and she gagged. "I killed them. I'm a ... I'm a murder."

Dalton pushed her back down. "It's okay, Stephania. You're safe now. It's okay."

As Dalton's face came into focus, Stephania sobbed, and tears welled up in her eyes. "Oh, Dalton." She threw her arms around him, crying into his shoulder and shaking in his arms.

"I'm so sorry, Stephania. I was too late to save you. If only I had been there a little sooner."

She pulled herself away from him, wiping her eyes and nose. "What? What do you mean?"

Dalton sighed, looking down at his hands, disappointment in himself plastered across his face. "I had a dream. A man—he said he was a messenger of the Great Lord—told me that you were leaving the house and that I needed to stop you. He urged me to go after you, but I thought I was just dreaming. He told me something was haunting you—a dark power—and that it was trying to consume you." He buried his face in his hands, and Stephania's heart broke for him.

She had never seen him so weak, vulnerable, and broken.

"I always knew something haunted you, with your nightmares and such." He choked back his tears, keeping his eyes anywhere but on her. "I could always feel something around you, something evil, but I couldn't do anything about it. It drove me mad. Even so, I didn't think much of it when I woke with that sense of evil permeating the house. I thought, maybe, you were having a nightmare or something. But then I felt it." His face paled. "Some sort of power had come into New-Fars. Everything was dark, darker than it should have been. And I didn't hear you or sense your mind anywhere near. I ran through the house, calling for you, searching for you, but you had already left."

He took a deep breath and wiped his face again.

Stephania, her own tears rising in her eyes, moved to his side, and put her hand on his arm. He took her hand in his, gripping it in his own.

"That's when I heard it. Screaming from the village. I nearly collapsed under the influence of the evil power, but that man kept it at bay. I saw you riding out from the village, and I grabbed my horse, following you and Braken here. You were completely unconscious when I caught up to you but—"

Stephania choked back her tears. "Dalton." She took a few deep breaths, forcing herself not to cry. "You did your best. I wouldn't have listened to a vision either. What happened, happened. I'm not sure you could have stopped it."

"Yes, I could have." His eyes blazed with anger. "I have before in the past. Many times I stood down a riot in your defense. Sometimes, I even used magic against them."

She shook her head. The taste of bile made her gag. "Dalton, you couldn't have stopped them. Nothing could've stopped them." Her tears spilled unchecked down her cheeks. She thought of the power that had overcome her. It was a rage, a blind, consuming rage that had driven them all to murder. "Dalton." A deep, shaky breath escaped her. "They killed—" She hid her face from him, ashamed. "They killed Jackson."

The Duvarharian man's face paled. "Jackson? They killed him?"

She could only nod.

"Why?"

"H—he defended me."

"Gods."

She couldn't bring herself to tell him everything. She felt dirty, tainted after the power had consumed her; it felt as if she had committed some great sin. As if she had sold a part of herself to something darker.

Silence replaced their voices and she eventually slipped into a restless sleep.

She woke up a few hours later. Her entire body hurt. It felt as if she had been dragged behind a horse. Her mind was foggy and slow. She looked around. Dalton was sitting, though his eyes were closed and his breath slow.

A rotten stench wafted in the air, and she recoiled; the stench was familiar. Red eyes flashed before her, and she quickly blinked them away. She knew those eyes. Was it a memory?

She looked above her. It was dark. Everything around them was dark. She realized that she couldn't see through the trees. It was as if they were in a room.

"Where are we?"

Dalton jolted awake and followed her gaze, squinting and pursing his lips. "Um, well, Braken took you to the waterfall in the dark forest, but when we got there and I got you off your horse, the forest kind of, um, swallowed us."

"What?" She couldn't help but laugh at how ridiculous that sounded. The movement caused her to wince as a shooting pain raced up and down her side.

"I'm not really sure what happened either, but the forest just kind of,"—he gestured to the trees, which could barely be seen above and around them in the dark—"hid us, I guess."

Her eyebrows furrowed. "Hid us from what?" The unsettling feeling that she had felt when she first woke up now grew, filling her with dread.

"Etas."

CHAPTER 28

A FAINT CRY RENT THE hollow air, and both Duvarharians' eyes darted from side to side, searching for something they couldn't see.

"Etas are *real?*" The name resonated inside her with burning hatred and fear. She could feel the vengeful magic grow inside her, but she was too tired. It fled, taking the unexplained emotions with it.

"Of course." Dalton's face was pale. "They are as real as you and me."

"I'm still having trouble really believing that we're Duvarharian, let alone the fact that shape-shifting demons really exist."

He laughed nervously. "Sometimes, me too."

"What time is it?"

"About noon."

Stephania's eyes widened. It was completely dark where they were. The forest was shielding them even from the sun itself, but why?

The unearthly screams grew louder. Their hands hovered uneasily over their weapons.

Stephania gently plucked her bow string. Its dull twang rang muted in the small clearing. Her heart pounded in her chest; her palms were slick with sweat. Any anger she had felt toward the Etas had vanished and was quickly replaced by stark fear. "You can use magic, right? To kill them?"

Dalton barely glanced at her.

She felt the blood rush from her face and her stomach dropped uncomfortably; her hands were trembling uncontrollably.

"Yeah, a little."

"Why are they here?"

Dalton moved closer to her, running his fingers through his hair. "They're following your magic trace. The man from my dream told me they were planning an attack on the village. That's why I met you out here."

"My magic trace? What exactly is that?"

Dalton's eyes narrowed. "Not now, Stephania."

An angry and frustrated energy instantly permeated the air.

"Seriously? They're hunting me because of my trace, and you won't tell me what it is?" She turned to him, her eyes flashing angrily.

"It'll just make it worse, Stephania. Not only that, but we don't have the luxury of time. You have to trust me. You can't know everything."

"Trust you?" Her voice rose to a high, breathy pitch. "Gods of all, Dalton, I trusted you my whole life, and you did nothing but *lie* to me! What reason do I have to trust you?"

A stab of pain filled his eyes, and his shoulders sank.

When she saw his hurt reaction, she regretted her words. She had let her mouth run away from herself again, but it was hard not to. Her whole world had been turned upside-down. She couldn't tell truth from lies anymore.

He opened his mouth to answer, his eyes begging to explain, but his voice was drowned out by the screams of the Etas that tore violently through the forest. The screeching, mixed with the terrifying thunder of running beasts and the flurry of wings, exploded all around them. It was almost deafening. The trees bent and cracked, moving closer together. Snapping wood joined in the noise as the Etas desperately tried to break through the barrier, but in vain. The trees were protecting the Duvarharians.

Stephania gasped in awe. Could something so wonderful, so magical really happen? Before she could appreciate the situation anymore, a piercing pain tore through her mind. Something was tugging her, pulling her toward the Etas. It was weak, but so was she. She groaned, dropping her weapon, and clutched her chest. "Dalton."

He caught her just as she collapsed, and he laid her gently on the ground. She twitched, convulsing at whatever was trying to control her. A second consciousness wrestled at the end of hers. She fought against it, repulsed by the fact that it was reaching out to her. It pierced through her wall and dove into her mind, tearing through her memories and visions.

She screamed.

"Curse the gods!" He muttered spells over her. "Not again. Please not again."

Brown magic twined from his hands and covered her, creating a shield around her.

Images of a man and woman holding her flashed before her. Their faces were a blur. She saw a mountain range and a glowing white palace. Brown sparks swirled around her, and the evil consciousness fled from her, leaving chaos in its wake. She sat up, gasping.

§

"DASE, ŻEBU," SHE GROANED, as she looked frantically around her. By the glazed look in her eyes, Dalton knew she wasn't seeing what was actually around her. She was trapped in another vision. By the words she had just spoken, the Duvarharian words for 'father' and 'mother', he guessed it had something to do with her parents.

He held her hand in his fatherly embrace and cradled her to his chest as she sobbed, shaking her head and moaning in pain and anguish.

After a long time, the rushing beasts around them faded into the distance, and her crying stopped as she fell asleep in his arms.

"If only there was some way I could help you." Tears sparkled in his eyes as he smoothed her soft hair, gently rocking her in his lap. "Just hold on for a little longer. Artigal will help you. He'll know how to heal you. He'll know how to protect you." His heart sank into despair. Tears filled his eyes. *Unlike me.*

He held her for a while longer, letting his tears fall unashamedly from his face. Then he packed up their little camp, using the slightest touch of magic to light the map he was reading.

"Where are we?"

Stephania's groggy voice startled Dalton, and he quickly shifted his position so she could sit beside him.

§

HER HEAD THROBBED. She felt only fear. She couldn't remember the things she had just seen. The last trails of the vision had all disappeared from her grasp. She did, however, remember terror and death. A lump rose in her throat. She could see the worry in Dalton's eyes, but she didn't know what to say. She didn't even know what had happened. The evil consciousness had left her feeling exposed, naked, raw. Her mind felt ravished—a strange, dirty feeling she wished she hadn't endured and would never have to endure again.

"I think we're here." He pointed to an obscure place on the map. "And that—" he said, as he drew an invisible line across the entire map to the top left quadrant, "is the Dragon Palace." Just above his finger was a minuscule drawn representation of the Dragon Palace. His worried gaze flickered across her face, and she quickly looked away, biting her lip against the tears. She knew he wanted to ask if she was alright, and she wanted him to; she almost let him. But before she could, she slipped behind the mask of false wellness she had gotten so used to wearing.

"Gods of all. We have to travel all that way?"

"Mm-hm."

She sighed heavily and frowned. *It's so much farther than I would have thought. Or wanted.* Her eyes lingered on a particularly imposing mountain range called the Filate Mountains. She recalled Dalton saying they were the steepest ranges in Ventronovia. By surveying the map, she concluded they would have to travel over them or spend years bypassing them. She had been looking forward to the adventure, but with that distance, and the obstacles that stood between them and Duvarharia, she wasn't sure if it would be so enjoyable.

She stood, feeling much too anxious to sit still, and paced the dark circle of trees they were trapped in. Her hand subconsciously ran across the branches that enclosed them. She turned her thoughts to anything but the wretched illness the evil presence had left in her. "How are we going to get out of here?"

Dalton stood beside her, having just finished packing their horses. "I don't know. The forest decided to protect us, so I guess it's up to the forest to decide when to let us go."

Well, that doesn't make any sense. She pursed her lips. "But how would it know to protect us? I mean, shouldn't it be impossible for it to know who we are? And why should it even care about us?"

Dalton studied her eyes. "Yes, it should be impossible, or the forest should be, at least, indifferent to us. Unless ... unless we have something that belongs to it that it wants to protect."

She frowned as a memory flashed before her. *"You must take this, Stephania, as a token of our allegiance."*

"The lyre," she whispered with wide eyes. "It's protecting the lyre. It must be."

She moved slowly, entranced by the sensation that the forest was pulling her to the instrument. Her fingers slipped open the satchel's straps and pulled the flap aside. She dragged out the neatly folded blanket, the curve of the lyre shaping the fabric. A shudder ran down her spine. Slowly, she lifted the edges of the wrapping until it slipped free and fell to the ground. The cold instrument rested delicately in her hand, its eerie, green light illuminating the forest around them.

Dalton took in a sharp breath, his eyes wide at the sight of the legendary instrument. Despite the fact that Nemeth had spoken of it to him before she died, he hadn't believed its existence until now.

"The *Zelauwgugey*."

"The what?"

Dalton moved to her side, his eyes fixed on the magnificent instrument. "The *Zelauwgugey*. That is the lyre's name—Forest Essence. It's supposed to contain the life of the forest. I didn't believe it existed. It was thought to have disappeared along with the last Fauns and all the forest children. I had sensed that you were carrying something foreign and powerful, but I hadn't been able to find it. It seems it is only physically visible to the holder, unless the holder is touching it. Then others can see it as well. Fascinating."

Before she could respond, he eyed her with suspicion. "How did you come to find this?"

She stuttered over her words, too captivated and entranced by the lyre to say anything for a while. "I, uh, I found, I mean, it was, uh, given to me when I came out here."

"Given to you?"

She nodded. "By a Faun, I think."

"Incredible." His eyes flashed with hungry excitement. "So she hadn't been completely delusional. She did have a son, and somehow, they both escaped the Sleeping."

Stephania frowned. "What do you mean?"

His eyes flashed, meeting hers briefly before shifting his gaze to the forest. "I was just remembering something Nemeth told me a long time ago, about the forest."

"What about it?"

His eyes narrowed. "I'm still not fully sure. It's all ... confusing." A heavy sigh escaped from his lips. "I'll tell you when I find out more about it. But until then, it's just rumors, dying words, and a few lost ballads."

She shrugged, disappointed that he wouldn't tell her more, but also feeling a little too tired to pry any more confusing information out of him.

For a few minutes, they did nothing but stare at the lyre in baffled amazement before Stephania shook herself back to reality.

"So, now what?"

Just as Dalton shrugged, and opened his mouth to answer, the forest creaked and moaned around them. The branches shifted and moved until a tightly woven tunnel appeared before them, stretching into the dark distance.

Dalton and Stephania looked at each other, their mouths gaping open in awe.

"I guess we follow the forest."

§

"HOW LONG DO YOU think we have to keep walking through here like this?" Stephania wiped her forehead before taking a drink of water. Braken stamped his hoof, and she swatted him away as he sniffed her pouch for treats.

Dalton had suggested walking for a while to give the horses a break, but he could tell Stephania was quickly tiring of the seemingly never-ending walk.

He looked up at the impossibly thick canopy of branches and leaves. If it weren't for his magic, which showed him they were still moving forward, he could have sworn they were going in circles. "I don't know. That is for the forest to decide." His own horse, a dappled gray gelding named Austin, was becoming more anxious and claustrophobic in the tight space. Dalton wondered how before it would be dangerous to be in such small quarters with two large beasts.

"Well, curse this forest." She shot a scathing look at the instrument in her hands, but its glowing green light neither dimmed nor wavered, and the forest didn't so much as sigh in return.

A small smile crept up on Dalton's face as he watched Stephania. She reminded him so much of Drox, with his headstrong, impatient ways. Andromeda had always been gentle and levelheaded, always careful to think things through. Though Stephania had inherited her mother's ability to overthink even the smallest, unimportant details, it seemed the girl had not a trace of the Lady's patience.

"What if we're just going in circles? I mean, how can we trust the forest? It's not like we," —she pursed her lips, looking for the right word— "*know* it."

252

He bit back his laughter and held his hand out in front of him. A brown, swirling, transparent compass formed out of smoke-like shimmering magic, the arrow pointing just barely north-west. "We're still moving in a consistent direction. Where that is leading us, however, I haven't the slightest idea."

She snapped her head around just in time to see the magic compass before he dissolved it.

"You're using magic." Her face contorted in an array of emotion, chief of which was frustration.

"Yes, I am." He stared calmly back, but the fire in her eyes had yet to go out.

"And what about your magic trace, Dalton?" Her voice had a sharp bite to it, as if she were trying to pick a fight. He winced.

Ever since she had started carrying the lyre, it had, along with the frustratingly dark and small tunnel, begun to weigh on her, making her extremely moody and grouchy.

Their patience and composure were wearing thin.

"I, unlike you, Stephania, can control my magic trace and cover it up."

She narrowed her eyes. "Then teach me."

"No."

"Why not? Because somehow covering my magic trace would make my magic trace bigger? How stupid is that? This whole magic stuff is so ridiculous." Tears brimmed in her eyes. She feverishly twirled a lock of her hair around her finger, ignoring the knots that were forming. Her eyes darted from side to side as her jaw worked against itself. Her eyes shone with a challenge.

Dalton bit back his stinging response, his hands balling into fists. "Yes, that is exactly what would happen. While I taught you, your magic trace would still be imprinting itself all over this land. That would only endanger the villagers. Not only that, but the Etas aren't following my trace. They're following yours. It's you they want. Not me."

"Curse those villagers," she hissed under her breath. "What if you covered my trace for me as I learned?"

He wanted to. He wanted to teach her so many things, but it was pointless to try.

"I can't, Stephania. That's not how that works."

"Then at least tell me how it works!" Her Shalnoa, the markings on her hands and neck, were starting to flare up due to her anger.

"I can't." His voice was flat. *So this is what Artigal had been fighting against when she lived with the Centaurs.* The Igentis had thought it best to teach her, but in doing even that small act, he had awoken the magic within her. It was impossible to win. It was impossible to both keep her safe and to let her understand.

"Why not? Because you just want another thing to hold over my head? Is that why you never tell me anything? Because you want to have some sort of control over me?" Her voice quavered with emotion. "Why is it so hard for people to tell me what's going on? Why do I always have to live in the dark? Why does all this have to be so confusing? I'm sick of having no control. It's my life, after all, isn't it?"

"I just can't." His own voice was choking with uncertainty. "Okay? Please just trust me. Please."

"No!" She furiously wiped away her tears.

He stepped back, shock and hurt painted on his face.

"I don't know if I can trust you anymore! What don't I remember? How can I trust someone who let my life and memories be taken from me?"

Her fists rested at her sides, but she looked as wired as a caged animal. "You've never done anything to help me! What if you stole my memories from me because you're the one who killed my parents? What if—" Fear flashed through her eyes as she took in a sharp breath. "What if you're Thaddeus?" The tears streamed down her face. Her voice was a bare whisper. "How do I know?"

Her words hit him like a spiked mace. He felt his heart shatter. *No. No. No.* What could he say to still her fear? "I never did anything to help you? Do you really think I could be Thaddeus? Please tell me you don't believe that."

She tried rubbing the tears from her eyes, but they only grew thicker. She hiccupped. He could see the regret crash over her as she looked into his face and saw the hurt and anguish there.

His voice was quiet.

"I raised you, even though I didn't have to. I kept all the villagers from murdering you from the first moment they met you. You have no idea what I have sacrificed for you. No idea! You think you're suddenly so grown up and entitled just because you found out that you are a Dragon Rider and because your parents were Lord and Lady of the Dragon Palace, but that's not how it works."

Tears drew rivers down his cheeks, catching in his stubble and wetting his shirt.

"You think that life is just so easy because you suddenly have magic or that any little thing is possible because we're Duvarharian. We're not *gods*, Stephania." He took a few deep breaths. "And you know what, you may be some sort of heir to an ancient throne, but you are nowhere *near* being their leader. You are still a child. You are still my niece, blood relation or not. I love you like my own. I always have, and I always will. I wish you would remember that."

She bit her lip, choking on her breath. She averted her eyes from his, her nails digging into her palms.

"Everything I have done, all the secrets I kept, no matter how painful for either of us, I only did to protect you. You can hate me for it. But it won't change that what I did was right, and Artigal too. And it will never change that I love you."

She wept, covering her face. "Oh gods," she whispered so quietly he could barely hear. "Why does everything I do have to end in suffering?"

Dalton clenched his jaw and shook his head, brushing the tears away from his eyes. He didn't know what to say to her. He tried to dispel the knot in his stomach, but it remained. He wanted to wrap his arms around her, to say how sorry he was, to tell her he loved her, but she seemed so far away. It was like her mask had turned into a castle. She seemed far beyond his reach. He stood in silence, feeling so alone. Finally, he spoke. "Come on. We have to keep moving."

She didn't move but instead wiped her tears from her face and sniffed loudly. "Yeah." Rubbing her arms and grinding her teeth, she bit her lip to stop the fresh wave of tears. Her shoulders slumped, and the disappointment in her eyes stabbed his heart. "Okay."

Just as she pulled herself together, the forest creaked and moaned around them once again, shifting its branches in a whirlwind of brown and green.

Stephania gasped.

They were standing in a clearing at the top of a small mountain, looking down at a valley. He recognized the valley and the town that was at its center: New-Fars.

"Gods of all." Dalton stumbled and fell to his knees, his heart slamming against his chest, dread sinking heavily inside him.

"What—" Stephania quickly made her way to his side and followed his gaze.

Their house and training arena were lit up as flames violently tore them apart, turning the buildings and all their belongings to ash.

Stephania sank to the ground, trembling uncontrollably. "Oh, gods."

Dalton bit his lip, his chest heaving with anger and anguish. His home, his belongings, everything he had worked so hard for steadily burned to the ground. Though they were many miles away, he could nearly see every detail as if he were there. His hands balled into fists, his knuckles turned white and his eyes burned.

The heat that rose to his face was almost akin to the heat of the blazing fire.

"Suluj źu sukuneruź ubaes." He forced himself to turn his face away from the scene. After all that he had done for the humans—taught them how to fight, improved their weapons, taken care of their children generation after generation—this was how they repaid him. Bitterness grew within him, but before it could settle in, an empty ache took its place. How many of his homes would he be cast out of? After taking Stephania to the Dragon Palace, where would he go?

"Come on, Stephania. We don't need to see this."

Her eyes were glazed, unseeing as they stayed fixed on the flames that consumed their home with an unquenchable rage. "How could they?" Her hands clenched into fists. Hot tears spilled down her cheeks.

Dalton held out his hand, offering to help her to her feet.

She snapped her head around, her eyes blazing.

"That is all your fault!" She jumped to her feet, snarling at him and shoving his hand away. "You're the one who forced me to stay in New-Fars. You always knew how much they hated me, and all the abuse I had to deal with. You might have tried to protect me, but why couldn't we have just moved? Why did we have to stay in this infernal place? You had it great here, but there was never anything for me here but hate. You're so selfish! Now look what's happened. Everything is gone. Everything!" She hugged herself. "Now I have nothing. I have no home. I don't know whom to trust. I don't know what to do. I just, I just—" She sobbed and cried out, shaking her head.

He bit his lip against his tears. Oh, how he had wanted to move, but a thousand reasons told him not to. All were reasons she couldn't understand. Not now, anyway. How could he make her see? Everything he had done was for her. He'd only wanted to make her happy, to keep her safe, to make her feel loved. Did she not know that it was his home as well that had been turned to ash? Why did he have to be at the center of her pain? Why did it have to be him who had to raise her? He had failed Drox. He had failed Andromeda. He had failed Stephania. He could offer her nothing now except his love—a love she didn't trust.

He couldn't hold back the tears. His heart stuttered weakly. He held his hand out to her, pleading for her forgiveness, for her understanding. "Stephania, please. I wanted to move, but we couldn't. Please try to understand."

She shook her head and stepped back. He stepped after her, wanted to hold her, to brush away her tears. "Please, Stephania. I've lost everything too. You're not alone. We have each other. We'll figure something out. Together. We just—"

"No!" She shoved his hand away from her and stumbled backwards, tripping over the rocks. A rock split open the skin of her palm. She stared blankly down at the blood. Her fingers closed over the cut and tightened into a fist, a rage and confusion building around her. The tears flowed fast down her cheeks. "Just—just—" She furiously brushed her tears away as she stumbled to her horse. "Just leave me alone!" She mounted Braken, though blinded by tears, and spurred him into a gallop, her sobs echoing hollowly through the still, silent forest.

CHAPTER 29

The Abandoned Mountain Fortress
Dragon Palace, Duvarharia

"WHERE ARE YOU?" an agitated, ragged man shouted into the early rays of the morning sky. His voice carried over the empty land beneath him as he stood on a sleek metal and granite patio that was suspended over the side of a looming mountain.

His hand tore through his long black hair as he ground his teeth. A blast of golden magic tore through the room behind him, sending a vase smashing into a wall. He cursed and cringed after hearing the glass shatter. Seconds later, gold magic twined around the shattered glass, mended it, and set it back on the table.

A deep sigh dragged down his shoulders. "Where are you?" he whispered softly into the wind, his hands gripping the railing, his broad, muscular shoulders tense.

His golden eyes slowly shut, and the images flashed before his eyes again.

A red-haired baby. A mother and father. Thaddeus. The child screaming. Blinding light. A mark flashing in front of him. Consuming him, burning him, judging him.

His eyes snapped open, and he jumped back from the railing, stumbling into his room. Crying out in pain, he pulled his shirt off, his hand flying to his shoulder. Curses hissed from his mouth as he desperately tried to sooth the burning pain on his skin. He turned in front of his large mirror. The mark shone mockingly. He couldn't bear to look at it. With a wave of his hand and a flourish of magic, the mirror became clouded.

As he paced his room, the mark on his back burning brightly and painfully, his eyes landed on a picture that rested on his table next to a vase of dead flowers. It was a *Qumokuhe*—an image made from magic. A handsome but tired and solemn man stared almost humorously ahead as his wife gently scolded their young redheaded daughter, who was carelessly waving a knife at them. It was Drox, Andromeda, and Stephania.

Stephania's flashing red eyes mischievously stared at the pacing man through the image, and the marking only burned more intensely.

Unbridled rage flooded through him. Storming over to the picture, he stared at it for a few minutes, his anger slowly evaporating as he looked once more at the few things he still had left from his deceased family. Tears glistened in his eyes, and his fingers slowly trailed across the still image.

Violently, he threw the picture face down onto the table so their eyes would no longer look upon him, and he banished the tears from his eyes.

Clenching his fists tightly, he stormed back out onto his patio and stared into the distance toward the human land, his breath heavy, his heart even heavier.

"By the gods of Ventronovia, wherever you are, I *will* find you."

CHAPTER 30

Common Road to Cavos Desert

Present Day

THE SUNS WERE BRIGHT. They were warm, oh so warm! The grass was soft beneath her feet. She stooped low, picked a purple wild-flower, and twirled it between her thumb and forefinger. It smelled like spring, like budding joy. She smiled and tucked it behind her ear.

A figure stood in front of her. It waved.

A grin spread across her face. Her feet dug into the soft grass and dirt as she ran, her hair streaming out behind her. The suns kissed her cheeks, and the wind hugged her gently.

"Uncle Dalton!" she yelled, as she jumped into his arms.

He caught her and swung her around. "Stephania, my child. You act as if you've forgotten what spring was like!"

A blush spread over her cheeks, and she played with a lock of her curly hair. "I did, I think. I forgot how warm it was."

He smiled tenderly. "It's wonderful, isn't it?"

She nodded, and he set her down.

"Now, shall we go home?" He held his hand out to her. She reached for it, but she could never grab it. He faded away from her, and the air became silent. The flowers were replaced by snow and the leaves by cold dead branches. The birds stopped singing, and it was cold, so, so cold.

Her eyes opened. It was dark. The ground was hard under her. A rock cut into her side. She shivered violently. The fire had died down to just coals.

A tear ran down her cheek.

Home. What is home?

She rolled over onto her side, wincing as another rock dug into her arm. The moon was just barely visible through the tops of the trees.

Will it snow? She drew the furs tighter around herself, but she couldn't rid herself of the impending chill.

How long had they been traveling? Four months or five?

It was winter now. It seemed like a lifetime since she had felt the warm suns shining on her back as she sat under a leafy green tree.

Instead, the crunch of leaves under their feet on the long road had turned to the snapping of frozen dirt and fallen branches. The wind was sharp, cutting deep through furs and clothes. The days were short, making their progress slow.

She stared at the dying coals. How long had it been since she had sat in front of a roaring fireplace, its warmth filling her whole being instead of this wretched, stabbing cold? How long had it been since she had drunk more than water heated over the fire or eaten more than wild foliage and game? How long had it been since she had slept in a real bed and felt its feathery bliss under her instead of rocks? How long had it been since she had called one place home?

She tried to swallow the lump in her throat. Sleep would not come. She sat up shivering. It mattered not the number of blankets or furs she pulled over herself, try as she might, she couldn't banish the cold.

A frown dragged down the corners of her lips. What would the winter be like so far up north in Duvarharia? Would it be worse than this? She wasn't sure if she would like that, though it would be nice to see more snow.

She dragged herself to her feet. Sparks flew up into the sky as she prodded the burnt logs with a stick, stirring up the coals. The crackling of new wood filled the air as she laid on a few more logs.

Shouldering her compound bow, she stamped her feet, blowing onto her chilled fingers. It would be morning soon. Trying to sleep would be fruitless now. She didn't want to stay and wait for Dalton to wake up though. Buttoning her coat up, she stepped quietly around his bundled, sleeping figure, pausing to look down at him.

His beard had grown out, his hair as well. He was looking thinner than he had back in New-Fars. It had been a long time since she had seen those thin lips smile. She knew he had taken the burning of their home, their arguments, and her accusations very hard, but she didn't know how to comfort him. She felt like a wall had been thrown up between them, and she felt just as much locked out of it as she felt locked in.

Thoughts that she had worked so hard to suppress in the last few months suddenly assaulted her. *Why? Why did this all have to happen? Why does this have to be so hard, so confusing?* She hated her destiny, magic, Artigal, and Dalton; she hated everything. And yet, she was so alone. Without Dalton, she had nothing. Nothing at all. She was trapped, caged, with nowhere to run, nowhere to hide from this nightmare that consumed her. She had to get away. She had to breathe. But she also had nowhere to go.

Shoving away the unwelcome tears, she patted the two horses and slipped into the woods, letting the darkness and the branches hug her like she so desperately wanted someone to.

§

"I DID NOT." Stephania gritted her teeth and forced herself to look away from Dalton.

"Yes, you did, Stephania. This is the fourth time you've disobeyed me now." He shook his head in exasperation. "Curse the Lavoisier stubbornness," he muttered none too quietly under his breath.

She resisted the urge to roll her eyes. "I didn't run off, though. I just went for a walk! I need my own space sometimes."

"I know that, child, but it doesn't matter. I can't have you just recklessly running through the woods by yourself. You have no idea how dangerous it is."

"I didn't go very far." Her voice was barely audible through the wind.

His lips drew into a thin line, and his grip on Austin's reins tightened. "I don't care, Stephania. All it takes is one time for you to be just far enough away from me and Thaddeus has his chance."

"And how are you protecting me now?" Her eyes flashed dangerously. *What good could he possibly do against someone as powerful as Thaddeus?*

"I put protective barriers around our camp, which scramble our magic traces. It makes it more difficult for enemies to pinpoint our exact locations."

Her eyebrows furrowed. "Oh. I didn't know that. Why didn't you tell me?"

"Because, once again, that knowledge increases your magic trace." He ran his fingers through his shaggy hair. "Gods of all, will you ever learn?" he muttered under his breath. His shoulders sagged, and he suddenly looked more tired than she remembered him looking.

"So then just keep covering it up. That's what you've been doing, isn't it?"

"Yes, in a way. Could you please stop using magic, though? It's a bit harder to cover up than you realize."

She looked around herself, her eyes widening. As they walked, she had been subconsciously levitating the twigs around them. Braken spooked at a particularly large branch and jumped. She yelped, grabbing onto his black mane, and the sticks all fell to the ground. Her heart pounded in her chest and an uneasy feeling settled in her. It wasn't the first time this had happened. Often, when she was upset, she channeled magic without realizing it. It unnerved her and made her question how much control she really had over her own power. She always felt like she was standing at the edge of a chasm and one step could send her falling into the darkness of the unknown.

"Sorry." She looked back at Dalton.

He was slumped over his gelding. The light had gone out of his eyes, and his hands were quivering.

"Uncle Dalton!" Her heart pounded in her chest, and she urged Braken forward until she drew even with Austin. She shook Dalton's shoulders, her heart pounding against her ribs.

He sat up, gasping for air.

"Are you okay?" Braken danced nervously under her, feeling her emotions.

Dalton groaned and clutched his chest. Silent tears streamed down his face. "I—I think so."

She wasn't convinced. "What happened?" Her eyes darted around to the trees, looking for the red eyes of evil. Their swaying, bare branches offered no answers or ominous motives.

A fake smile spread across his face, and he brushed her hand off his arm. His voice failed to stay steady. "I think it was just taking too much of my energy to cover your magic. You're much more powerful than I." He chuckled sourly.

"But how is that possible? You know more than me."

He shook his head and clenched his eyes shut so as to dismiss the pain. His words were barely audible. "Yes, but I've lost a part of myself." Through his tears, he looked down at his hand and her gaze followed his. His brown markings were faded. They weren't as bright and clear as Stephania remembered them to be.

Is his magic fading? A new dread settled into her stomach. *Is that even possible?*

Her eyes widened with realization. She remembered him saying something about the change riders undertook after bonding with a dragon. With the combination of the two souls, one would never be the same; they would never again be able to fully exist without the other. With dragons came greater magic. If one were to lose their dragon, one might lose their magic too. "Your dragon. You've lost your dragon. Of course."

He laughed quietly. "Yes. And in her place I have an empty chasm, a hollow pit of darkness where a piece of my soul once was. The more magic I use, the bigger it grows." His hand balled into a fist. He had never before talked about his dragon, and she had never pressed the subject. It had seemed a subject too dark to mention. Now she knew why.

Her heart ached with guilt as if it had been stabbed. She had willfully disobeyed him, using magic whenever she pleased, giving no thought to the possible consequences. He hadn't been telling her to use less magic out of spite or because he wanted to micromanage her; he had told her because he was losing the ability to protect her and even use magic in general. A blush burned her cheeks, and she gripped the reins tighter in her hands. How could she be so selfish?

"Don't worry about me, child. I'm the wizened, age-old storyteller. I can take care of myself." He smiled broadly, winking at her, but it did little to ease her fears.

She returned the gesture weakly, avoiding his gaze. How could she not worry about him?

"So, do you want to know more about magic traces?"

She snapped to attention, taken back by the shock. "What? But I thought—" she huffed. Had he not spent hours lecturing her about the dangers of learning more magic? "I thought it was dangerous."

He shrugged and a strange look of defeat flashed through his eyes. "It is, but it's about time you knew. It won't change too much anyway. If I can barely keep up with small spells, there's not much I can do about it anymore." He appeared nonchalant, but she could see the fear in his eyes. Even more powerful, she could perceive the sense of failure about him.

She balked. She'd waited so long to know more. She'd even gotten into so many fights with Dalton, trying to make him tell her. Now, however, she wasn't sure if she wanted to know. *Is it worth it? What price will we have to pay?*

"Why now?" The air carried her voice away, and she wondered if he had heard.

The silence stretched on. A branch laden with frost snapped, the sound echoing darkly through the woods.

"We're close to Trans-Falls."

All thoughts left her mind. *We're close to Trans-Falls.* A knot tied itself in her stomach. *Trans-Falls. With the Centaurs, and Artigal, and ... my family. My family. Oh, gods.*

"Artigal can keep you safe there. He'll be able to teach you and shield you." Jealousy laced his voice. "He promised to give you back your memories. Once he does, you will gain knowledge and experience in just a few months that I could never teach you. With that knowledge, you will grow powerful enough to protect yourself. All the puzzle pieces will have fallen into place. It will be complete." His voice grew even quieter. "You will be complete."

The saddle was suddenly uncomfortable, and she shifted her weight. "Are you sure?"

The warming sound of laughter rang through the forest, but its brightness did not travel far. "Yes, my child. I am sure. I have not much left to give you, especially since I cannot protect you, but I can give you my own knowledge."

She bit her lip.

"Okay, Uncle Dalton. Then teach me what you know."

He smiled sadly and cleared his throat. "As you know, when you were first learning about magic, you were unable to concentrate the power. Magic was being released chaotically, and you couldn't channel it enough to make a very simple spell like levitating a leaf. This is what happens to all young children, and is why, for good reason, you don't see children making spells at such a young age. Usually, an adult Duvarharian's magic presence is enough to subdue a child's magic. That is one reason why your parents wanted me to raise you. The Centaurs have no way of subduing your magic tendencies in the way I can."

She frowned. *I suppose that makes sense.*

"Now that you have strengthened your mind and are able to control the magic more, you can concentrate it into specific actions, like levitating sticks. Since all magic is just an unnatural transfer of energy, the bigger the spell, the bigger the difference between your unnatural effect on the environment and the natural effect. Make sense so far?"

She nodded slowly. This was a lot to take in. She hadn't realized it was so complicated.

"So how come magic isn't natural? I thought it was the dumb beasts of the forest who weren't natural in this land."

"That is true, to some extent. In reality, we are all the same. Depending on your worldview, it's all a little different. The majority of the Dragon Riders have always believed in some divine creator, as does the rest of the land, though each 'religion', so to speak, is a little different."

Thoroughly intrigued by this new topic, she sat a little straighter. He had never taught her religion, preferring to instruct her only that which he could prove with absolute fact. Instead of pushing for the direct answer to her original question, she inquired further. "How are they different?"

"Good question. The Wyriders, also known locally as Džoxsenä, meaning People of New Birth, live in Wyerland. They believe in many different divine beings that each have a role in the world, whether it be childbirth, animals, water, the afterlife, or anything like that. Then the humans, well, they don't really know what they think, and it seems most of them just don't even care. Even so, many of them, especially the scientific ones who are trying to destroy the magical world and who are inadvertently helping Thaddeus, tend to think that there is no divine creator or rulers of this world, and believe that they themselves are as mighty as it gets. And then, lastly, the Duvarharians. They believe in one great Creator, who made all that we see in the beginning of time and that he has blessed certain Kinds like the Fauns and Centaurs and the Dragon Riders. Through this blessing, they were given the extraordinary gifts of magic or reading the stars. Then there are even other legends that aren't tied to any particular race at all. Some say that those are the legends which are the truth, others say they came from a race long destroyed."

Her eyes slowly widened with awe. "What are they?"

Dalton shrugged and snapped off a low-hanging branch, slowly breaking bits off it and letting them fall to the ground. "Stories of huge, magnificent beasts which used to walk the earth—the first creatures, they were called. They destroyed or created whatever they wanted to, shaping the world and forming it. Out of their battles raged terrible death, but also the birth of new creatures, which became a part of the world."

Stephania's eyes sparkled. *I wonder what it was like before time itself.*

"Legends also speak of another realm just above us, the sky realm—Hanluurasa. It is a world made out of and in the cosmos with cities made of star dust and the hearts of young and old planets. They say it was the 'between' world of all other worlds, connecting them all together and watching their fate from the skies. During that time when the foundations of Rasa had yet to be laid, the legends speak of a gateway which freely opened between Hanluurasa and Rasa. The creatures of the land were able to travel freely to the sky and vice-versa."

"Woah." Her heart raced with excitement. *This land is so much more magical than I first thought. Is there really such a thing as a sky realm? Can you actually cross into it?* "So why isn't it still like that?"

He shrugged. "Some say the people of Hanluurasa finally closed the bridge and let Rasa rest in peace. Because the energy from the sky was cut off from the land, the great beasts which once roamed our planet either died or went to sleep. Others say that the great ruler of Rasa, whether it be the Creator of the Duvarharians or one of the many gods from the polytheistic Wyriders, closed the door and settled the foundations of the world, putting the beasts into a slumber until they will be needed again at the end of the world."

"The end of the world?"

Dalton nodded. "Some believe that the sky will be torn open once again and the creatures will be awakened to destroy and remake the planet once again."

"Incredible. That is just—" She shook her head, nearly squirming with excitement. "So what happened to the star people who lived here and the land creatures who lived there? In the sky realm, I mean."

Once again, Dalton shrugged and shifted his weight in the saddle. "I guess some were stuck in Hanluurasa. Most legends say they became the stars or that pieces of their souls were used to make new planets. But it also says the creatures who came down here were given the job of being mediators between Hanluurasa and Rasa. They were given the gift of understanding their homeland's language and dances, and are still thought to live among us."

"Wait, you mean they're the—incredible." Her eyes were wide. She didn't know if she could believe it all. It seemed too far-fetched, too fantastical. *Could something so amazing be real?*

His own eyes sparkling, Dalton nodded. "Yes. According to legend, the Centaurs and Fawns are originally from Hanluurasa, and while their physical appearances are different than they were so many years ago, they are essentially still children of the sky. But of course, remember this is all just myth. It isn't based on any facts and cannot be proven."

"Well, of course." She didn't let that dampen her mood. "But still. Gods of all.

That's—" She shook her head, unable to control her smile or find words for what she was feeling. "That's incredible."

Dalton turned his face to the sky. Though it was midday, it was unusually dark. "I wonder if it will snow?" he mused more to himself than her, but she hoped to any gods that might exist that it wouldn't.

She cast a sideways glance at him and took a deep breath. "So, what do you believe, and how does all of this tie into magic being natural or unnatural?"

One of his warm smiles from her childhood lightened his face. "That's where it gets tricky."

"For now, we'll just focus on the Duvarharian's way of thinking since that is the culture which you will soon rule over. So, if one all-powerful Creator made all of this and made everyone and everything the same, so to speak, then it's all natural."

He looked at her expectantly, and she merely nodded, not wanting to ruin this with one of her spontaneous, ill-timed thoughts.

"After certain Kinds pleased him, like the Centaurs and the original Dragon Riders, which, by the way, the humans and Wyriders later came from ..."

"Really?" Her mouth dropped open when he nodded. "Gods of all." It felt like her world had been turned upside down. *Humans, Dragon Riders, and Wyriders were all related?* It was almost too much to take in.

"Anyways, after those certain Kinds pleased him, the Creator blessed them with great gifts of power—the power of the Creator. That would make these powers *supernatural,* or unnatural. Do you still follow?"

Her eyes widened. It made perfect sense. She nodded violently. "But then, how do we have lesser races like the humans and Wyriders, if in the beginning, there were only the Dragon Riders?"

Dalton took a deep breath. "According to the Duvarharians, a rebellion occurred, but it wasn't just against the other dragons and riders, it was against the Creator Himself."

Stephania's dark eyebrows shot up. "That wouldn't go over well, I'm sure."

He shook his head, chuckling. "No, it didn't. According to their legends, those Dragon Riders became too prideful. They believed they were greater than the Creator Himself and thought they could be their own gods. They got their punishment. Banished from the ever-prosperous land of Adriva, they were stripped of their powers, and worst of all, their ability to bond with dragons."

"What's Adriva? I thought we were talking about Dragon Riders from Duvarharia."

A chuckle parted his lips, and he rubbed his cold hands together. "The first Dragon Riders lived in the country of Adriva, and the Dragon Rider's race is actually called *Ražužugub,* which means 'Chosen People' because they were chosen by the Creator. They were later driven out of Adriva and founded a new country—Duvarharia."

"Okay." Her face wrinkled as she pondered what he'd said. "I suppose that makes sense. So, why wouldn't the Creator just destroy them if they were so disobedient? That's what I would've done."

"I would have too." Dalton agreed. "But they say it was because He, the Creator, I mean, loved them like His own children, for they were His chosen people, having been the creatures He blessed in the beginning. And, rather than destroy so many lives, He let them go on in their ignorance, maybe to one day turn back to Him."

"By the gods." Her eyes widened. "He's got a lot of love. And patience."

Dalton's crooked smile caused his eyes to sparkle as he laughed.

"Yes, He does. At least, according to Duvarharian legend, of course. This is all just theory."

"Of course."

"After that, there were many peaceful years for a long time, until a different rebellion took place. This time, the rebels were only against the other dragon men. They fought and quarreled over rights and laws and what have you until the rebels just decided to leave. But because they were separated from the other more pure Dragon Riders, and because they didn't accept some of the laws that were supposedly laid down by the Creator, they lost a little of their power too. They can't bond with dragons and their magic isn't as strong. Since then, they have fallen from even that glory and are now considered by the Duvarharians to be an evil, pagan race. They loathe the Duvarharians with a deep and complete all-consuming hate; their children's children blame their fallen state on being kicked out of the dragon's land instead of the truth, which is that they left. Thus, you have the Wyriders. That is why Džoxsenä means 'people of new birth' in their language."

"Amazing. So, how do you know all of this? All the legends and religions, I mean. Do all Duvarharians know this?"

He chuckled quietly and played with a leaf, using a bit of magic to levitate it and send it spiraling though the air. "No. Gods, no. I was a historian at the Dragon

Palace. It was my job to make sure the legends weren't forgotten, were preserved, and properly recorded. Much knowledge can be derived from history, if only you are willing to learn."

A tender smile spread across his face when he recognized the excitement and awe she felt shining brightly in her eyes.

"Amazing." She took a few deep breaths and shifted her weight. Spikes of pain shot up her leg, and she slapped her thigh, trying to get her blood flowing again. "That's amazing." Her thoughts raced through her head over and over again as she processed them. Then she realized something. Dalton had yet to answer one of her questions.

"So, what do you believe in?" It was a risky question. She had always known Dalton didn't like talking about personal beliefs.

His demeanor instantly switched from excited and proud to anxious and irate.

"Uh, well," he said wringing his hands. "Oh, well, that's not really important. Let's just—" He turned his eyes from hers. "Let's just go back to the magic trace. Anyhow, so, in order to protect yourself from creatures that seek out magic traces, especially other Duvarharians, you have to actually release another spell—one that comes back through and wipes the trace clean. It is extremely complicated, seeing that you can't leave a trace with that spell. There is one other way to cover up a magic trace, and that is to make sure it's never even there to begin with."

The corners of her lips tugged down. "How do you do that?"

"By concentrating every ounce of the magic you release into the spell you are accomplishing. It's extremely rare to have the power and concentration to do such a thing though, and is widely considered impossible."

She nodded to show that she was following him. "So if it's all so hard to do, then how are you able to do it?"

He shook himself back to attention, and she could tell that his mind was still dwelling on her question about what he believed in.

He sneered. "I'm not able to. I'm only scattering our magic to make it more confusing. I have neither the skill nor the power to actually cover it up.

"Oh." She realized that meant he wouldn't be able to teach her. It was like he could read her thoughts.

"But don't worry." He smiled. "I'll teach you what I do know."

She grinned and let out a breath she didn't realize she had been holding. "Why do we call them spells? Is it the same as the spell-weaving that humans do?"

He scowled. "No. What humans do as spell-weavers is an abomination to themselves and magic. It's usually either a pact formed between a human and a magical creature where they serve each other, usually for an evil end, or a human traps a magical creature and forces the magic to work for them. Again, usually only for an evil end. The magical creature usually goes mad and dies because of the abuse."

Stephania recoiled in disgust. She couldn't imagine being trapped and forced to give up her magic. It only made her hate the villagers of New-Fars all the more for calling her that.

"So, now what?"

"Now you just need to practice."

For the rest of the day, she practiced under his careful supervision. By the end, she was able to sense her own and Dalton's trace and was able to scatter a minuscule fraction of her own trace. It was a useless amount, her magic trace was still like a shining beacon, but it was a start.

When she felt that she was too tired to even stand, they made camp, and she curled up in her blankets. The cold once more descended upon her, and she shivered, scowling bitterly, before rolling closer to the fire. As she stared into the hypnotizing flames, she wondered what tomorrow would bring—something she hadn't thought about in months.

She stared for a long time at the stars. They seemed so familiar but so distant. Sometimes it almost seemed like they were speaking to her, but when she listened to them, they fell silent.

Rolling over, she gazed tenderly at Dalton, who had fallen asleep almost as soon as his head had hit the pillow.

The unease settled back inside her. Her actions had more effect than she had known. Dalton was losing his magic because of her, and yet he didn't mind. He loved her that much. She rolled back over, tears stinging her throat and eyes. She remembered the pain, the loss she had seen in his eyes when he had talked about his dragon. *"In her place I have an empty chasm, a hollow pit of darkness where a piece of my soul once was. The more magic I use, the bigger it grows."* The furs were soft under her fingers as she gripped them to her chest. *Perhaps I have been too selfish. I am not the only one who has lost everything.* She frowned. *No, not everything. We have each other. That should be enough. But then why do I feel so empty and alone?*

She closed her eyes after gazing at the stars for a while, trying desperately to rid herself of the unease that clung to her like frost on grass. As she fell asleep, images of Wyriders, humans, forest children, and Duvarharians all danced around in her head, each with their gods fighting over who was right and who was wrong. Then, in one swipe, they were all knocked aside by a power greater than all others—a power both beautiful and terrible, one of creation and destruction. It filled the land and all inside of it, and nothing could exist outside of it.

Stephania turned over in her sleep, disturbed by her dream. What did it mean, if anything?

CHAPTER 31

New-Fars, Human Domain

Nearly 3 Years Earlier

STEPHANIA, THE MARES are over here." Dalton raised his eyebrow, a heavy sigh escaping his lips. He shook his head and followed the young woman's gaze to the snorting stallion.

"Amazing." Stephania's eyes sparkled with brilliant life. "He's ... perfect." Her hands gripped the wooden fence, her knuckles turning white.

The stallion snorted again, his nostrils flaring, the whites of his eyes gleaming in the mid-morning light. His strong, black hooves pawed the ground nervously. He pressed himself against the other side of the small pen, his sides heaving anxiously.

"Gods of all." He ran his fingers through his rough brown hair. Glancing quickly to his right, he cringed at the horse dealer.

The kind-faced trader only smirked back, showing he would wait for Dalton to restrain the eager girl before continuing to the more behaved mares and geldings.

"Stephania, there is no way I'm buying you that horse. It's impossible to get close to him, let alone ride him. Please, let's move on."

She shook her head, stepping up onto the first bar of the fence.

The horse screamed at the movement and reared up, pawing at the air.

Stephania pursed her lips. "Please, Uncle Dalton. He just needs someone to care for him." Her sparkling eyes dulled.

Dalton's own eyes roamed over the young horse's muscular but skinny body, stopping on its flanks and rear legs. Brutal signs across the horse's body told him that the horse had been whipped, beaten, and hobbled with spiked iron shackles. The horse's fear and anxiety were obviously the wretched result of that abuse.

Scowling, a flame of anger sparked in him for the horse's scarred body and horrific disposition, and Dalton turned to the dealer. "Where did you obtain this horse?"

The man's bright, kind face darkened. "Just east o' 'ere in a neighborin' town. 'E was dirty as a pig and being auctioned off for only as much as a chicken. I felt bad leavin' 'im. Thought I could get some coin off 'im if I could clean 'im up and break 'im in." He shrugged his shoulders and spat on the ground. "Thing's a beast. 'E won't let me near 'im. Almost broke my left knee two weeks ago. 'E barely eats 'e so scared. I'm 'fraid I'll 'afta put 'im down if 'e don't sell soon."

Dalton's heart sank as he turned his attention back to the stallion. The horse's coat was still dirty, though it seemed rain had helped wash some of the muck off. Dalton quickly took in the horse's measurements and qualities.

The stallion was of a fine breed and had excellent composition. And yet ... Dalton shook his head. He was no horse trainer, and neither was Stephania. The stallion would be impossible for either of them to tame.

"Come on, Stephania. There's nothing we can do."

He turned to leave, but when he didn't hear her follow, he turned back.

He was shocked to see tears in her eyes.

"I want him, Uncle Dalton. I think he needs me." She bit her lip and balled her hands into fists. She glanced back over to the stallion, to his wounded legs, to the tangled matts in his hair, to his glistening eyes. In some places, his coat shone honey brown through the dirt. His mane and tail were black, blacker than night.

Dalton sensed a strong emotion emitting from her. He tuned into it, listening for its essence. He frowned. It was familiarity.

The stallion turned to face Stephania, and briefly, their eyes met.

The horse stopped pawing the ground, and the fire in his eyes burned a little softer.

It was only for a moment though. He reared and screamed again when Dalton moved toward Stephania.

"Please, Stephania, there is nothing we can do for him." His own heart ached, now not only for the horse, but also for his adopted niece. He hated to see her hurt in any way. Her life was already so hard; she had already shed so many tears. But he couldn't see how this would end in anything but disaster. Neither of them knew how to train a wild horse and they would be forced to give him up eventually. It would be harder to give him up after they had taken him home and cared for him.

"Come on, child."

He grabbed her hand and pulled, gently leading her away from the scared stallion. Her eyes never left the horse until they rounded the stable and she could see him no longer. A pang tore through Dalton's heart as he saw her bite her lip against the tears brimming in her eyes.

She barely responded when he tried talking to her and seemed to not see the horses he showed her. He tried to excite her with the spirited geldings, but she brushed them off, her eyes trying to stray back to the stallion with every glance she could spare.

In a final attempt to change her mind, he even suggested that if she wanted to rescue a horse, they could look into going to the New-Fars horse auction. She refused. She didn't want just any horse. She wanted *him*.

From the corner of his eye as he paid for his dappled gray gelding, Dalton watched Stephania as she wandered back to the stallion's pen and stood up on the bottom rung of the fence; the stallion pawed the dirt across from her at the other end of the pen.

Slowly, Dalton stepped behind her. He hesitated to call her down, wishing he didn't have to tear her away from the unruly horse she so desperately wanted.

A deep sigh escaped her lips, and she rested her chin on the top rung.

Dalton knew she had been looking forward to this day for years. He had, long ago, promised to buy her own horse when she was fourteen. It should have been an exciting day, not a sad one. But something about this horse ... Dalton shook his head and was about to call her back when he heard her whisper, "Why are you so familiar?" He froze at her words. *Familiar.*

"Why do I feel as if I know you?" She reached a longing hand out to the horse, and it backed farther into the fence, the whites of its eyes sparkling in the suns.

Why indeed. His brows furrowed in a frown. He was just about to ask Stephania about what she had said when the trader interrupted.

"'E's the only 'orse that looks like that for miles." The dealer shook his head in mourning. "Don't really know the name for that color, but I thought 'e'd sell well, seeing how rare 'e is."

Dalton frowned, looking back and forth between Stephania and the stallion. Why was this horse so significant to her? Why couldn't she let it go?

"Stephania, please." He held his hand out to her, beckoning apologetically. "If you are going to pick out a horse, we should do it now. We've kept this kind gentleman long enough."

New tears glistened in her eyes as she tore her gaze from the stallion. She opened her mouth and then closed it several times, as if she just couldn't find the words.

"We can't afford a horse we can't tame, my child." His voice was soft and gentle, but he could see how deep they cut as her shoulders sagged.

"If I could just touch him," she muttered more to herself than him as her eyes drifted back to the horse. "If I could just feel him, everything would be okay."

The trader watched the horse and then watched the girl. His eyes narrowed as if he were thinking very hard about something, then he shook his head and chuckled. He leaned toward Dalton and whispered, "I'll let you take the 'orse, no charge, if she can pet it."

Dalton did a double take at the man, wondering if he had heard the dealer right. "What? No—"

Stephania's eyes widened. Despite the trader's nearly inaudible voice, she had heard his offer clearly.

She looked at Dalton, a wild glint in her eyes, her lips parted slightly.

"No, Stephania!" He shouted too late.

Before he could stop her, she had launched herself over the fence and into the paddock with surprising speed and agility.

As her feet hit the soft dirt with a muted thud, a cloud of dust rose around her, and everything went silent.

"Stephania," Dalton murmured, frightened that if he spoke too loudly or tried to rescue the girl, he would end up spooking the horse and getting her trampled.

She ignored him.

Her eyes locked onto the horse's. He watched her cautiously. Neither moved.

She took a step forward.

He pawed the ground.

She raised her hand.

He raised his head.

Another step.

A whinny.

Her foot inched forward.

Something changed in the horse's eyes; they shone with desperate fear.

Stephania's eyes widened in fear.

Time slowed.

Dalton saw the horse shift its weight to its hind legs. He knew if it reared up, its hooves would strike Stephania down like grass. But if he could distract the horse ...

Dalton yelled as loudly as he could, loud enough for both the trader and Stephania to cringe and cover their ears and for the horse to hesitate, just for a second.

A spark of magic left Dalton's hands, pushing the horse away with a small gust of wind.

The stallion screamed, jumping to the side, slamming into the fence. The sound of splintering wood mingled with the chaos.

For a moment, Stephania stood completely still, as if torn between two choices. Then suddenly, she bolted forward toward the stallion.

"No!" Dalton yelled as Stephania's feet dug into the ground, propelling her forward.

"If I could just touch him—" she pleaded.

The stallion's hooves raised, churning the air. Stephania ducked, rushing to his side, and placed her hand on the side of the horse's neck.

"*Woglawu!*"

Her shout hung on silent, still air.

Dalton's heart slammed in his chest, and his eyes widened with awe. "By the gods."

The fire had died out of the horse's eyes, and he suddenly was as meek as a songbird. Stephania's shirt was comically caught between the stallion's lips as he innocently nibbled the loose fabric.

Her lips curved into an elated grin. "Hey, bud. Are you alright?"

The stallion nickered, as if answering. His eyes were calm and warm, his breath had slowed. He stood still, his movements unhurried, gentle, and trusting. He pulled on her shirt and pressed his head against her chest as if asking for forgiveness for his earlier attitude.

"By the gods," Dalton repeated, unable to say much more.

A strong hand clasped him on the shoulder. "Well, looks like you got yourself a free 'orse."

Dalton scoffed and shook his head, but inside, he burned with pride. "Looks like it."

"You're alright. You're alright," Stephania whispered soothingly.

Dalton watched as her hands moved across the stallion's grimy coat, her fingers snagging on the matts in his mane. "And what should I name you, eh?" She stared deep into the horse's liquid caramel brown eyes for a long time, and Dalton leaned on the fence post, letting her take her time. "How about Braken?" She laughed when he pushed her with his face and nickered. "Braken it is, then."

"I suppose a halter and lead are in order then, if we have a deal," Dalton winked at the trader, and the man threw up his hands, still laughing with disbelief as he went off to find the tackle.

Dalton turned his attention back to Stephania as she touched the horse all over, delighting in how gentle the stallion was.

"Woglawu," he repeated for what seemed like the hundredth time. Where had he heard that word before? *"Woglawu."* It hit him. It was the word for "gentle" ... in the Centaur language, Sházuk. His smile turned to a frown. How could she have remembered that word? Or anything of the Centaurs? He sensed for her magic, praying against what he knew he would find.

A small trail of magic flowed from her. Not very much, nothing that could be traced, but it was there. She was growing up. The end was inevitable. One day, the magic within her would break free, and he could do nothing to stop it.

A sick feeling welled up in him and dampened the joy he should have felt as the trader handed Stephania the tack and she slipped the halter over the horse's head and led him out of the pen, gentle as a lamb.

As he led his own new mount down the road, just behind Stephania, he couldn't help but wonder where he had seen this sight before. Stephania, walking side by side with a golden-brown horse with a black mane and tail. He grunted and kicked a stone. *My memory is not what it was, even for a Rider. I guess I'm getting old.*

What color had the trader said the stallion was? Dalton frowned, wracking his brain. No, the trader hadn't known the name of the color.

What was the connection between Stephania and the horse? What did it have to do with her speaking Sházuk, which should have been impossible? Why had she insisted on getting this oddly colored horse?

His eyes flew open, and he gasped as he remembered. *Of course! The horse was a buckskin!* He grinned, proud of himself for remembering, but his triumph was quickly replaced by shock. He stopped walking.

"Dalton?" Stephania turned back to him, worry filling her eyes. "Are you okay?"

He ignored her. Of course. The stallion was a buckskin, and so had been ... he clenched his jaw, speaking the name under his breath, "Trojan."

CHAPTER 32

Present Day

S TEPHANIA! STEPHANIA, wake up!" Dalton's rough voice wrenched her out of dreamland as his strong hands unceremoniously shook her awake.

"Huh? What?" she groaned and pushed him away as she sat up, cursing under her breath. "What's wrong?"

Dalton wasn't looking at her. Instead, his gaze was now turned to a cluster of brush in the trees, a frightened look on his usually fearless, composed face. "Is it them? Oh, gods. I'd hoped they wouldn't find us. Not this soon!"

Scowling at his strange mutterings, dread filling her at his words, Stephania staggered to her feet and slowly approached him.

"What are you talking about?"

Ignoring her question, he unsheathed his sword. The early morning light glinted off the blade, shining in Stephania's eyes.

She squinted, feeling oddly disoriented.

"Get your bow." He muttered under his breath as quietly as possible.

Unaware of the danger, the haze of sleep fogging her mind, she slowly drew her compound bow, pausing to gaze at the intricate pulleys that the waxed string wrapped around. She pulled an arrow from her quiver but didn't nock it.

Then she heard it. The sound of hundreds of feet beating into the ground. The sound of mutated animals screaming and clawing their way through the brush.

Stark fear gripped her heart, and she leapt to her feet, feeling the adrenaline pounding through her body. She knew that sound. It was the sound of ...

"Etas. They've found us."

Stephania's mouth dropped open. She wished she hadn't heard him right, but there was no mistaking it. They were being hunted.

Her curly, red hair snapped around her shoulders as she frantically nocked the arrow to the string and drew another, stabbing it into the ground beside her. The string pressed into the curve of her fingers as she held the bow, her hands shaking uncontrollably.

A bloodcurdling battle cry in a beautiful but terrible foreign language rent the air. The sound of animals was replaced with the screaming of battle.

She turned to Dalton, her body going hot then cold. Any courage that she had once felt abandoned her.

An odd expression crossed Dalton's face. "Those are—" He frowned. "That language—"

"Uncle Dalton!" She thought her heart would race out of her chest. The noise of fighting was drawing closer. Why wasn't he doing anything? Were they going to fight or run?

"Shhh, Braken, Austin. It's okay." She let a small bit of magic extend to the two horses, and they stopped trying to pull their reins loose. Their hooves dug into the ground, the whites of their eyes showing. "Uncle Dalton we need to go. Please."

He waved her off and lowered his sword.

"Good gods. It *is* them. But are we really so close? I thought we were three days out. They must have followed the Etas to protect the tribe."

"Uncle Dalton!"

He snapped around to face her.

"What the Susahu is going on?" Her limbs burned with the instinct to fight or flee.

Another battle cry pierced the air along with a stream of commands in a foreign language.

Dalton grinned wildly and yelled back in triumph.

"Gods of all, what are you doing? Do you want them to come to us?" She started backing away from him. Had he tipped over the edge? Was he really not mentally stable?

"Oh, child. We have nothing to fear. The Trans-Falls army reached the Etas before they could reach us."

"Trans-Falls." The words were so familiar on her tongue, but they felt like a bad dream. "The tribe with my Centaur family?"

His eyes darkened. "Yes. I thought we were three days out. But it seems we were closer than I thought. And good thing too, or we'd be dead by now."

Her heart only beat harder. The thought of Centaurs being so near did not ease her fears like it had Dalton's; it only brought new ones. She began panicking. Her family. Her adoptive mother, father, brother—all of whom she wouldn't remember—were here. She was going to see them. *And Artigal. Oh gods.* She tasted bile. "No. No. No. I'm not ready. I don't want to do this now."

Dalton shook her shoulders. She couldn't hear his voice. Something stung her cheek, and she opened her eyes, realizing that she had fainted. She felt like she was going to throw up.

"Stephania? Stephania, are you okay? Can you hear me?"

She nodded and tried standing on her own. The sounds of battle had stopped, replaced by the thundering of hooves. It grew louder.

"Come on, child. They're coming. Can you stand? Are you okay?" His eyes pierced hers. He tucked a lock of hair behind her ear.

"I—I don't know."

"It's okay, child. I'm here. It's just the army. Don't worry. Just calm down. They'll take us to Trans-Falls, and you can meet your family when you're ready. Okay?"

She nodded. *It'll be okay. It'll be okay. I can see them when I'm ready.*

She planted her feet firmly on the ground and straightened. She would face them with pride. She was Stephania, daughter of Drox and Andromeda, Lord and Lady of Duvarharia. She could not show weakness. She had nothing to fear.

"Mu fud?" The commanding voice rang out again before repeating itself in the common tongue. "Who speaks?"

"Dalton Lefone and Farloon!"

More commands in the beautiful, wild language were shouted out, and the hooves thundered toward them.

The ground shook violently, and Stephania felt the hooves pound in time with her heart. Her newfound courage wavered, and she stepped behind Dalton, her hands once more shaking, and sweat beading on her forehead.

Braken and Austin screamed in fear, rearing and pulling on their ties. Dalton waved his hand, and they fell into a stupor, their heads hanging low.

Out of the brush ahead of them, a mighty buckskin Centaur, and many other different colored Centaurs behind him, charged into the clearing. In only seconds, Dalton and Stephania were surrounded by at least twenty of them, but the buckskin was the only one whom she saw.

His torso was bare, save for a plate of armor which rested over his heart and two others that covered his biceps. Straps holding the armor in place crossed his strong, muscular torso, and a thick belt girthed his waist. A quiver filled with an assortment of deadly arrows was strung across his back, his enormous, elegant, strong bow in his hand. An arrow was fitted to the string, the tip pointed straight at Stephania's heart. More armor covered his flanks and legs. His jet-black hair ran down his neck and gracefully transitioned into a long, silky mane that perfectly matched the long tail blowing softly in the wind. Strange markings, ones which looked oddly similar to the ones on Stephania's neck, decorated the side of his face, and down his chest to his arms and back. Splattered black blood glistened on his olive skin. Chiseled features on his battle worn face went hand in hand with his shining, steely blue eyes that seemed to pierce right into Stephania's soul. He was beautiful but terrible.

Her delicate eyes widened, her soft face displaying her terror at her first remembered sight of a Centaur. Her bow slipped out of her hand.

Dalton's eyes widened in horror. "Oh, gods." He fell to his knees, his hands trembling.

Stephania could barely hear him whisper, "Oh, Stephania. I'm so sorry. I couldn't have known."

She gasped at Dalton's reaction and retreated from the Centaur in horror. What was going on? She tripped on a rock and fell. She was too shocked and scared to stand back up. He seemed so much more imposing from down on the ground. She swallowed back the bile, forcing herself to take smooth, deep breaths.

"Faf ñá ashaif." The leader lowered his bow. His shocking blue eyes widened, and the bloodlust faded out of them. His face brightened with shock and disbelief.

Quickly, he slipped his bow over his shoulder and returned the arrow to the quiver. He stretched his hand out to her.

"Stephania?"

Stephania opened her eyes and met his gaze with caution. Though she felt as if she should know him, his face lacked any familiarity.

His face softened and broke out into a disbelieving smile. He slowly nodded, his eyes sparkling as they strayed first to her hair, then her eyes, to the markings on her hands and neck, and lastly to the pendant around her neck.

"It *is* you, Stephania. My Stephania. My baby sister."

A small gasp left her lips. *Oh, gods, no. This can't be happening. Not now. Please tell me this is a dream.*

She placed her hand in his. Effortlessly, she was pulled to her feet.

"Emperor be praised! I thought I would never get to see you again!" He laughed through his tears, his hands quivering with excitement. "There's so much to tell you! Mother and Father are going to be thrilled, Artigal too, I'm sure. Good gods!" He, still holding her hand, gently spun her around and admired her. "You're all grown up! And so beautiful too, just like you always have been, of course."

Stephania was still petrified with shock and fear, unable to make herself do anything but stare wide-eyed and openmouthed back at him, the air having left her lips long ago and her cheeks having reddened with growing embarrassment. *This is my brother. This is my brother. Trojan.*

"Trojan?" She barely heard her own whisper.

He nodded. Thick, fast tears began to pour down his face, and he choked with emotion, his eyes burning with passion. "Yes. Yes. It's me."

She was abruptly wrapped in his warm embrace, his arms pinning hers to her sides and her head on his shoulder. The warmth of his strong body failed to comfort her.

Her head spun and her ears rang as his strong arms crushed the breath out of her. His lips whispered words of Centaur endearments into her ear as if all the words in the common language could never be enough.

Oh, gods. What do I do? What do I say? He expects me to know him, and I don't! Gods of all, why did this have to happen this way?

He released her but kept her small hands in his.

At the sight of her horrified and embarrassed face, his smile faltered.

"Stephania!" His gaze pierced hers, and his grip on her hands tightened painfully. "What's wrong?"

He moved his hand to caress her face, and she couldn't help but shrink away from his touch. He snatched his hand back as if he had been burned. "You remember me, right? If you said my name, surely you must remember, despite the spell."

"I—I'm sorry." She forced herself to speak. It felt as if her very soul were rotting away with each word. "Uncle Dalton told me your name. I don't—I don't remember you. I don't know who you are."

She could have killed herself to take her words back, to have wiped that look off his face.

His beautiful, bright smile and the uncontrollable sparkle in his eyes faded. The intense passion and love he had so openly shown her at her return was instantly destroyed.

Now he stared back at her only in horror—horror and anguish.

"No. Of course you don't." He laughed hysterically. "Artigal's spell. Of course it's not broken." Tears flooded his eyes. He clutched his chest as he stumbled back. "You don't remember me. You remember nothing. Nothing." His voice was barely a whisper. Unchecked tears flowed freely down his tanned cheeks from his blue, blue eyes as he stared deeply into Stephania's, refusing to believe her. No sound came from his lips.

He shook his head in utter desolation. "Oh, gods." Violently, he shoved her away from himself and charged into the forest.

Her shoulders slumped, and she sank to her knees. Again, she had lost another family, another home. *Does everything I touch have to wilt and die?*

Dalton's arms wrapped around her. She sagged into his embrace.

"I'm so sorry, child. I wish I would have known. I'm sorry. I'm sorry." He smoothed her hair, tears sparkling in his eyes.

"Why? Why does everything always have to be this way? Why does it always have to hurt?"

He had no answer. "I don't know, child. I don't know."

She buried her face against his chest and wept. As the sickness of dread settled in her, she knew this could only be the beginning of the pain she would bring to these creatures.

DARKNESS AWAKES

Pits of Susahu

CREAMS FILLED THE rotten, dank air. Between the cries of the damned, silence was replaced with a constant screech akin to nails on polished granite. The Lord of Susahu knew most creatures would find the noise unbearable, but he found nothing less than solace in its formidable chaos.

"Lord Raythuz." The darkness morphed into a winged creature of daunting proportions as it fed off the fear and despair from its victims. "I have located one of the relics of Rasa you search for." Bones popped in its neck as it shook flakes of decomposing flesh from its mane and dragged its talons through the ground.

Raythuz collected a portion of his consciousness from the rotting hearts of the damned souls and drew himself into his throne room at the heart of his realm. A twisted body formed from the shadows, but he hardly noticed it. He was so much more than just a physical entity; he was the darkness in all living things—the disturbing, rancid, unwelcome thoughts and desires that twisted the minds of all creatures of Rasa. He was fear, he was destruction, he was the *Kijaqumok* itself.

"Let me see it," he hissed through rows of sharp teeth, a yellow tongue darting in and out of his dry lips as he tasted the scent of blood and hopelessness on the air.

A clear pool of metallic liquid gathered in the cracked rock below them. First, it reflected their appearances, but as the winged creature of fear dragged its claws through the liquid, an image began to form.

Bare tree limbs covered with snow shone under a pale moon. A young woman lay curled by a dying fire; her hair was as red as the embers.

"The savior of the Dragon Prophecy." Raythuz chewed his tongue until thick liquid filled his mouth. He spat into the reflection, and it darkened before clearing again. "Weak fool."

The Great Lord was so enamored with her, had staked so much hope on her with His Dragon Prophecy, but she was nothing to him. She was only a pawn in a small game the creatures of Rasa liked to play, balancing dark and light. She was one of many hundreds, no, *thousands* of creatures who were sent to purify the land of evil, to turn hearts back to the repulsive Creator and His false hope and life. She would fulfil her prophecy against Thaddeus, or she wouldn't, and then she would die.

The cycle of life for the creatures of Rasa was worthlessly short as they lived and then just as quickly died.

He was in search for things much more ... lasting.

"I have no need of the Great Lord's little puppet. I want to see the relic." Without batting an eye, he struck the winged creature before him, sinking his claws into its thick, black scaled neck. The creature screamed and thrashed against him. Raythuz watched its eyes turn from black to red, felt the rush of strength the creature's own fear and pain gave him, then ripped away a chunk of the creature's neck. Casting the flesh into the darkness, he spat on the creature's horse-like beaked face. "Be useful to me, or I will feed myself from your own fear and strip you of your power."

The creature whimpered, clutching at its wound with taloned feet. Dragging its other claws through the liquid, the creature used its power to see past the blankets wrapping what Raythuz wanted to see.

Green light filled the dark throne room; Raythuz's eyes glowed with greed and desire.

"The *Zelauwgugey*." He reached for it with all the desire of a lover, but without a single breath of tenderness. "The essence of the forest. The power to command every tree, Faun, and Nymph of Rasa."

The image in the metallic liquid disappeared, and with a wave of his hand, Raythuz healed the creature's neck. It gasped with relief and submission as it bowed low before him.

"Do whatever you have to." Raythuz gripped the creature's beak in his hands, crushing it until he heard it splinter. "Possess whoever you can." His other hand gently stroked the top of the creature's head. "Destroy the fabric of reality and mind if you must. Just bring me that Lyre."

"As you will, Lord Raythuz." The darkness swallowed the creature, and in a breath's time, it was nothing more than the fear in the minds and hearts of any creature in Rasa it chose to possess.

The image of a Centaur in Trans-Falls appeared in the liquid, and Raythuz watched as his eyes and the eyes of his two friends went dark, black veins trailing under their skin before fading from view.

A grotesque smile spread across his jagged teeth as he released his consciousness back into the desecrated, hopeless hearts of the souls in Susahu.

Within the next month, Stephania, with the Lyre in her weak, unassuming hands, would arrive in Trans-Falls where he and the *Kijaqumok* would be waiting.

The end of Rasa was near, the war over who would rule the new world only just beginning. This time, he wouldn't lose.

PRONUNCIATION GUIDE

&

GLOSSARY

PRONUNCIATION GUIDE

Adriva— uh-DREE-vuh
Aeron— ER-un
Artigal— AR-ti-gall
Braken—BRAKE-en
Duvarharia— DU-var-HAR-ee-uh
Elcore— EL-core
Eta— EE-tuh
Farloon— far-LOON
Filate— FI-late
Frawnden— FRAWN-den
Gauwu Zelauw— GAH-wu Ze-LOW ('low' rymes with 'wow')
Gauyuyáwa—GAH-yoo-YAY-wuh
Hanluurasa— han-loo-RA-sah
Igentis— aye-GEN-tis
Kijaqumok— KEE-jah-QUH-mock
Krystallos— kry-STAL-ohs
Kyrell— KY-rul
Lavoisier— lah-VOI-si-er
Leguows— leh-GWOWS
New-Fars— new-fairs
Quinlan— QUIN-lan
Salcon— sal-CON
Sankyz— San-keez
Saorise— SAY-oh-rise
Sházuk— SHAY-zook
Shushequmok— SHU-sheh-QUH-mock

Sleshqumok— SLESH-quh-mock
Stephania— Steh-FAW-nia
Susahu— Soo-SA-hu
Synoliki— SY-no-li-ky
Syrus— SY-rus (like Cyrus)
Tabor— TA-bore
Thaddeus— THAY-dee-us
Trans-Falls— trans-falls
Veltrix— VEL-trix
Ventronovia— VEN-troh-NOH-via
Wyerland— WHY-er-land
Wyrider— WHY-rider
Yufloy— you-FLOI
Zelauwgugey— ze-LOW-gu-gay ('low' rhymes with 'wow')

Glossary

Centaur/Faun *(Sházuk)*

Da me koyuwuk— My lover

Da rañ ñidauz yarazai zifezh— Our loyalty lies with you.

Elu— Ass

*Fadu, Igentis, mu shoz yásheň Sházuk.—*Hail Igentis. High leader of the *Sházuk*

Faf ñá ashaif— By all the gods

Fálaz— Dog

Fayum— Motherland, Homeland

Fom— Brother

Gaikuzh— Mountain

Gauwu Zelauw— Forest of Tombs (Also known as the Tomb Forest)

Gauyuyáwa— Tree of our Fathers (or ancestors)

Gubelæwur leňi rok— Please forgive us

Kodaazh— Warrior

Kofuz— Protector

Me koshoawázh— I am here, Igentis

Mewa— Friend

Me yuwuk fezh— I love you (to higher authority or with great respect)

Me yuwuk fu— I love you (to an equal)

Me yuwuk fu muyaa fáfád— I love you so much

Miw— Bay

Shaif zuru— Curse (as an expletive) the gods

Sházuk— Kin (Native word for Forest Children Kinds. Name of Kind, Centaur language)

Synoliki— Elite, honorary Centaur Warrior under the direct command of the Igentis whose dedication is to the protection of all Centaurs.

Talfindo— A common exclamation which translates close to "Eureka!"

Woglawu— Gentle

Yelar— Master

Yu'jac— A popular, Centaur strategy game

Yulu fe– Sweet child

Zháf wafu zhæk zi mazh— She will be safe with me

Zuru— Curse (as an expletive)

Zuru fuñofufe– Curse (as an expletive) this

Zelauwgugey— Forest Essence. Lyre of the Fauns

DUVARHARIAN *(Rażużugub)*

Dase— Father

Fubeżersufa— The strongest manipulation spell

Hanluurasa— Sky realm

Jok Kukeb— Instant Death

Juufu— An information recording device made of magic that transposes observed actions and personal reactions into words

Kijaqumok— Corrupt Magic

Kvażajo— Helper of the Dragon Prophecy

Nuse— Friend

Qumokuhe— Magic image

Qużech raż jin mraha— After our Lord

Rażużugub— Chosen People (Native word for Duvarharians, or Dragon Riders. Name of Kind)

Rilar— Love

Rilar że dachek— Love you too

Rumi— About/Around

Shalnoa— Markings similar to tattoos made with magic that are unique to each creature. Magical "fingerprints"

Shelesuujao— Savior

Shushequmok— Pure Magic

Sleo— Protector

Sleshqumok— Ancient Magic

Suluj— Curse (as an expletive)

Susokxoch— Commander

Suluj žu sukuneruž ubaes— curse (as an expletive) you, cursed humans

Susahu— The realm of darkness. Hell

Sužefrusum— Peaceful Forest

Zelou— Mother

ACKNOWLEDGEMENTS

BEFORE I LIST ANY of the incredible people who have supported me while re-publishing this book, I want to take a moment to give a HUGE shoutout to my fans! I literally never thought I would have fans or be able to talk to them and meet them, but I ran into a young woman in an ice cream shop who wanted a picture with me because she loved Child of the Dragon Prophecy. Literally made my year. My great aunt pulled me aside just to talk to me about this book which she is absolutely loving. It's people like you two who I've written these books for, and I sincerely hope you continue to love them as much as you are and as I do!

Exceptional thanks to H.A.Pruitt who continues to support me and my series, who edited the first edition of Child of the Dragon Prophecy, and helped touch up some leftover work I needed help with for the second edition.

GC Annison was so sweet to reach out and offer to proofread this edition of Child of the Dragon Prophecy one last time before its newest publication. I was so grateful to have an extra set of eyes to make this book the best it can be.

As always, Docuprint in Fort Smith Arkansas was an integral part of getting this book printed and re-published. They always do a splendid job of printing all my art, bookmarks, business cards, and books for editing, and on top of that, they've given me so many free "samples" and discounts that have allowed me to do more with my books than I ever could without them. Thank you so much!

Thanks to Bookish in Fort Smith for being the first physical store to stock copies of Child of the Dragon Prophecy and host some of my book signings.

Lastly, I want to shout-out myself because I'm a prideful hardworking little author of course. I formatted Child of the Dragon Prophecy for its second edition, did all the new cover designs, and founded Dragon Bone Publishing to fulfill my publishing dream. This is proof that if you, the reader, have a dream that you want to accomplish, don't let anyone tell you it can't be done. You can do whatever you want and whatever you need to do to make your dreams come true.

Thank you, reader for picking up this book and believing in it enough to read it. I hope it's an exciting beginning to a series that will stay in your heart for the end of time.

May the suns smile upon your presence.

—Effie Joe Stock

About the author:

EFFIE JOE STOCK

Effie Joe Stock is the author of The Shadows of Light series, creator of the world Rasa, publisher of the Aphotic Love Anthology, and head of Dragon Bone Publishing. When she's not waitressing at a local café in Arkansas, you can usually find her in front of her computer, hacking away at her never-ending list of projects. She also enjoys playing music, studying psychology, theology, or philosophy, playing fantasy RPG video games, riding motorcycles, or hanging out with her farm animals. Her publishing journey only just beginning, she hopes to release her first children's book soon along with another Dragon Bone Publishing Anthology.

Instagram: @effie.joe.stock.author
Facebook: Effie Joe Stock Author
Website: www.effiejoestock.com

For more books like *Child of the Dragon Prophecy,* visit:
www.dragonbonepublishing.com

Read Heir of Two Kingdoms Now!

DUVARHARIA AWAITS.

THE PAST CALLS.

THE HEIR OF TWO KINGDOMS FACES HER INHERITANCE.

Stephania is destined to rule Duvarharia, but when she stops in the Centaur tribe of Trans-Falls on her way to the land of dragons, her past snares her. As she lingers in her childhood home, a traitor, a brother, supernatural evil, a mentor, nightmares, and new friends remind her of who she was while also urging her to move forward. While she fights between her memories and destiny, she also battles the darkness growing in the land and in her soul. When loss threatens to shatter her, will Stephania remain behind the mask of her past, fall victim to the darkness, or step forward to inherit her destiny?

Available internationally on major retailers such as Amazon, Barnes&Noble, Books-A-Million, Kindle, and more.